Praise for the Novels of Leslie Parrish

Black at Heart

"Dark, edgy, fantastic romantic suspense that readers and reviewers all over the Web are buzzing about."
—All About Romance

"The emotional layers in this book, the descriptions, the plotting, the characterizations are rich and satisfying."
—Armchair Interviews

Pitch Black

"Parrish's Black CATs novels are taut, exciting, sweet, dark, and hot all at the same time."
—Errant Dreams Reviews

"Superbly written and thoroughly engrossing."
—All About Romance

"The ultimate edge-of-your-seat thriller."
—Romance Junkies

continued . . .

COLD SIGHT

EXTRASENSORY AGENTS

LESLIE PARRISH

A SIGNET ECLIPSE BOOK

SIGNET ECLIPSE
Published by New American Library, a division of
Penguin Group (USA) Inc., 375 Hudson Street,
New York, New York 10014, USA
Penguin Group (Canada), 90 Eglinton Avenue East, Suite 700, Toronto,
Ontario M4P 2Y3, Canada (a division of Pearson Penguin Canada Inc.)
Penguin Books Ltd., 80 Strand, London WC2R 0RL, England
Penguin Ireland, 25 St. Stephen's Green, Dublin 2,
Ireland (a division of Penguin Books Ltd.)
Penguin Group (Australia), 250 Camberwell Road, Camberwell, Victoria 3124,
Australia (a division of Pearson Australia Group Pty. Ltd.)
Penguin Books India Pvt. Ltd., 11 Community Centre, Panchsheel Park,
New Delhi - 110 017, India
Penguin Group (NZ), 67 Apollo Drive, Rosedale, North Shore 0632,
New Zealand (a division of Pearson New Zealand Ltd.)
Penguin Books (South Africa) (Pty.) Ltd., 24 Sturdee Avenue,
Rosebank, Johannesburg 2196, South Africa

Penguin Books Ltd., Registered Offices:
80 Strand, London WC2R 0RL, England

First published by Signet Eclipse, an imprint of New American Library,
a division of Penguin Group (USA) Inc.

First Printing, July 2010
10 9 8 7 6 5 4 3 2 1

To my big, wild, crazy "Smith" family: Dad, Toni, Lynn, Chris, Donna, Paul, Karen, Cheri, Lee, Holly. Thanks so much for your constant support and enthusiasm.

No author ever had a greater cheering section.

I love you all. And your kids are pretty cool, too!

ACKNOWLEDGMENTS

To Bruce—thanks for being such a great sounding board . . . and husband! Up for another screenplay?

To my editor, Laura Cifelli—I really appreciate your encouraging me to test and stretch my writing boundaries on this one.

As always, thanks to the Plotmonkeys—Julie, Janelle, and Karen—for your invaluable assistance in plotting this story, and in helping me work out the kinks along the way.

Many thanks to Silver, Heather, Liza, Paula, Stacey, and other bloggers who were so supportive in helping to get word out about my books. Your efforts are sincerely appreciated.

Prologue

Until last night, nobody had ever read Vonnie Jackson a bedtime story.

Though she'd lived for seventeen years, she couldn't remember a single fairy tale, one whispered nightie-night, or a soft kiss on the cheek before being tucked in. Her mother had always been well into her first bottle, her second joint, or her third john of the evening long before Vonnie fell asleep. Bedtime usually meant hiding under the bed or burrowing beneath a pile of dirty clothes in the closet, praying Mama didn't pass out, leaving one of her customers to go prowling around in their tiny apartment.

They definitely hadn't wanted to read to her. Nobody had.

So to finally hear innocent childhood tales from a psychotic monster who intended to kill her was almost as unfair as her ending up in this nightmare to begin with.

"Are you listening to me?" His pitch rose, her captor's voice growing almost mischievous as he added, "Did you fall asleep, little Yvonne?" But that mischief was laced with so much evil that it almost seemed to be a living, breathing thing, as real as the stained, scratchy mattress on which she lay or the metal chains holding her down upon it.

Most times, such as now, the man who'd kidnapped her spoke in a thick, falsetto whisper, his tone happily wicked, like a jolly elf who'd taken up slaughter for the sheer pleasure of it. Every once in a while, though, he got angry and dropped the act. Once or twice, when he'd said a word or two in his normal thick, deep voice, she'd felt a hint of familiarity flit across her mind, as if she'd heard him before, recently. She could never focus on it, though; never place the memory.

Maybe she was crazy. Maybe she just recognized the twisted, full-of-rage quality that made men such as him tick. She'd seen that kind all her life. She'd just never landed in the hands of a homicidal one. Until now.

"Sweet little girl. So weary, aren't you? I suppose you fell asleep, hmm?"

She shook her head. Even that slight movement sent knives of pain stabbing through her skull and into her brain. Whether that was from the drugs he'd been shoving down her throat or from the punches to the face, she couldn't say. Probably both. The pills he'd given her hadn't made the pain go away. Instead they'd intensified it, brought her senses higher until every word was a thundering cry, every hint of light in her eyes as blinding as the sun. And every cruel touch agonizing.

The first beating had hurt. The subsequent ones had nearly sent her out of her mind. Only the solid, steel core of determination deep inside her—which had kept her going despite so many obstacles throughout her life— had kept her from giving in to the urge to beg him to just kill her and put her out of her misery.

"You must want to go to sleep, though."

"No," she whispered. "Go on. Don't stop. I like it."

Oh, no, she didn't want to fall asleep, as welcome as it might have been. Because it was while she slept, helpless against sheer exhaustion, lulled by his singsong bedtime stories or unable to fight the effects of the drugs, that he came in and *did* things to her. She'd awakened once to find him taking pictures of her, naked and posed on the cot. Though his face had been masked—one of those creepy, maniacally smiling "king" masks from the fast-food commercials—he'd rechained her and scurried out as soon as he realized she was fully conscious. As if he didn't have the balls to risk letting her get a good look at him.

Maybe he's afraid you'll escape and be able to identify him.

Yeah. And maybe a pack of wolves would rip him to pieces in his own backyard tomorrow. But she doubted it.

One of these times, she suspected she would wake up and find herself in the middle of a rape. So, no, she did not want to fall asleep.

"I don't know—we've read quite a lot. I'm worried you might have nightmares. Did you, last night, after hearing about the little piggies who got turned into bacon and sausage patties?"

She suspected the story didn't end like that. If it did, parents who called it a bedtime story had a lot to answer for. As for her nightmares . . . Well, she was living one, wasn't she?

Vonnie swallowed, her thick, dry tongue almost choking her. "I'll be fine. Please read to me some more."

The words echoed in the damp, musty basement room in which she'd been imprisoned for three days now. Or four? She had been unable to keep track, even though she had noted the sunshine coming and going again through the tiny window in her cell. She had been too out of it, couldn't make herself focus.

How long had it been since the night he'd grabbed her? And when had that been? *Think!*

Monday. He'd attacked her while she walked the long way home from a nighttime event at her new high school, to which she'd just transferred because they offered more AP classes than her old one. Mistake number one. Her old school had been a block from her crappy home.

"Well, if you're sure, I suppose we can read a little more about those naughty children."

Knowing he expected it, she managed to murmur, "Thank you."

"You're welcome, dear. I'm glad you like this story. It's no wonder their parents didn't want Hansel and Gretel—awful, spoiled brats, weren't they? Most parents hate their children anyway, but these two were especially bad."

If it wouldn't have caused her so much pain, she might have laughed at that. Because he was saying something he thought would hurt her, when, in truth, he'd just reinforced what she already knew. Her mama had made that clear every day of her life.

Most parents would be proud of their kid for doing well in school, but not hers. All she'd said was that Vonnie had been stupid to transfer. Stupid to go to the evening event. Stupid and uppity, thinking getting into the National Honor Society mattered a damn when she lived on the corner of Whoreville and Main.

Normally she'd have been at work serving chicken wings and fending off gropey drunk guys by that time of night on a Monday. But no, she'd had to go to the meeting, had to act as if she was no different from the smart, rich white kids with their trust funds and their sports cars. She'd been cocky, insisting it was no big deal to walk home alone after dark through an area of the Boro where no smart girl ever walked alone after dark. Not these days, not with the Ghoul on the loose and more girls missing from her neighborhood every month.

The Ghoul—the paper had at first said he was real, then that he wasn't. Vonnie knew the truth. He was real, all right. She just wasn't going to live long enough to tell anybody.

"Hansel and Gretel didn't know that the starving birdies of the forest were eating up their bread-crumb trail, waiting for the children to die so they could poke out their eyes," he read, not noticing her inattention. "It was dark and their time to find their way home was running out."

Time. It had ceased to have any meaning at all. Minutes and hours had switched places: minutes lengthened by pain, hours shortened by the terror of what would happen every time he came back from wherever it was he went when he left her alone in the damp, cold dark.

And Vonnie knew, deep down, that her time was running out, too.

"Did you hear me?" he snapped.

She swallowed. "Yeah."

"Good. Don't you fall asleep. I'm reading this for you, not for myself, you know."

She suspected he wasn't reading at all, merely Wes Craven-ing up a real bedtime story.

"Now, wasn't it lucky that they were able to find shelter?" he added. "Mm, a house made of gingerbread and gumdrops and licorice. Imagine that. Do you like sweets, pretty girl? Want me to bring you some candy? Sticky, gooey candy?"

She swallowed, the very thought of it making her sick. Not that she wasn't hungry, starving even. But the foul-smelling air surrounding her, filling her lungs and her nose, made the thought of food nauseating. She didn't like to think about the other smells down here—the reek of rotten meat, the stench of human waste. And something metallic and earthy, a scent that seemed to coat her tongue when she breathed through her mouth.

Blood. At least, that was what she suspected had created the rust-colored stains on the cement floor.

Those stains had been the first things she'd noticed when she regained consciousness after she'd been kidnapped. And ever since, they'd reiterated what she already knew: This guy had killed before, and he intended to kill her. It wasn't a matter of if; only when.

There was no escape—she was chained, drugged, and had been terrified into utter submission. She had no idea where she was, or when it was, or if the door led to a way out or just another chamber of horrors.

Vonnie didn't even try to comfort herself with thoughts of escape. It did no good to pump herself up with the memories of all the other times she'd gotten herself out of difficult situations—put there through either her own gullibility or by her mama's greed.

Don't go there, girl. Just as much darkness down that path.

No, she didn't want to think those thoughts. Not if they were going to be among the last ones of her life. Because so far, at least, this nightmare hadn't included sexual assault.

"Well, maybe the candy shouldn't be too sticky," he said, tutting a little, like a loving, concerned parent, not that she had firsthand experience with one. "I know your jaw must hurt from when you made me hit you the other day. Maybe I could chew it up, make it nice and soft for you, then spit it into your mouth just like a mama bird with her little chick."

Though she hadn't figured there was anything left in her stomach, she still heaved a mouthful of vomit. But she forced herself to swallow it down. She wouldn't give him the satisfaction of seeing that his mere words had made her sick. Nor could she let him know just how disgusting she found the thought. Giving the monster ideas to try on her when she finally did pass out was a stupid thing to do, and Vonnie Jackson might be beaten and chained, she might be poor and the daughter of a drug-addicted prostitute, but nobody had ever called her stupid.

"Why was she doing it, do you suppose? Why did she want them to eat all those sweets?" When she didn't reply, his singsong voice rose to a screech. "Answer me!"

"Fattening them up," she said, the words riding a puff of air across her swollen lips.

"Yes! You're so clever; that's what they say about you. Such a smart, clever girl who was going to escape her pathetic childhood." He *tsk*ed, sounding almost sad. "And you nearly made it—didn't you, Yvonne? Oh, you came so close! High school graduation next May, then off you'd go to college on one of your scholarships, never to see your slut mother or the hovel you call home again. All that work, all that effort. Wasted."

She didn't answer, didn't even flinch, not wanting him to see that his words stabbed at her, hurting almost as much as his fists. Because getting out was all Vonnie had worked for, all she had dreamed of for as long as she could remember. And the fact that this filthy monster had taken that chance from her made her want to scream at the injustice.

"Ah, well, back to our story. Yes, indeed, the witch was fattening them up," her captor said. "But do you know why?" He hummed a strange tune, repeating himself in discordant song. "Why, why, why? Do you know why?"

Her eyes remained open as she listened to that crooning voice deliberately trying to lull her into much-needed sleep. Her body wanted to give in to it, to let go. If she thought there was a chance she might never wake up, she would have gladly embraced the chance.

But she wasn't that lucky. And she knew she would regret it when she awoke and found out what he wanted to do to her. So Vonnie forced herself to shake her throbbing head, knowing the sharper the pain the less she'd be inclined to give in. "Why?"

He laughed softly, not answering. Just as well. She probably didn't want to know the answer to that question, given the way he was turning these nightly stories into tales from his twisted crypt of a mind.

"You'll just have to wait and see. Patience, sweet . . ."

His sibilant words were interrupted by the sound of banging coming from somewhere above. Before Vonnie could even process it, she heard a clang of metal. The small sliding panel in the door, through which he watched her, talked to her, and tormented her, was slammed shut. The narrow column of illumination that had shone through it, one single beam of blazing light in the darkness, had been chopped away like the head off a snake.

Another bang from above. She tried to focus on it, tried not to let the relief of his leaving make her give in to exhaustion. That noise, the way he'd reacted to it, was important, though it took a second for her to process why.

Then she got it. He had been startled. The creature had been surprised out of his lair by something unexpected. Or someone?

Oh God, please.

Hope bloomed, relentless and hot. What if someone else was out there? For the first time in days, she realized he hadn't taken her to the bowels of hell but to somewhere real, a place that other people could come upon. A mailman, a neighbor? Anyone who could help her?

An internal voice tried to dampen her hopes. That might not have been someone banging on the door at all, but merely a loose shutter or a tree branch. Besides, it was dark out, maybe even the middle of the night—no mailman worked these hours.

The police. Maybe they're looking for me.

It was a long shot. But long shots were all she had right now. "Help me. Somebody, help me," she whispered. "Please, I'm here!"

She didn't think about what he'd do when he came back. Didn't stop for one second to worry whether he'd find some new way to punish her.

No. Vonnie Jackson simply began to scream as if her life depended on it.

Chapter 1

Aidan McConnell awoke to the smell of gingerbread and the sharp, piercing sound of a woman's scream.

The scream ended the moment he opened his eyes. The smell did not.

It took him a minute to place the scent, which had invaded his head and his dreams as he tried to grab some sleep just before dawn on Thursday. At first, in those early moments between asleep and awake, he assumed he'd been dreaming of some long-forgotten holiday visit to his grandmother's house; her kitchen had always been rich with all the delicious aromas any sugar-deprived kid could desire. But when he sat up on his couch and realized the cloying, sickeningly sweet odor of ginger and spice was truly filling his every breath, he knew he wasn't dreaming.

He was connecting.

"Damn it," he muttered, not wanting this, not now, not again. Not so soon after last night's mental invasion. Bacon, for God's sake. The reek of fatty, greasy bacon had seemed to permeate every inch of air in his house a few hours ago, and now it was gingerbread.

Forcing himself to focus on his other senses, he stared at his huge, antique walnut desk, which sat in the dead center of the room. Its surface was hidden as completely as the top of a freshly buried casket. Files, notepads, research books, his laptop—they consumed almost every inch of space. A few random items finished the job: A coffee mug that read, "Psychics do it when they're not even there." A colorful sand pail filled with pencils in varying lengths. A paperweight. An old-fashioned wind-up clock that dinged violently when the alarm went off.

Aidan stared; he focused; he thought about the coolness of the brass on the clock and the heft of the stone base of the paperweight and the way freshly brewed coffee tasted when sipped out of that mug. He thought of the thousands of doodled sketches he'd made with those pencils, trying to capture images he'd seen while mentally connecting with someone before they shortened and finally disappeared from his mind like a shadow at high noon.

It didn't work.

Spice. Cinnamon. Sugar. But bloated, vile, thick, and putrid like the remnants of a Thanksgiving pie buried in a garbage heap with rotting turkey and moldy stuffing.

He focused harder, rubbing the tips of his fingers across the grain of the leather couch, craning to hear the faint tick of that clock, staring at the desk, ordering his other senses to combine and smother the smell. But still the stench enveloped him. He could taste it now, the sting of too much ginger, the vile, rancid sugar melting on his tongue. His stomach rebelled.

Closing his eyes, he gritted his teeth, resorting to his oldest tricks against the familiar invasion into his psyche. He visualized a sea of sturdy cement building blocks. One by one, he began piling them up, erecting the psychic barrier between his mind and the one with which he was unwillingly connecting. Building mental walls in order to protect himself wasn't just an expression when it came to Aidan; it was pure survival. He'd have gone insane long ago if he hadn't learned how to protect himself.

His maternal grandmother—the one who'd slipped him usually denied sweets—had taught him the trick when he was eleven or twelve. Teaching him how to survive in a world that didn't like kids who were "different," she'd given him just about every coping skill he had. She had been strong-willed, had fought for him when nobody else would and Aidan was too young to do it for himself. They'd made quite a team. The old woman had been different, strange, had seen things she'd never truly seen, known things she couldn't possibly know.

Like him.

In another era, she would have been burned as a witch. In modern-day Georgia, however, she'd been deemed a quack and hidden away like the proverbial skeleton in the family's closet. She was seldom spoken of, but would never allow herself to be completely banished. When she felt like it, she inserted herself into her family's lives, whether they wanted her there or not.

That was lucky for him. Because she had been the only one Aidan could talk to about his unexpected, unwanted abilities. The only one who'd understood and helped him. She was also the one who had never called him a demon from hell when he was eight years old.

That'd been his oh-so-devout parents. Who said radical Southern Baptists didn't know how to raise a kid right? They'd reacted by locking him away with his grandmother . . . who made the best gingerbread. *That smell.*

"No, build, damn it!"

He mentally built—row by row, layer by layer, foot by foot. His head ached, but he forced every brain cell into submission. The cement wall was almost touching the clouds by the time the spicy stench began to gradually dissipate like steam off a mirror. Until finally he could breathe again without smelling anything but the normal leather of the couch and the faintly old air of the closed-in house in which he lived.

He could also think again. Unfortunately, his thoughts went to one place: Who was it? Who had he met, touched, interacted with in the past? Whose thoughts were filled with stink and rotting garbage? And gingerbread. Why was that person's mind consumed with it—so consumed that Aidan was overwhelmed by their thoughts, which translated into physical scents, from far away?

He didn't doubt he'd met the person with whom he was connecting. He'd touched him or her; perhaps just a faint brush of hand against arm as they passed on the street, but they had physically connected. The sensory reactions were never this strong without real, personal contact. Studying a photograph or holding an item used by someone he was seeking might bring a quick sensation, a breathful of odor, a flash of mental imagery. But for it to go on like this morning's nightmare meant skin-to-skin contact.

Thank God the scream hadn't rung in his ears for as long as the stench had filled his nostrils. *Maybe it wasn't connected.* Perhaps the scream had merely been a last remnant of one of his own forgotten nightmares. He preferred to think that, not wanting to imagine the scream was really happening anywhere else but in his own mind. Aidan didn't want to picture the screamer in agony, desperate for help. *His* help.

"Forget it," he muttered, not letting himself go down that path. He didn't do that anymore. Once crucified, twice shy. He did everything he could to stay in his own head these days, and stay out of everyone else's. Where he'd once used psychic ability, he was now quite content to use his own highly tuned sense of intuition and reasonable deduction.

Right now, he reasonably deduced that the smell had been noticed and thought about by somebody he'd briefly met, somebody who was walking by a garbage dump. And the scream was a product of his own tortured memories running rampant in his dreams. Period. He refused to consider any other options.

The sudden ringing of the phone came as a jarring surprise. First because it was so early, and second because he so seldom received phone calls. He liked it that way, having isolated himself in this old house in Granville when he'd decided to get out of Savannah after everything went down so badly last year. He rarely shared the number, and when he saw who was calling he heaved a heavy sigh. So much for staying out of the mind-hopping business. Because one of the few people in the world who could occasionally rope him into working missing persons cases again was on the other end of the phone line.

Julia Harrington hadn't given up trying to get him to come back to work for her, at least on a part-time basis. She knew him well enough to know he still had his fingers in a few pies out there, that he couldn't completely stay away from the world of crime solving, even if he did it without the "woo-woo" stuff, as she called it.

With this morning's incident fresh in his mind, he was tempted to just let the machine pick up. If he did, however, he'd be letting himself in for more calls, every half hour, around the clock, until he finally answered, and it didn't take any psychic abilities to know that. They'd played this game before. His former colleague was relentless about getting what she wanted.

"Hello, Julia," he said as soon as he lifted the phone to his mouth.

"How did you know it was me? Admit it—you're doing your psychic thing again, right?"

"Ever heard of a little invention called caller ID?"

"Oh, that. How mundane."

"Welcome to the twenty-first century."

Julia was one of the few people he kept in touch with from his old life. When everything had gone to hell with his last case, she'd been right there, standing beside him, ready to fight for his reputation if he asked her to.

He hadn't asked her to. Though he'd certainly appreciated the offer, Julia had her own issues. Ex-cop or no, she now owned a company called eXtreme Investigations, and led a team of psychic detectives. So she wasn't exactly the most staunch and upstanding of character references. Whenever her name came up, the media was almost as vicious toward her as they were toward Aidan.

Almost. Had she been working with him on that last case, she might now be living in the old house next door, just as wary, just as vilified.

"So, whatcha working on?"

"I don't do that anymore; remember?"

"Yeah, uh-huh, sure you don't. I thought about you the other day when I saw a story out of Charlotte about an 'anonymous tip' that led police to the killer of a local carpenter."

He stiffened, wondering how she could possibly have connected that to him.

"Morgan."

Ah. Morgan. Of course. Julia's business partner definitely got around.

"Reasonable deduction," he admitted grudgingly. "Nothing supernatural about it. I merely hacked into the case file, read the witness statements, and found some inconsistencies. It was all right there."

"Just can't stay out of it, can you?"

"If by 'it' you mean dabbling in cold-crime solving, I'll admit that I haven't lost my interest. But as for the rest? Hell, yes, I can stay out of it. So you might as well not even start."

"Hold on, before you go getting your excuses lined up about why you can't come back to the real world, and have to keep wearing your hair shirt and indulging in self-flagellation—"

"That was a mouthful."

"I'm just saying, don't panic. I'm not calling to beg you to come back to work, or to lure you into working a *special* case, or even to pick your brain."

He couldn't deny a flood of relief. She didn't want him for a job. He'd never worked for her exclusively, but he'd done a lot of contract jobs for Julia when she and her partner were getting eXtreme Investigations off the ground. Since his "retirement" she'd come to him a few times, strictly for advice—so she said—or trying to lure him into work via the back door of consultancy.

But not this time. Which meant she was probably calling to try to reengage him in a social life, like she had a few weeks ago when she and two of her other agents had shown up at his door. Aidan wasn't the type who enjoyed surprise visits, nor did he ever go to beer-and-wings joints like the one to which they'd dragged him. Despite the fact that he'd almost had a good time, he had no desire to repeat the experience. Because even here in Granville, where he was a newcomer and a stranger, people knew him by reputation—and oh, how they did like to stare.

"Aidan?"

"Okay, so why are you calling?" he asked, not sure he wanted to know.

"I got a call last night from a reporter."

"We don't use that word anymore, remember?"

"Oh, sorry. I mean, I got a call last night from a lying, manipulative media cockroach."

"Better."

"It's about the Remington case." The words sounded like they'd ridden out of her mouth on a deep sigh, as if she hated to be the bearer of bad news.

"Wonderful." Aidan lifted a hand to his face and rubbed at the corners of his eyes. Of all the names he didn't want to hear ever again, Remington topped the list. "Go on."

"He wanted to get in touch with you to see if you'd heard Caroline Remington tried to commit suicide last week, on the anniversary."

"Jesus." Aidan sagged against the back of the couch, a well of emotions surging through him. Anger, pity, frustration. Regret. Such regret. It was like his worst nightmare, only it just kept going and he couldn't wake up from it.

"I know; it's awful."

He'd never even met Mrs. Remington; she'd been well protected by her husband from the minute their son disappeared. But from the pictures he'd seen in the paper, she looked like a pretty, fragile woman whose world had been shattered, leaving her confused and heartbroken.

"Is she all right?"

"Apparently. She took some pills, but her husband found her in time. I thought you'd want to know, in case the cockroach from the morning news manages to track you down."

Finding out his general location probably wouldn't be too hard. He hadn't made it a state secret that he was moving to Granville, fifty miles west of Savannah. Or that he was giving up his role as prominent author, speaker, and expert on psychic phenomenon to become a hermit who growled at the world whenever it dared to intrude on him.

But at least his number was unpublished and his address unlisted. Anyone wanting to reach him would have to do some digging, and hopefully the reporter wouldn't bother.

Wishful thinking. In his experience, there was no place too low for most reporters, no dirt they wouldn't claw through, no muck they didn't want to rake up.

"I hate that this is coming up again," Julia said. "I'm really sorry."

"I figured it would, with the one-year mark. Besides, I'm not the one you should feel sorry for; Caroline Remington is."

First, for the loss of her six-year-old son, and second, for being married to a controlling, manipulative bastard like Theodore Remington.

Thrusting the anger away, he forced himself to think of the fact that, even though he was a rich, spoiled, overbearing asshole, Remington was also a grieving father. He had good reason to bear a grudge against Aidan. Whatever petty revenge he'd taken, using his contacts and power to make Aidan's life hell, it had been justified. After all, in Remington's mind, Aidan had been responsible for his son's death. And Aidan couldn't entirely disagree with him.

"Aidan?"

He sighed heavily. "As if I have anything to add on that subject? Haven't I said enough to and about that family?"

"It wasn't your fault."

"Yeah, yeah."

He'd heard those words a thousand times in the past twelve months, since the Remington boy had been found dead, trapped inside an old antique freezer in his own grandmother's garage. At least, he'd heard them from his friends and colleagues.

From strangers, the media, the boy's parents? Well, their words weren't nearly as comforting and their attitude not nearly as understanding.

"You are not responsible; it was a tragic accident."

"An accident," he repeated.

Maybe. Probably.

Or maybe not. Sometimes he wondered. Though, of course, he couldn't voice his curiosity now, couldn't ask the questions the investigators should have asked back then. Because he had zero credibility and nobody gave a damn what a disgraced former psychic thought.

"What you do isn't an exact science."

"No, but if I had stayed out of it, maybe—just maybe—somebody would have thought about how much the kid loved to play hide-and-seek, actually done a proper search and found him in time, rather than going on a wild-goose chase into every orchard in eastern Georgia."

All because when he'd focused all his thoughts and psychic energy on young Teddy Remington, he'd smelled peaches. He'd also felt the brittle spray of rain on his face, the press of hard wood against his back, and the sting of splinters puncturing his skin.

"You're repeating your own bad press," Julia insisted. "You didn't send them running around like a bunch of idiots. You told them what you were feeling and Ted Remington decided what it meant—that his son had wandered into one of the local orchards and gotten lost. You didn't put that boy in that freezer."

"I sure as hell didn't help him get out of it," he replied, hearing his own bitterness.

"Look, if the cops had been doing their jobs, it wouldn't have mattered if you had visions of a convicted pedophile snatching the kid." Her righteous anger exploded through the phone lines, snapping and hot. "Searching everyplace he could have gone, including his own damn grandmother's house down the street, was the first order of business. They should have been fired for letting Ted Remington's money and influence browbeat them in the wrong direction."

They should have been fired. And *he* should have been run out of town on a rail.

At least one of those *should haves* had come true. Not that he'd actually been run out of Savannah; he'd left of his own free will. But the effect was the same—Aidan McConnell was no longer in the psychic business. Never again would he let himself be responsible for the well-being of someone else's child. Not ever.

He'd had misfires before. Like Julia said, it wasn't an exact science. There had always, however, been some bit of truth, some small element that had been correct, just misinterpreted.

But in the Teddy Remington case? Nothing.

The top-opening, chest-type freezer had been ancient, unused for years. It had held no fruit, much less sweet, fragrant peaches, and the garage itself had smelled of nothing but stale air and mothballs. The unit hadn't been plugged in. It contained no moisture at all, so the child certainly hadn't felt the hard, punishing spray of cold water on his face. Rusty metal, sagging plastic—no hardwood, certainly no tree limbs, nothing to cause splinters. All wrong.

"You okay?"

"I'm fine. Thanks for the heads-up," he told Julia. "I'll

be sure to activate my electric fence and charge up the cattle prod."

"Ha-ha. No torturing members of the press, as tempting a target as they may be."

Considering how brutally the media had dissected him last year, stopping just short of accusing him of murdering a child, they were indeed a tempting target. Still, he said, "Got it."

"We've got a lot of cases, Aidan. Let me know when you're ready to get back to work."

"Let *me* know when you're ready to stop asking."

"Not gonna happen."

A bitter laugh emerged from Aidan's mouth and he shook his head. "Ditto."

Not gonna happen.

Thursday, 8:15 a.m.

As she typed her article on the community playhouse's production of *Annie*, Lexie Nolan somehow managed to refrain from punching her fist through the computer monitor. It took some effort, real willpower. But the urge faded when she reminded herself of a few pertinent truths.

First, it would hurt. She might slice off a finger, which would make typing a real chore.

Second, she wasn't using her own computer; this one was owned by the newspaper for which she worked. Considering the reporting pool for the *Granville Daily Sun* had a sum total of three creaky old desktops for use by the entire staff, she would not only have to pay to replace it, but would greatly inconvenience the other four reporters who worked here.

The main reason, though, was because punching anything—a monitor, a wall, the mayor—wouldn't change the fact that she'd gotten herself into this situation all on her own. It wasn't the PC's fault. Nor was it the fault of those chirpy, perky little orphans singing their guts out in the local musical. It was all her own doing.

She was the one who'd insisted on writing a story she knew would anger a lot of people. The one who'd convinced her editor to let her. The one who'd researched and worked seven days a week and sacrificed any kind of personal life for months. She'd poured her heart and her soul and every intuition she owned into what she'd been sure would be a shocking, sordid tale that would soon draw the eyes of the entire world to this small Georgia town.

She'd been so utterly positive . . . right up until the moment she'd been proven wrong.

So she was also the one who got to watch as her career blew up in her face. Lexie Nolan, the former big-fish-in-this-little-reporting-pond had been busted down to guppy. She'd been demoted from her position as the hard-news reporter on staff to covering local theater productions and basket bingo fund-raisers.

And it was all on her head.

"Aren't you finished yet?"

Another punch-worthy target popped into her field of vision. But just as she couldn't fling her fist at inanimate objects, she couldn't pummel the smirk off Stan Brightman's face, either. The fact that the other reporter had enjoyed her downfall, and had been the one to most benefit from it, since he was now covering the crime beat for the paper, was just part of the biz. He hadn't stolen her job—she'd handed it to him on a platter of unprovable suspicion, unconfirmed rumor, and pure journalistic frenzy.

"I think every little girl in town is in this show. Lots of names to get right or those stage mommies won't be happy."

"Oh, yeah, you definitely wouldn't want to get anything *wrong* in this one."

She forced a tight smile as the obnoxious man, who smelled of the ham-and-eggs special he'd had for breakfast, entered the cubicle. Stan was one of those middle-aged guys who thought a droopy mustache, sideburns, and a comb-over would prevent anyone from noticing his blossoming bald spot. The buttons of his disco-era polyester dress shirt bulged under utter duress.

He'd played the big-newsman-takes-newbie-under-his-wing game six years ago when she'd landed this job, right out of college. When that hadn't worked, he'd started hitting on her. Since that had been a no-go, too, he'd resorted to hating her guts and plotting her downfall.

That was when she'd started mentally thinking of him as S(a)tan.

"I'll be finished with the computer soon," she said, pretending she didn't know he'd come in here only to be a dick.

"No worries; take your time." His voice could serve as the audible definition of smarmy.

Stan clearly delighted in Lexie's fall from grace and she suspected that only the loss of her job would have made him happier. Stan had probably wallpapered his bedroom with copies of the retraction and public apology Lexie had been forced to write for the paper last month.

That retraction had earned her stares of hatred and resentment nearly everywhere she went. She'd terrified an entire townful of people. She'd not only blown her career; she had made herself a pariah in the process. Probably only one other person in Granville was more regularly vilified from under the blow-dryers at the Blow-N-Go Salon or across the aisles at the local churches. Considering that guy was a disgraced psychic who'd moved here from Savannah after being accused of costing a child his life, that wasn't much comfort.

She wondered what the locals would think if they knew how she really felt about what had happened, and her role in it. Because she wasn't the heartless fear-mongerer she'd been made out to be. A big part of her had been relieved, hoping deep down that she *had* been wrong, that the missing local teenagers she'd written about were out there somewhere, safe and sound.

Something deep inside her, however, had never fully accepted it. A few questions had been answered, to the satisfaction of most people around here. But Lexie had a lot more. She just wasn't allowed to ask them.

Oh, how they haunted her, even now. Especially now. Because every single night, Lexie still went to bed thinking about those lost girls.

"Lex? I need you in here!"

Saved by the boss. "Guess I gotta go. Computer's all yours."

Rising, she saw by the quick narrowing of Stan's eyes that he didn't like her being called into Walter's office. Walter Kirby, the editor of the paper, might have bowed under pressure and demoted Lexie, but he hadn't fired her, and she remained his closest confidante on staff.

Stan had once floated the rumor that it was because something was going on between them. If he'd understood anything about their boss, he'd have long since realized that Walter, the father of four daughters, simply stepped into protector mode around young women he viewed as vulnerable. When he'd realized she was being subtly harassed, he'd put the fear of God into S(a)tan, and had taken Lexie under his wing as if she were his own.

So maybe it was quid pro quo. She'd given him her job, but Stan had contributed to the close relationship Lexie now enjoyed with their editor. She blessed that relationship; Walter was the closest thing to a father she had, since her own dad had passed away when she was twenty.

Stan pivoted, pushing past her. "Yeah, boss, I actually needed to talk to you about—"

"Later." Walter crooked a finger at Lexie, beckoning her into his office.

She recognized that stiff finger and Walter's frown. Something was bugging him, but she didn't worry. She had been playing the part of Good Girl Friday lately and hadn't done a damn thing to jack up Walter's blood pressure. Or to rescue her own savaged career.

It had been hard, almost painful, but she'd let it all go. Journalistic fervor was well and good, but in this economy, so was being able to pay her rent.

Besides, you were wrong; they're all runaways. Just runaways.

That didn't help. No matter how many times she repeated the mantra in her mind, she never felt better about having given up on the poor kids whose story she'd tried so hard to tell.

" 'Scuse me, Miz Lexa," a voice said.

Lexie glanced over and realized her anxious, sneakered feet had almost met the business end of a sopping mop, which was being pushed by Kenny, the maintenance guy.

"Whoops. Sorry," she said.

He ducked his head, not meeting her eye, as usual, as if he knew how hard it sometimes was for people to look at him and not reveal the dismay the sight of his face usually wrought. "S'okay. Just be careful. Wouldn't want you to slip and fall. Somebody spilt coffee."

Kenny seemed to operate in his own world and was left alone, either because everyone sensed he was a bit slow, or because of the scars on his wrecked face and hands that made him an object of pity to those around him. The scars and that pity were probably why Walter had given him a part-time job when he'd shown up several months before looking for work.

"Will do. Have a good day, Kenny."

Stepping around Kenny's work area, she entered Walter's office. "Hey, boss." She kicked the door shut behind her, though it wouldn't stop Stan from trying to eavesdrop. The other man was a lurker. She had no doubt he stood right outside the office glaring at the closed door.

"What's up?"

Walter merely gestured toward one of the two stiff,

uncomfortable chairs fronting his overloaded desk. Lexie lowered herself into one, but didn't prompt him. Walter always needed to bluster a bit before coming to the point.

"Stubborn kids," he mumbled as he walked around the desk and sat in his well-worn chair. It emitted a long groan as he leaned back, lacing his fingers together on his barrel chest.

"Problems at home?"

"Would it really have been too much to ask for one of my children to have been born without any estrogen?"

She hid a smile. The lament was a frequent one. "Sorry."

Mournfully shaking his head, he added, "It's hard now to remember how sweet they looked when they were little, in their Sunday dresses and princess costumes, because now they do nothing but hold out their hands for money."

"You keep putting it there," she mumbled.

Walter continued as if she hadn't said a word. "Or they scream, 'I hate you,' because you say they can't go to a rock concert in the next state with a tattooed, ear-gauge-wearing slimeball who rides a motorcycle." He paused for breath after the rant, rubbing a weary hand over his eyes. "I shoulda quit after the twins were born. Or halfway through—after Jenny, before Taylor."

Taylor was younger than her identical twin sister, Jenny, by about fifteen minutes. To hear Walter tell it, over the past several months she had segued from Sweet Valley High senior into Stephen King's Carrie-the-psycho-prom-queen.

"That child drives me crazy and will end up being the death of me."

Lexie grunted, seeing through the grousing. Walter was a human-sized marshmallow when it came to his girls. He adored all of them, from the seventeen-year-old twins down to the thirteen-year-old baby. "She'll snap out of it. Now that Ann-Marie is doing so much better, and she's not afraid she's going to lose her mom, Taylor will get over this rebellious kid thing."

A brief smile softened his features. Ann-Marie, Walter's wife, had recently been pronounced in remission after a long battle with lymphoma. Things were finally looking up for the man—at least at home. At work was another story. After the scandal, he'd had to do some fast-talking to keep his own job as well as Lexie's, of that she had no doubt. Even though he was part owner of the paper, he was the minority shareholder.

"I got a call this morning from Chief Dunston."

"Wow, what a nice way to start the day."

Despite the flippant words, every cell in her body reacted to the name. Her ears still stung from the insults she'd endured the last time she'd come face-to-face with the jerk who swaggered around wearing a police chief's uniform.

"I've had better."

She didn't doubt it. Dunston hated to be questioned, and Lexie was all about asking questions. Considering her questions had led to a lot of speculation about whether he was actually doing his job, she had no doubt she held the number-one position on his shit list.

"So what'd Chief Dunce want? I haven't done anything," she insisted.

He waved an unconcerned hand. "I know."

"Then what's the problem?"

"He wanted to remind me how much better it would be if you no longer worked here."

"What'd you say?"

"I reminded him how much better it would be if he had a set of balls."

She snickered. "Zing."

"It's only the truth. Jack's not a bad man, just a weak one."

Not knowing the man, she'd have to reserve judgment on that. "So what's got him on the warpath again? You haven't printed a single story accusing him of having no balls or speculating on whether a serial killer is operating right under his nose in, oh, a month, at least."

His eyes gleamed. Walter was a newsman through and through, even if he did live in a town of twelve thousand, where the biggest crime news usually involved sleazy jerks dealing drugs or addicts stealing money to buy them. For a little while, he'd relived his city desk days, joining Lexie in the thrill of chasing down what might have been the biggest story of their careers. Their failure had been as huge as their effort, but damn, what a ride.

"Apparently Chief Dunston got a call yesterday from a woman who lives down in the Boro. This 'drunk ho'— to use his description—was all riled up. Seems she read the articles last month and was calling about her teenage daughter, who disappeared earlier this week."

A jolt of almost electric fear shot through her. How could it not? Every journalistic bone in Lexie's body had been sure, utterly certain, she'd been onto something. It was hard to let go of that certainty, even under indisputable proof and extreme duress.

If this girl's disappearance was anything like the others, her mother might as well give up hope right now of ever seeing her again. The Boro had become the Bermuda Triangle for poor young women who seemed to round the wrong corner and disappear forever. She didn't care what kind of "drunk ho" the woman might be. Losing a child was, in her opinion, the very worst thing that could happen to any parent.

"Apparently she insists her daughter didn't run away but was a victim of the Ghoul."

Lexie rolled her eyes. "The Ghoul. That's so stupid. I didn't come up with that, *he* did!"

"I know."

During a press conference in which he'd vivisected Lexie, the chief of police had accused her of searching for spooks, inventing a serial killer, whom he dubbed the Granville Ghoul. Ridiculing her speculations had helped discredit her. A little spiteful humor and two or three pieces of evidence and he'd succeeded in shutting her down completely.

Oh. The fact that he regularly golfed with both the mayor, and with Walter's partner, majority owner of the paper—and therefore Walter's boss—didn't hurt, either.

A thought suddenly made her frown in confusion. "Wait, why would the chief tip you off? Another missing girl sounds like the last thing he'd want us to know about!"

"Actually, he didn't tell me. I heard last night. Word is spreading throughout the schools and the girls were upset." He shook his head, not liking anything to upset his daughters, despite how he griped about them. "As for Dunston, I think he was going for a preemptive strike. He suspects the mother is going to call you and wanted to make sure I had you under control."

Lexie lifted one brow at that word.

Laughing, Walter held his hands up, palms out. "Hey, I would never dream of claiming such a thing. With four daughters, I know better than to think I control anything in my life except the amount of time I get to spend in the bathroom."

Lexie snorted. "With four daughters, I'm surprised you actually have your own bathroom." Her laughter faded as did his. Then, as much as it pained her, Lexie gave him the reassurance she assumed he'd called her in here for. "It's okay. If she calls, I'll . . ."

"You'll hear her out."

Lexie hesitated, seeing a look of determined defiance on Walter's face.

"How many?" He slammed his hand down on the desk. Though he kept his voice low, in acknowledgment of the in-house spy, it shook as he added, "For God's sake, how many young women can go missing without somebody other than you and me starting to wonder whether there's a darker reason for it than our police chief would like us to believe?"

Lexie's mouth dropped open. For weeks, she'd been tiptoeing around the building, remorseful, regretful, certain she'd let her boss down and had deserved the scorn that had been heaped on her head. Equally certain Walter felt the same way, or at least wished he'd kept her on a shorter leash. Now the realization that he hadn't simply shocked her into silence.

"Lex, they wanted to shut you up. And I let them." He leaned over the desk, twisting his thick fingers together tightly until the knuckles grew white. "I let them."

"What haven't you told me?" she asked softly. "Something else happened. What is it?"

He stared at her for a long moment, then cast a quick glance toward the door. Whatever it was he wanted to say, he wouldn't do it here, no matter how low the whisper.

"Why don't you come over for dinner tomorrow night?" he asked, his voice at a normal level. "Ann-Marie and the girls would love to see you."

Nodding, she was just as normal in her reply. "Sounds great! I'd love to see them, too."

She had been a frequent guest of the Kirbys before Ann-Marie's illness. But she didn't doubt why she was receiving this invitation. In the privacy of his house, Walter would tell her whatever it was that he was afraid to reveal here.

"Why not tonight?" she mouthed.

He leaned over his desk to whisper, "I need more time to confirm what I'm hearing." Then, loud again, "Of course, I can't promise the kids will actually be around for long on a Friday night. Biggest game of the season, you know. Two hometown teams going head-to-head."

Meaning Taylor and Jenny would both be donning

their cheerleading uniforms. Hundreds of kids and their parents, who wanted to relive their own glory days, would crowd the stadium of Granville High to roar for their football heroes.

Her smile was slightly cynical as she thought of how nice and quaint the old-fashioned Friday-night ritual was. Because nice and quaint didn't describe the Granville Lexie had come to know recently. No, they weren't the words one would associate with missing teenagers or with the shut-down of the local press.

Given the usual tensions between the residents of the Boro and those in the north side of town, she could only imagine rumors of another disappearance would make things even more tense when Granville went up against Hoover High. "I suppose the missing girl went to Hoover. That's where I'll start . . ."

Walter shook his head. "Not Hoover. She was from GHS. My daughters know her, Lex." His throat worked as he swallowed, hard. "Jenny was one of the last people to see her. She's the one who told me the girl was missing."

Wow. No wonder he was in a state about this. "I'm sorry," she murmured. "But it's really interesting that she's from the other school."

All of the other missing teens had gone to the "poor" high school, or they'd been dropouts. This was the first from the snooty side of town. No wonder the chief was panicking. North Granville was the only part of the area he seemed to give a damn about.

"Here." Walter reached into his desk and drew out a sheet of paper.

"What's this?" She took the paper, opened it, and read the name and address. Genuinely surprised, she asked, "You really want me to contact *him*?"

Walter nodded once. "I have my reasons. I don't know that he'll talk to you, but I think he might be able to help with this."

Huh. She had her doubts. But she wasn't about to argue with her boss now that he'd given Lexie her journalistic legs back. "I guess it makes sense. I considered interviewing him before we broke the story, after I heard he used to specialize in missing persons cases."

"I wish we had reached out to the man."

A few days ago—hell, an hour ago—she would have responded with a pessimistic, *Why? Because he could have saved us the trouble and told us we were chasing people who weren't really missing?*

Now, though, she didn't. All the scorn and the accusations that she'd been creating news, or seeing boogeymen, the spiteful laughter at her expense of the past month—they had suddenly evaporated, become completely irrelevant. Things had changed. Yet another girl had disappeared. And Walter had stumbled across something important. She knew it.

"I don't know how much of that supernatural stuff I believe, but there's no doubt this guy is smart. Even if it's just intuition, this McConnell guy comes up with some amazing insights."

She lifted a surprised brow. "You know him?"

"Know of."

"Yeah, quite a rep he's got."

"You should know better than anyone not to believe everything you read in the papers."

"Touché."

Lexie rose from her chair, tucking the piece of paper into her pocket. Not leaving yet, she offered her boss a genuine smile. "I can't tell you how much I appreciate your trust and your faith in me. And thanks for believing me to begin with."

The big man waved off the humble thanks. "See what you can find and we'll talk more tomorrow at dinner. Come around six thirty."

Suddenly thinking of his wife, who was recovering, but certainly not yet healthy, she felt a stab of embarrassment. She'd been so interested in whatever information Walter had to share, she hadn't considered the imposition on his wife. "I don't want to put Ann-Marie to any trouble. How about I bring some pizzas?"

He chuckled. "You really think my wife does the cooking? Puh-lease. Her meatloaf could be used in place of a cement block to hold a Mafia hit man's victim underwater. The girls threatened starvation protests if she ever went near the kitchen again. I'm still chief cook and bottle washer these days. Ann-Marie's strictly the supervisor."

His bluster didn't fool her one bit. The tenderness in his voice and on his face when he talked about his family was something to behold. Whatever Ann-Marie's skills in the kitchen, her husband wasn't about to let her take on too much.

What a good man. The nicest, most decent one she knew. Again, Lexie had to acknowledge how blessed she'd been the day he'd hired her.

"And listen to that mother if she calls," he added softly.

She nodded. Oh yeah, she'd take the call and listen very carefully.

If that call didn't come, she'd go one step further. She would do what she did best: dig around to find out which girl had missed school all week and go find the mother herself.

As she left the office, she wanted to skip with relief. For the first time in a month, she allowed herself to fully believe she hadn't been wrong, hadn't been the sleazy reporter making up juicy scandal, finding salacious stories where there were none.

Deep down, she'd always known it. She just hadn't allowed herself to think too much about it, knowing those thoughts would lead her to bitterness and even more worry about things she knew were happening but was powerless to change.

Now, the man she respected more than anybody else

had given her his blessing to remember who she really was and what she did best.

Lexie sought the truth. She almost always found it. And this time, she would not rest until every ugly secret in this town was brought out into the light.

Including the fates of all those missing girls.

Chapter 2

Aidan should have been bored.

The change in his lifestyle from Savannah to here had meant removing himself from the day-to-day regularity of work. He didn't need the money, having made a lot over the years, with book royalties still coming in and several recession-proof investment choices.

That meant he didn't live on a schedule, didn't pencil in meetings or go into the private office he'd kept near Wright Square. There were no more visits to crime scenes with the SPD, no trips out of state to help a family in need, no interviews with witnesses, lawyers, or the media. No explorations of the lives of missing people, no careful touches of their hairbrushes, their pillows, their clothing, all in an effort to find out where they were— and if they were still alive.

None of that.

The house, which he'd bought for next to nothing, was old, but not in need of significant repair. He certainly wasn't involved in the local community, and he sure as hell wasn't the type to have a cold one over the back fence with the neighbors. So after almost a year of solitude, he probably should have gone crazy out of sheer boredom.

Fortunately, though, he'd found a way to keep himself busy, challenged, and almost entertained. He'd also occasionally managed to make the cops look like idiots. That was a plus.

Which was why he was now calling a complete stranger, a rich widow in Atlanta who lived with her equally rich, equally widowed sister. The women might be about to help him solve an armed robbery that had taken place in her neighborhood. They just didn't know it yet.

"Hi, is this Millicent Weinberg?" he asked, tucking the phone into the crook of his neck.

"Yes? Who is this?" asked a demanding voice.

"This is Charlie. I work for Tony's Pizzeria and deliver pizza to your house."

"You must be mistaken," the old woman said. He could almost hear her frowning; snobby old ladies from Buckhead didn't order pizza. Especially not extralarge pizzas with half a pig sitting on top. Mushrooms, onions, double sausage, double pepperoni—either the woman had a cast-iron stomach or she hadn't been the one who'd ordered the artery-hardening pie that had been delivered to her door one night eight weeks ago.

"I don't think so, ma'am. I got the record right here that says at seven thirty on the second Friday of September, an eighteen-inch pizza with the works was brought to your back door."

"Ridiculous . . ."

"Your purchase means you've won a coupon to try our new triple-bacon, sausage pizza."

The woman's gasp made him fall silent to wait for the payoff.

"First of all, young man, if it was a Friday evening, I was at temple. Which, unless you're as uneducated as you are uncouth, means I am not a customer who would be interested in bacon or sausage pizza. I did not order anything from your establishment. I never have."

"But—"

The woman harrumphed. "Wait. The second Friday of September, you say? I wasn't even in town! We didn't even come back from our summer place in the mountains until a week later."

Score. "Maybe somebody else at your house placed the order?"

"Impossible! My sister and I took our live-in housekeeper with us."

Interesting. Aidan had to wonder whether that housekeeper had happened to lose her key to the Weinberg house one day before she'd left, or whether she'd merely misplaced it for a few hours—long enough for her sleazy, drug-addicted half brother to have a copy made.

Said sleazy thief had been looked at by the local cops for the violent break-in near the Weinberg house, but they hadn't connected him to the housekeeper who worked right up the street from the vic. Dumb mistake; Aidan had put them together with a one-hour records search.

The guy had an alibi for that night. A false one, Aidan had felt sure. Now he thought he could prove it—with some help from the real pizza delivery boy, with whom he'd already spoken.

The local PD could have done that, too. Instead, they'd ignored one of the witness statements about a pizza delivery vehicle being spotted in the neighborhood two hours before the robbery, dismissing it as irrelevant. In Aidan's opinion, when working violent crimes, nothing was irrelevant. Every lead deserved to be followed.

He might have to remind the detectives of that when he dropped the info he'd gathered into their ears. Maybe it would teach them a lesson. It should certainly cause a little embarrassment for the investigators whose work had been so shoddy. Win-win.

"Well, ma'am, thanks for your—"

He was interrupted by a loud knock on the front door. Startled, as he was so unused to visitors, Aidan almost dropped the phone.

"Mr. McConnell? I need to speak with you!" called a muffled voice from the front porch. The person didn't wait for a response, knocking again and adding a sharp jab of the doorbell.

He flung his hand over the mouthpiece of the phone, but apparently not in time.

"Wait a minute. Where did you say you're calling from?" Mrs. Weinberg asked, her tone sharp. She'd obviously heard the doorbell, not exactly standard background noise at a pizza joint.

"Uh, I better go. Got some deliveries to make. Thanks a lot!"

"Young man . . ."

He hung up, swinging around to look out the arched doorway between his office and the foyer, frying the front door with his heated stare. Not even putting the cordless phone down, he stalked to it and swept the door open.

"Aidan McConnell?" the woman asked, flinching, as if surprised at how suddenly, and forcefully, he'd answered.

He didn't reply, taking a moment to assess his unexpected visitor.

She was pretty. Very pretty. Looked to be in her late twenties. Her fine blond hair was swept into a ponytail that brushed her shoulders, her cheeks a little pinkened by the strong autumn breeze that had turned his deep, covered porch into a wind tunnel. Of average height, she had to tilt her head back to meet his angry stare.

Her dark green eyes had quickly narrowed with determination when she'd seen him. The woman's small jaw was thrust out a tiny bit, as if she'd been steeling herself for something, and the way she held her slim form—squared shoulders, stiff back, frown—indicated she knew he wasn't going to want to speak to her.

The car parked at the curb looked fairly new, the hood wasn't up nor were any of the tires visibly flat, so she wasn't a stranded motorist in search of a phone. Of course, he'd already known that, since she'd called him by name.

Her clothes—a Bulldogs hoodie, jeans, and sneakers— didn't scream door-to-door salesperson, Bible pusher, or census taker. Despite the backpack hanging off one shoulder, she was too old to be a student. She looked too casual to be a professional, yet too determined to be a neighbor.

One thing left.

Reporter.

Aidan didn't give it another thought. Reacting purely on instinct, he slammed the door right in her face.

Surprisingly, the media bloodsucker didn't waste one minute on being shocked or insulted. Instead, she immediately pounded on the door, using her fist this time. "Mr. McConnell, please, I just want to talk to you. My name's Alexa Nolan. I'm a—"

"I know what you are," he called from inside. "And I know what you want. Get in your car and go back to Savannah. I have no comment."

"I'm not from Savannah."

National media? It seemed a bit much for a ghost like him from a year-old news story, but he wouldn't put anything past some of those scandal-stirring shows, especially with Mrs. Remington's suicide attempt.

"Mr. McConnell?"

"Go back to whatever hole you crawled out of and get a life, why don't you?"

"That hole would be right here. I'm with the *Granville Daily Sun*."

Oh, great. So much for trying to keep a low profile. The local yokels had jumped into the action, looking for a titillating headline. *Fake Psychic Drives Mother to Attempt Suicide*. It would probably appear in the weekend edition, below *Mayor Hooks a Ten-Pound Catfish* and above *Congregation Sick After Eating Old Potato Salad*.

At least, that's what he imagined the local paper would look like. He'd certainly never picked one up. Aidan didn't read any papers within a hundred-mile radius of his current location, though he closely watched the crime reports in dozens of other major cities across the country. He especially avoided the rag from Savannah, and the dinky small-town ones that loved to fling innuendo while wearing the mantle of folksy human interest.

"Please, I need help."

"Yeah, no kidding," he said, thinking just about everyone who chose her manipulative, vicious profession needed help—of the mental variety. "Try a shrink. Or a priest."

"Mr. McConnell?"

"Get off my porch before I call the police."

"Good luck getting them to answer," she said. "The inattention of the police is one of the things I want to talk to you about."

That caught his interest, albeit briefly. Not the biggest fan of those in blue these days, he was up for hearing from almost anyone else who had similar stories to tell.

There was one exception to the *anyone*, however. Because there was one group of people he disliked even more: reporters. "The answer is no. And this conversation is finished."

He turned and headed back into his office, sure she'd leave once she realized he wasn't going to open the door again. Even if she did stick around and wait for him to come out, she'd be waiting for a long time. He seldom went anywhere, knowing the only place he was entirely safe from intrusion was behind his own closed doors. He'd learned that lesson well in Savannah.

But this wasn't Savannah. No longer did he live in an exclusive condo with a friendly old doorman guarding the entrance. His new home was an old Victorian with a verandah that wrapped around three quarters of the house. He'd never quite understood the ramifications of that until he realized the damned woman was following him from the outside. She suddenly appeared at the French doors behind his desk. There she started tap-tap-tapping on the glass like a veritable raven out of Poe's nightmare.

The woman had brass ones.

"Mr. McConnell, please, give me five minutes. I really need to talk to you. I have nowhere else to turn."

He gaped at her, kicking himself for tearing down the filmy sheers that had been left by the previous owners. They might have afforded some privacy from the determined woman. That was something he'd remedy just as soon as he could pick up some long blinds. Hell, he might just have to tack up some old sheets in the meantime.

"I'm not leaving until you hear me out."

Lifting the phone again, he called, "They do have 911 in this town, don't they?"

"So I hear."

He punched the 9 button. "How long will it take them to get here, do you think?"

Frustration washed over her face and her full mouth twisted. "Would you just shut up and listen for one second?"

He had to give her credit. She wasn't like the typical attractive female reporters he'd dealt with—the ones who used smiles and low necklines to forward their agendas. She hadn't started flirting, hadn't used her pretty face or her admittedly curvy body to get a foot in the door with him. But that was about the only positive thing he could say about her so far.

"It's about a missing person."

At the words "missing person" Aidan's muscles tensed to rock hardness. He'd once made a name for himself off that term. Now it was stricken from his vocabulary—the mental one and the verbal one. The surefire way to guarantee she didn't cross his threshold was to try to cajole him with that kind of bait.

"I've been looking into this on my own for a long time; the police don't care that this young woman is missing. I know you've got experience with this type of thing. I'm not looking for an interview; I just need some help."

Aidan hesitated, though he didn't lower the phone. She could be lying, making up some story to get in so she could hit him with the Remington crap all over again. But something about the sheer frustration in her voice told him she wasn't.

"I'm not lying to you, or trying to talk my way in," she said, correctly reading his skepticism. "Her name's Vonnie Jackson, she's seventeen, and she disappeared while walking home from an event at her school Monday night."

A few convincing details. She was either good at her job, or believed what she was talking about. Of course, there was one big hole in her story. "How long can you have been working on this if she just disappeared Monday?" he asked with a smirk.

She didn't even hesitate to think up an answer. "She isn't the first. Something strange is going on in this town, and nobody else seems to want to find out why."

He thought for a second, suddenly remembering a few of the whispers of conversation he'd heard in passing when he'd had to make a trip to a local grocery store. There had also been some serious gossip floating that night a couple of weeks ago when he'd gone out to dinner with Julia and the other XI agents. People had been talking about some big local scandal. He'd tuned out as much as possible, but the echoes lingered.

Other echoes were louder, however. The grief of an anguished father, the helpless scream of a heartbroken mother, the accusations of an enraged public, the blame and condemnation of a city police force, and the glee of a rabid press. Yeah, those all came through loud and clear.

"Five minutes," she pleaded.

No. Not again. Never again.

"I don't do that anymore," he said, keeping his voice raised, both as a self-reminder and so she could hear him from outside.

The woman stared at him, something haunted and desperate in her vivid green eyes. "It's a matter of life and death!"

"That I *especially* don't do anymore."

"You did once," she snapped. "I know you did. I've spent the day reading about you."

He leaned against his desk, crossing his arms and staring at her with a jaded smile. "Then you know why I don't talk to reporters."

Her hand flattened against the glass door panel and he could see the slimness of every finger. "I'm not here to do a story about you. Please, I'm desperate."

Something about the pleading tone in her voice got to him, grabbing at him, at least for a second. He'd almost swear she was telling the truth. The fear in her eyes wasn't a simple reporter's worry about not getting the story. She looked genuinely worried about someone else.

A matter of life and death, she'd said. Maybe she'd even meant it.

But he couldn't give her what she wanted, couldn't make himself responsible for anybody's life ever again. He simply wasn't willing to carry the weight of one more death.

"I'm sorry," he told her, knowing she probably wouldn't believe him, though he meant it.

"You won't even hear me out?"

He shook his head, resolute, certain, and forbidding.

She finally got the message. Acceptance mingled with disappointment made her shoulders sag and her anxious frown deepen into one of anger.

"Yeah. Whatever," she said, raking him with a look of disgust. "You stay locked up safe while that poor teenage waitress disappears off the face of the earth like she was never born."

The woman, this Alexa Nolan, turned as if to leave, but then hesitated. She reached into her backpack, dug out a sheet of pale green paper, and slid it into the crack between the doors. It hung there, half inside, half out, resting on the lock. The page flapped in the breeze, looking like a Greenpeace flag, cautionary and guilt-inducing, demanding notice.

"Try looking at her face and still getting to sleep tonight," she said.

If only she knew. He didn't need any more faces of the lost to keep him from sleeping. He'd waged a life-long battle with insomnia.

Their eyes met one more time, hers green and stormy; his, he knew, dark and unyielding. Aidan didn't move toward the door, didn't say a word. He merely crossed his arms and watched until, finally, the reporter shook her head, turned and trudged away. Her shadow moved past the windows in front, and her footsteps came heavily on the steps as she descended. Other than that, the only noise was the faint rippling of that single sheet of crumpled paper she'd left behind.

Damn it. He knew what was on it, knew why she'd left it. She was trying to suck him in, grab his interest whether he wanted to allow it or not. Or else she thought she could guilt him into getting involved.

"Nice try, but it's not happening, lady," he mumbled, crossing the room. He didn't touch the paper she'd left, not because he expected he'd get any kind of feeling off it—his abilities didn't work that way. He had to be focusing for it to kick in, almost to invite the connection.

Except when somebody smells gingerbread.

He flung off the thought. That episode had been an aberration. Thankfully, it hadn't been repeated, either. There had been no further incidents. That mental wall was still sky-high, his abilities in safe mode.

Flicking the lock, he pulled the handle, opening the door an inch, trusting the wind would take the missing persons flyer without him having to lay a finger on it. Somehow, though, the Georgia air wasn't cooperating, or else the antilittering gods had other plans. Instead of whipping the document outside where he never had to think about it again, a gust carried it in. The page twirled and spun lightly, like a leaf riding a current of air, then came to rest on top of the mountain of manila envelopes piled on his desk.

Aidan shook his head, his jaw stiff. The cursed thing had landed faceup, right-side up, too, in the dead center of his work space. His files and other documents almost framed it. To Aidan's eyes, it resembled the lid of Pandora's box, just waiting to be opened.

Pressing his fingers to his temples, he felt the deepening throb of his pulse, each beat accompanied by a sliver of pain. The first hints of a headache. He so did not need this.

"Forget it," he snapped aloud. He didn't give it another thought before he grabbed the green menace, crumpled it into a ball, and tossed it right into the trash can.

Then he froze. His breath caught and he stared down into the depths of the metal can where that one damned scrap rested alone. Not because he'd felt anything when he'd touched it, but because of the picture—the photograph of the missing girl. He'd caught a glimpse of it as he'd swooped the flyer up and the wheels and cogs in his brain processed it almost against his own will. The pieces had clicked into place even as he'd tossed the unwanted page away.

Poor teenage waitress.

He knew her. He'd met her. He'd touched her less than three weeks ago.

And if she had, indeed, been kidnapped and was being held against her will somewhere, he greatly feared he might have mentally connected with her mind. He might even have heard her scream.

Though Aidan wanted to, he knew he could no longer ignore the reporter. Not without learning more. Not without finding out whether he already had information that could, indeed, help save a young woman's life.

Thursday, 4:10 p.m.

Though they looked identical, the Kirby twins weren't very much alike.

Taylor was tough and gutsy, Jenny sweet natured and considerate. Taylor squeaked by with Cs, Jenny's name had never given up its permanent spot on the honor role. Taylor routinely barreled into trouble, Jenny carefully avoided it. Taylor took crap from nobody and loved dishing it out. Jenny usually let people walk all over her and seldom stood up for herself.

So, really, it should have been Taylor who'd gotten them into this current sticky situation. Only, it hadn't been. It had been the "good" twin for once.

"Oh God, what are we going to do?" Jenny asked, her chin trembling.

The two of them sat on the floor in Taylor's room, behind a locked door that meant their two younger sisters needed to stay out and let them do their "weird twin" thing, as their siblings called it. The rest of the family was used to giving them their space, and even though Taylor had insisted she wanted some independence, and had moved into her own room when they'd started high school, more often than not they still spent the night together.

"Calm down. It'll be fine," Taylor insisted.

She didn't like seeing such weakness on her sister's face, mainly because it was too much like seeing it in herself. And she didn't even want to consider being weak, not when she'd always been the fighter.

Besides, somebody needed to stay calm and rational about this. She had looked after Jenny all their lives and would continue to do so.

"I swear, it's going to be all right. It's not like there's anything we can do about it, anyway. We just have to stick to our story."

Jenny grabbed her hand. "You don't have to cover for me. It was my fault. I should come clean about it; that's what you'd do."

Taylor knew she meant it. Jenny would take the fall alone if she had to. Because, in her own way, Jenny always looked out for her, too. The only time her twin ever showed any kind of temper was when she rose to Taylor's defense.

They were mirror images, people said, two halves of

the same whole. Despite how much her sister's niceness got on her nerves sometimes, Taylor knew she would absolutely lay down her life for Jenny if it was ever necessary. She also knew the feeling was mutual.

"We should just tell Dad," Jenny added.

Taylor shook her head, horrified by the idea. "What's the point? I mean, it's not like I really saw anything, or know anything. I don't have one tiny little idea what happened to Vonnie Jackson. And if you'd been at the meeting, like everyone thinks you were, you wouldn't know anything either."

Monday certainly hadn't been the first time the twins had changed places. Usually, it was for Taylor's benefit—like when they'd first started high school and she'd been flunking out of Algebra and needed her sister to take a couple of her tests.

That hadn't lasted long. Their teachers had gotten pretty good at telling them apart because of their personalities and the one feature that distinguished them: the nickel-sized birthmark at the base of Taylor's throat, just above her collarbone. Last year, their teachers had even gone to the school administrators, demanding that the Kirby twins be restricted from wearing turtlenecks, as ridiculous as that sounded.

But when they weren't going to be closely scrutinized, they still pulled switches now and then. And Monday night, at the honors society meeting, nobody should have cared enough to tell which Kirby twin was there. It had been no big deal for Taylor to sit with the nerdy kids and pretend to be interested in all that academic junk. In fact, she'd liked it, smiling to herself as she thought about how she'd contributed to the delinquency of her straight-laced sister.

Monday night *had* been a very big deal for Jenny. She'd desperately wanted to spend a little more time with a hottie from Georgia State whom she'd met last summer at cheerleading camp. The guy was twenty-two and was staying at a local hotel, having driven down for the weekend just to see Jenny. So there'd already been a made-up sleepover at another friend's house.

All of which, had he found out, would have caused their father to totally lose his shit.

Neither of them had wanted to upset him, or Mom, and figured one little switch so Jenny could have a couple more hours with the guy she was crazy about wasn't such a major thing.

Who would have imagined somebody would kidnap Vonnie as she walked home from school that night? Or that Taylor—posing as Jenny—would be the last person to ever speak to her?

"What should I say if the police question me?"

"Exactly what I told you. You tell *my* story, as if it were yours. Every detail I told you, just pretend you were standing there, not me. Vonnie was in a great mood at the meeting, she got along with everyone, didn't have any kind of disputes or fights. Afterward, she and I walked out together. I offered to drive her home, but she said her mom was coming to get her."

At that point, Taylor probably should have insisted, or at least volunteered to wait until the ride showed up. Everybody knew poor Vonnie's mom was a crackwhore. And, judging by what they'd all learned later, there never had been any scheduled pick-up. Vonnie had just made it up, probably so she wouldn't have to let anybody from GHS see where she really lived.

I wouldn't have cared.

She really wouldn't. Damn, how she wished she had waited. But she hadn't done it—for one reason. All the kids at school knew which twin drove which car, and she and Jenny had forgotten to switch before they'd gone out. She hadn't wanted to answer any questions about why she was driving her "sister's" Beetle—which might get back to a teacher, and then to Dad. Being totally paranoid about it, she'd even kept her headlights off as she'd driven across the huge parking lot, not flipping them on until she'd turned the corner heading away from the school.

"You're sure you didn't see anything that could help her?"

"No," she said, probably for the twentieth time since yesterday. "I left her there by the exit, went to get my car, and by the time I drove back, she was gone. I figured maybe her mom had actually shown up. Now, looking back, I guess she just started walking."

"And that's it?"

"That's it," Taylor said with a nod, absolutely certain. "I promise you, Jen, otherwise we wouldn't be having this conversation. I'm not a psycho bitch. I know the kind of trouble Vonnie's in. If I knew anything that could help find that girl, I woulda gone to Dad myself. But I just don't. Meaning you couldn't have either."

Except, if she'd been there, Jenny wouldn't have had the car worry and would absolutely have insisted on driving Vonnie home, or waiting for her ride. Taylor shifted uncomfortably at the thought. That guilt had been nagging at her, a lot. And it probably would for a long time.

That didn't, however, mean there was anything she could do to change what had happened.

"It's decided," she said. "Until there's some massive, compelling reason for us to tell somebody, we'll just leave it as it is. You repeat what I told you and that'll be the end of it."

Jenny didn't look entirely convinced, but at least that chin quivering thing had stopped. Still, she sniffled as she asked, "What do you think happened to her?"

"To Vonnie?"

"Yeah."

Taylor frowned. "We both know what happened. That psycho ghoul got her."

Her eyes looking shiny and wet, Jenny lay down on her side and curled up with a pillow, like a kid who couldn't let go of her favorite stuffed toy. Honestly, Taylor couldn't blame her. Retreating back into childhood, where stuff like this only happened in scary dreams or movies they weren't allowed to watch, sounded really nice right now.

"I can't stop thinking about her. Do you think she's still alive?"

"I don't know," Taylor replied. She wanted to console her sister, answer as a hopeful kid. She couldn't. Because the adult in her knew the truth.

"Even if she is, I don't think anyone in this town is ever going to see Vonnie Jackson again."

Chapter 3

With every step she took toward her car, Lexie's indignation grew. Yes, as a journalist, she'd become used to having doors slammed in her face, euphemistically speaking. But this was the first time it had ever *really* happened.

The guy was totally rude. Incredibly good-looking, yes, but talk about a bad attitude; his made the average angry teenager seem like a barrel of sunshine.

She had already called Aidan McConnell a whole lot of names in her head; now a few choice ones spilled out of her mouth. "Condescending, arrogant ass."

To think she'd almost felt sorry for the man before she'd come here this afternoon, her hat in hand, her hopes high. After having researched him online as much as she could today, she'd almost come to the conclusion that he'd gotten a raw deal in Savannah. She'd definitely begun to rethink her psychic-stuff-is-garbage opinion, having read about the dozens of cases he'd proved instrumental in solving.

She'd been feeling self-righteous; not only was she going to find Vonnie Jackson and learn what had happened to the others, she could help redeem a crushed man in the process.

"Only the crushed man turned out to be a major jerk," she muttered.

A handsome jerk with the most hypnotic blue-gray eyes she'd ever seen, but a jerk nonetheless. She shouldn't have wasted the trip over here; she should have just kept on doing research into Vonnie Jackson's life, trying to find some connection between her and the other girls who'd gone missing, beyond coming from the same general area.

There had to be something. Some tiny link that had drawn the eye of a monster.

She had a few ideas, and planned to tackle them as soon as she got back to her place. This wasn't the kind of work she could do at the office, not with Stan reading over her shoulder. She'd gotten Walter's blessing to work at home and had spent much of today there, other than breaks for a successful trip to Yvonne Jackson's school and an unsuccessful one to the girl's run-down apartment. Oh, and this total waste of time.

She glanced at her watch and considered heading back over to Berna Jackson's place. Vonnie's mother hadn't been home earlier and a neighbor told her she'd been hitting the bars pretty hard in her "worry" over her missing child. Either she hadn't come back at all or she hadn't gotten the note Lexie had left in her door.

One more possibility: She'd gotten cold feet and wasn't going to call.

"I hope you didn't believe every word Chief Dunce said," she muttered, having no doubt the chief would have browbeaten the woman to get her to keep her mouth shut.

Lexie reached the curb and was about to step off it when she heard a sound from behind her. Recognizing the low squeak, she jerked in surprise, glancing over her shoulder at the front of McConnell's house. The door was swinging open.

He didn't say a word as he stepped into the doorway, the late-afternoon sun framing him in fiery gold so he almost seemed to be surrounded by an otherworldly glow.

Knock it off. So much for the hard-hitting journalist.

Her overactive imagination was having a field day. She'd read all about his amazing abilities, noted his dark good looks, and was a little too curious about him, so now she was half fancying the man as some mystical being.

McConnell said nothing; he merely stared at her, long and hard, as if he hated her for making him take an interest in what she had to say. Well, that's exactly why she'd left the flyer. She just couldn't believe it had actually worked. Excitement made her heart skip a beat as she realized the reclusive mystery man had taken an interest.

He lifted a hand, palm out, all his fingers spread.

She understood. *Five minutes.*

Not about to waste one of them, Lexie turned and jogged back up the walk. By the time she got to the porch, he'd already disappeared into the grand old house, which, from the outside, looked just as secretive and mysterious as its owner. She walked right in behind him, unable to resist taking a quick peek at the soft, golden oak floors, the plastered walls and decorative crown molding. The house had once been a grand Southern showcase and was about four times the size of her 1970s-era duplex. Though clean and updated, it hadn't been fully restored. If it were hers, she'd be spending every spare minute bringing this old beauty back to her former glory.

"Lock it, please," he called from the closest room— the office in which she'd spied him a few minutes ago from the side doors.

She entered to find him standing beside a front bay window, gazing outside. A deep frown pulled at his brow, but didn't detract from his strong, handsome profile, with a square jaw, slashing cheeks, and slight grizzle that said he hadn't shaved today. She'd seen in her research that he was thirty-four, but he looked a little older. Not only because of his somber demeanor—his all-black clothes and the frown—but also because of the slight premature gray at his temples, stark against the rest of the thick, dark brown hair.

It was not unattractive, not in the least. The silvery

gray matched that same hint of color in his eyes, which reminded her of a blue summer sky caught between sun and storm. And though she stood on the other side of the room, she still wasn't sure she could hold an even stare if he leveled all that attention, that intuitive, other-worldly focus, directly on her. Because he was a little too knowing, as if he'd already done some kind of psychic stuff and figured out all her secrets, or would, if she let down her guard.

That's crazy. She'd met him fifteen minutes ago; they hadn't even shaken hands. It had obviously been way too long since she'd been with a good-looking guy if this one could have her emotions all jumbled up just because of the way he looked at her. Well, and the way he looked.

"Say what you have to say." His deep voice sounded more melodious than it had when he'd been barking at her from the other side of a closed door.

She shook off the strange sensations that had been washing over her since she'd first seen Aidan McConnell and focused on what she'd come here for. Not even wasting time on niceties or taking a seat, she jumped right in.

"Again, there's a missing girl, whose name is Vonnie Jackson. She's a senior at Granville High and she disappeared while walking home after an event at her school Monday evening. The school secretary told me Vonnie's mother showed up there yesterday, a full day and a half after Vonnie went missing, to say she'd never come home Monday. Her books were found on the ground not far from where she lived." She dug another flyer out of her backpack, waving it at him. "These were already up all over the school by the time I arrived this morning. The principal's one of Chief Dunston's cronies, like the guy at the other high school. But the vice principal's more reasonable and isn't as quick to believe whatever Dunston says. He's very worried and has kids lining up to help form search parties."

When she stopped to heave in a breath, he immediately began asking questions.

"Why aren't the police taking an interest? Are they saying she's a runaway?"

"How did you know . . . Oh, duh, I said that before, didn't I? Well, they're not taking an interest in any of the *other* missing girls. But as far as Vonnie goes, I don't know if they're interested or not, because they won't talk to me. The chief made it clear to my boss that I am to stay out of it."

He held up a strong hand, stopping her with a gesture. "I don't want to hear about any of the others. Stick with Vonnie Jackson."

Swallowing, not allowing herself to be intimidated, she did as he asked. "She's an incredibly smart girl. Ivy League smart. She transferred to GHS this year because she'd already gone through every advanced class she could get down at Hoover."

He lifted a curious brow.

"Hoover is the other local high school, filled mostly with kids from the Boro. The principal apparently hasn't noticed his student body has been shrinking." Still seeing his confusion, she realized he hadn't spent much of the past year getting to know the place in which he now lived. "The Boro is what they call the area just south of Woodsboro Avenue. Granville's wrong side of the tracks. That's where all the girls . . ." She cleared her throat. "That's where Vonnie lives."

"I see."

"From what I hear, the cops haven't been over to GHS to talk to anyone, so they could be trying to sweep this one under the rug, too. Or they might be keeping their heads buried in the sand."

"Something the police are often very good at," he muttered.

Remembering some of the comments made about him by a few of Savannah's finest, she understood his dislike. She also suspected it was extremely mutual.

"But it's not going to be as easy this time." She ticked off a few pertinent facts, which had convinced her this girl was no wanderer, no vagrant, as the chief had made the others out to be. "Vonnie is well liked and highly thought of. She was sixty points shy of a perfect SAT score, and already has a bunch of scholarship offers. She's not somebody they can write off as just another no-good runaway like the other victims."

"Just. Vonnie. Jackson," he said tightly, as if slicing off the words from between clenched teeth.

Yeesh. The man obviously did not want to be having this conversation. Which meant she was going to have to interest him a little more in what was going on in his new hometown. But despite having been accused of sometimes having the tact of a double-barrel shotgun, she did know how to work a story, build it to the high point.

"Okay, Vonnie. She's an only child, not a bad word said about her by anyone. Definitely one of those kids who overcame a rough childhood—the mother has a record of drug abuse and prostitution and lost custody for a year when Vonnie was in elementary school."

"Where'd she end up?"

"Foster home."

"Father?"

"Whoever he is, he has never been a part of her life."

He didn't appear particularly surprised. Nor did he ask more questions, as if knowing she wouldn't stay quiet for long.

Lexie pulled a pad of paper out of her backpack, glancing at the notes she'd taken while doing research on the missing teenager all day. "She doesn't party, rarely dates, hasn't had a serious boyfriend since last year."

"The ex-boyfriend . . ."

She cut him off, knowing where he was headed. "According to one of her friends, that breakup was mutual and pretty friendly, as far as teenage romances go."

His frown deepened. "Continue."

"Her records don't show a single disciplinary mark at any school. In the short time she's been at Granville High, she's already become active in the drama program and in the debate team." She flipped the page and continued. "She worked at a restaurant downtown. A place called—"

"Ranger Joe's Wings and Things," he murmured.

Surprised, she felt her jaw fall open, wondering how on earth he could have known that. The information certainly hadn't been on the flyer she'd left.

For the first time, McConnell's stern mouth softened with what might have been amusement, although it had a long way to go before it could actually be called a smile. "No, Ms. Nolan, I didn't read your mind."

"Lexie," she automatically murmured.

"Lexie?" He swept an assessing stare at her, top to bottom, with those piercing, knowing eyes. "I don't like it. That's a little girl's name; it doesn't suit you."

"Gee, thanks. Why don't you go ahead and read my mind this time and see how appreciative I am that you pointed that out?"

Ignoring her sarcasm, he crossed his arms, leaning one hip against the over-laden desk that looked like it could double as a two-person life raft. "You misunderstood."

Didn't seem like there was much to misunderstand about his saying her name was stupid.

"I don't *read* minds at all."

She should have known he wasn't apologizing for the name crack.

"Now, as I was saying, Ms. Nolan, I know Vonnie Jackson worked at Ranger Joe's because she waited on me when I ate there with some friends a few weeks ago."

Huh. The abrasive, snarly guy, who'd just insulted her nickname—which her father had bestowed on her when she had been, okay, a little girl—actually went out in public on occasion. With other people. Guess anything was possible.

"Yes, even shut-ins get out to a restaurant once in a

while," he said dryly, again as if he could look into her head and see her thoughts.

She shrugged, then, always blunt, couldn't help adding, "Frankly, I was thinking how strange it is that you actually have friends."

His dreamy, mesmerizing eyes widened; then a bark of laughter emerged from those tightly compressed lips. His face softened, a year of resentment and mistrust disappearing in an instant. This was the Aidan McConnell whose picture she'd seen in a couple of old online articles—the one who hadn't yet been lynched in print. Suddenly, instead of a handsome, stern, forbidding man, she saw a very sexy, mysterious young one. A good-humored guy who didn't mind being the butt of a snarky joke.

The change was pretty remarkable. Not to mention distracting. It made her wish, for a moment, that she'd met Aidan McConnell before last year.

"Do you have a filter, Ms. Nolan?" he asked, shaking his head and staring at her in surprise. "Any kind of off switch between brain and mouth?"

"Do you have an *on* switch?" she countered. "Any button that allows you to drop the tough, reclusive, mystery man act and become human?"

"I think you might have just pushed it," he admitted with one more amused chuckle.

"I push your buttons, huh?"

"Guess that's in your job description."

The last remnants of laughter quickly faded, as did the smile. That was good. She didn't need distractions, especially not sexy male ones. Not now when she might again have a crack at the biggest story this town had ever heard. Not when there was still a chance for Vonnie.

Suddenly realizing the implication of what he'd said, she prodded, "So you already know Vonnie. That's why you invited me back in here."

"I don't actually know her," he clarified. "She simply brought food and drinks to the table at which I was sitting." He breathed in deeply, then slowly exhaled. "Her fingers brushed against mine when she handed me a beer."

That apparently meant something to the man, though Lexie didn't understand why he seemed so bothered by it.

He turned his back to her, walking over to the expensive-looking leather couch and sat down. Tapping the smooth top of a coffee table—obviously a refurbished antique, like most of the other furniture she'd spied since entering—he said, "The flyer, please?"

She glanced around for the sheet she'd given him, didn't see it, then dropped the one she was holding onto the table in front of him. "That's her senior picture," she murmured.

He leaned forward, his elbows on his knees, and studied the paper. "Her birthday's tomorrow," he said, obviously focusing in on the details, including the date of birth, listed below the photo. "Eighteen."

"Yes. Hell of a way to spend your eighteenth birthday."

He ignored her, apparently having been talking to himself. "I don't suppose they make their own desserts in that restaurant where she works."

"At Ranger Joe's? Yeah, right. Only if unwrapping a Ring Ding or a Twinkie and dumping it on a chipped plate counts as *making* them."

He muttered something under his breath, something about bread.

"I somehow doubt they bake their own bread, either."

"I was talking about gingerbread," he muttered, though he didn't explain.

"Unless Sara Lee makes it and the Piggly Wiggly sells it, I'd say that's a definite no."

Falling silent again, he continued to study Yvonne Jackson's grainy photograph. The man went still, though his posture wasn't stiff and angry. It was strange, the intensity of his pose. He didn't glow, his eyes didn't roll back in his head, nor did he start speaking in tongues. This was no psychic trance, just the focused concentration of someone able to lose all sense of time and place and disappear deep into his own thoughts.

At least, she didn't think he was doing his seeing-visions thing. She'd read a lot about the cases he'd worked on, but none of the interviews or articles she'd read talked about exactly *how* he did what he did. She somehow suspected his shtick had to involve touch—mainly because he hadn't touched that sheet of paper, nor had he extended his hand to her in greeting. She got the feeling reaching out and shaking hands wasn't something that came naturally to him. Plus, he was sitting on the far end of the couch, as if making sure they would not be too close should he ever get courteous enough to invite her to sit down.

Touch. He'd mentioned his fingers and Vonnie's had touched.

Lexie sucked in a breath, understanding his worry. He'd touched her, and suspected he might be able to help find the missing girl. He just didn't know that he was willing to.

Well, she didn't have time to watch him decide what to do. Thinking about the case was all well and good, but the clock was ticking. She wanted to have a few answers—or at least some better questions—by the time she saw Walter again tomorrow.

Besides, long, introspective silences weren't exactly her thing.

To hell with it. Without invitation, she sat down beside him, though she did maintain his personal bubble by a good ten inches, at least. That was probably for her own sake, as well as his. Aidan McConnell was too mysterious, too interesting—too attractive—for her own good. She didn't need to get any closer; that would only tempt her to accidentally-on-purpose brush against him, just to see what happened, what made him tick. And, she had to admit, to see if her skin tingled in utter electric excite-

ment when it touched his. Not because of what he did,
but because of the sheer sexiness of the man.

He didn't glare her away or growl in frustration that
she'd interrupted him, so Lexie pointed to the home address printed beneath Vonnie's photograph. "That's a
particularly bad block she comes from. I went over there
today, trying to track down her mother, but a neighbor
said she's been hitting the bars all week, day and night,
and hasn't been home much."

"Drowning her sorrows, drinking away her grief and
worry, I presume," he said, a hint of dry sarcasm in that
deep voice.

"Guess so," she said, noting that he'd already formed
the same impression she had. "From the sound of it,
when the woman finally figured out her daughter hadn't
made it home, and went to the school to look for her,
she seemed more interested in threatening lawsuits than
finding her child."

"Mother of the year."

"Exactly. I suppose it's no wonder Vonnie worked so
hard to do well in school. She was willing to brave the
sneers from the neighborhood, the potential rejection
from her new classmates, even the disdain of her own
mother in order to get a better education. She knew she
had one ticket out and she wasn't letting anybody stop
her."

"How eloquent," he said, though the mildly mocking
tone meant he wasn't offering her a compliment. She
immediately realized he thought she was exaggerating,
playacting about how concerned she was for the missing
teenager.

Given his track record with the media, she supposed
he had reason to doubt her motives. But he was wrong.
In truth, the girl's story broke Lexie's heart. She had
never even heard of Vonnie before that morning, but
she already felt almost protective of the girl.

She'd cared about all the others, but with Vonnie,
there was a little bit more. Lexie admired her spirit, her

determination, her bravery. It was unjust for somebody's dreams and hard work to come to this. Unjust, unfair, untenable.

"Look, I don't know what happened to this young woman," she said, hearing the way her voice shook with emotion, "but no one will convince me Yvonne Jackson sabotaged her entire future, threw away all she has worked for her entire life, and ran away. Not when she was so close to achieving everything she wanted. She just wouldn't do that."

He didn't tear his gaze off Vonnie's senior picture, and she wondered if he saw that same spark of brilliance and boundless energy in the girl's dark eyes. It was as if she'd looked into the lens of the camera and seen the path to her own perfect, successful life laid out in front of her, waiting for her to take that first step. How wrong that a single footstep off the path had put her in the hands of a monster.

"Teenagers do run away," he said, though the words lacked real conviction.

"This one, though? Come on. Are you buying it? That she took the time to go across town to her school at night, sat through a dull meeting for new students in the National Honor Society, *then* ran away? What kind of sense does that make?"

"Not much," he said, rubbing at his strong jaw. He didn't like admitting it, but at least he was thinking along the same lines.

"I know the chances aren't good that she's still alive after three days," Lexie said, hating to voice the thought out loud.

"Most kidnapping victims don't make it past twenty-four hours."

"I'm aware of the statistics. Still, if there's any chance of saving this one girl, I intend to take it."

McConnell straightened, leaning against the back of the couch, staring toward the center of the room. She could almost see the thoughts churning away in his head, but they weren't as deep and intense as before, when he seemed to be so focused on figuring out some great puzzle. Now the tension in him told her he was arguing with himself. Knowing how little he wanted to be involved in this, she could only think he was trying to find a way to convince himself Lexie was wrong, or that this wasn't his problem.

Part of her wanted to snap that murdered girls were everyone's problem. But she knew it wasn't cowardice or lack of caring that kept him from offering to help. She'd read about the cases he'd been involved in. The man had seen both brilliant successes and a few losses. He'd been fearless and driven. Right far more often than wrong.

That last case, though, had been beyond wrong. It had robbed him of his confidence. Wounded him. And he wasn't ready to go back to his real life—a look around this stuffy, closed-in mausoleum in which he'd entombed himself made that clear.

Too bad. Whether he was ready or not, she needed him. But she knew of only one way to get him to keep considering getting involved.

By leaving.

"Well, I think I've used up a lot more than my five minutes," she said, standing abruptly.

She knew better than to push this man. He'd come around and let her in earlier only after she'd shown herself willing to walk away. If he had to take some time to come to the realization that this poor, missing girl—and the fate of all the others—did involve him, that he was a part of this community and should care what happened here, she'd give it to him. She only hoped he didn't take too damn long.

"Thanks for listening, Mr. McConnell."

He stared up, surprise and confusion widening those eyes.

"The only way you will understand why I am so sure something has happened to this girl is if you understand what's been going on here in Granville over the past three years." When he opened his mouth to protest, she shook her head, not allowing him to refuse. "Not that I'm going to sit here and force you to listen to it."

Lexie reached into her backpack, pulling out the thick folder full of clippings of articles she'd collected in recent months. Articles from the high school paper about the increase in runaways from the Boro. Articles she'd written for the *Sun* connecting those runaways and offering another possible explanation for their disappearances. The file also included her research, bios of the missing, photographs, notes, transcripts of her interviews with the victims' families, a copy of the chief's press release rebutting the story and her own retraction. Everything she had.

If it wasn't enough to interest this man, well, there was nothing she could say to change his mind. She just had to trust that if she got out of his hair, he'd take the time to read it over, realize she was right, and then get back in touch. It was a risk, but journalism was all about taking risks, going out on a limb for the sake of the truth. This was one risk she had to take—the stakes were too high to blow it by pushing him.

"I left my card inside. My numbers are on it," she told him as she bent and lowered the folder onto the coffee table. "I'll show myself out. Thanks again for your time."

She almost made it, almost slid away on that final line, making a grand, classy exit. But when McConnell *tsk*ed and shook his head, slowly rising to his feet and eyeing her with something like amusement, she had to snap, "What?"

"You're good."

Compliments didn't seem like something that fell naturally out of this man's mouth. Then again, his expression said he hadn't really been making one. "What do you mean?"

"You assessed the situation, figured out the best way

to get what you want, and went for it." He reached down and picked up the folder, not opening it, but not shoving it back into her hands, either. "You know I don't want to look at this."

"I know," she admitted, though begrudgingly.

"You also know if you sat here and tried to force me to hear you out about it, I'd have shown your ass the exit."

She offered him a sweet smile. "Would you at least have opened the door before tossing me out?"

He hesitated, then finally told her something she already knew. "I don't like reporters."

"No, really? I never would have imagined."

"I guess I'm wrong and you're not very good at your job. That's pretty unobservant," he said, almost sounding as though he were teasing her. If he was capable of such a thing.

Challenged, she retorted, "I'm an excellent reporter."

"I have my reasons for not liking people who do what you do."

Remembering everything that had been said and written about him, much of which had made him look like a hunk of bait encircled by an entire circle of vicious sharks, she understood and respected those reasons. "Not all members of the media lose their morals and principles in order to get the story."

One fine brow went up, debating that.

He didn't have to say anything; she knew he had a point. She'd seen some pretty nasty things in the news business, and she'd only ever worked at Granville's small-town paper. There wasn't, for instance, much Stan wouldn't do if he thought it would get him ahead, or even just give him a leg up on her.

"However, some do. And to be completely honest, I don't like some of them myself," she had to admit.

"Honesty? Not something I usually associate with those in your profession."

She didn't take the insult personally. "Yeah, well,

I never associated callousness with people in yours. I thought psychics were supposed to be more empathetic than the rest of us."

Looking more surprised than offended, he crossed his arms, pressing the folder against his broad chest. "You think I'm callous?"

"Either that or cowardly."

The insult didn't faze him; not much seemed to. "I'm neither. Just burned out, and maybe a little gun-shy."

She got that. God, if anything, last month's public humiliation should have her feeling the same way. Though she had only been accused of scaring people, not being responsible for the death of a child. In his shoes, she'd probably be more gun-shy as well.

"I don't ever want to feel solely responsible for someone else's life," he admitted. The words were open and honest, his dark, almost mournful expression saying he meant them completely. The weight he carried must be impossibly heavy and her heart twisted as she wondered if he ever allowed himself to put it down, even for a moment.

"You can't be responsible for somebody whose life is already lost," she told him. "And there's no doubt in my mind Vonnie's life is over if we don't at least try."

Silence descended, broken only by the loud ticking of an antique grandfather clock standing in the hall. Each tick served as an audible reminder that time was slipping away, every second brought Vonnie Jackson closer to taking her last breath, feeling her final heartbeat.

He glanced down at the folder, hesitated, then sighed heavily. "I'll read what's in here."

She didn't smile, wasn't flooded with triumph. This was a momentous thing he'd offered and she knew it. "Thank you."

"I'm not promising anything," he cautioned.

"You don't have to."

"All right, then. You're welcome."

He placed the thick bundle of documents back on

the table, then walked toward her, passing right by and heading out into the foyer. As he moved, she couldn't help noticing the height of the man. Not to mention the breadth of him. He was the brainy sort, classically handsome and intellectual looking, so she hadn't really acknowledged before just how well formed he was—broad shouldered, slim hipped, with a hard chest, strong arms, and powerful-looking hands.

Now she noticed. Which was sort of like noticing for the first time that the sun was yellow. And hot.

Also noticeable was the warm, spicy scent of his cologne, and the way his hair was a little disheveled, as if he'd run a frustrated hand through it more than once today.

Yeah, now that he'd stopped growling at her, she was noticing quite a lot about her unwilling host. She was also liking the things she noticed more and more. Especially the fact that, even though he resented her showing up here and trying to drag him into something he wanted no part of, he was still willing to keep an open mind.

She couldn't ask for more than that.

"I'll be in touch tomorrow," he said as he unlocked the door and opened it for her.

"Either way?" she asked, wanting some assurances that she would hear from him again, either because he intended to help her, or because he couldn't. *Or wouldn't.* Besides, if his answer was no, at least the contact would give her an opportunity to try to change his mind. Having met the man, she truly believed Walter was right—he could be a big help with this and she would do whatever she could to get him to see that.

He nodded once.

"No sooner than tomorrow?"

He rolled his eyes and heaved a sigh. "Reporters."

Lexie couldn't prevent a tiny grin. "Sorry."

Aidan McConnell's mouth lifted a bit at the corners, flashing that small smile that made the years and the so-

berness and the hardness melt away until he was nothing but sweet-looking, sexy man again. "There's a lot in
that folder. But if you give me until tomorrow, I'll read
every word of it. I promise." He raised his index finger.
"But I want one promise from you."

"Anything!"

"My involvement, anything I do or say or think, is
totally off the record."

"I don't understand. I mean, if you help solve this
case, don't you want . . ."

"If my name never shows up in the news again, it will
be too soon," he insisted. "My name stays out of it, or
you can take this folder with you."

Yeah, fat chance of that. "Okay, Mr. McConnell, your
involvement is completely off the record. You have my
word." She thought about sticking her hand out so they
could shake on it. But remembering his thing with touching, she decided not to.

"Good-bye, Ms. Nolan. I'll talk to you tomorrow."

"I'll hold you to it," she said as she stepped outside
onto the porch.

He didn't come out with her, as if loath to emerge
from his sanctuary, merely watching her from one step
above as he said, "I would expect nothing else."

Thursday, 5:10 p.m.

After watching the attractive young reporter drive away,
Aidan retreated into the shadowy house, locking the door
behind him. He didn't proceed immediately to his office,
instead heading into the kitchen. Dumping a handful of
aspirin into his palm, he tossed them into his mouth and
washed them down with some bottled water.

The headache that had been digging at his temple
with sharp metal spikes had increased into a full-out
hammering over the past half hour. It felt as though
something had burrowed into his brain and was trying

to punch its way out, as if his skull could crack under the pressure.

You know why. Or, at least, he suspected.

She was onto something. That reporter, Alexa, so strong, so passionate, so damned stubborn, had come to his door to enlist his help, bringing complications and obligations, worries and bad memories in with her. In doing so, she had forced him to stop thinking of this morning's episode as some kind of strange aberration and acknowledge what it really had been.

His gift wasn't one that switched on and off at random. Nor was it ever caused by anything as simple as somebody walking by a trash can and smelling something unpleasant. He'd been kidding himself. Only severe emotional distress could cause such a solid connection between his mind and another's. That distress had to be extreme for those images, those smells, to claw through his standard mental blockades and insert themselves into his sensory input.

He'd met that girl. Touched her. And now she was missing.

He needed to know if hers was, indeed, the mind he'd been connecting with.

"Vonnie?" he whispered, staring at the closed refrigerator door, though he was picturing something else. A restaurant, a crowd of people, a pretty African American girl with braided hair, a pencil stuck behind her ear, shiny gold hoop earrings, a deep laugh, and a big smile for everyone who walked in the door.

He didn't want to do this, didn't want to even think of doing it. But he had no choice.

Aidan closed his eyes. Visualizing that protective wall he'd spent so long building, he reached for one cement block, dead center, and began tugging, digging it out inch by inch. He worked hard, pulling with all his strength. Finally, it popped free, leaving a single rectangular hole in the barricade. One small opening through which anything could intrude and his own imaginative thoughts could escape.

He drew a steady breath. Then sent them flying.

Wishes and demands, fears and instincts . . . all spewed out of him and raced in search of answers to his deepest questions. His questing mind was like an enormous blanket held aloft by a flock of soaring birds. They dove closer to the earth and slowly draped Aidan's consciousness over the entire town, insinuating itself into others' conversations, thoughts, private moments.

He shrugged off the familiar sense of unease, ignoring the barrage of images that charged back at him through that small hole. Snippets and ideas, half-lost memories of people who didn't even know they still existed deep within their brains, they all had to be sifted through.

"Vonnie," he murmured. The name became a chant. "Vonnie, Vonnie."

He looked for her, searched, trying to find *just* her thoughts, just her memories in the ocean of them that were flooding his mind. He pictured her face, heard her laugh, remembered the moisture on the glass as he'd taken it from her and the faint brush of their fingertips.

He wanted to see her alive and well, sitting on a bus somewhere. Anything that would allow him to let this go.

The tension grew, until he felt like he was being pulled toward that hole in the wall. Aidan was being drawn by a powerful rubber band that was wrapped around his chest, squeezing the breath out of him. It was so strong, it could suck him through the tiny opening, even if it had to crush him in the process.

One more tremendous push. *Vonnie!*

And suddenly he found her. It was brief, so brief, just a few seconds. He didn't see her, didn't feel her or gain any insight as to where she was, even if she was still alive. But he heard her, heard two words repeating over and over in her voice. Her terrified voice.

The king. The king. The king.

He dug deep for the strength and drove harder, needing more, trying to grasp the meaning of the words. Was she saying them? Thinking them? Were they real, or literal? Was she alive, or was this some echo of the last words she'd whispered days ago?

He had to know.

But he pushed too hard. The band snapped. The cement block flew back into place, cutting the connection instantly. He went flying, too, stumbling across the kitchen until he ended up sprawled on the kitchen table with her words echoing in his brain. *The king.*

The word came with a faint whiff of gingerbread.

God help him. God help *her*, for the terror in that voice.

It took a few minutes for him to regroup, to bring his raging heart back into a normal rhythm and stop gasping in shallow mouthfuls of air that did little to fill his lungs. But slowly, minute by minute, he returned to normal, regained control not only of his body but of his mind.

Finally, when he was able to think again, he straightened and allowed the truth of it to fill in all the last doubtful places inside him. He'd heard that girl and she was in trouble. No more self-denial, no more theories. And if the reporter was to be believed, she wasn't the only one.

Aidan hadn't wanted to be dragged into this, or anything like this, ever again. Yet he couldn't blame Alexa Nolan. She had brought an explanation to his door, but he'd been sucked in before he even knew she existed. Though she might have borne the news, she hadn't thrown the rope around him and dragged him kicking and screaming into this case.

Though she didn't even know it, Vonnie Jackson had.

Chapter 4

Lexie worked from home on Friday. She had a lot of digging to do, phone calls to make, and nowhere private to do any of it at the office. She'd already spoken with Walter to get his approval, and to see whether she could get any more out of him. His voice had been guarded. After their call, he'd e-mailed her to say he was doing some more investigating and would definitely fill her in on everything this evening.

She hoped Walter had a good password. Honestly, she wouldn't put it past Stan to do a little e-mail spying. He was probably having a field day over her absence, and desperate to find out what she was up to. But she had a lot more to worry about than a petty coworker. One of those worries, a broody psychic, was foremost on her mind.

She hadn't yet heard a word from Aidan McConnell.

"He said today, not first thing this morning," she mumbled as she forced her attention back onto her computer screen. She'd been exchanging e-mails with the school secretary over at Hoover, who'd pretty much echoed everything the one from GHS had told her yesterday. Vonnie was a great kid, no enemies, extremely well liked by her teachers and fellow classmates. And everyone was just devastated that she'd disappeared.

"Everyone except the cops."

She put her fingers on the keyboard to type a response, but was interrupted when her Instant Messenger box popped open with a ding. At first assuming it was Walter, she had to think for a second when she saw a strange ID: AidMcC.

Yes! Her AIM ID was on her business card, and Aidan had used it.

AidMcC: Are you there?

LexieWrts: Yes. Glad 2 hr from u! Have u bn reading?

AidMcC: Yes.

LexieWrts: Interesting, isn't it?

AidMcC: So far.

LexieWrts: I'm right, aren't I?

AidMcC: Are you always so cocky?

LexieWrts: R u always so cranky?

AidMcC: Touché. Have a ? for you.

LexieWrts: Yes?

AidMcC: Why include Jessie L as vic # 1? 6 mos before the others start?

Lexie stared at the question, not surprised he'd asked it. Jessie Leonard's disappearance had been a long time before the others, which had come more frequently, one every two or three months, beginning six months later. But she'd had good reason—the victimology and the way she'd disappeared.

LexieWrts: Have u read her bio?

AidMcC: Yes. Very similar. That the only reason?

She hesitated before answering. At the time, she had wondered if Jessie really was one of the victims of the same attacker. Remembering her initial investigation, she recalled one more thing that convinced her of that, beyond the fact that she was so much like the rest of the victims in every other way.

LexieWrts: The intervu w/ her mom.

She couldn't remember the exact details, but she definitely remembered feeling Mrs. Leonard's passion when she'd spoken about the disappearance of her only child, and how out of character it was. The woman had convinced her Jessie had been victim number one.

LexieWrts: Hello?

AidMcC: Yes. Already read transcript of that & others. Do you have actual recordings?

LexieWrts: Yes.

AidMcC: Would like to hear them. Can you burn them to cd for me?

LexieWrts: You got it. Offer me coffee & I'll bring them over in 30.

AidMcC: Done.

LexieWrts: I take it w /cream & sugar.

But her message didn't go through. McConnell had already signed off without another word. "Typical," she groused, not offended at the abrupt end to their online conversation. The niceties didn't matter as much as the fact that she'd gotten him to read the file. She just hoped that once he had finished reading it, and listening to the recordings, he'd be able to help.

Burning the audio files he'd asked for, she was in her car within ten minutes, the drive taking another ten. When she arrived at his house, she parked out front, right where she'd been the previous afternoon. Only this time, as she walked toward the house, it wasn't with any sense of nervousness or worry about being rebuffed. The fact that he'd asked for these recordings meant he was interested in the case. Interested was one step from involved.

The door opened before she even reached the front steps. "That was fast."

"I don't live too far from here."

He appeared puzzled. "Weren't you at work?"

"Not exactly." Rolling her eyes, she added, "We have an in-house spy."

"Ah. And he might tell someone you're working on this story again."

"Bingo."

Stepping back, he gestured her into the house. "Coffee's ready."

"Thanks."

"It was no trouble. I never start the day without brewing a gallon," he said as he turned to lead her toward what she assumed was the kitchen. "I don't sleep well at night."

"Maybe because you drink a gallon of coffee during the day?"

He was walking ahead of her, so she couldn't be sure, but she'd swear by the slight movement of his broad shoulders that he laughed.

The short hallway opened into a huge, modern kitchen that had obviously been recently renovated. Judging by the top-of-the-line appliances, marble countertops, and walnut cabinetry, the man obviously had a little money put by. Whatever he hadn't updated about the rest of the house, he'd made up for with this fabulous room. "Wow. Very nice. You could cook an entire flock of Thanksgiving turkeys in that oven."

"I can live with creaky floors, but not with forty-year-old appliances."

Lexie leaned against a cabinet, watching as he poured her a cup of coffee, his movements smooth and easy. He seemed comfortable today, definitely less on guard, the handsome face not set in a permanent frown and those amazing eyes more blue than gray. Even the all-black ensemble didn't seem so much dour as super-mysterious now.

By God, the man was something.

He pushed the cup across the countertop. "So I've lived up to my end of the bargain?"

Inhaling the strong, heady scent coming off the steaming cup, she could only nod in appreciation. She loved good coffee. The stuff at the office was about one step up from brown water. Helping herself to the cream and sugar he'd already put out, she replied, "More than."

He held out his hand. "Okay. Have the CD?"

Grabbing it from her purse, she handed the disc to him. "I took thorough notes for the transcripts."

"I don't doubt it. I just want to hear the voices, the tones. Catch the nuance."

"That a psychic thing?"

He shook his head. "A cop thing."

Her jaw fell open. Fortunately, she hadn't just taken a sip of coffee; otherwise it would be all over her front. "You were a *cop*?"

"Well, not officially. I majored in criminology in college, then went through the police academy in Little Rock, but never put on a badge."

She definitely hadn't turned up that tidbit in her research, having spent much of her time reading about his recent cases. Ever blunt, she asked, "Why? Just couldn't cut it?"

"Thanks for the vote of confidence," he said, his brow rising in amusement. "Actually, I was at the top of my class. I wasn't interested. Did it for the experience but never wanted to wear the uniform."

"Bet the police in Little Rock aren't too fond of you."

He grinned, that quick, sexy grin he'd flashed once or twice yesterday. "Not as unfond as the ones in Savannah."

She only hoped he soon became the bane of the local police force, too. Because right now, it was her and Walter against the rest of the town. They could use some reinforcements. Especially reinforcements with investigative backgrounds and psychic powers—if such things really existed. Now that she'd heard Aidan had studied criminology, she had to wonder if his successful record was more a product of really good investigative skills and excellent intuition rather than any supernatural know-how. Either way, the man's involvement could be important.

Though she wanted to savor the excellent coffee, and also wanted to pick the brain of her host to see what he thought about everything he'd read so far, she knew better than to push. If he wanted to tell her, he'd have told her. She had only met him yesterday, but she already knew that. So she didn't take her time, or even finish the coffee, before pushing the cup away.

"I've got to run. I'm heading over to Vonnie Jackson's mother's place."

He crossed his arms over his big chest. "In the Boro?"

"Yeah."

"Maybe I should go with you."

She chuckled, amused by his sudden worry for her. Yesterday he'd seemed ready to toss her off a high building. "I'll be fine. I live in Granville and have been south of Woodsboro Avenue plenty of times. Heck, my favorite bakery is down there! You just stay here, read, and listen." Flashing him a flirty grin, she added, "Maybe I'll bring you back a peach pie. Theirs is amazing."

"I don't do sweets."

She lifted a hand to her chest and gasped. "No!"

" 'Fraid it's true."

"You just lost a lot of points, mister. There's something wrong with a person who doesn't like dessert."

One of those sexy grins tilted the corners of his mouth up. "But you have to admit, I do make good coffee. Doesn't that earn me a couple of brownie points?"

"Do you like brownies?"

He shook his head, appearing rueful.

She blew out a disgusted breath. "Well, then, no points for you. But you do make excellent coffee," she conceded. "So I guess I'll let you slide. Now go read."

He held up the CD. "I want to listen first. I have a feeling there's something important on here. Something I caught in the transcripts but can't quite nail down."

Following him to the door, she said, "I hope you're right. Because that clock keeps on ticking." Three and a half days since Vonnie had been taken. The thought made all humor slide right out of her.

"I'll be in touch," he said, opening the door and stepping back out of the way.

She'd noticed that before, of course, that he was careful not to get too close. Now, however, she wondered whether it affected every aspect of his life. Whether he ever allowed himself to touch anyone.

Any *woman*.

Sex had to be something he was very careful about. And if he never had it, well, that was just a crime against half of humanity. Not only incredibly hot, the man was also charming, intelligent, and had a good sense of humor lurking behind all that sternness.

So, no, an abstinent Aidan McConnell was unacceptable. It would be a complete travesty.

The very idea was also something she, personally, didn't want to contemplate any longer.

Because combining Aidan McConnell and sex in the same thought was way too dangerous for her peace of mind.

Friday, 4:55 p.m.

As Chief Jack Dunston strolled out of the police station, he had high school football on his mind, the thirst for a cold beer in his mouth, and a pleasant couple of days to look forward to. At this time of year, Friday afternoons were all about taking off early and starting the weekend the all-American way.

The street was quiet, traffic through the small downtown area light. Lots of folks would be heading home to have an early supper so they could then go out to the stadium to cheer on the Granville Giants. Football was big in this town and he didn't know a single person who wasn't looking forward to this particular game.

After a short nap, he'd enjoy a cold one and a Manwich, then head over to the school. Sitting on his blue and gold cushion in the home-side bleachers, he'd wave his big foam finger and smile in self-satisfaction as the townspeople cheered and enjoyed the comforting pastime—a pleasant, old-fashioned benefit of living in a place as nice as Granville.

Other people were welcome to Savannah and Atlanta, crime ridden and fast moving, filled with people who didn't give a damn about anything but getting ahead. He'd take this place with its neighborly outlook, family values, and laid-back lifestyle any day of the week.

He'd nearly reached his squad car, parked in a reserved spot out front, when he spotted the sheet of paper stuck under his windshield wiper. And suddenly he was no longer smiling.

"Some people got no respect," he muttered, stalking over to remove the offending flyer. His blood pressure went even higher when he saw what it was, and he immediately tore it out, balling up the offending flyer in an angry fist.

"Hey, Chief, I saw one of those signs in the drugstore window earlier," a voice said.

Jack clenched his teeth, wishing he hadn't lost his temper in front of Harry Lawton, who managed the biggest bank in town. Lawton had probably been heading toward the Blue Duck Diner for the early bird dinner special. A widower, the man was a regular at the place, which specialized in the best country-fried steak in the county.

"Hey there, Mr. Lawton."

"Have you been investigating?"

"Enough to know the girl's eighteen and has a piece of garbage mother and a lot of reasons to leave home."

Before Lawton could reply, another loud voice intruded. "Good afternoon, gentlemen!"

Damn. Mayor Bobby Cunningham, who had just parked his Lincoln Continental two spaces down, was getting out of his car to join the game of let's-bother-the-chief-on-a-Friday-afternoon. What a hell of a way to start the weekend.

"What's this I hear about another girl goin' missin'?"

Cunningham asked as he walked around the car and joined Jack and Lawton on the sidewalk.

Forcing away his instinctive reaction, which was to curse over the insult of coming out of the damned police station and finding that on his own squad car, he managed to shrug instead. "You know kids, Mayor. Just another Boro tramp taking her act on the road."

Harry Lawton, who, Jack quickly recalled, sang the loudest every Sunday in the church choir, frowned at the description, the expression on his chubby face reproachful.

Always quick to smooth things over with the local businessmen, Jack added, "What I mean to say is, she probably got herself in trouble and left town to go have an abortion or something. These kids nowadays, it's just shameful."

The picture of a concerned, devout citizen, Lawton shook his head. "Poor child." He stepped closer, looking nothing less than serene and pious, as if he was about to spout platitudes about loving thy neighbor. So the next quiet words to come out of his mouth definitely caught Jack by surprise. "Make sure that cunt from the newspaper doesn't make a big thing out of this."

Jack froze, stunned into silence for a second. "Uhh . . ."

The mayor jumped in, his heavy accent growing even thicker with his irritation. "This town's finally settling down after that mess she caused last month. We don't wanna draw any outside attention he'ah." He patted Jack on the shoulder. "Gotta protect our way of life. Don't you agree, gentlemen?"

"Yes, indeed we do," said the banker. "Things are just about perfect in Granville and we want nothing changing about our little piece of Georgia heaven."

"Little piece of heaven," Jack repeated, trying to figure this out. Were Cunningham and Lawton merely concerned citizens, or more than that? Jack wasn't stupid. He'd heard rumors about the secret goings-on of some of the more prominent townsmen. And he suddenly had to wonder if these two had been nominated to speak for that shadowy group. Honestly, he had no way of knowing. Nor did he want to. Some things weren't worth finding out, and in the dark wasn't such a bad place to be. Especially when the light shone garishly on things he'd rather not think about. As long as he kept opening the small beer fridge on his back porch and finding a small stack of twenties every weekend, he was more'n happy to not know any damn thing the rich folks in this town wanted to keep secret. They were welcome to keep their skeletons in their closets.

He shifted uncomfortably, not liking the direction his thoughts suddenly went. To skeletons. Some strange things had been going on lately. It was getting harder to keep his eyes focused straight ahead and not glance at the strange occurrences taking place on the sidelines.

The money provided a nice blinder when it came to secret affairs and a little creative accounting. But murder? That was a whole different ball game. One he really didn't want to think about playing.

"So y'all are gonna stay on top of this he'ah situation?" Cunningham asked.

"You bet. No worries about that reporter," he said. "I already put a muzzle on her." He waved the crumpled flyer. "I'll have another talk with the girl's trashy mother, too. I bet she's the one stirring up this trouble. Woman's got a record as long as my arm."

"Not surprising," Lawton said. "Trashy parents, trashy child. It's the way of the world, isn't it?" Not pausing, he turned to offer a gentlemanly little bow at two women who walked out of the nearby diner. "Evening, ladies."

After they'd nodded their hellos and passed by, Cunningham smiled at Jack, wearing his politician's face. "You gonna make it to the game tonight, Chief? Watch our North Granville boys whup on those Hoover hoodlums? I hear they're dedicating the game to Coach White."

"You bet your sweet ass I am," he replied, thinking about the former Granville coach, who'd died in a car crash a few years ago.

Harry Lawton frowned and *tsk*ed, looking at the choir-singing banker again. "Cursin's a crutch, son." As if he hadn't just called a local woman a cunt. It was like a switch went on and off in the man, light to dark and back again. Mayor Cunningham had the same ability.

They weren't alone in having that ability. Jack had seen it in a few other high rollers in this town. They seemed to have hiding what they were really thinking down to an art form. It was a skill that came in handy for them, or so he suspected, since few people around Granville had any idea at all what really went on behind closed doors of their respected neighbors' houses.

And as long as they never found out, and that fridge kept getting visits from the money fairy, that was okay with Jack Dunston. Because a neighborly outlook, family values, and an old-fashioned lifestyle were all well and good. But if the day ever came when he decided to stop bowing down to men he didn't particularly like, and lost his job, nothing beat a whole lot of cash.

Friday, 6:30 p.m.

Walter Kirby and his family lived in a pretty, woodsy subdivision just north of town, filled with huge lawns and dozens of modern-looking houses. The place had sprung up prerecession, when people were looking to upgrade to McMansions. It had yet to recover from the downturn, which had seen a third of the homes in the neighborhood go to foreclosure. A few of the yards were overgrown, old, swollen newspapers rotting on the curb like big dead rats.

There weren't quite as many For Sale signs as a year ago, though. Apparently a few upwardly mobile locals and newcomers to town were taking advantage of the bargains. Still, it didn't look great.

Lexie wondered if Walter had thought about getting out. With Ann-Marie's cancer treatments going on for well over a year, he had to have considered looking for a job elsewhere, where he wouldn't have to commute an hour to get to and from the best hospitals.

But when she turned her car onto his block and saw the teenagers hanging out in his driveway, she knew he wouldn't have done it. He'd never have made the girls change schools, not with the twins being in their senior year. He'd just done his good-dad-good-husband thing and made that drive, trying to keep everyone happy and the balls of his family life up in the air.

"Hey, Lexie!" one of the kids called when she pulled up in front of the house, parking at the curb. There were already four cars in the driveway. She expected a couple of those, Taylor's VW Beetle and Jenny's PT Cruiser, to be pulling out soon. It was almost game time.

"Hey, girls," she said, nodding to Walt's younger daughters as she exited the car. The other two were probably inside donning their makeup, uniforms, and their school spirit. Rah-rah.

Cheerleaders had never been among her favorite people, not even when she'd been in high school herself. But somehow the Kirby twins managed to be okay despite their perkiness. Probably had something to do with the good parents who were raising them.

"Seen any serial killers lately?" asked one of the smirking boys from the neighborhood.

"Only the one hiding under your bed, waiting for you to go to sleep tonight," Lexie immediately replied, used to the snark. Hell, at least the kids would say such things to her face.

"Dad said for you to go on around back. He's firing up the grill," said Christy, Walter's youngest child, who was still snorting over the way her male friend's face had gone a little pale.

Lexie smiled at all the teens as she worked her way through them, holding a brown bag containing a six-pack in one arm, and a bunch of flowers in the other. She emerged into the backyard just in time to hear Walter muttering something about his propane. "What's that, boss?"

He glared down at the grill. "Might as well be in the kitchen. Damned gas grill doesn't taste much different than the stove. But they say it's healthier than charcoal."

"Ugh. Grunt. Caveman must cook meat over flame," she teased, handing him a beer.

He twisted off the cap and took a long pull. "So," he asked when he was finished, "how did you spend your day today, other than pretending to be sick?"

She tilted her head in confusion.

"Stan. He came in to tell me he felt sure you weren't ill and I should talk to you about the importance of not calling off work on a Friday just because you don't feel like coming in."

"Frigging tattletale. Did you tell him I hadn't called in sick?"

"Actually, no. More fun to let him stew about my lack of interest."

"Evil man. I like it."

"Any luck today?" he asked.

Shoving her unpleasant coworker out of her mind, she admitted, "I saw our local psychic again. He had more questions and promised to read everything I left for him."

"I still can't believe he even talked to you."

"Yep. He wasn't happy about it at first, but he eventually even let me in his house." She grinned. "Not a shrunken head, voodoo doll, or crystal ball anywhere in sight."

"You haven't really told me what you think of him."

She considered the question, going over the time she had spent at McConnell's house again. "I think he's very interesting," she mused, knowing that was putting it way too mildly. But she didn't necessarily want her boss to know her thoughts about their local psychic were as much personal as professional. "He's also incredibly smart."

"His record proves that. You look at some of the cases he's worked, and you can see a lot of what he comes up with is pretty remarkable."

"That's why you wanted me to go talk to him," she said, understanding why her boss had put that note in her hands. "It had nothing to do with the weird stuff."

"He's an experienced investigator and brilliant to boot. Hell, I don't care if he claims he can put on thick glasses and channel Buddy Holly's ghost, we could use his help."

She agreed. After meeting him, she had gone back and studied all those reports about the cases he'd helped solve. How sad that it appeared one hugely unsuccessful one had completely overshadowed all the ones on which his aid had proved instrumental. "One thing—he is adamant that his involvement remain completely off the record, during and after this investigation."

He waved an unconcerned hand. "Done." Casting a quick look toward the house, he added, "Ann-Marie will be out in a few minutes."

She knew what he meant and didn't waste any time. "Tell me why you brought me here."

Sitting down on a cushioned outdoor chair, he gestured toward an empty one opposite it. "I heard a rumor that some human remains turned up out on Old Terry-town Road."

She shook her head, hard, sure she'd heard him wrong. "What?"

"You heard me. Human remains."

Stunned, she whispered, "How have I not heard about this? Why aren't we covering it?"

Walter simply stared, waiting for her to figure it out.

"They're not reporting it? A body?" She leapt to her feet. "This is unbelievable."

"Not a body. Some bone fragments." He glanced toward

the still-closed sliding-glass door, and gestured her back to her seat. "An old friend of mine, wishing to remain anonymous, said he was out walking his dog and found some strange-looking bones. Called the chief, who said he felt sure they were—are you ready for this?—from a bear."

Lexie dropped back into the chair. "Oh, now he's a freaking mammalogist?"

"My friend said he got a really good look at what he was sure was a human jawbone. Said if he was wrong about that, he would give away his entire collection of *CSI* DVDs."

She closed her eyes, the idea of a human jawbone being discovered by the side of a local road a little sickening. Especially if that bone belonged to one of the missing teens.

She'd speculated about it, written about it, and she'd firmly believed she was onto something, but hearing about actual remains made everything that much more real, more tragic. Theorizing on paper that a serial killer was murdering young women right here in Granville was one thing. But she'd been so caught up in the investigation, in the story, she hadn't really let herself think of things like shallow graves and bodies.

Finally, once she felt sure she could speak calmly again, she asked, "So what happened?"

"Dunston took the remains," Walter said. "He didn't bother setting up any kind of crime scene, showed no care in collecting evidence. He threw the fragments in a plastic grocery-store bag and said he'd have the coroner take a look to 'confirm' his theory that they were from an old dead bear."

Muttering an obscenity, she wondered if she'd be able to eat dinner at all. She had lost her appetite. "It's like living in a comedy where the bumbling cops couldn't find a wall if they ran into it."

Walter's bushy brow pulled down over narrowed eyes. Again, though, he didn't tell her what was on his mind, he let her figure it out for herself.

It didn't take long. "You're thinking it's more than stupidity," she whispered.

"I made a few calls today, including one to the coroner's office, asking if they'd been asked to examine the bones." Walter paused long enough to sip his beer—or to get control of his own anger. "They had no idea what I was talking about. Hadn't heard a word about it."

She let out a long, slow exhalation, her heart thudding so hard she almost felt her rib cage shake. "My God, what if he's not being careless? Are we talking about a deliberate cover-up?"

"I don't know," Walter said, shaking his head. "I always thought Jack was weak, but still basically a decent man. I have to wonder whether he really has got himself convinced there's nothing to this, so he doesn't *want* to see anything that contradicts his story."

That was certainly possible. She'd spent the past month thinking Chief Dunston had reacted so badly to her articles because he'd been embarrassed, caught with his pants down. Men like him excelled at ass-covering. She'd believed his response had come purely out of anger and self-protection, that he wasn't willing to see the truth being dropped into his lap.

Now, though, she had to wonder if there was more to it. If he knew what he'd found—knew enough to intentionally take the evidence and not let the coroner see it—something much deeper was at work here. Would the police chief really ignore a crime like murder just to avoid embarrassment? It seemed crazy, completely irrational.

"We have a very serious problem," she said, talking as much to herself as to Walter.

"I know."

They stared at each other. She had no doubt her boss was thinking the same thoughts, and wondering, like Lexie, what to do about this whole ugly mess. For her part, she wanted to throw a spotlight on the situation. A front-page article asking, "Where's Vonnie?" for starters.

Walter, however, would want to proceed more cautiously, quietly. With a family to protect, and insurance to maintain on his sick wife, he had more at stake here. He could not afford to be pushed out of the editor's chair.

"So are y'all out here talking about the way you're gonna make the dickweed chief, the mayor, and everyone else sit up and pay attention to what's going on in this mean little town?"

Lexie jerked her attention toward the door, seeing Taylor. The sarcastic tone would have told her which twin it was, even if she didn't know to look for the girl's small birthmark.

Taylor bounced down the outside steps, her brown ponytail swinging, her short cheerleader skirt fluttering in the strong breeze. She was the strong-willed one, the one who tested her parents every single day and had from the time she had taken her first step.

She was also, Lexie suspected, secretly the absolute apple of her daddy's eye, even though he was now casting a reproving glance her way. "Language."

The teen shrugged, confident in her ability to wrap her dad around her little finger. "Call 'em what you want, somebody has to wake up around here."

"What do you mean?" Walter asked.

"Everybody at school's talking about it." Taylor sat on the arm of her father's chair. "About your articles, the serial killer. Wondering if the Ghoul's got Vonnie Jackson."

"Do you know her?" Lexie asked, forcing herself to ignore the stupid nickname.

Taylor nodded. "Not well, but she seems nice. She's in Jenny's AP Chem class."

"She hadn't been acting strangely at school?" Lexie asked.

"No. She was fine and excited at the National Honors Society meeting Monday night."

Walter raised a brow. "How do you know? Got something to tell me about your grades?"

The girl frowned and looked away. "No, Dad, sorry, I'm still the dumb one. Jenny's your honors kid. *She* said Vonnie seemed fine that night. They walked out together afterward. Jen offered her a ride, but Vonnie said her mom was picking her up." Taylor shook her head, her pretty face set in an unusual deep frown. Sounding grieved, she added, "Jenny feels like shit."

This time her father didn't correct her language. His face had grown pale, as if he'd finally put together the fact that his own child had been the last to see Vonnie before her disappearance. Her path may have come within minutes of crossing a monster's.

Taylor continued. "How can somebody just vanish off the planet? It's so scary."

Walter reached out and grabbed his daughter's hand. "Yes, it is. Which is why I don't want you going anywhere alone for the time being. Stick with your sister or your friends. And don't forget, midnight curfew."

"I'll be fine, Daddy. I'm a big girl."

Lexie cleared her throat. "I'm sure that's what everyone of those other girls said."

Nodding, Taylor kissed her father's cheek, promising, "I'll be careful!"

She headed for the door as her sister came out of it. The twins touched as they passed on the walkway, lightly, just a brush of hand on hand. It was always that way. From the outside, they appeared physically identical but different in every other way—from personality, to brains, to dreams. But there was always that connection that made them reach out to each other. Not having a sister, and never having been close to her brother, Lexie could only wonder about that kind of relationship. They were incredibly lucky to have it. Having spent a lot of time with the girls, even spending weekends with them occasionally so Walter could stay close to Ann Marie in the hospital, she suspected there wasn't much the Kirby twins wouldn't do for each other.

"Hi, Lexie," Jenny murmured as she joined them.

The older twin was always quieter, more bookish, though she still wore her uniform like she meant serious cheering business. Now, however, with her genuinely adult brush with tragedy, she appeared even more subdued. When asked, she confirmed what Taylor had said about Vonnie, appearing on the verge of tears.

Well, who wouldn't be? The north side of Granville had been pretty well insulated from what had been going on here for the past few years since none of the other missing girls had gone to GHS. But now things were different. Even though Vonnie Jackson lived in the Boro, she'd been grabbed walking home from the "good" school. It had changed the whole ball game.

Jenny was saying good-bye to her father, making the same promises to be careful her sister had, when Lexie heard the trill of her cell phone. She tugged it out of her pocket, glanced at the screen, and immediately began to put it away. People who blocked their phone numbers from caller ID deserved to have to leave a message and be called back whenever she felt like it.

Then she hesitated. It had been hours since she'd heard from Aidan, time enough for him to finish reading through the folder and listen to the recordings. Plus, he seemed like the type who would protect the privacy of his number. So she answered. "Hello?"

"Ms. Nolan?"

Smiling, she replied, "Hello, Mr. McConnell."

Walter, who had been watching his daughter walk pensively back into the house, jerked his attention to her, mouthing, "It's him?"

She nodded.

"I'd like to talk to you again," the psychic said. "I've finished reading through all this information and I have a few questions."

Her reply was sardonic, but true. "A few? That's about a hundred less than I've got regarding this case."

"Is there any chance of me getting copies of the police reports on these other missing teenagers?"

This time she actually laughed. "You must be kidding. *If* he wrote up any reports, I assure you Chief Dunston isn't going to let you, me, or anybody else near them."

Silence; then he asked, "How wired is the police station?"

"Wired?"

"I mean, the town's pretty small. Is the station's computer system up-to-date?"

Understanding, she asked, "Are you a hacker as well as a mind reader?"

"Sometimes to the first, a definite no to the second. Do you know?"

"Well, I know they're computerized." She put her hand over the mouthpiece and asked Walter, "How good's the IT guy who handles the police department?"

Walter sneered.

"Okay," she said into the phone, "security's probably not great. Are you really going to hack into Chief Dunce's files?"

He was silent for a moment, then smoothly said, "Of course not, Ms. Nolan. That would be illegal. If I do come up with any information that's in those reports, you're just going to have to assume I used my super-psychic brain to get it."

She heard another hint of that dry humor in his voice, like she'd noticed once or twice yesterday afternoon. It suited him, somehow, and she imagined that when he was in a good mood, the under-the-breath one-liners were probably wickedly funny.

"How soon can you come back over here?" he asked.

"I'm at my boss's right now, and I was thinking of going over to the high school after dinner." She'd been thinking about Taylor's passion regarding Vonnie's disappearance, and Jenny's obvious sadness. Considering their school was playing against Vonnie's old one tonight, she had to wonder if it might be worth going to the field, seeing if anything happened when Granville's two worlds collided.

"Isn't the school closed by now?"

She explained her thinking, noting Walter's nod as he silently approved the plan.

"If you want me to, I can come by later, after the game. Might be a little late." Suddenly realizing he might be of some help, she added, "Or else you could meet me there."

"I don't think so," he immediately replied. "I don't do well in crowds."

"I get it. It would be like walking into an all-you-can-eat psychic buffet, right? Too many minds to read?"

He sighed, not amused by her poor jest. "Maybe you should get out your notebook and write this down since you keep forgetting. I am not a mind reader."

"Sorry, just joking. But seriously, why don't you come? This game is one of the social events of the year. Almost everyone in this town will be there. If you ever wanted to get a look at the chief, the mayor, the rich business owners, as well as a lot of people from the Boro, plus Vonnie's friends, that would be the place to do it."

"You might have a point," he murmured, not sounding happy about the prospect, but at least considering it.

How his world had changed in the one day since she'd invaded it. From his absolute lack of knowledge about the basic geography of Granville, she suspected he'd seldom left his own house since moving here. And now she was trying to drag him out into one of the biggest crowds that ever gathered around here.

She expected him to refuse, figured he might even be having second thoughts about calling her at all. Opening her mouth to tell him to forget the idea, she was stopped by the sound of his deep, resigned sigh.

"All right, Ms. Nolan. I'll meet you at the high school. Look for my car, a black SUV with tinted windows."

She subdued a triumphant exclamation. "It'll be crowded, so park in the far north lot, away from the field. And speaking of black, can you maybe dress a little more, umm, cheerfully than you were earlier? You and I are going to draw enough attention as it is."

"The two outcasts of the town, hmm?"

"Something like that."

"Mightn't people just assume we wanted to watch the ball game?"

She couldn't prevent a snort. "Mightn't people also just assume you're an undertaker? Look, face it, you're not the small-town-football-fan type and everybody and his mother will know I'm there because another girl has gone missing. So I'd rather not draw any more attention than necessary. Meaning, I'd appreciate it if you'd lose the head-to-toe black ensemble and try to blend with the sea of denim and flannel, especially since you want your involvement to stay off the record."

He sighed again. "Fine. I'll meet you in the parking lot; we can talk inside my car before we go in." He sounded thoughtful as he added, "And from our anonymous vantage point, you can point out everyone I need to know about. Including this infamous Chief Dunston."

"Sounds good. See you then."

Lexie disconnected, meeting Walter's eye. "I think he's in."

If he was going to a high school football game in the middle of Nowhere, GA, the man was definitely *in*.

"Excellent," her boss replied. "I'd love to go with you, but Ann-Marie's just not up to it yet and I hate to leave her alone after being at work all day."

"I totally understand."

His expression grew more serious. "Listen, Stan'll be at the game tonight."

She expected nothing else, since his son played for Granville High. Since his divorce a couple of years ago, during which his teenage son had asked to stay with his mother, Stan had been trying to make up for being a total waste as a father throughout the boy's childhood. Too little, too late, in her opinion, but she had to give the man props for not giving up.

"If anyone asks," he added, "say I sent you out there to do a human interest story. The girls tell me tonight's game is being dedicated to the memory of Coach White."

She vaguely remembered the man, who'd led his team to a state championship some years back. He'd died in a single-car accident and was still hailed as a local hero. "Okay."

"And, Lex, do me a favor, would you?"

"Anything."

He answered not as her boss, not even as her friend, but simply as a concerned father. "Keep your eye on my girls tonight, would you?"

"I will." She leaned over and patted his hand. "But don't worry, this guy isn't grabbing his victims from big, crowded events. He's taking them when they're alone in secluded places."

"I know." He glanced toward the door through which the twins had gone. "That doesn't mean I'm not scared to death and won't do everything I can to keep my daughters safe."

Lexie nodded in agreement. "As should every parent in town."

Chapter 5

Vonnie didn't think she was going to last much longer. How long could someone survive without food or hydration? Food, probably several days. But if she didn't get some fluids into her body, her organs were going to start shutting down.

It had been more than a day since she'd taken her last sip of warm, rusty water. Now she was so thirsty, she probably would have tried licking the dampness off the cement walls.

But she couldn't even do that. Not with her mouth duct-taped closed.

Oh, he had been angry that she'd screamed for help. Far from being rescued, her last-ditch effort to save herself had earned her only more abuse, and enforced starvation. When the bastard had returned from wherever he'd gone—without any strong, heroic rescuer storming in behind him—he'd burst into her cell with a big roll of tape. He'd wrapped it around and around her head, sticking it to her face, her hair, her mouth, her nose.

She'd felt certain she was going to suffocate. He'd let her think it, too, watching her closely from behind the awful, smiling mask. She'd been writhing on the cot, her body struggling for air, her lungs burning, screaming, when he finally pulled out a long, slim metal skewer and held it up in front of her terrified eyes.

Vonnie had screamed behind the tape when he

moved the skewer to her face, sure he was going to stab it through her eye, up into her brain. Instead, he'd poked a hole in the tape beneath one nostril for her to breathe through, then another on the other side.

The holes were small, the air they allowed in barely adequate to keep her alive.

Yet she was still breathing. *Still breathing*.

"I suppose you're thirsty."

She didn't turn toward the door at the sound of his voice, not surprised she hadn't even heard the metal panel sliding open. She couldn't hear much of anything anymore, except the slow, sucking rasp of her inhalations, which were never enough to really fill her lungs.

"I might be persuaded to take off the tape and let you have something to drink. That is, as long as you promise you're going to be a good girl."

Vonnie nodded desperately, willing to promise absolutely anything if she could just get the tape off and take one long, deep breath. Suddenly that seemed even more important than taking a gulp of water.

The door opened and she turned toward it, seeing only his big, dark form enter. He didn't approach as he closed and locked the heavy metal barricade behind him, remaining on the other side of her cell, melting into the shadows. He could be holding a knife, an ax, anything over there, just waiting for the right moment to leap forward and use it. She couldn't see, couldn't tell, could only hope that whatever he was going to do, he did it quickly.

She wanted this to end.

"Do you know what the witch did to Rapunzel to keep her from calling for help from up inside her tower?"

That singsong voice. Another damn story. That told her his mood wasn't as bloody as it had been since she'd screamed for help. So maybe he wasn't here to kill her after all. Whether that was a good thing, or a bad one, she just didn't know. Part of her desperately wanted release, even if that release came because she'd lived her last moment.

Another part, the hard, determined core of her that had taken on so much, fought so hard, was suddenly desperate to stay alive, if only to keep him from winning. Funny, she didn't mind so much losing—dying. But, oh, she did not want him to win.

"Well?"

She answered with a small shake of her head, not wanting to do anything to antagonize him.

"The witch chopped out the ungrateful girl's tongue and fed it to her dog. Do you think I should do that to you?"

Is the dog as hungry as I am?

That answer came from the old Vonnie's brain. The sassy Vonnie. Not this beaten, broken one.

She replied with another head shake, pleading at him with her eyes. Finally, he came closer, the white king mask emerging out of a dark corner into her line of sight like a pale skull out of a crypt. The plastic smile was as insane as the person behind it.

He was holding two things. In one hand, a big plastic cup with a lid and a bendable straw. In the other, a small knife. The knife wasn't so small it couldn't be used to slit her throat, but Vonnie suspected he hadn't come here for that. For some reason, he wanted to keep her alive.

She wished she knew more about his other victims—how long they'd stayed down here, how long he'd kept them imprisoned, telling his sick stories. But there was no way to know. None of them had carved any last words into the wall or hidden any journal of their tortured, final days. At least as far as she could tell.

"I'll show mercy," he said, "because I like you."

He liked her. She'd hate to see how he treated those he didn't like.

"You remind me of myself, you see, the way I reacted to being down here in the dark. The others were so stupid. So weak. But not you. You're so smart—always thinking. You don't cry; you don't plead. You play along and don't do anything until you think you have a chance, like when you screamed yesterday. Very naughty, but a good effort."

Now that his anger had faded, he sounded almost approving, admiring even. Like he'd been glad she'd bided her time and done nothing, waited until she had an actual chance of rescue before crying out.

The truth washed over her. She had been involved in a game of wits with the man from the very start.

He had no pity, so all the others who might have pleaded for help had earned nothing but his disdain. Because she hadn't, because she'd been smart enough to know that would never work, she was still alive. Though probably not for long.

"You haven't once begged me to kill you and get it over with," he added.

If only he knew how often those words had repeated in her mind.

"You haven't even begged me to stop, or to let you go. I never begged, either. Not for myself, anyway. Hmm . . . would you beg for someone else, like I once did? What will it take to crush you completely, pretty Vonnie?"

Something in the tone told her he looked forward to finding out. His next words confirmed it. "The anticipation of it has me quite excited. What will be the final straw that breaks your pretty back?" He chuckled behind the mask. "We have to get you stronger so we can start playing our games and find out."

Oh God. Please help me.

Her tormentor finally drew closer. "And it's not just that you're smart, you know. You've pleased me in other ways, too."

Vonnie didn't take her eyes off the knife, knowing that when he cut the tape away beautiful, blessed oxygen would fill her lungs. Who cared if it was painful, if the tape ripped out her hair and tore her skin? She just wanted to breathe.

"Did you hear me?" he prompted, his voice hardening. "I said you've pleased me in other ways."

Not wanting to drive him away now when he appeared on the verge of giving her what she needed, she focused on what he was saying. She tried to swallow, but there was no spit left in her mouth and her dry throat screamed with the pain of it. But even as she grimaced, she concentrated on tugging her brow down harder over her eyes, hoping she looked deep in thought and puzzled.

He got the message and laughed. "You don't know how; I understand. But if you think about it long and hard, I bet you'll remember. You'll recall how you pleased a lot of people."

Not giving her a chance to dwell on it, almost as if he didn't want her to remember just yet and had only intended to tease her, he knelt beside the cot. The knife came up, but she couldn't muster any terror, not even when he ran the flat blade along her forehead, just above her eyebrows. She was wise to him now, knew he wasn't going to plunge that knife into her eyeball or any other part of her. Not now when he'd started this new game of figure-out-how-you-know-me. He liked his games and he wanted her lucid enough to play.

She was proved right when he moved the knife to the tape covering her mouth and started to cut. He sawed carefully, layer by layer, as if not wanting to nick her lips—strange since they were probably still swollen and fat from when he'd punched her. Within a few moments, he'd created a small opening.

Vonnie couldn't hold back, immediately sucking in a deep breath. The oxygen hit her lungs and shot through her blood, her heart sending it in every direction to nourish all the starving cells of her body. She grew light-headed but didn't care. Nothing in her life had ever felt as good as that one long inhalation.

He watched approvingly from behind the mask. Lifting one hand, a hand she didn't recognize, that could belong to any white man she knew, he carefully poked the hole a little, widening it. He took his time, blocking her oxygen again with his finger, just to fuck with her, she had no doubt.

"Ready for your drink?"

She nodded, for the first time wary of the plastic cup. There could be anything in it.

It's water. Just the same nasty water he was bringing you before.

Or it could be drain cleaner.

She prayed that whatever it was it didn't hurt as he slid the opening of the straw into the hole. Live or die, she just didn't want to hurt anymore.

"Sip slowly. You don't want to throw up. I don't know if I'd be able to stick around to get the tape off before you suffocate. I have somewhere to go and will be out late."

She did, tentatively drawing the fluid up the straw. It hit her mouth, cold and sweet, and she realized he'd brought her some kind of energy drink. Just as that one deep breath had been the best she'd ever inhaled, so, too, was this mouthful of liquid the best she'd ever tasted. As difficult as it was, she sipped slowly, feeling the icy relief slide down her scratchy throat. It landed in her empty stomach, which churned but didn't rebel, and then she sipped again.

With every taste of that sweet drink, a truth hammered home in her brain, causing her both hope and despair. He could have given her water. Instead, he was giving her something with nourishment. Something that might help fend off starvation for a little while longer than mere H_2O would have done.

Which confirmed what he'd been telling her all along. He wasn't ready for her to die yet.

Because he wasn't finished playing with her.

Friday, 7:40 p.m.

Aidan arrived at the local high school about twenty minutes before his arranged meeting time with the reporter.

Parking where she had told him to, he watched as cars poured in, many of them spilling laughing teenagers out into the evening. Many also, however, contained adults. Middle-aged couples, corpulent businessmen, entire families with young children. Alexa Nolan hadn't been kidding when she'd called this one of the social highlights of Granville's year. The stadium looked well on the way to being packed.

Something else he noticed. For every upscale-looking Lexus driven by a stay-at-home soccer mom came a rusty, smoke-belching rust bucket owned by someone who lived in a completely different world. These, he assumed, were the residents of the Boro, who ranged in ethnicity but not in economics. Poor didn't have its own color.

Sitting behind his tinted windows, he was able to see the way the groups eyed one another with wary mistrust. There were no jovial greetings between fans of the opposing teams. And he doubted it had anything to do with what was about to happen when their sons and brothers came face-to-face on the field.

This looked more like an example of class warfare, the have-nots of Granville resenting the haves. Only, in this case, the have-nots did have something: a slew of murdered girls and a community full of fear. While the other half of the town had remained immune, protected, safe in their cocoon of money and a close-knit society with their oblivious police chief and their complacent officials.

Until Vonnie, the girl who'd somehow managed to straddle the line between them. He only wondered whether her disappearance would make things better or worse.

Hearing a tapping sound on his passenger's-side window, he glanced over and saw Alexa standing outside, hunching close to the vehicle as if not wanting to be seen.

He flipped the automatic lock and she got in, quietly closing the door behind her. Her curvy form had barely landed in the seat when he hit her with his first question.

"How did this start? Go back to the beginning."

"Well, good evening to you, too."

He cleared his throat, suitably chastened. He hadn't done the social thing in a long time and barely remembered the rules of it, one of which was, on occasion, to say hello. "Sorry. I don't get out much these days. Guess my conversational skills are a little rusty."

"It's okay. I'm a pretty no-nonsense person myself."

"Pushy one, too," he couldn't help muttering.

"I'll cop to that. Just don't call me perky. Ever. I hate that word."

He gaped. "You? Perky?" He didn't see that at all. Stubborn, tenacious, inquisitive, yeah, all of the above. But not perky. She was too dark and sarcastic to ever be something so cutesy.

"I've seen perkier pit bulls." He meant that as a compliment. Sort of. Maybe.

"I know, right? Crazy. My mother always used to say if I wanted to get the *right* boys to like me, I needed to try to be more perky. Which, I think, is why I went out of my way to be a scowling bitch throughout high school."

Scowling bitch? That he couldn't see, either. Despite her in-your-face toughness, the woman was soft underneath. She cared about people and took things personally. Still, part of her comment amused him. "Not interested in boys, huh?"

"Not the 'right' ones."

He didn't doubt it. He suspected Lexie had rebelled at anyone who tried to put her in a nice, good-girl box from the time she was old enough to ask *Why?* "Yeah, I somehow picture you as a bad-boy magnet."

"You got it. And bad boys aren't interested in perky chicks."

"Got it. Perky is right out. No problem. If I had to choose an adjective that starts with the letter P to describe you, I can come up with several more. *Pushy* is a much better one. Or *persistent*."

"Persistent I can deal with. You could even have called me a pain in the ass."

"The evening is still young."

"Fair enough; consider me warned." She shifted in the seat to look at him, bending one leg and tucking it under herself. "As it happens, I think of persistence as a good quality, especially when someone as no-nonsense as me is willing to go begging for help from a guy who dabbles in the supernatural."

"I don't dabble in anything," he replied flatly. "What I do is just part of who I am."

"What *do* you do?" she asked. "I mean, exactly?"

He should have known that by opening the door an inch, she'd kick it in and storm through. Not knowing this woman for long didn't mean he couldn't figure her out. And it didn't take any psychic skills to know she would be like that pit bull after a buried bone when it came to getting at a bit of juicy information she wanted. Like all her kind.

She's not like all her kind. He needed to keep reminding himself of that. Because after reading through her files, he knew this story was more than a big-news feature to Alexa Nolan. It had become personal—he could read that in every line of her articles, in her hand-written notes and in each question she'd asked. Especially her jotted speculations about the unanswered ones.

The files had changed his perception of her. Before, he'd seen a tenacious, incredibly attractive young woman. Now he saw that same woman—with a heart. It was a stunning combination. He'd spent a long time this afternoon thinking about it, about all the different sides to her. Though a stranger to him two days before, she had succeeded in doing something even his oldest friends had been unable to do: get him involved again. That alone made her pretty unique. When combined with all the rest, she became fascinating.

"I mean, you know, the psychic stuff?" she prodded. "Do you have to look at someone's picture, or be in their house or touching their pillow or something in order to get any impressions about them?"

How to explain that to someone who'd never experienced it? Most people's exposure to the more unusual possibilities in this world came from shows like *Ghost Whisperer* and the one about those demon-hunting brothers with the cool black muscle car. Few ever realized they had a glimmer of the same ability he had, they simply mistook it for something like intuition, déjà vu, or lucky guessing.

She continued to wait, so he gave her his most basic answer to that very common question. "I am sometimes able to mentally connect with other people."

"So you're Mr. Spock. Vulcan mind-meld stuff."

He sighed. The woman's mouth was always three steps ahead of the conversation as she tried to fill in the answers to her own questions.

"I can't put my hand on someone's temple and know just what they're thinking. In fact, I don't have to be in the same state as the person I'm connecting with. But I am sometimes able to catch images, scents, or the physical sensation of things that have been filling their minds lately."

"And that would be different from mind reading . . . how, exactly?" she asked, a little accusingly.

"Look, I can't see their real-time thoughts, can't experience *precisely* what they're seeing or hearing or feeling at any particular moment." He ran a frustrated hand through his hair. This was damned hard to explain. "Sometimes I catch snippets of people's memories, even after they're dead. They're left behind, like a mental fingerprint on the world."

"That's gruesome."

"It can be."

"But I guess it comes in handy for solving crimes."

"On occasion," he admitted. "The problem is, it's not

a sure bet. I get flashes of things that might represent what's been on someone's mind, not necessarily a real picture of what they're seeing or experiencing. Think of it as recording your favorite show on your DVR, only the power went out and you only caught part of it. It's cut off, plus it's a rerun, not real-time. Not the whole thing, never the entire story."

She nodded slowly, getting it. "Frustrating."

"Yeah. For instance, if I were to mentally connect with you, I imagine I'd see . . ."

"Don't even go there—I was not thinking that about you!"

". . . a random scattering of girls' faces. Or I might catch the scent of ink and paper." He couldn't help raising a curious brow. "What, exactly, were you *not* thinking about me?"

"Nothing right now." Her eyes shifted down at her hands, which were twisted on her lap. "But if you went back in the DVR of my mind to yesterday when you slammed the door in my face, you might see me thinking about a whole overflowing bucket of assholery."

Unable to prevent it, he laughed, wondering how this blunt woman had so quickly worked her way around the stern, protective walls behind which he usually barricaded himself. "No wonder you're a writer, Ms. Nolan. You certainly have a way with words."

"And no wonder you're a psychic. You certainly have a way with that whole mystical thing. By the way, if you can't bring yourself to call me Lexie, how about Alexa? The Ms. business is a little too 1970s women's lib for me."

He considered it. Alexa was too formal, too junior league for her. Just as Lexie was too young and carefree.

"Or you can call me what my boss, Walter, does. Lex."

He nodded, repeating, "Lex. As in the cape-wearing superhero's nemesis. I think I can work with that."

"Does that make you the cape-wearing superhero, Mr. McConnell?"

Sneering, he replied, "Hardly. And call me Aidan."

"Yeah, I can't see that, either, Aidan. Maybe the dark, brooding guy surrounded by bats, but definitely not the squeaky-clean one."

Not knowing whether that had been a compliment—*probably not*—he said, "I'm not your nemesis. Not anymore, anyway."

"No, you're not." A small smile told him how glad she was of that.

He noted the prettiness of that smile, the way it brought a sparkle to her green eyes.

"Speaking of Walter," she said, "he asked me to thank you." She quickly explained what was going on with the man, her tender tone revealing how close they were. "He would be a lot more active with this investigation himself, but with his wife, he just can't."

"It's okay," he said. "Now, can we go back to the question I asked before I neglected to say hello? Can you tell me how this all started?"

"You read the whole file?"

"I did." He reached into the backseat to grab his briefcase. As he retrieved the folder, his forearm brushed against her shoulder. It was just the lightest brush of clothing, no meeting of skin, and yet he reacted strongly, yanking his arm back.

Touching was something he tried to avoid as much as possible. Even with his mental walls in place, as they were now, sometimes people could slip in between the cracks. With a personality as strong as hers, he suspected Lex could come barreling through.

She either didn't notice, or pretended not to. Hunkering down a little in the seat, she cleared her throat and pointed at the ticket booth set up near the field. "Wait! That's Chief Dunston."

He stared out the windshield at the uniformed police chief. Younger than he'd imagined, maybe in his early forties, the man wasn't the tubby blowhard he'd been picturing. "Who's that walking up to him?"

She moved a little closer to get a better look, leaning over into his side of the car to see around a truck blocking her line of sight. He shifted closer to the door, pulling away as instinctively as he drew breath. She noticed, looking up at him in confusion. He could only imagine what she was thinking. His innate desire to avoid touching anyone had to come across as either extreme paranoia or snobbery.

Actually, it was neither. He just didn't want to open any lines of communication he wasn't prepared to deal with.

She shook her head, as if chasing away some dark thought. With that shake came a hint of the light scent of her perfume, or her shampoo, flowery, clean and fresh. It suited her.

Why he'd even taken note of that, he honestly didn't know. He was working with the woman, not contemplating sleeping with her.

Lie.

Okay. The thought had crossed his mind once or twice. He'd been alone for a long time, and from the minute he'd answered her demanding knock yesterday, he'd been very much aware of that fact. As aware as he'd been of her silky hair, her husky voice, her curvy form, the sparkle of her smile.

He liked sex. A lot. But physical attraction usually led to mental vulnerability, so Aidan seldom allowed himself to give in to it. When he did, even more self-protection was required. Because actual physical connection demanded strength and stamina to prevent someone else's thoughts, feelings, and emotions from overwhelming him.

So it said a lot that he'd been wondering how smooth her skin would feel beneath his fingertips, how her mouth would taste and how well her soft body would fit against his.

She might just be worth the risk.

"Would you move?" she snapped.

He jerked, wondering whether he'd inadvertently done something to reveal his incredibly personal thoughts. Then he realized she'd been addressing a group outside, who had stepped between her and the chief. Once they had left, she pointed out the window again.

"The one on the right is Mr. Lawton, who manages one of the downtown banks. On the left is"—she sniffed in disdain—"Ed Underwood, who is my boss's partner in the paper. He stays out of it when things are going the way he wants them to. When he's unhappy, he becomes extremely bossy."

She didn't have to elaborate; he got it. The man had become very bossy about Lex's articles. He'd probably been the one who'd demanded that public *mea culpa* of a retraction, in which the woman sitting beside him might as well have asked to be smeared with tar and rolled in a field of feathers.

"The game's starting soon," she said, returning fully to her seat. "We should wait a few more minutes, try to slip in after it starts and get lost in the crowd."

"Sounds good. Meanwhile, fill me in. I read the file; now I want to hear it through your perspective." Black-and-white text was all well and good, but the nuances and subtle impressions she might have formed could prove very important.

"As you read, fourteen teenage girls from the Boro area have gone missing in the past thirty-six months," she explained, her deep frown signaling how she felt about the subject. "All aged sixteen to nineteen, starting with Jessie Leonard."

He nodded. "The one that stood out from the rest. She disappeared three Halloweens ago. Six months before the others."

"Right. Like you, I wasn't entirely certain she was connected at first because there was that big gap."

"I can see why you decided it was."

"You listened to the interview?"

"Yes." It hadn't been easy, but he'd listened to each and every recorded discussion.

"Six months after Jessie, it was boom-boom-boom," she said. "They started happening pretty steadily, one every other month or so. All under circumstances very similar to that first one. Add Vonnie Jackson this week and you have fifteen."

He opened the folder, recalling some of her notes. Thumbing to one particular photocopied sheet, he tapped it and glanced at her. "Only fifteen?"

She met his even stare. "You noticed that, did you?"

Yes, he'd noticed. One page, copied out of what looked like her own journal, had a hand-written list of the fourteen names mentioned in her newspaper article. It also, however, contained three additional female names, all with question marks beside them.

"I can't say for sure," she admitted, "but these three missing teenagers from other parts of Georgia have aroused my suspicions. The cases were from before this time period, and they are a little different, but they do have a few things in common. Same type of girls—pretty, from poor backgrounds. Same circumstances surrounding their sudden disappearances. Their families are completely clueless as to what happened to them."

"You didn't mention them in print."

"Nor did I even talk about them to anyone else, not even my boss. My own intuition led me to note those cases, nothing else."

"Trust that intuition," he told her, pleased that she'd included the journal entry in the file she'd left him. Again, every detail mattered. "Always."

She nodded, silently assuring him she would. Then she continued to explain, quickly and concisely. First how she'd begun hearing whispers about a lot of runaways from the Boro, then details of her own interviews with family members, friends, teachers, and the uninterested members of the police force. She told him that the missing never took anything with them—leaving clothes, personal items, even cash behind. That not one of them had mentioned any thought of running away, even to their closest friends. The plans made and events skipped. Everything that had led her to write the original piece, headlined "Mysterious Disappearances of Local Teens Concern Residents." It was followed by two more, during which it was clear that the town's mood had grown from concerned to frightened.

Which brought them to the next document in her folder: the press release from Chief Jack Dunston. He pulled it out, reading it over, intensely disliking the man just for the arrogance of his tone that came through loud and clear, even in print.

"Dunston tracked down two of the missing girls," Aidan said, already knowing it.

She nodded. "Yes. Rosa Chavez and Carrie Marks. Rosa was an illegal who went back to Mexico to be with her father and Carrie was picked up on a prostitution charge in Atlanta a few months after she skipped town."

"And based on proof that those two had left of their own volition . . ."

"He was able to convince everyone *all* the rest were simply runaways, criminals, or transients, as well," she said with a disgusted sigh.

"People believe what they want to believe."

"You got it. Dunston didn't have to offer any proof or even conjecture about any of the others. Providing a definitive explanation for what had happened to these two was enough to satisfy most people I had let my imagination run away with me. Or I'd made the whole thing up to get attention. It was easier than believing the alternative, I guess."

Noting her frustration, he nodded in sympathy. "As if a dozen disappearing teenagers is just the norm in a town this size."

Obviously hearing his skepticism, she said, "Exactly!

And if you narrow down the geographical area to just the Boro, which only makes up about a third of Granville's population, the odds against this are even worse. But nobody gives a damn."

"The girls' families?"

She frowned. "The ones I interviewed for the article don't want to talk now. That could be because they're holding out hope that I'm wrong and their daughters are fine."

"Or because Dunston got to them?"

"Yeah. These aren't exactly pillars of society. Rosa wasn't the only illegal, and Vonnie wasn't the only one who'd spent time in foster care because she had the misfortune to be born to crappy parents."

"Sounds like whoever's taking them is counting on that."

Her mouth fell open on a soft gasp; he'd surprised her. That hadn't been his intention. It just seemed a no-brainer to him that somebody was making these girls disappear. Any decent law enforcement officer should reach the same conclusion.

"You really believe that's what's going on?" she asked, her voice shaking the tiniest bit, as if she wasn't quite prepared for someone else to come over to her side in this whole ugly situation. From the sound of it, she and her editor at the newspaper had been fighting a two-man battle for a long time. It really was no wonder she'd sought him out, if only to bolster the number of people on the side of the good guys.

Huh. He was thinking of a reporter as one of the good guys; maybe because he already liked her. This was, indeed, a banner day. Physical attraction, now actual liking? All wrapped up with a woman whose profession he loathed? He never would have believed it.

"Aidan?" she prompted.

"Yes. I do think you're right. I certainly don't believe all these missing teenagers left of their own free will. Someone took them, though I'm not certain that means we're dealing with a serial killer. We can't reach that conclusion yet."

"What else . . ."

"There are a lot of places in the world—including some right here in this country—where attractive young women command a high price."

Every last bit of color fell out of her face. "Human trafficking."

"It's possible," he said, trying to be gentle. "The girls could have been kidnapped and sold. And the chances of them ever being heard from again are very thin, Lex."

Her eyes drifted closed for a long moment as she acknowledged that reality. It was the first sign of helplessness he'd seen in the woman since he'd met her. But he wasn't sure whether she found that possible explanation better or worse than the one she'd convinced herself was true: that the missing teenagers were all dead.

"They could be alive, then," she finally said.

"I doubt it," he admitted, sounding as grim as he felt, "but it is a possibility."

Even if they were still drawing breath, he couldn't be sure that would count as living. Existing, at most. Sexual servitude couldn't be called much more than that.

"There's something else," she said softly. "Something Walter told me tonight."

As she told him about her boss's story regarding the discovery of human bones, her face paled. It had become real to her, all too real. Until recently, she'd been focused only on the professional aspect, the story, the mystery. She hadn't fully allowed herself to consider the missing girls as murder victims.

Now it was hard to do anything else.

"I'd wanted to keep a low profile for a day or two, but we're going to have to confront the chief on those remains," he said.

"I know." A long exhalation said she didn't relish the prospect, though he knew she wanted the information. "At least I know it can't be Vonnie. Not this soon."

Very doubtful, but technically not impossible. But he wasn't about to go there. Discussing methods of dissolving a human body down to bone just wasn't a conversation either of them needed right now.

She cleared her throat. "About Vonnie."

He knew what she was about to ask. It was the one question he had been waiting for. The one he still wasn't sure how to answer, mainly because he didn't know the answer himself.

"Have you had any feelings about her? You mentioned that your hands touched when she waited on you at the restaurant. Does that mean you could possibly 'connect' with her? Wouldn't that be one way of finding out what's happening here?"

Aidan hesitated, not sure how much to share. Yesterday's experience in his kitchen remained strong in his mind; if he focused, he could still hear the missing young woman's voice. He no longer doubted that he had opened a channel of communication with Vonnie.

But the evidence was so thin, the clues so tantalizingly obscure. A few scents, the word *king*, that strange, breathless sensation just before they'd been cut off? Those things could mean just about anything. Or, as much as he hated to admit it, nothing. After all, the last big case he'd worked on had shown him just how unreliable these visions could be. Still, it was worth at least checking one thing. "In your research on Vonnie, did you happen to stumble across anyone named King? Or somebody with that nickname?"

She shook her head. "No, nothing. Why?"

"Just a possibility that occurred to me," he said.

He heard her sucked-in breath as excitement hit her. "Something happened. You felt her, didn't you?"

"I haven't experienced anything that leads me to draw any conclusions," he finally said, not telling her the whole story, but not lying, either. "She might be alive; she might not. The best way to find out is through good, intensive detective work. For instance, paying attention

to the tiniest details, which might not seem important at
the time. Especially if you're so close to a case you can
easily miss them."

She stiffened. "Are you saying I overlooked something?"

Flipping through the file, he pointed to the disc that
contained the audio files she'd brought over earlier today. "Have you listened to these again? Once the heat of
the story wore off, I mean?"

She shook her head. "Not since I got shut down. It
seemed pointless. Not to mention frustrating. Why? What
do you think is on there?"

Aidan didn't know for sure that anything was, but
he had a suspicion. "It seemed to me that several of the
missing girls had something else in common."

"Beyond having crappy home lives and living in the
Boro?"

He nodded.

Appearing anxious, she reached for her own hand-
written transcriptions of the interviews. "What? What
did I miss?"

"It didn't stand out quite as much in your notes, but
it definitely did in their voices." Wondering if she'd feel
the same tingle of interest he had when he'd stumbled
across the common refrain that had so interested him,
he explained. "Most of the girls' parents commented
that it wasn't the first time their daughters had dropped
out of sight."

Her lips tightened and her green eyes flashed as if
he had accused her of some wrongdoing. "For no more
than a night, two at the most, and always with warning
that they were going, or else a reason they might go. This
is a completely different . . ."

"I'm not criticizing you," he said, waving off her de-
fensive explanation. "Not accusing you of intentionally
leaving out details. It wasn't every girl and you're right, a
teenager fighting with her mother and being gone over-

night is not the same as one who goes out on a normal day and never comes back."

She relaxed a little in her seat, but continued to eye him, still somewhat wary.

Aidan pulled the transcripts from her hand and thumbed through the pages, pointing at small sections he'd highlighted. "It's the way they said it. Not 'Sometimes we'd fight and she'd stay out all night,' but 'One time she left a note that she had somewhere to go, then disappeared for two nights and we never found out where she'd been.'" He found the next one he'd noted, reading aloud again. "'She scared us once, disappearing one Saturday night and she just seemed really unhappy when she came back.'"

That one had bothered him. A lot.

"Then there was the mother who said, 'Something happened last summer. She was supposed to be at a friend's one weekend, but she wasn't. She would never talk about it or admit where she really was.' A total of seven of the families made similar comments. Strange, don't you think?"

Her brow was furrowed as she thought about it; then she slowly began to nod. "Okay. I see what you mean. That's not the standard my-teenager-threw-a-fit-and-took-off complaint."

"No, it isn't."

She closed the file, her slender hand resting on top of it, murmuring, "So what does it mean? Where did they all go, and what happened while they were there?"

"That's an excellent question."

Maybe it didn't matter. Perhaps it had nothing to do with the disappearance of all these girls. But it was a link among them, a tiny red flag, and often in an investigation, those small flags led to interesting discoveries. "It's definitely something that will require some good detective work."

She snorted. "Not one cop who works for Chief Dunston will help us."

"I wasn't talking about those detectives."

No, he had a much more highly specialized group in mind. After all, Julia Harrington had asked him for plenty of favors over the years. It was about time he called in one of his own.

EXtreme Investigations had resources police departments and other private investigation firms lacked. Their investigators were uniquely qualified to handle things like this, where the questions of the case far outweighed the leads. Not to mention where the circumstances were highly unusual. If there had ever been a crime meant to be solved by the XI group, this was it.

Strange that just a few hours ago, he was determined to stay out of anything resembling a missing person's case. He didn't know whether it was because he'd met and remembered Vonnie, or because he truly believed Alexa Nolan had uncovered a mass conspiracy, or because there were just so damned many of these girls. Maybe also because it was a chance to show the local cops for the corrupt fools they were. All of these, perhaps. But most likely it was because he felt Vonnie's terror for himself. Whatever the reason, he suddenly found himself anxious to get back to work.

Julia had been saying for months it would happen, that he could never give up his old life completely. He'd thought doing a little crime solving from afar would be enough. He knew now it wasn't. Not when a case this huge, this important, had landed right in his own front yard.

For some reason, he had chosen to pack up and move to a town that had turned out to be a deathtrap for teenage girls. And Aidan's own background, his intense curiosity and his strong sense of justice demanded that he try to do something about it.

Which meant it was time to get to know a few more of his new neighbors.

Chapter 6

Now that the cat-and-mouse game with Vonnie was becoming so entertaining, he had hated to leave her there, all alone in the pit. He had obligations, however. He couldn't miss tonight's big football game at the school, not without somebody noticing.

Then again, perhaps it was just as well that he'd had to leave the girl alone. Keeping his pretty guest on her toes made her that much more interesting. Besides, he'd wanted to see how people were taking the latest disappearance.

"Hey, everyone, great night for football, huh?" a passing parent called to the crowd.

He smiled slightly, mumbling, "Every night's a great night for football!"

Too bad Vonnie wasn't here to enjoy it.

He'd known this one would get more attention. Her disappearance was bound to reignite the fire that had been doused by that idiotic, bought-off puppet of a police chief, who'd managed to shut down the investigation right when it seemed about to begin.

Funny that he liked the spotlight now, considering he'd spent the past couple of years trying to avoid detection by anyone except a very choice few. At first he'd wanted to arouse the suspicions only of those who knew *exactly* what all those missing girls had in common. He wanted them afraid, wanted them to realize someone else knew their secrets.

Most of all, he wanted to punish them. Slowly, deliberately. He intended to drive away their security, their sanity, one chunk at a time until they turned on each other like rabid animals, wondering if they had a traitor in their midst.

Tormenting those men had given him a great deal of pleasure. It was just what they deserved for what they'd done, the murderous lengths to which they'd gone to protect themselves and their diseased friends.

Of course, his other pleasure was in having all those pretty girls to play with. How lucky for him, since torturing pretty girls had been one of his favorite pastimes even before he'd moved here to Granville.

He'd been satisfied with all of that—revenge, and his time spent with those young ladies. Fear of his own capture had been enough to keep him from ever going further. All had been well, until Alexa Nolan had begun putting things together.

When that had happened, he hadn't panicked. He'd simply watched. Soon realizing his revenge plan had been helped by the attention, not hindered, he'd loved thinking about all the others in this shit-heel town who *would* be in a panic. Not because they gave a damn about the missing teenagers, but because any investigation would almost surely shed light on their own dark, dirty doings. Their fears were coming true. He could almost hear their whispered phone calls and secret meetings, could see it even through the public masks they wore over their hideously ugly, true faces.

What fun.

Then the chief had fouled everything up. Sure, Dunston had inadvertently provided *him* protection from discovery by shutting the story down. But he'd also removed that thrilling, exciting element that had him watching as his enemies squirmed.

He'd known he had to get people around here talking again. And that's exactly why he'd chosen her: Yvonne Jackson. Pretty Vonnie. Because while it upped the danger for him, it also put a lot of pressure on other men in this town . . . men who owned that police chief and pulled his puppet strings. Men who were undoubtedly pissing into their expensive leather shoes, wondering if this might be the card that knocked down their entire wobbly, degenerate house.

"Can I get you something from the snack bar? Popcorn, or a hotdog?" asked a kindly voice.

How nice. The locals were so thoughtful, the ladies predictably feeling sorry for him, a man alone with no little woman at home to take care of him. If only they knew he had a little woman locked in his basement right now, fulfilling his most deadly needs.

"Thanks, but I'm okay." He patted his stomach and grinned. "Gotta watch my figure."

The woman—who had never realized that she'd known him previously, the last time he'd lived in this hellhole of a place—chuckled a little awkwardly, not sure what to make of his joke. Just as he'd wanted.

He wondered how hard she'd laugh if she could see what he really thought of her. What would she say if he tore off the nice, easygoing mask he wore, as deceptive and tricky as the ones worn by so many others in this town?

She'd die of fright, he didn't doubt. So he kept his thoughts hidden, his dreams his own. He smiled and mingled and conversed. And all the while, he glanced at the clock, thinking about what was going on one floor below the ground back in the dark, damp basement. He longed to be there, watching on his closed-circuit monitor, seeing Vonnie's every move courtesy of a few hidden cameras.

Are you still fighting?

The girl had such amazing strength. That hadn't surprised him initially; most of them had been strong when he'd taken them. Every one of his guests had been street kids, tough and hardened by their sorry, pathetic lives. And each of them had fought physically, which had provided a few worrying moments and the occasional bruise. Because street kids tended to fight dirty.

That was okay. He'd been a street kid himself once. He'd learned how to fight at a young age, too—though not young enough to stop certain unpleasant things from happening.

Unlike most of the girls, however, he'd also been incredibly smart, learning how to get along, how to do what had to be done in order to fit in, to survive. To thrive, even.

Before now, none of his captives had exhibited that same ability. None had even been clever enough to play his game, to humor him in an effort to get him to keep them alive a little longer. They'd all been full of bluster and rage, then terror and pleas. Until now.

Vonnie was different.

Oh, she'd been full of bluster and rage at first. And she was most definitely terrified. But she'd kept her head about her, pretending to like his stories, playing meek and mild when she'd still had the strength to scream the roof down at the first possible opportunity.

Fortunately for him, the old house he'd lived in as a child had been soundproofed long ago, in the days when *he* had been a frequent captive in the pit. The place now used to house reluctant young women had once been used to discipline recalcitrant little boys. Or simply to rape and torture them.

He knew better than anyone how futile it was to scream. He and Jed had bloodied their vocal cords screaming before realizing it would do them no good. Vonnie had learned that lesson already, too. She was a quick learner. Brilliant. It was almost going to be a shame to kill her.

A pleasurable one, though. Breaking her would give him more satisfaction than he'd had in a very long time.

She had to be wondering if and when he would rape her—and that would probably happen. It always had before. But sexual release was never as pure and perfect as when he choked the life out of the person he was fuck-

ing at the very moment of orgasm. And he just wasn't
ready for Vonnie to die yet.

Yes, she'd been a wonderful choice, serving so many
purposes while giving him so much enjoyment. Taking
Vonnie had been a calculated risk, and judging by the
tension here tonight, it had paid off beautifully. In fact,
everything had gone beautifully.

"Except one thing," he whispered with a frown, knowing any passing fan would think he was merely sending
up whispered support for their team.

Yes, there might have been one little hitch. One un-
foreseen circumstance.

Nothing had come of it yet. Maybe it never would. Still,
he couldn't help thinking about that car he thought he'd
seen in his rearview mirror as he'd slowly driven down
the street to follow Vonnie home from school Monday
night. The car whose headlights hadn't been on.

Had it really been there? If so, why had the lights
been off? Had the driver seen him following his target?
What other reason could there be for the clandestine
driving?

Could just be a careless teenage driver.

Maybe. Maybe not. The vehicle hadn't been there a
few minutes later when he'd pulled over, clubbed the
girl, and thrown her into his trunk; he knew that for certain. But someone could have seen him turn down that
street just a few minutes before Vonnie disappeared,
and could start asking questions.

Damn it. Not knowing was driving him insane.

He couldn't put it off, couldn't wait to see if anything
came of it. He had to act, eliminate the threat before it
ever became a legitimate one.

Fortunately, the car had had a distinctive shape. He
had a pretty good idea of the model, and knew of a few
locals who drove them. He also had a good idea of where
to go to look for this particular one, and he intended
to do just that during halftime. Because if he really had
seen that car, on that night, in that area, odds were it be-

longed to a student from Granville High School. Even better odds said it had been one who'd been at that honors club meeting.

The vehicle was probably right now parked in the school parking lot. Which meant the potential witness against him could be here in this crowd, mere feet away.

His heart thudded; he knew what he had to do. This one would be far different from his usual type, another honors student who didn't have the background of the Boro to give him or her—oh God, he hoped it was a her—the strength to fight him.

How interesting it would be, bringing Vonnie a playmate, especially given what he'd asked her tonight: *Will you beg for someone else?*

Like he had once begged for Jed after a particularly brutal beating, when he'd thought the younger boy would die?

What would it do to the strong, tough girl if she had to watch while another was tortured to death? Would she plead? Finally break down and stop pretending she liked his stories and wanted him there?

He also wondered about something else. Which would horrify her more—seeing he'd brought her a friend? Or the moment when he took off the mask and let her see the face of her tormentor?

He shivered at the thought, not with fear, not with worry, but with pure excitement.

Like he always did when things were about to get especially bloody.

Friday, 8:35 p.m.

As she'd predicted, the stadium was packed. Easing in a half hour into the game, Lexie and Aidan were able to skirt the crowd so none of the enemies of truth and justice, as she'd begun to think of Dunston and his cronies, had seen her yet. They headed toward the small building that housed the concessions stand and restrooms, and from there would be able to mix with the fans making their way along the track back to the visitor's-side bleachers. Having a ringside seat to the action on the field, and off it, she hoped Aidan's impartial eyes would notice something hers might miss.

"Oh, hell, it's Stan," she whispered, seeing a familiar face not ten feet from where she and Aidan stood, trying to sidle their way along the outer fence.

"What?"

"Somebody from work."

"Your boss?"

"Don't I wish."

She thought for a second Stan wouldn't notice her, but his gaze shifted and he suddenly spied her. His eyes narrowed, one lip curling up, and he wove through the crowd of people standing between them, obviously intending to put her in her place.

"Should somebody call the 1970s and tell them they let one escape?"

Lexie sucked her lips into her mouth to prevent a startled laugh from spilling out right into Stan's face. Damn, Aidan could get off a really unexpected remark now and then.

"Well, if it isn't Sexy Lexie. What are *you* doing here?" Stan asked, not trying to hide his true personality since nobody who really mattered was close enough to hear. "Thought you were too sick to work."

"I wasn't sick," she replied, keeping her tone pleasant. "I was working at home. I had to do a lot of research and I didn't want to tie up one of the office computers."

Stan's eyes narrowed, as if he didn't believe her. Or, more likely, he wasn't happy that Walter hadn't shared that tidbit with him earlier today. "Well, why did you come tonight? You shouldn't be here. Nobody wants you around. Haven't you gotten that yet?"

Aidan moved closer, until she actually felt the warmth of his tall, lean body just an inch away from hers. They weren't touching, but almost could have been.

Heat rolled off him, and she realized he was genuinely angry—on her behalf.

Interesting. Even more interesting was the sense that despite the inch of air separating them, she would almost swear she could feel him pressed against her. Her skin tingled beneath her clothes and her entire left side felt hotter than the right.

Maybe it was just his presence, solid and powerful. Or his emotions—the sudden, roiling anger and his immediate dislike of Stan, combined with his apparent need to come to her defense. They had become almost tangible.

Her breath caught for a second and she let the sensations wash over her. Lexie knew, somehow, that if she stood here long enough dwelling on it, this strange, nonphysical connection was going to arouse some very definite physical reactions in her.

Not the time, not the place. Definitely not the man.

"Who are you, exactly, to tell her where she should and should not be?" Aidan asked, his voice low, his tone as hard as his stiffened jaw.

Stan, though big in the gut, wasn't particularly tall. He didn't take a step back, but he did lean backward as much as possible; he was trying to pretend he wasn't intimidated as hell by Aidan's glower, broad shoulders, and imposing height.

Knowing Stan didn't have the nerve to answer him directly, Aidan went on. "As for who wants Ms. Nolan around"—his smile glittered under the field lights, though it held no hint of humor—"I do. Now, do you have any more stupid comments to make?"

Stan's innate pompousness wouldn't stand for being spoken to like that, no matter how intimidated he was. He shot Lexie a dark glare. "Who's he?"

Man, the guy just didn't know when to quit. Aidan's voice grew even softer, even more dangerous as he replied, "*He* is a friend of Ms. Nolan's. He's also not deaf."

Stan's throat bobbed as he swallowed hard. "Sorry," he mumbled.

"If you have any questions to ask me," Aidan said, "you can make an appointment sometime next year. Now, would you get the hell out of our way so we can go sit down?"

Realizing he was outmanned in every way, and that Lexie was doing absolutely nothing to call off her angry companion, Stan took a step backward. He plucked at his sleeve, fussily, trying to appear unconcerned, then said, "See you in the office, Lexie."

"Sure."

They watched as the other man turned and hurried away; then Lexie smiled up at her new friend—he'd used the word first, not her. She liked that. Heaven knew she would not have imagined it yesterday when they'd met.

"I am certain I'll pay for it Monday when he gives me the third degree and plays the he-was-mean-to-me card, but I must say I quite enjoyed that."

"Not a fan of yours, I take it?"

A barked laugh emerged from her mouth. "Hardly. I don't think he'd waste a drop of spit on me if my hair caught on fire. He tries every single day to make my life a living hell."

Aidan's eyes narrowed and the icy gray overtook the warm blue. His earlier annoyance had segued into near anger on her behalf. "Forget it," she said. "We've got other things to worry about. Oh, by the way, remember those things you can and cannot call me?"

"Yeah."

"Well, uh, Sexy Lexie? Don't even think about it." She shuddered, still grossed out that S(a)tan had used the term. "Not *ever*."

His tension seemed to ease up, as she'd hoped it would. "Sexy, huh? That's a little cocky."

She quirked a brow. "You saying I'm not sexy?"

"Uh-uh," he replied, not even hesitating. "That's one thing you will *never* hear me say."

She'd been trying to tease him out of a dark mood, but Lexie had to admit, hearing Aidan say that was a nice side benefit. Especially since his innate sexiness had definitely drawn her attention on more than one occasion.

"Now, shall we try this again? Our target is the opposite side of the stadium."

"After you.'"

She started walking, drawing in a quick, relieved breath when they reached the small concessions building and were blocked from the view of the home-team bleachers. The relief came a moment too soon, as it turned out, since she almost ran right into another familiar person.

"Kenny!" she said, surprised to see the janitor here. He didn't seem the type who would like to go out in public, knowing he'd draw his own kind of attention. Her heart twisting with pity, she saw the way he hovered in the shadows of the building, separate from everyone else, trying to remain unobtrusive. Whether for his own protection or other people's sensibilities, she didn't know.

"Miz Lexa," he said, his eyes wide, stricken, as if he feared he'd get in some kind of trouble for doing something as innocent as going to a local sporting event. "I was just watching. Mr. Walter's girls are doing their cheering, and Mr. Stan's boy got a little playtime."

"Of course, I'm sure they appreciate you being here to support them," she said, smiling warmly. God, she just couldn't imagine that kind of life, always skulking in the shadows. People joked about journalists living that way, but Kenny's life was no laughing matter.

"Gotta be here, anyways," he mumbled, pointing to a groundskeeper's cart parked between the building and the fence. He apparently had more than one part-time job. She could only imagine how hard it would be for him to come to work and be surrounded by hundreds of teenagers, who could be so incredibly cruel. Fortunately, most adults treated the man with kindness.

"Okay, then, good seeing you," she said.

He touched the brim of his cap as they moved away,

melting into a group laden with popcorn and drinks. As they walked, Aidan murmured, "So what's his story?"

"Kenny? I don't know," she admitted. "He works part-time for the paper, doing odd jobs and cleanups. Walter has been good to him; obviously he was in some kind of accident."

"Very sad. It takes courage to come out in public like this." His voice lowered and he sounded thoughtful as he added, "He must really like football."

"Well, he works here part-time, so he probably had to be here for the post-game cleanup. But coming early and being part of the crowd can't be easy."

As they reached the bleachers and picked their way up to a couple of vacant seats at the very top corner, Lexie took note of the atmosphere. The home team was winning out on the playing field. But in the stands, among the crowd, there was such a sense of anger, mistrust, and resentment, that nobody was doing a lot of cheering. Glares and sneers had replaced cheers and applause. Noticeably absent were any hints of sportsmanship, community, or camaraderie.

The divide at the fifty-yard line had absolutely nothing on the separation between the residents of "old" Granville and those from below Woodsboro Ave, who eyed one another across the expansive field like two opposing armies sizing up a battlefield just before bloodying it.

The tension was so thick, the two sides so distinctly separated, it was like being in a gangland turf war rather than at a high school stadium. Lexie had lived in Granville for six years and had never seen anything like it. People in line for the bathroom or snacks jostled and shoved, insults were shouted, elbows flew. Several members of the police force were on hand to watch the game, and while they didn't wear uniforms, they made their presence known, shouting down anybody who got a little too aggressive. Especially anybody from the opposing team's side.

"It's not usually like this," she mumbled to Aidan. "I mean, there's always the typical tension, but I've never felt this much . . ."

"Rage?"

"Yeah," she admitted. "You can almost smear it on, it's so thick."

"Powder keg," he said with a matter-of-fact shrug. "People are afraid, pointing fingers. The tension's going to cause an explosion if something doesn't happen to release it. Dunston's a fool not to see it."

She only hoped they weren't in the vicinity when it all exploded. Since she and Aidan were sitting on the visitor's side, with those Dunston would undoubtedly call "rabble," the last thing she wanted was to be caught in a riot. She'd probably get arrested for incitement.

Lexie had drawn a few curious glances, and wary nods from those sitting around them when they'd arrived at their seats. People were whispering about her articles, wondering if they'd been too quick to believe the chief who, the Boro folks now recalled, they pretty much hated anyway. Sensing their desire to question her, she figured if she'd been alone, a few would have done it. But Aidan's presence at her side kept them from asking anything. They didn't recognize him, saw only a stranger in their midst. With his dark good looks, his frown, and his deep, gleaming eyes, he didn't inspire quick trust and ease. More like excitement and wary interest.

While he'd done as she'd asked and gotten rid of the black-on-black-on-black look, the dark jeans and navy jacket didn't make him look any more like a typical guy next door. She didn't think he was capable of that look. Not unless one lived next door to a mysterious wind-swept old mansion on the English moors. He resembled one of those alpha men who would inhabit an old Gothic novel.

She laughed at herself for the thought, knowing it was as much his personality—his innate draw—as his looks that put that strange image in her mind. But not entirely.

Because even if she had no clue who he was, and just walked past him on the street, she somehow knew goose bumps would rise on her skin and she would tingle with awareness. He was just so there. Intense. Unlike anyone she'd ever met before.

Lexie had enjoyed her share of sexual affairs, though none recently. But she'd never known a man, not even one with whom she'd been intimate, who could glance at her and cause shivers of excitement to run up and down her spine. Not until Aidan.

This was utter physical attraction at its most pure, basic level.

"The chief's making the rounds. Who's that he's talking to?" he asked, nodding toward the other side of the field, where Dunston stood with a small group of men.

"The one bursting the seams of that letterman's jacket is Mayor Bobby Cunningham."

"Reliving his own jock glory days?" he asked.

She rolled her eyes. "I think he bought that jacket at a thrift shop or on eBay. I snooped into his background a little bit and he never made it higher than batboy when he went to school here. That's our illustrious mayor, all flash and show, nothing underneath to justify it."

"The others?"

Shifting in her seat, she peered at the chief and his cronies. After naming two she recognized as members of the town council, she added, "The gray-haired guy is Principal Steele, and the tall one in the navy sport coat is his vice principal, Mark Young, who I told you about."

"The one organizing search parties," he said, quoting her.

"Right. The one with the Jay Leno jaw is Principal Ziegler from Hoover. I don't know as much about him, except that he wouldn't meet with me when I was working on the story."

"At least the school administrators haven't come to blows," he said.

"Not yet," she muttered. "Though the evening is still young."

The only place the hits seemed strictly sports related was out on the field. Lexie wasn't much of a football fan, but she knew a little about the game. Though she watched for any after-the-call strikes or low blows, she didn't see any. The teams were playing their hearts out, just like any other Friday night under the lights; they seemed oblivious to their parents' bad behavior.

Or maybe not so oblivious. She had to wonder when halftime rolled around. Because instead of running off the field with their teammates, suddenly the captains of each team, as if by unspoken agreement, strode to the fifty-yard line. They met face-to-face, each removing his helmet to engage in a serious conversation, appearing tense but cordial.

"What's going on?" someone nearby whispered.

"Probably getting ready for a speech for the late coach they're supposed to be honoring tonight," she said, pulling a small notebook out of her pocket so she could jot down a few comments. Walter had given her a story to cover, after all.

"I don't think so," Aidan murmured.

The two boys—young men—spoke for a few moments, ignoring the shouts from their coaches. Gradually, everyone in the stands noticed. Conversations quieted, the spectators watching closely as the boys were joined by two teenage girls, one from each side's cheerleading team. Lexie immediately recognized one of the Kirby twins, likely Taylor, who was captain of the squad. By virtue of her peppiness as opposed to her sister's academics, Lexie assumed.

"This should prove interesting," Aidan said.

"What?"

"I believe we're about to see these kids put their parents to shame."

She understood, and suspected he was right when the four young people moved in unison toward the sidelines, where a microphoned announcer had been calling the game. Though the two school principals waved the coaches over and tried to intercept the kids, they would not be deterred. The young man in the red and black Hoover uniform muscled past all of the adults, pulling the microphone right out of the volunteer announcer's hand. He said something, realized the microphone was turned off, and flicked a switch. A sudden blast of screechy feedback got the attention of the few oblivious people who hadn't already been glued to the unfolding spectacle.

"We got something to say," the boy said into the mike, his voice echoing across the suddenly quiet stadium. "All of us."

He waved an arm back, gesturing toward all the other students. Every member of both teams, and all the cheerleaders, had come forward, shoulder to shoulder in one long, uninterrupted line of solidarity across the football field. The coaches appeared beside themselves, running back and forth, shouting at their players, who completely ignored them.

The boy was joined at the mike by the other three, and Taylor handed him a folded sheet of paper, nodding her encouragement and squeezing his hand.

Lexie muttered, "That oughta send the old-guard racists running for their white sheets."

"No shit," said a woman sitting beside her. They exchanged a smile.

Unfolding the paper, the boy began to read, his voice a little shaky—nervous—yet his posture firm and resolute. "We the students of Granville High School and Hoover High School want to dedicate this game to . . . Vonnie Jackson."

Even from here, Lexie heard the collective gasp rising from a number of people sitting over in the opposite bleachers. That had not been the name anybody had expected to hear.

The first boy offered the microphone to the captain

of the Granville team. He took it, and the note, and read, "Today is Vonnie's eighteenth birthday. We ask all of you to join us in a moment of silence to show our solidarity in hoping that she's okay and that *somebody* finds her, and all the other missing kids, and brings them back home."

Wow. Direct hit, right at the chief of police. And right in front of his most rich and powerful constituents.

"Nice," Aidan whispered.

"Very nice," she agreed. "Especially because that kid from Granville High is the son of a well-known local attorney."

The four students took each other's hands, boy-girl, boy-girl—different races, schools, and backgrounds—looking like a commercial for racial harmony and peace. They lowered their heads and fell silent. As Aidan had predicted, they humiliated everybody else in the place, including the inept police chief and the pig mayor, into doing the same thing.

Lexie joined them, pausing to send heartfelt good wishes to Vonnie. But as soon as it ended, she knew she would need to get to work. Though Stan would be covering the game itself, she would tell this part of the story in the paper, no matter what anybody had to say about it.

It was going to be a lot harder now for Dunston to try to keep her quiet. A big spotlight had been shone on the darkest corners of the town, courtesy of a group of teenagers who were able to see past their own differences to that which united them: Vonnie and the other victims.

It was one of the bravest things she'd ever seen, a moment she would never forget. And one she suspected also would be remembered by all the mostly decent, rational people who lived in this town and were sitting quietly in their seats, joining in the resounding silence.

*   *   *

Friday, 9:05 p.m.

You've pleased me in other ways.

At first when she woke from her brief, fitful sleep, Vonnie thought the monster was back, that his evening had ended sooner than he expected and he'd returned to read to her some more.

Or to beat her. Or to kill her.

But it was merely a whisper in her mind, the echo of the words he'd said earlier lingering like a wisp of smoke in her memory.

You've pleased me.

She focused on the words, her head a little less spinny than it had been over the first couple of days. The tape he'd put over her mouth to keep her from screaming, and to teach her a lesson, had actually helped her in one way. He hadn't been able to shove any pills down her throat. Nor, she suspected, had he laced her drink with anything. She had noticed no strange taste, and right now felt more clearheaded and in control than she had since she'd first woken up in this hole.

Had he simply made a mistake by not drugging her? Or had he merely assumed she was so weak, so broken, that she would no longer even try to escape, knowing how close she'd come to death after the screaming episode?

She had no way of knowing; she only knew it was damned nice to feel smart and focused again, even though she had a bitch of a headache. But the pain didn't matter, only the clarity did. She had a chance to try to think her way out of this and she intended to use it.

Vonnie decided to start with her hands. Though her arms had long since gone numb from being bound behind her back, the tape he'd used to bind her wrists was getting a little old. She had felt its restrictive hold loosen over the past few days, and he hadn't replenished it.

Rolling onto her side as much as she could beneath the chains looped around her body, she tried to flex her fingers. They didn't feel a part of her anymore, just lumps of dead meat dangling from her hands, all sensation gone. She curled them, fisted them. Again, and again. Until prickles of sensation returned, stinging and hot.

Blessing the sensation, since it proved he hadn't cut off her circulation to the point where he'd done permanent damage, she flexed and stretched, just her fingers, then just her hands.

She had no idea how she would get free, but knew her hands—and the looser binding at her wrists—was a good place to start.

You've pleased me. The damned voice popped into her mind, interrupting her concentrated efforts.

"Not by choice, you son of a bitch," she tried to say, though she could barely move her lips because of the tape.

He'd widened the hole before he'd left, as if finally realizing by her desperate, deeply indrawn breaths that she had been close to suffocating. And what fun would it be if he came back and found her dead? He'd get no pleasure out of that, was definitely not the type who wanted to achieve her death in any but the most personal, intimate, close-up of ways. Even a gun would be too distant, too easy. Not that he'd shown any evidence of having one. A few punches to the head had been all he'd needed to kidnap her. That and an open car trunk.

No, it wouldn't be a gun, nor an accidental death.

He was a knife kind of guy. Or an ax, a chainsaw, a hammer. Or even just his bare hands. Something bloody and messy, brutal and satisfying. Something that would bring her incredible pain.

Sick motherfucker. Sick motherfucker who she'd pleased, somehow.

But how? By playing along with him, pretending to listen to his stories? By acting beaten, as if she'd thoroughly learned her lesson and wouldn't scream for help even if she heard the FBI storming into the next room?

Hell to that; if her mouth were uncovered and she heard a plane flying somewhere overhead, she'd scream her guts out.

You pleased a lot of people.

He was talking about something else, something more than this battle of wits. She knew it.

Blinking hard, Vonnie shook her head, trying to clear her slightly blurry vision, deprived of real light for so many days. Not to mention wake herself fully and get her brain up to speed. Her hands were waking up; her mind needed to as well.

He had said he'd be out late, but she'd drifted into a fitful sleep and didn't know how long ago he'd left. Maybe an hour. Maybe three. She needed to get busy.

But his voice kept intruding.

A lot of people.

Who else had she pleased? What was he talking about? He seemed to think she'd figure it out. She had the feeling once she did, she'd learn more about why she'd ended up in this situation. And maybe the identity of the man behind the plastic mask.

"So who?"

She'd spent a lifetime doing whatever she could to improve her chances, and sometimes that meant bending over backward to please people who had authority over her. Teachers, bosses, friends who would watch her back when times got tough—in a neighborhood like hers, everybody needed a few solid friends. Vonnie even managed to please her abusive mother twice a month when she handed over most of her paycheck to cover the rent.

She sensed, though, that the monster wasn't talking about any of them. There had been something so malevolent, so darkly amused in his voice. Knowing the memory he wanted her to recall was an especially ugly, painful one, he'd enjoyed tormenting her with his cryptic clues.

You pleased a lot of people.

A lot of . . .

Oh, Lord.

Vonnie gasped, at least as much as she could through the small opening in the tape. Because she suddenly thought of a possible explanation for his words. A place where she'd *pleased* a lot of people.

"No," she groaned, shaking her head back and forth as tears spilled out of her eyes. Images washed over her and she became overwhelmed with the ugliest memory of her life—before now. "No, no, no."

Yes.

It had to be. What other explanation was there? What would "please" a cruel monster like him, as well as a bunch of other deviant bastards whose motives might be a little less deadly but whose pleasures were every bit as corrupt?

She'd pleased those men, all right. Over and over. Not out of the goodness of her heart, oh no. But because she'd been sold by her own mother.

Chapter 7

"Here I go. Wish me luck," Lex said, leaping to her feet as the marching band took the field for the halftime program. The teams had gone to their locker rooms after their moment of silence, and Dunston had immediately been surrounded by a mob of curious, worried residents.

"I'll stay put and observe. No point tipping anybody off that we're working together."

"Good plan. Plus you have an eagle-eye view from up here."

"And maybe a nosebleed," he said, his tone dry. "Fortunately I have pretty good vision."

"Yeah, I heard that." A slight wag of her eyebrows said she was joking. Her mood was considerably lighter, with good reason. The restraints were off. She knew it, everybody knew it.

"Be sure to make a note of anybody who acts suspiciously," she added.

He couldn't help chuckling. In Aidan's somewhat jaded experience, everyone acted suspiciously on occasion. "Will do. Be careful," he admonished, though as soon as the words left his mouth, he wondered if she'd question his right to say them. Again hit with that sensation that things were spiraling too fast, he forced himself to remember he barely knew the woman. They weren't involved, and the connection they were feeling was a result of being thrown together in an ugly situation and, on his part, anyway, immediate, raw physical attraction.

That didn't help, though. He still worried about her.

"Go get 'em, girl," said a Hoover parent. "Don't let 'em shut you down again!"

Lexie turned back and smiled over her shoulder. "Not a chance."

Aidan watched her progress all the way down the bleachers and around the long curve of the track. Though he still had no use for any other reporter, he couldn't help admiring this one's tenacity as she strode on, her steps determined, her shoulders squared. People melted out of her way when she approached; she was a force of nature and nobody was going to shut her up again.

The man she'd identified earlier as the mayor saw her coming and did a one-eighty. A few of the puffed-up-looking businessmen, including Underwood, the newspaper owner who was, technically, her boss, departed as well. There seemed to be a small exodus heading through the gates. Their zeal for the home team appeared to have faded once the burly players proved they had brains and hearts to go along with the muscles and testosterone.

Lex did manage to corner both high school principals. The two men stepped to a quiet corner with her, talking for several long minutes, each nodding and even, occasionally, smiling. Aidan didn't have to wonder why. Despite the lapse of protocol, as an educator, it had to be nice to see the usually thoughtless, self-absorbed teenage students become so passionate about a cause. If he'd been the parent of one of the kids on the field, his chest would be bursting with pride over a hell of a lot more than their prowess with a ball or a pom-pom.

He suspected a lot of people felt the same way. Despite the quick exit of some, the majority had stayed put. The excited chatter in the visitor's section firmly illustrated that the bubble of anger and tension enveloping the first part of the evening had popped with the students' brave display. He listened to bits of conversation, trying to thin out the gossip and wait for any nugget or kernel of useful information. But it proved fruitless. He just didn't know enough about the area to winnow out the good information from the bad.

Finally, when the game came to a close and Lex had just about run out of police chiefs and officials to face-off with in front of an appreciative audience, he slowly followed the rest of the fans down the metal steps and across the playing field. The home team had won, but nobody really cared anymore. Both teams were being celebrated.

Stopping beside the refreshment building, he watched as a long stream of humanity moved through the exit gates. Lex stood at the base of the bleachers with a tall, middle-aged man wearing a tweed jacket with elbow patches and rumpled pants. He might as well have the words *disgruntled high school teacher* tattooed on his forehead. They'd been speaking intently, standing close together in order to be heard over the last remaining voices of the crowd.

When Lex looked down at her notebook, furiously jotting some notes, Aidan watched the man shift even closer, well within her personal space. He also noted the look on the guy's face.

Noted it. Interpreted it. Was infuriated by it.

Mr. Wannabe College Professor might as well have licked his lips, he was so visibly awash with sexual interest. Alexa wore perfectly respectable khaki pants and a light sweater, but there was no disguising the sensual fullness of her lips, the feminine shape of her face, or the shape of her nicely curved body beneath the clothes. The guy standing beside her was mentally filling in any mysteries her concealing clothes contained, trying to figure out how to get at them.

Without giving it another thought, he strode the few yards to the two, stepping to Lexie's side and casting an assessing stare at the man she'd been talking to. "Lexie, are you ready to go?" he asked her, knowing his intimate tone hinted that they were here together, as a couple.

She jerked her attention toward him, lifting a quizzical brow, apparently not noticing that the guy she'd been with had been studying her ass and trying to get close enough to cop a feel.

Something else he didn't have to be a mind reader to know. Sleazy men all thought about the same thing: how to be sleazier.

"Hey, you called me Lexie," she said, wagging an accusing index finger at him.

He shrugged. "What can I say? You're growing on me."

"I have that effect," she said.

The sleazy teacher frowned. "Please, take my number in case there's anything else you need. I hope you can keep me updated and would be happy to meet with you again."

Lexie merely gave him a friendly shrug. "That's okay. I can reach you through the school. Thanks for talking to me, Mr. Wilhelm. I appreciate your thoughts."

"Anything I can do," he said pleasantly, though his smile was tight at her obvious disinterest. "Vonnie was one of my favorite students. A brilliant girl."

"Is," Aidan interjected.

"What?"

"*Is* one of your favorite students," he said, wondering if the other man realized how cold he'd sounded. He had no idea whether Vonnie was alive, but the very least her own supposed "favorite" teacher could do was presume so. A small point, perhaps, but the man irritated him. Wilhelm made the hairs on the back of Aidan's neck stand up.

"Okay," she said, staring back and forth between them, grasping the sudden tension. "We'd better get going. Looks as if they're trying to get things cleaned up for the night."

She reached for his arm, thought better of it, and simply walked away. He leveled one more stare on the teacher, snapping, "Why don't you wipe your chin," then walked after Lex.

They were among the last to leave, along with the volunteers who'd worked the concessions stand. Kenny, the scarred man they'd run into earlier, was already piercing trash with a long, spiked pole. As they passed, the guy in the navy blazer, who Aidan recognized as Vice Principal Young, called to the janitor, "Would you hurry the hell up? I'd like to get home before midnight, and I can't leave until your sorry ass gets out of here!"

Lexie cleared her throat. The man glanced over, realized they'd been close enough to hear the ugly tone, and put on one of those plastic smiles that all future high school administrators had perfected by the time they graduated from college. "Long night," he said, rubbing a hand over his brow, as if fatigue was enough to explain being a shit to a maimed, scarred underling. "After a long week. Thanks again for your help with this, Ms. Nolan."

Uh-huh. Oily. The man would be running for school board someday; Aidan had no doubt. Willing to set up search parties or no, the man seemed as fake as the rest of the bureaucrats in this town.

"No, thank *you*, Mr. Young," she called, not breaking her stride. Once they had gotten a few yards farther, out of earshot, she said, "So, shall I prove my psychic abilities now? You didn't like Mr. Wilhelm."

"No," he growled, "I did not. That vice principal is a piece of work, too."

"But you disliked Wilhelm because he wouldn't stop staring at my butt."

He froze.

"I'm not stupid. My scum-dar is quite high, actually. But he's the honors society advisor and was at the meeting Monday night; otherwise I wouldn't have given that pig the time of day."

Glad she'd noticed, he nodded to accede his own overreaction. "Sorry."

"It's okay."

"Did you have any luck?" he asked as they headed toward the parking lot.

She smirked, looking more than a little self-satisfied. "They hate my guts."

"It's good to be hated for the right reasons."

"Don't I know it. It's also good to be liked for the right ones."

"How so?"

"There are some people in this town who have both honor and integrity. A few of them are in positions of power, including that prosecutor, whose kid spoke earlier, and the medical examiner. Two members of the town council demanded meetings with the chief, plus the mayor just got his ass reamed out by his own sister, who wants to know why he hasn't started a community watch program to protect our young people."

He raised a surprised brow. "All because of some kids?"

She considered it, then slowly shook her head. "Not because the kids convinced them this was happening, but because they had the guts to actually say it out loud and take a stand. How can the adults not do the same? I never realized before tonight how many people saw right through Dunston's actions last month. A lot of them just didn't know they weren't alone in thinking we've got a nutless loser for a police chief."

He was about to reply when Lex stopped midstride beside him. They had reached the parking lot, heading toward the far corner where his SUV was parked. Her small sedan sat just beyond it, and had been out of sight until a moment ago. She'd spotted it first.

"Son of a bitch," she muttered.

Following her stare, he felt his muscles tense with wariness as well. Though it almost never came naturally to him, Aidan gave in to his first impulse and put a steadying hand on the small of her back. It was the first time he'd really touched her, and there were no jolts, no shocks, nothing at all unusual. Not that he'd expected them, especially not since she was wearing a sweater. But with a personality as strong as hers, and with the sparks they'd set off each other from the moment they'd met, he hadn't been entirely sure what to expect.

Fortunately, he got nothing except the sensation of a woman who needed some support.

That was good. Because right now, he just wanted to offer her that support. "You obviously got under somebody's skin," he said, trying to contain the anger building inside him as he eyed the carnage visited on her cute little car.

Whoever it had been, he'd been pretty thorough given the short time frame and the public location. Aidan's tall SUV had been the only thing hiding the vandal from the view of anyone else heading toward their cars either during or after the game. He'd not only snipped the valve stems on the tires, he'd gouged long scratches down the side and had smashed in the windshield.

"Okay, so sometimes it's not so great to be hated," she said, her heavy sigh hinting that her reaction was more resigned than enraged.

"Insured?"

She nodded.

"So you'll deal. But do it tomorrow. Let me take you home."

He steered her toward the passenger's side of his SUV, not wanting to stand there doing a postmortem of the night that had led to this vandalism. Both because she had enough to think about, and because they needed to go. It wasn't smart to stand under the overhead lights in a deserted parking lot where somebody filled with rage toward Lexie could be watching them.

She couldn't take her eyes off her car. "This sucks. I just paid the thing off."

"I know. But I assume you aren't in the mood to call the police back out here tonight."

"If I have to see Dunston's smirky face as he pretends to give a damn, I might throw up."

"Yeah. That is if he even shows up after having arranged for it to be done himself."

Not surprised by his words, as if she'd already considered the possibility, Lexie allowed him to open the door and help her into the seat she'd vacated a few hours earlier. Joining her inside, he glanced over, seeing the weary tilt of her head and the way she rubbed her slim neck. She'd been so strong all day. Now she didn't look so much weak as simply exhausted.

"Where do you live?"

She gave him the address, and he punched it into his GPS, being totally unfamiliar with the area. Maybe he needed to get out a little more. He'd certainly been given reason to today.

"I can give you directions," she insisted.

"It's okay. Just relax. Close your eyes. Let it all go for a couple of minutes."

She sank deeper into the leather seat. "Mm. You have a nice voice, Aidan. Do you have a hypnotist act on the side?"

Laughing softly, he started the car and pulled out of the lot. "Not a chance. I've met too many hypnotists to even consider it."

"You mean in your line of work?"

"Not exactly." He shifted, not thrilled with the direction of the conversation, but not hung up about it, either. "A few of them tried to cure me of my 'delusions' when I was a kid."

He didn't have to look over to know she'd opened her eyes and was staring at him. "Oh."

"They came on the scene after the religious wing nuts who tried driving out whatever demons must have taken over my body."

She jerked upright. "Good God!"

"Whatever," he said with a shrug. "Some people hear

about psychics and see fraud. Some see magic. My parents saw demonic spirits."

"They really held exorcisms?" she asked, sounding shocked.

"'That's those crazy papists,'" he said, quoting his father. "Southern Baptists hold prayer circles." His tone dry, he added, "It was that or call the *National Enquirer* and make a fortune touting me as the half-alien mind-reading boy. And they're just not the type."

"Thought you didn't read minds, alien-boy," she said with a deliberate snicker, as if knowing they were skirting the edges of a difficult subject.

"I don't," he replied, smiling as well. "So feel free to think whatever you want about the bastard who trashed your car."

"Huh. I don't have to hide those thoughts. I'd be happy to share them, as long as you have a dictionary full of four-letter words to refer back to."

"I've got a pretty extensive vocabulary."

He didn't blame her. A few choice words had entered his mind when he'd seen the car, too. Not all four-letter ones, though. At the top of his list was coward. Only somebody who had no guts would take such petty revenge on a woman who was just doing her job.

Though maybe the vandalism was something to be thankful for. It beat somebody taking a pair of scissors or a sharp object to the car's owner. His hands tightened on the steering wheel at the thought of it, his stomach churning and a faint red haze appearing before his eyes.

"So," she said, getting back to the fun topic of his whacked-out family, "the folks don't like having a psychic for a son, huh? I can sympathize—my mom hates that I'm a reporter."

Deadpan, he asked, "Why would she feel that way about such an *admirable* profession?"

She swatted him lightly in the upper arm. He didn't even stiffen at the contact. Progress.

"She wanted college and a career for my brother. House and babies for me. Now he's a trucker and lives in her basement, and I never married, moved away, and will never go back."

"To?"

"Chester, Indiana, population twelve hundred."

One-upping her, he said, "Freemont, Arkansas, population twelve. All of them members of my father's congregation."

"What a couple of big-city big-shots we are to have ended up in this metropolis." She gestured out the window as they drove downtown. Sounding a little less amused, she added, "Though, of course, you are a newcomer, most recently of Savannah, as I recall."

He stiffened reflexively.

"I'm not going to pry."

"You already have, I assume?"

"Only through the public record."

"And that's always so reliable."

"Maybe you'll tell me your side of the story someday." As if knowing where his mind immediately went, she clarified, "Off the record. Just like everything else."

He nodded slowly. "Maybe." Then, knowing he owed her one, he added, "I'm sorry I was so abrupt with you yesterday."

"Career hazard."

Perhaps, but she didn't seem like the rest of the people in her career. Maybe it was just because of this one case, this particular story, but Lexie seemed bigger-hearted than most of her brethren. "You're not supposed to get so personally involved with something like this, are you?" he asked. "You need to remain detached to do your job."

"Hello, pot, I'm kettle," she said, sounding tart. She obviously had been reading about him, had seen the truth lurking in his own history—Aidan had almost always become too personally involved with the cases on which he worked.

"Touché. But I've learned my lesson."

"I hope not," she murmured, gazing out the windshield at the oncoming headlights. "I mean, I hope you haven't stopped caring about the people you're trying to save."

"You can't save them all, kettle."

She wrapped her arms around herself, as if cold, though the evening was balmy. "Maybe that's why I so desperately want to save this one."

"Vonnie?"

She nodded. Falling silent, as if considering whether she wanted to say more, she finally continued. "There was this girl who lived in the next town over from where I grew up."

Ahh. He'd half wondered whether she had a story, something that drove her on, pushed her to do more than another person might in this situation. "Someone you knew?"

Shaking her head, she continued. "A few years older than me, but still in elementary school. She disappeared while riding her bike home from the park one day."

He knew this sad tale. Or at least dozens like it.

"It was all any of the adults were talking about. Neighborhood watches started up. We weren't allowed to walk to friends' houses alone or go to the playground by ourselves anymore. Everybody was in a panic. My parents included."

She hadn't mentioned her father before, just her mother. But he didn't want to interrupt by asking for more details than she was already providing.

"Who wouldn't be?" He didn't really expect an answer, the question was rhetorical. He had plenty of experience with hysterical parents. Discovering your child was missing was something one never got over. Caroline Remington certainly hadn't.

He buried that memory, focusing on the here and

now, not to mention the road. They were turning into what he assumed was her neighborhood and would be at her door momentarily. Soon she'd exit the car and he'd go home and maybe tomorrow they'd go back to being a little more formal, a bit more aloof. He wouldn't be putting his hand on her shoulder and she wouldn't be baring her soul about a bad childhood memory.

Which, for some reason, made him lift his foot ever so slightly off the gas pedal as they cruised slowly down the block. "So how did you react? What were you thinking?"

"I was afraid. It was all anybody talked about. I remember being terrified for months, having nightmares. Probably like every other seven-year-old girl in the area."

Seven. Jesus. "Did they ever find her?"

"Yes," she said, her voice thick. "Her body was found in a neighbor's shed, rolled up in an old rug. Guy was a convicted sex offender; he'd killed her a few hours after taking her."

Aidan wasn't at all surprised. If parents knew just how close monsters like that were to their nice, normal homes and neighborhoods, they'd probably never let their kids out the door.

"Hell, I'm sorry," he said.

"Me, too."

He listened for the softly spoken instructions from the smooth, computerized voice on the GPS, which told him to turn into the next driveway. No more delaying. They had arrived at her small, one-story house on a quiet street with dozens of other homes that looked just like it.

Pulling up in front, he moved the gearshift to park, and waited. Lexie didn't hop out right away, nor did he move to go around and open the door for her. As if they both just wanted to sit here in the darkness and talk for a few more minutes.

"There was one thing that always stuck with me," she finally said. "A conversation I overheard one night when my parents thought I was asleep."

He turned to look at her, noting the way the dash lights brought reddish highlights to her blond hair, which had tumbled out of its ponytail at some point today and now fell around her shoulders in soft waves. He'd found her pretty before; now, seeing the strength of her profile, the softness of her cheeks, the fullness of her lips, he acknowledged that she was, in truth, a beautiful woman. Her passion and drive only made her more so.

"My mother said it would have been better if they'd never found her. That knowing how awful her final hours were was too much for a parent to bear, and it would have been kinder for them to go on believing she was still alive somewhere, hoping they'd see her again someday."

He'd heard the theory before. Didn't agree with it, but he'd heard it.

"My father, though, felt the opposite. He said knowing the truth, and knowing she couldn't ever be hurt again, would be better than going to bed every night for the rest of your life wondering if your child had just endured another endless day of brutalization and torment. With nothing but more days just like them ahead of her."

He swallowed hard, having met people whose minds filled with that very thought every single time their heads touched the pillow. "Your father sounds like a smart guy."

"He was," she murmured.

Filing that tidbit away—that she'd been especially close to her father and he'd died—he said, "That's why this is so personal to you, why you have to find them. Find *her*."

"Yes, that's why." She finally lifted her gaze from her own clenched hands. "And I'm not going to give up until I do, whether Vonnie Jackson is alive or dead."

He let the words sink in, noting her will and her determination. Aidan understood so much about her now. He already knew her relationship with her boss had a lot to do with the loss of her father, and her recklessness had probably come about from rebelling against her mother.

He also knew that every single day she waged a battle against men in power who wanted to control her, or men without it who wanted to hurt her—or merely objectify her. Lexie's life was a constant balancing act as she tried to follow her conscience and do her job, despite obstacles and enemies. Every day she kept on going, kept fighting.

Knowing her, even for such a brief time, was suddenly making him question every choice he'd made in the past year. Because *she* could have run; she could have quit, could have given up. But she hadn't. So what did that say about him?

"Okay, Lex," he finally said, "we do this together."

He knew she understood everything he was trying to convey. That he was with her, that he wasn't giving up, either. That she was no longer alone.

She glanced over, her eyes gleaming, moist. He sensed the woman didn't cry often—didn't *allow* herself to cry often. Seeing the way her lashes fluttered and her lips quivered, he couldn't help reaching out, giving her a bit of the human connection she seemed to need.

Aidan touched her in the darkness, brushing his fingertips against her soft cheek. He didn't think about what it might cost him, how her thoughts and memories might later invade his consciousness. He merely thought of the now. Of her need. Of the attraction he'd felt for her from the start, which had built every minute since.

She hesitated for the briefest of seconds, as if knowing a touch was something he never offered lightly. Then she curled her face into his hand, and her soft hair fell over his wrist. Her warm exhalations flowed across his skin, her breaths deep and steady.

They remained still, motionless for one long moment. But he had the feeling it was one of those moments when everything changed.

Neither of them spoke, nor did they move closer, try

to change or deepen the connection. This was enough. At least for now.

"Thank you," she finally murmured, her lips brushing ever so lightly against the fleshy part of his palm before she lifted her head and stared at him.

"You're welcome. Good night, Lexie."

Saturday, 5:45 a.m.

Lexie couldn't remember the last time she'd had such vivid dreams, the kind that were so intense, it was hard to know where fantasy ended and reality began. She only knew that as she woke up, she had to sit straight up in bed and blink a few times, plus pat her hand on the pile of rumpled sheets beside her, just to be sure she wasn't still asleep.

Because in her dreams, she hadn't been alone beneath those sheets.

"Good God." She swung her legs off the bed and sat in the darkness, trying to slow her rapid breaths. She'd had nightmares a lot lately. Bad ones. But last night was the first time she could recall dreaming about hot, sweaty sex with a guy she hadn't even known a few days ago.

If Aidan McConnell really had the kind of skills and talents she'd dreamed about, he didn't have to worry about going back to work as a psychic. He could get a job providing satisfaction to women. She'd hire him. Dream Lexie had taken every little bit of physical pleasure she could get from the man until she'd been totally wrung out and unable to move.

Her breaths evened out, but nothing cooled off the heat in her. She was hyped up, her nerve endings afire, every feminine part of her in thrall to the fantasy delights of the night before.

Considering they hadn't even kissed, and Aidan had done nothing more than gently touch her face, she couldn't understand why her nighttime rest had been consumed by him. Yes, he was incredibly good-looking, but she'd met good-looking men before and her subconscious hadn't spent entire nights indulging in wild fantasies about them. It seemed like it had gone on for hours, dream after erotic dream about being with him, touching him, having Aidan in every way a woman could have a man. Thinking about it, she suspected she'd actually been rocked awake by a real orgasm about an hour ago, but had interpreted it as part of the illusion.

"You are losing it," she told herself as she got up and stumbled to her bathroom. "And you need to get laid." Preferably by someone who could satisfy her and then be easily forgotten.

Which left Aidan McConnell out of the picture. He wouldn't be easily forgotten. The man had already taken up residence in the most secretive, hidden part of her brain, where her deepest fantasies and sensual wishes resided. Though she hadn't communicated with that part of herself for a long time—it had been eighteen months since she'd slept with anyone—she knew she wouldn't be shutting it down again soon. Not when it had been so thoroughly awakened.

Standing at the sink, she eyed herself in the mirror, seeing the tangled hair, the moist, parted lips, the pucker of her nipples against her T-shirt. She didn't look like a woman who'd had erotic dreams; she looked like one who'd had an actual erotic night. As if she'd truly given herself over entirely to her new lover and he'd given her immense satisfaction.

But now she was awake. And very—*very*—needy.

Part of her wanted to go back to bed, to lose herself in that decadent bliss again. This time, she wasn't even sure she'd have to fall asleep before the images overtook her thoughts. She was, for once, easily remembering every detail of her dreams.

Wow, the details. Obviously she had a wild side she'd never tapped into before.

A worried thought flashed through her mind, because everything about last night—and now—was so out of character for her. "Did you do this to me?" she asked, speaking not to her reflection but to the man she'd dreamed about. Had he somehow caused last night to happen?

Crazy. Whatever he might be able to do when it came to the woo-woo stuff, she definitely could not. Psychic ability wasn't catching. The simple touch between them in the car might have left him with some residual sensations, but it shouldn't have done anything to her beyond feeling nice at that particular moment.

And it had. Really nice. But there hadn't been any mystery, any otherworldly stuff about it. From the minute she'd met Aidan, she'd been overwhelmed by his magnetism. He hadn't used any powers to arouse her, beyond his own strong sexual appeal.

She didn't breathe a sigh of relief yet, however. Because the way he'd described his abilities brought another worrisome thought to mind. What if he tapped into her dreams? Were they floating around, her own invisible lust-print on the world, waiting to be discovered? Could he see what had been on her mind throughout the long night hours, envision the erotic moments that had played out behind her eyes? If so, how would she ever face him again?

"Naked and on a flat surface," she immediately whispered, not giving it a second thought.

She didn't know where the response had come from; she knew only that she meant it, as if she'd always known that's where they would end up. No, she hadn't gone to bed imagining he was with her. She'd liked his touch, liked the warmth that had been building between them. Still, she hadn't truly thought about them having sex, beyond the general he's-so-damn-hot stuff.

Now, however, when she did think about it, she had to wonder whether her subconscious was telling her to just drop any mental barriers and go for it if she had the chance.

Okay, so he wasn't an unchallenging, no-strings guy.

She didn't see him as the type who would indulge in meaningless one-night stands, not when intimate touching opened him up to so much potential conflict. She already knew he wouldn't be easily taken and forgotten. But that didn't mean she shouldn't want to go right ahead and take him.

So take him. Her heart beat a little faster and she went soft inside. Oh, yeah, she definitely wanted to take him. She just wasn't sure how. Or when.

Unfortunately, she had no time to think about it. The only thing she had time for right now was a long, hot shower. But hell, if that shower included a little erotic daydreaming and some flirtation with her shower massage, well, there were certainly worse ways to start the day.

Chapter 8

Having long been a victim of insomnia, Aidan was used to sleeping in short increments. He took rest when he could get it, not even attempting to shut himself down unless his mind was devoid of any pressing thoughts. Which meant he'd done very little sleeping the previous night.

But at some point he had drifted off. He'd last looked at the clock at three. Checking it now as he jerked awake, he realized he'd managed almost three solid hours, which was good for him these days. Yet he didn't feel rested. God, no. In fact, he felt more edgy and tense than ever.

Because of his dreams.

"Shouldn't have touched her, man," he told himself as he sat up on the couch in his office, where he almost always slept these days. "You should never have made contact."

Too late. He *had* touched her, cupped her cheek, felt the brush of her hair on his skin. And though he'd been honest that he couldn't do any kind of Vulcan mind meld, that simple connection of his fingertips to Lexie's face had created a hell of an opening between their minds.

Maybe not. Maybe it was just a normal dream. And just yours.

Maybe. After all, he'd never experienced anything like that before, sharing actual real-time mental images with another person while they both slept. It never worked that way, his ability. There had never been an actual open channel with thoughts, feelings, and sensations flowing back and forth between him and someone else.

So, yeah, it probably had been just his dream. A hot, sexy dream about a sexy woman who'd intrigued him from almost the very start.

"Yeah, dream on," he muttered.

Because, somehow, he knew it had been real. Last night hadn't been some standard sex dream. It had been so physical, so tangible. He was out of breath, as if he'd completed a hard workout. His heart was pounding. He could smell that spicy shampoo of hers, plus the sweet, pungent aroma of steamy sex. He was sweating, his skin sensitized. And he had a huge hard-on.

"More than just a dream," he admitted aloud.

There had been communication, give-and-take between them. Each intimacy had been returned with an equally erotic one, and they'd moved together like long-time lovers.

They'd met in the night. Her mind had been swept up with midnight visions and he'd barged into them. The details were too clear, the sensations too extreme to mean anything else.

Though he'd walked her to her door last night, he hadn't gone in. Yet he knew the sheets on her bed were a soft yellow and the bedspread had daisies on it. He knew the ceiling fan above the bed squeaked, but that the breeze it generated felt good against their sweat-tinged bodies.

He knew Lexie had a small birthmark just below her right pelvic bone, that it was shaped like a crescent moon, and that his lips would fit perfectly against it. Just like he knew she loved having him tangle his fingers in her hair when he was inside her.

He knew all of that. Because he'd been there, in her mind, sharing every experience as it had happened. He'd slipped inside her dream and upped the stakes, answering each of her fantasies with mind-blowing attention, fulfilling every one of his own at the same time.

He knew something else, too. They hadn't been sharing one dream about some could-have-been kind of encounter. They had jointly anticipated a someday-soon one.

And though he knew he was nowhere near ready to let anybody—any woman—into his life on a real, permanent basis, especially one who was upbeat, energetic, outgoing, and his total opposite, his bed was a completely different story. There, he didn't think it mattered how different they were, or whether he was even capable of connecting emotionally with anyone ever again. He was definitely interested in connecting physically.

So if he had his way, that someday soon would be very soon indeed.

Saturday, 10:55 a.m.

"Ms. Jackson? Berna Jackson?" Lexie asked, knocking on the warped apartment door. She'd intentionally arrived at the dilapidated building at midmorning. Her hope was to be late enough that Vonnie's mother would be awake, but early enough that she hadn't yet left to go out for a liquid lunch that would last dozens of courses and many hours. "I need to talk to you!"

She got no answer. Lexie considered pounding harder, yet she hesitated. The building was quiet. On arrival, she'd seen none of the residents smoking on the outside stoop like there had been yesterday, nor did any children play on the rusty swing set outside. The dingy halls, lit by bare, weak bulbs, were deserted. No ragged women watched with suspicious, bruised eyes; no thin, jittery men tried to hide the needle they'd just used to shoot up. It was a ghetto ghost town.

She suspected she knew why. Lots of people would be sleeping off hangovers or recovering from a wild Friday night that lasted until dawn. Children had probably been plopped down in front of Saturday-morning cartoons and told to stay quiet for fear of waking up somebody who wouldn't be happy being awakened. What a life. What an awful, tragic life.

Vonnie. God, no wonder she'd so desperately wanted to get out. For her sake, she couldn't give up. Hopefully, now that Aidan seemed committed to helping her, and the whole town was starting to demand answers, the truth would come out.

She couldn't deny it felt good to have allies. Especially allies who could stare down a belligerent jerk, or touch her and make all the anxiety melt away.

She knocked again. "Mrs. Jackson, please open the door. I have some information. I think you're going to want to hear about what happened at the game last night."

Mentioning the game reminded her of the rest of last night. As in, her car. She still had to deal with the legalities of that. She'd called her insurance agent this morning, who'd told her she'd need to file a police report. Not up to that, she'd arranged for a rental car. To her knowledge, her poor little Honda still sat on its four flat tires in the school parking lot. It wasn't going anywhere and could be dealt with this afternoon—when she didn't have to do it alone.

Somehow, the image of going to the police station and reporting the vandalism seemed a little easier when Aidan was included. He'd made the offer last night, and while it hadn't seemed entirely necessary then, now she intended to take him up on it. It would be one of their first stops after she met up with him at his place at noon. Hopefully by then she'd be able to meet his eye without revealing that she'd spent all night dreaming of doing wild things with him.

Glancing at her watch and realizing Vonnie's mother was either dead to the world or already gone, she gave it one more shot. She knocked again, a little harder, and raised her voice as much as she dared. "Please, Ms. Jackson, I know you wanted to talk to me!"

Still nothing, but she did hear a creak from behind her. Swinging around, Lexie saw a robe-wearing neighbor, eyeing her through a cracked door across the hall. This wasn't the same woman she'd talked to previously, who'd been weary but worried about her neighbor's daughter. This one looked hard and bleary-eyed, as if she'd been on an all-night bender. And Lexie had woken her up. Not a good way to begin an acquaintance.

"Hi. I'm sorry to—"

"She ain't home. Ain't been home since yest'day mornin'."

A vicious-sounding dog barked from behind the closed door of another apartment in the rundown building. A thin wooden door, a chain, and a dead bolt didn't sound strong enough to keep it away should it choose to sic. It might, however, keep random drug dealers and thieves from coming too close, which was probably the animal's entire purpose in life.

Honestly, Lexie found it hard to believe the girl she'd been learning so much about over the last forty-eight hours had grown up here. How had she done it? How had Vonnie had the strength to overcome this when so many could not?

"Do you know where she is?" Somehow, Lexie suspected Vonnie's mother wasn't out there holding candlelight protests.

"She got the notes you left," the woman said. "Was supposed to call you."

"She didn't."

"Look, I know fuck-all about where the woman is. She said she was gonna call, so why don't you stop pounding the door down and get on back to your side of town?"

"Ma'am, I'm sorry I disturbed you, but Ms. Jackson's daughter is missing."

"I know that," she snapped. "Everybody knows Vonnie's gone."

"I want to help find her."

"You wanna help? Get that pussy chief to pay attention to what's goin' on down here."

A familiar refrain. She'd heard the same thing a month before when researching the original story. Dunston had few fans south of Woodsboro Avenue.

"I think he'll have to, given what happened last night at the football game," Lexie said. She briefly explained, concluding, "Believe me, ma'am, he's not going to be able to ignore this any longer. The rest of this town won't let him."

The door may have eased open another inch. But that could have been her imagination.

"So if you have any idea where I can look for Vonnie's mother. . . ."

"She said last night she was goin' to confront the cops," the woman admitted, begrudging every word. "Gonna handcuff herself to the flagpole to get them to pay attention."

Lexie frowned. "How much had she had to drink when she said that?"

The other woman's lip quirked up on one side in jaded amusement. "Just enough to think it sounded like a good idea, but not enough for her to pass out and forget the whole thing."

"Not good," she muttered.

"Nope. So I'd prob'ly start by lookin' in the closest jail cell. And while you're there, you can ask Dunston 'bout what else is goin' on down here."

"Are you talking about the other missing girls?"

"Yeah, well, missing ones ain't all I'm talkin' about. Lot more happening in this town that nobody gives a damn about, least of all the po-lice."

The dog barked again, and the woman froze. As if realizing she'd been about to say something she shouldn't, she stepped back into her dark apartment, her eyes wide with fear.

Lexie followed, crossing the hall to the other door. "What are you talking about?"

The woman shook her head. "Go on, now," she urged. "Get outta here."

"Please, I just want to help!" she said, keeping her voice low.

"Tina?" a male voice bellowed from somewhere inside. "Who you talkin' to?"

Her mouth fell open, her bottom lip quivering. Lexie recognized that tone, and the terror it brought to Tina's face. "I'm sorry." Lexie stepped back, holding her hands out in supplication, not begging for more answers. Not if it was going to land this woman in trouble with that man.

Tina watched her closely, as if waiting for Lexie to push her, demand more. When she realized that wasn't going to happen, her compressed lips softened a bit. She glanced to the right again, starting to ease the door closed, whispering, "Talk to the fresh fish on the corner."

"What?"

"The underage hookers," the woman hissed.

Then the door slid closed with a decisive click. From within came another male bellow. Lexie bit her lip, appreciating the woman's help, wishing she could come to her aid. But the best thing she could do for her was to get out of here and never let her husband or boyfriend know she'd been talking to a reporter about things he would say were none of her business.

She might not have been raised in a building like this, but she knew how things went here. And once again, as she left the shabby hallway, the shouting voices, the barking dog behind, she could only think about Vonnie.

Just how hard would the girl fight to stay alive if this was all she had to return to?

Saturday, 11:05 a.m.

Aidan wasn't surprised when Julia Harrington knocked on his door a little after eleven a.m. He'd called her last night to fill her in on what had been going on in Granville and to see if she was interested in helping out. She'd asked a few questions, then said he'd see her today, promising to spread the word and find out if any of the others minded working on a Saturday.

Apparently, they hadn't minded. Because as soon as he answered the door, two of her three employees walked in behind the energetic, dark-haired woman. Barging into his house, they acted as if they'd all worked together every day for the past year. They tossed their jackets on the coatrack by the door, making themselves at home like they'd been here dozens of times.

"I see you rallied the troops," he said, knowing how persuasive his former boss could be.

She shrugged, a twinkle appearing in her soft brown eyes. "Most of them."

"Where's Morgan?" he asked, lifting one brow, knowing she had to hear the overly innocent note in his voice as he inquired about her mysterious "silent" partner in the agency.

She waved a hand in the air. "Out getting the lay of the land. And Derek sends his apologies—he had another obligation today, but said he'd come tomorrow if we need him."

They would need him, though probably not by tomorrow. Aidan felt sure several murders had been committed in Granville, but finding out where they had occurred would be tough. Not something that could be accomplished in just twenty-four hours. There was no point in bringing Derek Monahan down until they had a crime scene, where he could do what he did best.

"As for the rest of us," Julia added, "it's not like we have real lives or anything better to do on the weekends. Now, do I have to say it, or is it simply understood?"

He knew what was coming and sighed. "You might as well get it over with."

"Okay. I told you so."

"So you did."

"Crime solving is in your blood, and doing it from a thousand miles away was never going to be enough for you. You live for this."

Maybe, though he wasn't ready to jump back in with both feet. Now he just wanted to get through this one case, find this missing girl. Then he could do a big Zen self-evaluation on all the choices he'd made in recent months and decide if he wanted to make any changes.

"Are we done now?"

"Not quite." She squeezed his shoulder. "I'm really glad you've taken off the hair shirt. If only you hadn't bought this white elephant and could move back to Savannah."

He took no offense, knowing she had decided that his getting involved with this case meant he was ready to go back to everything about his old life. He wasn't there yet and didn't know if he ever would be. Going backward seemed a little pointless. Since last night, during those charged moments in the car with Lexie, he'd begun to think a lot about going forward.

"I appreciate your coming," he said. "*Now* are you done?"

"Yep," she said with a cheerful smile.

The others had been exploring inside. Liv had been here once, Mick not at all. Seeing them, hearing them talk as he walked through his usually silent home, he felt a little like the winter warlock from that old kid's Christmas show. Crowded—but at least part of a group again.

"Hey, man, long time, no see!" said Mick Tanner, who had been the last person to come to work for Julia before Aidan's departure last year.

They didn't know each other well. Mick hadn't come with the others a few weeks ago for their dinner at Ranger Joe's—the one that had turned out to be so important in linking him to Vonnie Jackson. He wasn't even entirely sure whether Mick's abilities had been of help in any of eXtreme Investigations' cases. But Aidan had thought from day one that he could like the guy, whose unusual background had left him with a great sense of humor and a lot of cool stories.

"Good to see you, Mick. Thanks for coming down." Aidan extended his hand in greeting, realizing it was the first time, both of them cautious in the past, both having their reasons. It was as if a simple handshake meant they'd passed each other's test.

He didn't for one second worry he wouldn't be able to control his ability to stay out of Mick's thoughts—or anyone else's. Even Vonnie's terror couldn't permeate and catch him unaware because of that mental wall he'd rebuilt. He had to open himself up to it—as he had this morning when he'd again tried to find the girl, with no luck. Lexie's thoughts and fantasies were the only ones that seemed able to invade his psyche whether he was ready for them or not. And that was because he wanted her as much as she wanted him. He knew it.

"Lots of old stuff around here," Mick murmured, eyeing the room. He studied the antiques, the art, the period furniture—mostly things Aidan had bought off the previous owner because he didn't want to deal with shopping once he moved in.

"Yeah. Sorry about that."

Mick shrugged, used to these situations, especially in the South where tradition meant holding on to remnants of the past until nobody remembered what they'd once been used for. Not that Mick ever wondered. Once he touched something, he knew. The older the object, the deeper the history. Which was why the other man would have to be careful here.

Judging by the way Mick reached into his pockets, withdrew a pair of thin leather gloves, and pulled them onto his hands, he already knew that, too.

"Hello, Aidan," a woman said, the voice warm, yet

reserved. That described Olivia Wainwright very well. Of all of them, she had the most reason to be cautious, to protect herself emotionally from what they did for a living.

Hers was a talent he did not envy, an ability that seemed straight out of a horror movie. He wasn't sure he'd have the strength to use her dark gift had he been cursed with it. That she was still working for Julia after two years said a lot about how well she was able to handle it.

"Hi, Olivia."

The redhead kissed his cheek. "I'm so glad you called. We've missed you a great deal."

He smiled his thanks, realizing he'd missed them, too. More than he'd been willing to admit as recently as a few weeks ago. Funny, he had to wonder whether it was spending so many hours yesterday in the company of someone as vibrant and alive as Lexie that had made him realize how much he had once enjoyed the energy of interacting with other people.

"Make yourself at home," Aidan said. "Julia filled you in on what's going on here?"

Mick dropped a pile of printed pages onto the coffee table. "After she called last night, I did some digging on missing persons statistics in Granville." He whistled and shook his head. "Talk about an anomaly. It's crazy that nobody has noticed and tried to get to the bottom of this."

"Someone has," Aidan replied, sitting in a chair opposite the other man.

"The reporter?" Olivia lowered herself to the arm of a chair, poised and graceful, almost like a perched bird. That was pretty appropriate. She had always seemed a little fragile to him, as well as often giving the impression of being ready to take flight. Considering the things she had seen and felt, he couldn't blame her. He probably would have run away screaming long ago.

"She's the one who brought you in, right?" Olivia added.

"Yes," he said. "Lexie Nolan. She came over yesterday to enlist my help."

Mick pointed a gloved finger at a few pages of printouts—Lexie's articles. "She really got the shaft . . ."

"I know."

"Kinda like you," the man added, sounding more matter-of-fact than sympathetic.

Aidan appreciated the sentiment, but didn't feel the need to dwell on that mess just now. If he decided to return to work after this investigation, maybe he'd be ready to revisit the Remington case, do a play-by-play of what had happened and his culpability in it. But not now.

"After I read this stuff," Mick said, "I did what any detective with half a brain would have done. I looked all over the country for every missing girl named in this article and got the hits on the same two that the dimwit local police chief did."

"Unlike him, you didn't decide that was enough and stop there," Aidan said.

"Right."

"And you discovered?"

"Nothing. Absolutely nada. Not an arrest, not a single bank account, not a speeding ticket, not a credit card application, not an unemployment claim. The paper trail ends here in Granville. It's like they were just scooped up by aliens and removed from existence."

Not aliens. A human monster. But the result was the same. "Yeah, that's what I figured."

"So tell us about this reporter," said Julia, who had been nosing around the room, flipping open magazines and peeking unrepentantly into cupboards. The woman had a lot of energy and was always on the move. He sensed she was enjoying getting out from behind her desk, away from the administrative stuff, back into an active case. "Why'd she let herself get shut out?"

He told them what he knew, everything Lexie had shared, including her boss's problems. Right up through last night's drama on the football field, and in the high school parking lot.

He didn't mention the ride home. Or those moments they'd sat in the car, just breathing the same air and connecting in ways he couldn't yet define. And God knows, nothing about the shared dream. None of that was relevant to the case. Besides which, it was way too personal.

As he spoke, he found himself thinking again how tough this must have been on Lexie. He'd gone through his own trial by fire, but at least he'd had friends and colleagues ready to stand by his side if he asked them to. From the sound of it, she'd had no one. Her one ally, Walter, had been distracted, dealing with his own family crisis, so she'd been on her own. One woman trying to do battle with both a corrupt system and, Aidan greatly feared, a serial killer.

"Sounds like she made quite an impression," Julia said, eyeing him closely.

Olivia was just as bad. "*Quite* an impression."

Mick seemed oblivious to the undertones. Probably because he didn't have that know-it-all gene most women had when they sensed a guy might be interested in a female.

"Ms. Nolan is coming over at around noon," he said, glancing at his watch, ignoring the smirk on Julia's face as he suddenly called Lexie by her proper name. Damn, she was like a bloodhound. "She wanted to go back over to try to talk to the girl's mother today."

"I'm looking forward to meeting her," Julia said. "She sounds tough."

"Tough, yeah." His lips widening, he couldn't help adding, "Just don't call her perky."

Julia's speculative gaze intensified. "My, oh my."

His smile, combined with the tone of voice she'd heard probably had the woman ready to give Lexie the third degree about her love life, her marriageability, and her stance on kids. Which was ridiculous since he'd never been interested in love, marriage, or kids. Not with what he'd seen throughout his life, from his own family to every other fucked-up one he'd worked with.

God, why on earth did he decide he wanted these people back in his life and his business?

"We'll be good," Olivia said softly, knowing exactly what he'd been thinking.

"Okay, no clue what you guys are talking about, but can we get back to work?" Mick asked. "Aidan, what are you feeling about this missing girl?"

He wasn't asking about Aidan's emotional feelings. They all knew that. With these people, who understood just how capricious their abilities could be, there was no fear of building false hopes or expectations. They knew as well as he did that visions could have many meanings and didn't always lead to the right answer in time. So he had no problem sharing what he knew.

"First," he said, looking at the women, "you should know you've met the latest victim."

They both appeared surprised, but when he reminded them of their evening out a few weeks ago, immediately remembered their pretty, friendly young waitress.

Olivia appeared stricken. "Did you touch her that night? Have you connected with her?"

"I think so." He quickly told them what he'd experienced—the scents, the scream, the words repeating in his brain. He also told them about this morning's utter silence, nothingness, which had left him feeling even more concerned about the teenager's welfare.

"The king?" Mick asked doubtfully. "Are we talking an Elvis impersonator here?"

"No clue," he said, not willing to discount anything as ridiculous or improbable.

Julia, who'd still been circling around the room like

a shark, suddenly jerked her attention toward the front hall. "Will you excuse me?" she asked.

Aidan nodded, used to these types of interruptions. He didn't direct her to the bathroom, knowing something else had caught her interest. Something only she could see or hear.

"Tell Morgan he owes me ten bucks. The Redskins lost!" Mick called after her.

Julia glanced back, wrinkled her nose at the other man, then strode out of the room.

"You been able to collect on one of those bets yet?" Aidan asked, curious and a little surprised at how easily Mick kidded his boss about a subject everyone else treated very carefully.

"Hell, no. I keep threatening Julia that she's going to have to make good on them if she keeps letting him bet against me. For a guy with all the answers, he's got no head for football."

"Very funny," Aidan said.

After less than a minute, Julia burst back into the room, reaching for her purse and tugging her keys out of her pocket. "We gotta go. You ride shotgun."

Seeing her tension, he immediately rose, as did the others. "What's wrong?"

"It's your reporter friend," Julia explained as she turned and stalked back out. Aidan's heart skipped a beat. He stormed after her and overtook Julia at the front door, grabbing her arm, every muscle in his body snapping to attention. "What about Lexie?"

"You said she went down to talk to the victim's mother. Is that in a bad part of town?"

The tension rose. "Yes."

"You know how to get there?"

"I'll figure it out," he growled, ready to explode if she didn't tell him what was going on.

"Okay, let's go. Morgan says she's about to get in some kind of trouble."

That was all he heard, all he needed to hear. Aidan didn't hesitate. Nor did he look back to see if anybody else was coming. He flung open the front door and stalked toward his own car.

"Let me drive!" Julia called. "So you can jump out when we get there."

The way she said it made him realize they had no time to waste. "Fine. But go fast."

She chuckled as she ran toward the driver's seat. "I don't know any other way to go."

Chapter 9

Lexie thought she had seen the worst of life in the Boro when she'd gone to Vonnie's apartment. Now, though, as she stood at the mouth of a narrow alley thick with trash and bejeweled by flecks of broken glass, she began to know better. In the shadowy channel between two ugly brick buildings, she was trying to talk to two suspicious, hostile teenage girls wearing platform shoes, booty shorts, and push-up bras.

They were young—one sixteen or so, the other probably a bit older. But their eyes held the misery of much longer lives. One was white, one black. Both were utterly broken.

She'd definitely hit rock bottom.

Honestly, if she hadn't gone looking for them, it wouldn't have occurred to her that girls this age were walking the streets of Granville. Of course, every town had its pros and everyone knew the inn out by the interstate rented rooms by the hour. But she'd never envisioned a thriving climate for teenage prostitution here.

Unfortunately, once the girls had realized she wasn't a paying customer looking for some kinky, same-sex thrills, they'd wanted nothing to do with her.

"Please, I just want to talk to you. I'm a reporter; I'm not here to cause any trouble." She dug for her wallet. "I'll pay you for your time."

The teens looked at each other, then around the alley, as if suspecting a setup. Finding a couple of twenties, she shoved the money at them. They took the cash, then both crossed their arms, visibly belligerent, but no longer attempting to walk away.

"I'm trying to find out what happened to Vonnie Jackson."

One of the girls immediately frowned. "Fuck Vonnie. Thinking she was all better'n us."

"Chill, Ruby," said her younger friend.

"And the others," Lexie quickly added. "All the other missing girls."

"Wait!" said the younger one. "You're the one wrote them articles about the Ghoul."

The Ghoul. Damn you, Dunston. Gritting her teeth, she replied, "Yes."

"He's real, ain't he? You had it right all along."

"I think so."

"And now he got Vonnie?"

She could only nod.

The older one—Ruby, whose lips were as red as her name—rolled her eyes. "Who gives a shit? Vonnie got what was coming to her, being stuck up and too good for the neighborhood."

Though she certainly disagreed, Lexie wasn't about to antagonize them now that they were talking. "What about the rest? Brittany and Shayna, Tracy, Jessie. . . ."

When she said that last name, the two prostitutes exchanged a quick, secretive look. Not one other word had inspired the reaction, just the mention of the first victim, Jessie Leonard.

"You knew Jessie?"

"She was . . ."

"Can it, Tyra," said Ruby. "We don't know jack shit, lady. Ain't our business to know."

Lexie wasn't about to give up, not when Tyra looked ready to share something important. The girl's eyes were huge, and her mouth trembled. She was completely cowed by her friend.

"Please, Ruby," she urged, "don't you want to get this guy off the streets before he comes after you or somebody you do care about? He's targeting girls from the Boro, more than a dozen in the past few years. How long do you think it'll be before this becomes your business, when it's your sister, your cousin, your best friend?" Staring hard, she added, "Or *you*?"

Ruby's lip curled up a sneer. She opened her mouth, as if to say something caustic, but not a word came out. Slowly, reluctantly, she closed it again. Though anger still shone clearly on her face, she had conceded the point. For all the toughness and swagger, this was still just a kid. Grunting and shaking her head, she looked away, giving tacit permission for Tyra to speak.

"What can you tell me about Jessie?" Lexie asked.

"I heard stories 'bout where she was goin' that night. The night she disappeared."

"What kind of stories?"

Tyra visibly swallowed, looking around again, toward the shadowy depths of the alley into which they'd ducked for their conversation. "That she was joinin' the club."

"At school?"

Ruby snorted. "Hell, no." She glared at her friend. "And she wasn't joining it, any more than any of us *join* it."

Not following, Lexie pressed them both. "What is this club? Where?"

"Middle'a nowhere," Tyra said. "They blindfold us on the ride out so I don't know for sure. Big ol' fallin'-down house out in the country—can't even see the road from the front of it."

"Who's in the club?" she asked, knowing she was onto something.

"No idea," Tyra said. "Just know girls like us is invited to come along sometimes and there's lotsa men."

Girls like them. "Prostitutes?"

Ruby's mouth tilted up on one side, though her ancient smile held no humor. "Uh-uh. They like their girls sweet. But after you leave the club? Well, that's a whole 'nother story."

"What the hell's goin' on?" a harsh voice suddenly called.

Seeing the girls' faces twist in fear, Lexie spun around and saw a man, probably in his mid-twenties, heavily pierced, wearing leather and chains. Burly and scowling, he looked less like a greasy TV pimp than a Hells Angel. But judging by the way the girls began explaining what they were doing—and how much they'd been paid for it—that's exactly who he was.

"Get back out there," he snarled at them, encircling Ruby's upper arm in one beefy hand. He squeezed hard, then shoved her toward the entrance of the alleyway. Neither of them looked back, hurrying on their impossibly high heels out to their corner.

"I was just talking to them," Lexie said, edging after the girls. She was in trouble here, serious trouble. It hadn't even occurred to her that she could be attacked on a sunny Saturday morning on the streets of dinky little Granville, even if she was in the Boro. "I'll be going now."

He grabbed her arms, just as punishingly as he'd grabbed Ruby's, and pushed her toward a brick-walled building. Lexie tried to twist away from his brutal grip. She was in pretty good shape, but her three-times-a-week-Zoomba class was no match for his bulging muscles.

"Let me go," she insisted, knowing he was trying to scare her. "I'm working on a story."

"'Bout my girls? You better keep your mouth shut." He shoved her against the wall so hard her back screamed. Her head thunked against it, hard enough to make her vision spin.

"No," she said, blinking away tears of pain, "not about that. I'm looking for the Ghoul."

"You found one." He released one arm so he could grab her throat. And squeezed.

Lexie tried to swallow, but was thwarted as he pressed harder. Her breaths were shallow. She couldn't seem to draw a full one as he closed his hand tighter against her windpipe.

This guy wasn't just trying to scare her off. He could really hurt her.

Though terrifying, that thought chased away any remnants of simple fear. There was no thought, no considering. Instinct just kicked in. No way was she giving in without a fight.

Leaning back against the wall and letting her eyes droop, Lexie sagged a little, as if losing consciousness. As she'd hoped, his grip on her throat loosened. When she felt him start to pull back, maybe to see if he'd actually killed her, she reacted. Jerking a knee up hard, she aimed for his groin, shoving at his chest with her free hand at the same time. She didn't make full-on contact, but judging by the pain in her knee, got him with at least a glancing blow.

He bellowed in pain. "Bitch!"

Kicking at him, she grabbed at the hand holding her throat, but couldn't hold it away for more than a few seconds. Her ploy hadn't gotten her free and now his rage made him squeeze harder, as if he fully intended to kill her. His eyes bulged and his face had reddened with utter fury. She began to feel light-headed, and her legs wanted to give out, in truth this time.

Lexie couldn't believe this was real. She was a few feet away from a major street, a block from her favorite bakery—a place she'd been to dozens of times. *Can this really be happening?*

"Let go of her, you bastard!" a voice snarled.

Strange, that had sounded like Aidan's voice. Which was crazy, since he couldn't possibly be here, and she didn't think he was capable of that kind of fury. Maybe she was having some kind of hallucination as she lost consciousness.

Then her attacker was violently yanked away. Bending over, Lexie heaved in several deep breaths. Her throat ached, and so did her head, but right now she could only think of how grateful she was to the strange man who had saved her life—the man who was now brutally punching her assailant.

"Oh my God," she whispered, her voice hoarse. Because the strange man *was* Aidan.

"Lexie, are you okay?" a woman's voice asked.

Blinking, she looked into the pretty face of a dark-haired stranger, who eyed her with worry. That made her again wonder if she was dreaming this, having one big hallucination as she dangled by the throat from some brutal psycho's fist.

"You're going to be fine," another woman said, putting an arm around her. The two pulled her away from the wall, toward the end of the alley where a car waited, its doors open as if all the occupants had leapt out in a rush.

"Aidan," she whispered, pulling away. Maybe this was real. If so, no matter how strong her dream-lover was, she seriously doubted he was a match for a thug who could be armed and almost certainly would not fight fair.

"He's all right," the red-haired woman said.

Turning around to see for herself, she nodded in relief when she realized Aidan wasn't alone. Another man was with him. Together, they had wrestled the burly pimp to the ground and were whipping her assailant's own leather belt out of his pants to bind him with.

"I've called 911," one of the women said. "Let's go sit in the car and wait for help."

But she wasn't moving. Now that she could breathe easily, Lexie felt much more clearheaded. She had a headache and a sore throat, but was otherwise fine. And what she most wanted right now was Aidan, who was bent, with one knee on the pimp's back.

When he finished lashing the man's hands together, Aidan finally looked over at her. Their eyes met and locked. His were slate-gray and livid, fury etched on his handsome face. Remote and cold, he looked more than capable of ripping apart the man who'd attacked her, or anyone else who happened to get a little too close.

She would not have imagined it if she hadn't seen it with her own eyes, given his usual calmness and intellect. But right now, Aidan looked utterly primal, as capable of brutal violence as any embattled soldier.

As their long stare continued, the bloodlust began to leave him. She saw the movements of his chest slow as he took a few deep, calming breaths. Then he slowly rose to his feet. Not sparing a single disdainful glance at the man on the ground, he walked toward her. With each long stride, his anger seemed to further melt away. As his gaze moved over her—the tangled hair, the probably bruised throat—his rage was replaced by almost tangible tenderness. Protectiveness. As if they were much closer than either of them would have believed possible.

The dreams.

He was treating her like a lover, enraged for her, fighting for her. Now wanting only to see for himself that she was really all right.

When he reached her, he didn't pause, didn't slow in his steps. He merely walked right into her, putting his strong arms around her shoulders and drawing her tightly against his chest.

"You're okay," he whispered as he tenderly stroked her back. "You're fine. You're safe, Lex. I've got you."

She slid her arms around his waist, burrowing tighter against him, certain she had never felt more secure in her entire adult life. They had barely touched before now—except in her dreams. But stepping into this man's embrace was like trying on something new and discovering it was exactly what you most needed and had been seeking your whole life. They just fit.

His heart thudded against her chest, and they were

so close her lips brushed against his warm neck. Aidan's spicy scent filled each breath and their bodies molded together, softness melting into hardness, until they were like one person standing in the alleyway.

Lexie let it happen, took the silent comfort he was offering and lost herself in it. It had been a long time, so very long, since she'd leaned on anyone, or felt anything other than completely and totally on her own. For years, she had relied on only herself. She'd been proud and determined, certain she was up to any challenge and while it was nice to have other people around, she hadn't let herself need them.

That was all well and good, and she'd done a fine job of living that way. Until today. When she'd been shown that things could get really ugly, really fast, and she wasn't always able to take care of them all on her own. Sometimes, she really did need someone else.

Funny, though. It suddenly felt it wasn't him hauling that beast off her that she'd so needed. It was this: this moment, this embrace, this connection. Having a welcoming pair of arms to step into and a strong hand on her back, a powerful heart beating against her and his voice whispering tender reassurances.

This was what she'd most needed.

She knew Aidan was every bit as affected. There was no reserve, no stiffness. He held nothing back. Gone was the strong sense of self-protection that usually kept him from getting too close to anyone. He'd thrown off all restraints. Inviting all the trouble and anxiety that touching anyone could cause, he'd not only touched her, he'd imprinted himself on every inch of her and didn't seem to care one damn bit that he might suffer for it later.

"It's all right, angel," he murmured.

The truth washed over her and rather than sucking in a shocked breath, she could only sigh as she acknowledged it was true. This mysterious man had shared her dreams. Because in them, while making the most erotic, intense love to her, he'd called her that. Angel.

She tilted her head back to look up at him, getting a little lost in the blue-gray channels to his soul, and whispered, "It was real."

He shook his head once. "No. It was just a dream, Lexie."

"But you were there? You were part of it?"

He hesitated, then slowly nodded. "I was there. Not intentionally, I promise you, but yeah. I experienced it, too."

Mortification should have flooded her. She should have at least looked away to try to collect her thoughts and figure out how to deal with something so blatantly embarrassing. Or maybe she should have gotten indignant, worried about her loss of privacy. She could have made a joke, slapped his face, run away, anything.

She did none of those. Instead, she rose up on her tiptoes and lifted her arms to wrap them around his neck, twining her fingers in his hair. His eyes widened, as if he had been expecting some other reaction. Maybe an hour ago, he would have gotten one. But not now, not when she'd had a brush with danger that had reminded her of just how alone—and how lonely—she had been for so long. Embarrassment and privacy were one thing, but needing physical connection, and wanting it from a man who'd excited her beyond belief from the moment they'd met, meant a hell of a lot more.

"Aidan?" Lexie smiled at him. "I'm glad you were there."

Without saying another word, she lightly brushed her lips across his, a first kiss that wasn't their first—one that was much more demure than those they'd shared in the richness of her heated imagination.

She didn't intend for it to be more and would have let herself drop back down after that brief meeting of their mouths. But she couldn't. Aidan's arms tightened around her and he held her up.

They shared a breath. Then he kissed her back.

Lexie closed her eyes and savored the connection.

This wasn't a quick brush of lips. Yet they didn't engage in a kiss of deep, hungry passion like they'd shared in her dreams. Instead, it was a sweet joining that asked questions and made promises, a kiss of familiarity and longing. His mouth tasted familiar—warm and welcoming. And his tenderness revealed far more than words ever could have about how glad he was that she hadn't been hurt.

In another place, at another time, without an audience, it would have deepened. Feeling a low, insistent hunger rising inside her, Lexie knew how much she wanted it to. But they were not alone and the circumstances were less than ideal. So they finally ended the encounter on a mutual sigh.

Aidan let her down, but he didn't step away immediately. Rubbing a thumb across her cheek he whispered, "I'm glad, too."

A sharp trill of a siren suddenly echoed down the alley and they both realized this was over, for now. It was time to get serious again, time to deal with what had happened to her, and to utilize the information she'd gained this morning.

And time to focus on all the realities she'd totally ignored while indulging in a first real embrace with the man of her dreams.

Saturday, 12:25 p.m.

"Do you feel better now, dearest?"

Vonnie didn't answer right away, not wanting him to realize how alert and aware she was of what was going on around her. After having left her alone since last night, the monster had returned an hour ago—she'd heard a car pull up outside. Now that he wasn't drugging her, she was much more aware of what was going on, and was able to prepare herself for his arrival.

He'd come in, offering her another energy drink through a straw. Then, apparently convinced by her apathy and listlessness that she wasn't much of a threat, he'd gone a step farther. He'd actually cut the tape away from her entire mouth, ripping it off her cheeks. Judging by the pain, he'd taken some skin along with it. But she hadn't cared. She could breathe—really breathe—at last. The air was dank and stale, reeking, but she drew in deep mouthfuls of it, absolutely delighted, though careful not to show just how panicked the taped mouth had made her. Because then he'd just put it back on.

"Ahh, feels good, doesn't it?" he asked, a smile in his high-pitched voice to match the one on his awful, cheerful mask.

"Yeah, thanks," she muttered, knowing he expected gratitude.

He patted her head, like she was some kind of dog. "You should have told me yesterday was your birthday," he said, reproaching her. "I might have taken it off then, as a special gift from me to you."

Her birthday. Her last one, she had no doubt.

He reached for a bowl of water and a rag and began wiping the blood off her cheeks. Working carefully, he acted like he actually gave a damn whether he hurt her or not, which was funny since he'd caused every one of her injuries.

"Poor little girl," he cooed.

The man was insane. One minute murderous, the next nurturing. But always underneath the surface was utter insanity.

His mood seemed good—as good as a psychotic killer's mood could be, she supposed. Since his return, he'd been chuckling and muttering about how grand a time he'd had at the football game. How much fun it had been, how entertaining. And how much she'd been missed.

Yeah, sure. Her own mother probably wouldn't notice she was gone until the first of the month when she came scratching for Vonnie's paycheck so she could pay the rent.

She couldn't contain the bitterness, thinking that her eighteenth birthday had arrived, and she wouldn't be able to finally flip her mother the finger and move into a place of her own.

"I think I'll sit with you awhile," he said once he'd finished cleaning the blood off her cheeks. "If you're good, I might let you get up and use the potty. You must really need it."

If she had anything left in her that could feel embarrassment, maybe she would have, since he knew she'd been chained flat on her back for days and was just taunting her. Funny, though, embarrassment was long gone. Survival was the only thing that remained.

She didn't reveal those thoughts. The fact that he wasn't leaving the small cell right away didn't terrify her, it gave her hope. Having had a couple of days to heal, to clear her mind, Vonnie knew the only way to escape death was to trick him into making some kind of mistake.

If he unchained her so she could use the makeshift toilet, maybe she could find some kind of a weapon. He couldn't do that from the other side of the door. And he *wouldn't* do it if he thought she didn't appreciate it, so she mustered up a weak smile and whispered, "Thank you."

"You're welcome. Now, shall we talk a little?"

She tensed. Talk could be dangerous. Since figuring out what he'd meant about her "pleasing" him, she hadn't been sure if she should let him know she remembered. Would that heighten his concerns, make him worry she might be able to identify him? She doubted she'd be able to, not unless she heard that hateful, squeaky voice he used around her, and she knew it wasn't his regular one.

Hell, maybe if he pulled down his pants she'd have a clue. Then again, one disgusting prick looked just like any other, and the night he was referring to, she'd been forced to endure the sight of a whole lot of them. Just like now, the faces of the monsters had been hidden; the vile men had worn black hoods. And nothing else.

"Have you ever heard of Snow White and Rose Red?"

She almost sighed in relief. Fairy tales. Okay, she could deal with his damned fairy tales. He could invent a story about Santa Claus cannibalizing his elves and it would be a whole lot better than thinking about that other night—the night she'd become a member of the club.

"Well, have you heard about those evil girls, Vonnie?"

Hearing the tone that said he was growing irritated, she cleared her throat. "No."

He *tsk*ed. "Well, it's not as popular a story as some. Though I've always liked it."

Probably because he was about to tell her his version of the tale, in which two girls got gang raped and gutted at a biker bar.

"My mother used to read it to me sometimes when I was lying right there in that spot and my stepfather was raping me. Oh, she did like to read bedtime stories, especially when she was drunk."

Vonnie hated this man. She loathed him with every fiber of her being. But something inside her twisted a little, a purely instinctive, human reaction to whatever must have happened to him as a boy to turn him into the adult monster he had become.

"Do you know what made me think of it?"

"What?"

His dark brown eyes sparkled behind the mask and she had the feeling if he removed it, she'd see a smile as wide as the phony plastic one. "I'm going to have my own version of it!" He clapped his hands together. "Right here in my secret hideaway. My own Rose Red"—he playfully pointed a finger at her—"and a Snow White who will be joining us very shortly."

Oh God. She didn't have to think about it, she knew exactly what he meant. He was going to kidnap another girl, bring somebody else into the pit with her. She gagged, unable to help it, and almost lost the liquid she'd been so happy to get a short time ago.

"Yes, I can see you've already figured it out. You're going to have company, sweetie." He rose from the chair, folding it and putting it against the wall. "I've never had two guests at once, so it might take a little getting used to for all of us. We'll have to muddle through together."

Vonnie couldn't deny it—part of her felt a sudden rush of relief that soon she would no longer be alone in this awful nightmare. She'd have an ally. But a much bigger part wanted to scream in terror, to beg that unknown, faceless girl to run and hide while she still could.

"Won't that be fun?"

Hot tears rose in her eyes. Though she blinked rapidly, she couldn't stop them. They slid from the corners and streamed down her cheeks, wetting the rough pillow on which she lay.

"Oh, dear!" he said, rushing back over. "You're crying! What is it? Are you jealous, pretty girl? Afraid you won't get as much attention?"

Jealous? *Jealous?* The man was completely delusional.

Vonnie shook her head, asking him questions she hadn't asked for several days. "Why? Why are you doing this? Why me? Why her?"

He stood above her, motionless, and she almost bit her tongue for speaking so coherently. Vonnie held her breath, counting the seconds, wondering if he was going to storm out and return with handfuls of white capsules, blue tablets, and little yellow pills. All of which would land in her empty stomach and send her flying, rendering her as useless as a butterfly riding a breeze.

Finally, he shrugged. "That's easy to explain."

She didn't ask him to, wasn't about to remind him that she could follow a conversation.

"I took you because of a little party you attended a couple of years ago."

The club.

Confirmation, though she hadn't really needed it. She'd known. Last night, after the possibility had occurred to her, she'd begun to think about the other girls who'd gone missing over the past few years. She didn't know them all, but she'd known a few.

They'd been guests of the club, too. That was the connection.

Most girls brought to "entertain" there did it for the money. They knew what they were doing. Maybe they didn't quite realize how bad it was going to get, or how many men would be attending, but they knew. And most of them were experienced.

Vonnie hadn't known, and she hadn't been experienced.

She had to close her eyes and swallow just to get the thoughts to leave her mind. Both of that long, ugly, demoralizing night, and of the harsh sense of betrayal that had changed her forever. Before then, she'd known her mom was unreliable and weak, but she'd always believed the woman whe she said "I love you," and "I'll change, baby; it's just I need the stuff."

After that, she had never believed another word that came out of Berna Jackson's mouth. She'd grown up overnight, lost any sense of the girl she'd once been after the brutal trick that had been played on her. She supposed that's what she got for trusting someone so twisted. But God, what fifteen-year-old girl would suspect her own mother of selling her into a nightmare?

"Ah," her attacker said, sounding almost sympathetic, "I see you've put it together."

She swallowed, then slowly nodded. Forcing the flood of images away, knowing she didn't have the time or the emotional strength to deal with them now, she asked, "Is that the only reason?" He'd chosen her to be his victim because she'd once been a victim of others? Was there any motivation more sick than that?

"Isn't it a good enough one? The members of that

club have been very nervous lately, which makes me very happy. They did something very bad to someone I cared about and I'm punishing them."

He cared about someone? Seemed impossible to believe. "So why not kidnap and murder *them*?" she spat, unable to help it.

He chuckled. "I considered it, believe me. But I do like girls ever so much more than men. And, as you should have realized by now, sometimes the psychological torment of not knowing what is going to happen—or when—is more frightening than anything else."

He was right about that. Wasn't that why he'd been playing this game with her?

"Do you know that club has been active here in Granville for over a hundred years?"

She shook her head, a little surprised but mostly not. Evil seemed to thrive in some places and the weird old house where she'd been taken that night had throbbed with it.

"My stepfather was a member."

"Is he one of the ones you want to torment?"

He laughed behind the mask. "Oh, no, he's dead. Jed sent him straight to hell years ago. Right around the time I sent my mother there."

Jed. She focused on the name, thinking frantically, wondering if she'd heard it before. Some clue to who he was could help her in this psychological battle.

She'd taken psychology in school and her first thought was to wonder if there really was a Jed. If her tormentor had been that badly abused as a child, maybe this Jed didn't even exist—maybe he never had. Abuse had certainly caused split-personality disorder in some cases.

"There is one other reason I chose you. I suspected your disappearance would get attention, which it did. I'm taking *her* for the same reason—attention. She'll get even more of it. Granville is about to tear itself apart in utter terror." The man casually reached down and fluffed the nearly flat pillow beneath her head, carelessly adding, "But I'm also taking her because she might have seen me when I followed you as you left school Monday night."

As she'd left the school . . . meaning, several blocks before she'd reached the Boro where he'd grabbed her. The man had stalked her a long way.

The rest of what he'd said sunk in, too. A girl who might have seen him as she'd left the nearly deserted school? There weren't many possibilities about who that could be, and the most obvious one became immediately clear. He wasn't talking about some random girl. He meant one of her classmates, someone who'd been with her at the meeting last Monday. Maybe one of her new friends.

"Please don't," she whispered.

A sly chuckle emerged from his mouth and she realized she'd been a fool to act like she might be worried about this other unnamed girl. Thinking quickly, she added, "Don't bother on my account. I mean. If she saw you, you'd know by now, right?"

His noncommittal shrug said she hadn't mollified him.

"Besides, I kinda like it as it is. I never had anybody give me as much attention as you do. My mom sure didn't."

Clapping his hands together in delight, he chortled, "Oh, you are jealous! Isn't that just the cutest thing?"

No, actually, the cutest thing she could think of would be looking up and seeing a sharp spike being plunged into his eyeball. But she merely forced a tiny smile.

He bent down and patted her hip. Vonnie couldn't help tensing, even though, so far, he'd limited his abuse to beating her, not raping her. If he'd once been a member of that club, however, she knew it would probably be only a matter of time. She honestly had no idea what he was waiting for.

Don't question it; just be thankful.

"Well, don't you worry your pretty little head about it, sweet one. I doubt she will be here for long. I suspect she's not going to be quite as adept at entertaining me as you have been."

She stared up at him, not asking what he meant. She already knew.

Because he was twisted and because he liked her terrified, he explained anyway.

"So I'll probably have to kill her much sooner than I'm going to kill you."

Chapter 10

The paramedics who had responded to Julia's 911 call had insisted on taking Lexie to the small local hospital to be checked out. She had tried to refuse, but Aidan had overridden her protests. Her throat was bruised and swollen, her back scraped and abraded from rubbing against the brick wall. No way was he letting her just leave the scene, despite this "new information" she'd discovered, not until he was sure her windpipe hadn't been seriously damaged and she wasn't going to suffocate the next time she lay down.

He'd wanted to ride with her in the ambulance, but had instead remained behind to talk to the two cops who'd responded to the 911 call. They were young, not entirely poisoned by their idiot boss, and had taken the situation with the seriousness it demanded. Lexie's attacker, who was well known to them, was taken off in handcuffs and they'd said they would be by the hospital to take her statement once she'd been looked at.

That was how it should have gone, anyway. But when he got to the hospital a short time later, having driven over in the rental car she'd asked him to retrieve, he realized things hadn't gone as planned. Because as he reached the curtained area in the emergency room, where he'd been directed by a nurse, he heard the irritated voice of someone who had to be Chief Dunston.

"Just can't keep your nose out of trouble, can you?

Had to go down there where you don't belong and try to stir up trouble."

Shaking with anger, Aidan grabbed the curtain and flung it aside. "What's going on?"

The police chief spun around, startled and more than a bit irritated. "Who are you?"

"I'm the man who found this woman being attacked and nearly killed on a public street in your supposedly safe town," he snarled, pushing past the chief. Seeing Lexie's pale face, he put a hand over hers. "You okay?"

She nodded, squeezing his fingers. "The doctor says I'll be all right. I'll just have this supersexy voice thing going on for a while."

It was supersexy. It also sounded superpainful.

And he really wanted to hurt someone superbad for that.

The chief was the closest target. Aidan whirled around to face the man, and jabbed an index finger toward him. "Instead of berating the victims of crime, or just ignoring their existence altogether like you have all the girls who've gone missing, why don't you try doing the job you're being paid to do for once?"

Dunston stuck out a belligerent jaw. "You can't talk to me like that. I want your name."

"You can have it," he snapped, "and you can have the name of my attorney as well. I'm quite sure he would be happy to represent Ms. Nolan should she decide to pursue a complaint of harassment and negligence against you and your whole department."

"It's not negligence that she gets herself attacked while consorting with criminals!"

Aidan's jaw clenched so tight he thought he might crack a tooth. "Again, I remind you, a public street. Broad daylight. Your supposedly 'peaceful' town. Several witnesses who saw her nearly strangled to death. How do you think accusing the victim will play on *Larry King Live*?"

Steam almost flew out of the man's ears. But like all bullies, the idea of being made to look like a fool on a bigger stage than the one on which he already stood was too much for him to bear. Casting one final frustrated stare at Lexie, he said, "You'll be hearing from one of my officers. Don't leave town."

She managed a cheeky smile. "I'm not going anywhere." The words were hoarse and she had to be smiling through a lot of discomfort.

The chief spun around, his footsteps so hard, they heard him throughout his entire march across the ER. Once the sound had died out, Aidan released his tight grip on Lexie's hand, but didn't let go entirely. "I'm sorry I didn't show up sooner."

"It's all right. He was here only a couple of minutes." She moved her eyebrows up and down. "I notice you never did give him your name."

"No, I guess I didn't. Forgot all about it."

Snickering, she swung her legs over the side of the thin, gurney-type ER bed and rose to her feet. That was when he realized she was fully dressed, ready to go. She scooped up a small tube of ointment and some medical papers and said, "Let's roll."

"You're not going anywhere."

"Clean bill of health, I swear." She raised two fingers in a Scout's promise. "The doctor already cleared me. I was just waiting for you to pick me up."

"Don't they have to wheel you out?"

But he was talking to air. Lexie had left the examination room, heading toward the exit. Sighing, glad the incident in the alley hadn't robbed her of her independent streak, but also wishing she'd let somebody take care of her for a while, he strode after her.

He flinched when he saw the rips on the back of her shirt—and the white bandages underneath. Damn that man.

"Would you hold on?" he asked, reaching out and

putting a hand on her shoulder. He did it carefully, not knowing where else bruises might be hiding on her body. "Where are we going?"

"I was talking to Walter on the phone," she told him. "Right before Dunston showed up."

He rolled his eyes. "Ignoring that whole no-cell-phones-in-the-hospital rule, are we?"

"No, Mr. Smarty-Psychic, I used the one in the room." Looking a little sheepish, she admitted, "I can't find mine. I think I dropped it in the alley."

Knowing her relationship with her boss was a close one, he had to ask, "How did Walter react to what happened?"

She nibbled the corner of her lip, not quite meeting his eyes, which was when he knew she hadn't told him. She'd called the man she considered her closest friend from a hospital bed, and hadn't mentioned she'd nearly been murdered.

Then he thought about that friend, what he'd been going through, and admitted, "I guess he wouldn't have handled it very well. And there's nothing he could have done."

Lexie's mouth fell open, as if she'd expected him to criticize her decision. In truth, though, he understood it and probably would have done the same in her situation. It sounded like this editor of hers was a good man, with a lot of problems. Not wanting people you care about to worry about you when there's nothing they can do was human nature.

"Thanks for understanding."

"So why'd you call him?"

She glanced around, seeing a few patients and staff members milling around. Nodding toward the exit, she said, "Why don't we talk in the car?"

He nodded his agreement, put an arm on her elbow—funny, how easy it was to touch her now—and led her out the doors of the stuffy, medicinal-smelling hospital into the bright sunshine. It was one of those beautiful

Georgia fall days, clear and warm, the air free of the haze that usually hung around during the long, brutally hot summers. Lexie's smile seemed a little more relaxed out here, as if just the change in scenery was helping her to recover. Obviously the woman strongly disliked hospitals.

"Wait here and let me pull up, okay? The car's right over there."

"Look, I'm fine, Aidan."

He'd had enough of the bravado. She might have desperately needed to get out of the hospital—in fact, he suspected the way she'd hurried up to do so had as much to do with needing to feel in control and strong again as it did with getting back to work. But the woman had limitations. Everyone did.

He put both hands on her shoulders. "Lexie, you *are* fine."

"I know . . ."

"You're fine physically," he said, cutting her off. "I believe you. But you were attacked. You can't ignore that. You have to deal with it."

She stared up at him, her beautiful green eyes a little bloodshot from her ordeal. And those bruises on her throat, God, just the sight of them—ugly and dark against her creamy skin—made him want to drive over to the police station and beat that animal all over again.

"I will," she said, her lips trembling, her whole body tight as if she was holding on to her control by a thread. "However, right now I just need to work, okay? I *need* to. I'll deal with all of this later—I swear. When I'm a little more pulled together."

She wanted to postpone the crash, the fear, the moment when she allowed herself to acknowledge that she could have *died* today, could easily have been strangled to death and dumped in that alley, her vibrant life cut off in its prime. Just another violent statistic.

He got that. He'd been around enough crime victims, and enough grieving family members, to understand the sentiment. Putting off "dealing with" things was a reaction as normal and human as reaching for a light switch to banish the darkness.

Thing was, when she flipped that switch on and allowed light to shine on the dark places of her mind, she was going to *have* to face them. All of them. It would be neither easy nor pretty. Facing your own death was a momentous thing. She just hadn't yet realized how momentous.

"Okay," he said, mentally vowing to be there with her when it happened. "But humor me, would you? Wait here while I get the car? I'll be right back."

"Thanks," she whispered. She lifted a hand to his face and ran her thumb along his bottom lip. "I wasn't unconscious, right? I didn't imagine what happened between us?"

"Well, you dreamed it," he told her. "But no, you didn't imagine it."

She lifted her face to his and persisted. "I didn't dream that kiss, though."

"No, you didn't dream that." The kisses of Lexie's dreams had been far more intense than the one they'd shared on the street. But not as important. Reality made it incredibly important.

"Whew," she said, still gazing up at him, lovely and sexy, despite the bruises and the weariness and the tangled hair and torn shirt. Just lovely.

Knowing what she wanted, he lowered his mouth to hers, kissing her again, as carefully as he had before. This time, he gave in to his deep need to taste her and swept his tongue between her lips. She sighed, turning her head and kissing him back, their tongues tangling, warm and lazy like this slow Georgia afternoon.

She tasted familiar and so damn sweet. They embraced as if they had always done this, had always been like this, and Aidan simply didn't allow himself to question it or second-guess it. Maybe things had started strangely, maybe it had taken a shared dream to make them realize they wanted each other, but right now he didn't care. He just wanted to keep standing here kissing her in the sunshine, both because he liked it and to protest the darkness that had drawn them together.

Good things had to end, however. Finally, thinking of the place and her physical condition, he ended the kiss. "Wait here."

She sighed. "If you insist."

"I do," he said, already turning to stride across the lot toward the rental vehicle.

The car was small, not easily accommodating his tall form, but it would do to get her home. Then he'd get Mick and Julia to bring over his SUV. While he'd headed to the hospital, the others had gone back to his house to go through the files and recordings he'd studied yesterday. With so many sets of eyes and ears, hopefully they'd find something he'd missed.

Pulling up, he was about to get out to help her, but she was already climbing in the other side. He waited until she buckled herself in, seeing how careful she was not to let the seat belt brush against her throat. Clenching his hands on the steering wheel, he had to look straight ahead, not wanting her to see how affected he was by her every pained movement.

"It doesn't hurt that much," she murmured.

Okay, so apparently he hadn't hidden his reaction well enough.

"Did they give you any pain pills?" he asked.

"A prescription. But seriously, I don't even know if I'll need to fill it."

"Fill it, then decide if you need to use them."

"Yes, sir," she said, cocky and amused. If not for the Kathleen Turner voice, someone might not even realize she'd almost had the life choked out of her a few hours ago.

Aidan forced himself to let go of those dark thoughts and drove out of the parking lot onto the main road. He'd only driven to her home once, but remembered the way. It wasn't like Granville was big enough to ever really get lost in.

Unless you were a teenage girl from the wrong side of town.

They didn't speak; he wasn't sure what was on her mind. Them? The dream? The reality?

"I called Walter for an address," she said, answering the question he'd asked inside.

The case . . . her story. That's what was on her mind. Work. It figured.

He liked her for that. Liked her a lot. He also knew she needed to focus on something—anything—else.

"You're such a romantic. Whose address?" he asked, not hiding his amusement.

"I'm very romantic," she retorted. "You wait and see: When this is over, I'll outromance the queen of hearts."

He frowned, mumbling, "Wasn't she a psychotic, head-lopping megalomaniac?"

"Don't make me hit you before I've even seen you naked."

Shifting in his seat, remembering they had absolutely seen each other naked in every way except in reality, he had to say, "You know, I don't quite know what to make of all this. I've never experienced anything like it."

"Like what?"

"Like *you*. How you make me feel. I don't know what to do with you. I'm not usually so . . ."

"Peppy?" she asked, sounding mischievous. Because peppy he was not. No more than she was perky.

"Oh, here we go with the adjectives again. Let's just ban words from our vocabulary that start with P and end with Y, all right?"

She tapped a finger on her cheek. "Like play?"

He thought about it, conceding, "Okay, that one can stay."

"Party? Pretty? Paltry?"

"They gave you a sample pack of that pain medication, didn't they?" he asked, eyeing her suspiciously.

She grinned. "Not a bit. But even if they had, I could outdo you in any word game."

"My luck to go up against a writer."

Laughing softly, she said, "Since you think I'm medicated, can I ask you something else, and then later we'll chalk it up to the medicine I didn't have?"

He had a feeling he knew what she wanted to ask.

"Last night. Has anything like that happened to you before? I mean, I can certainly see you inspiring them, but do you routinely go around inviting yourself into women's wet dreams?"

He choked on a mouthful of air. "Uh, no."

"Never?"

"Never. I was just as surprised as you were. Thought it was all my own dream until I realized it couldn't be."

She thought it over, then nodded. "Good. I have to say, it certainly beats beer and pizza for a first date."

"Oh, please," he said, scoffing at the notion, "you obviously haven't been out with anyone other than an overgrown frat boy in a long time."

She twined her fingers in her lap, looking down at them. "I haven't *been* with anyone in a long time. Not in any way, shape, or form."

He got the message. Found it hard to believe, given how vibrant and beautiful she was, but was also grateful she was completely free and unencumbered now. Free to explore with him, help him recall all he'd been missing about a normal life.

Clearing her throat, she changed the subject. "As much as I enjoy flirting with you and taking advantage of the fact that you think I'm a little high on meds, we do have other things to discuss."

"I know," he said, knowing there would be moments to look forward to later, when this pall wasn't hanging over them, and the town. "Whose address did you want from your boss?"

"The friend of Walter's who found the bones. He told

me the guy lived out on Old Terrytown Road, and I got to thinking about what those prostitutes said."

He almost skidded right through a stop sign at that one. *Prostitutes?* They hadn't even talked about that part of her adventure. He could only shake his head, wondering if she was always so ballsy. He liked that about her, but it also scared the hell out of him. "Maybe you should back up a little and tell me everything that happened today."

She did, quickly and concisely, that husky tone making her day sound like an adventure.

Yeah. If only it hadn't ended with her getting brutalized by a thug.

The only time she showed any emotion was when she spoke of the fear and plight of the teenage girls, but even then she was able to focus on the information they'd provided rather than what might be done about them and others like them. There was nothing spacey or woozy about her. She hadn't been kidding about the medication; she was entirely sharp, focused, *on*.

"And they said a lot of local girls—including Jessie Leonard—went out to be 'entertainment' at this mysterious club?" he asked.

"Yes. One said it's out in a big, falling-down house in the country. I got to thinking about those remains Walter's friend found. Terrytown Road's an old plantation route that winds out toward the ass end of nowhere. There are a number of abandoned houses near it."

He had to admire her quick thinking. "It's possible these human remains came from near one of those old places."

"Yes. Find out who the victim is, and who belongs to the club, and maybe we'll be able to narrow in on Vonnie's location."

It made excellent sense and was a strong lead. So he didn't even take the time to caution her about her hopes for finding Vonnie alive after five days.

Nor did he reveal that he'd tried again to reach out

to the girl, sending his thoughts soaring over Granville before he'd come inside the hospital. He hadn't gotten a scent, nor her voice. Just the sensation of moisture on his face.

Hot moisture—the kind caused by tears.

Not wanting to think of Vonnie crying, desperate and alone, he got back to the point—trying to save her. "What did Walter tell you about the location?"

"He wanted to protect his friend's privacy. But he told me to check between mile markers ten and eleven." With a smile, she added, "With a strong emphasis on the ten-and-a-half point. I'm thinking we can drive out there and explore, see if we can find any overgrown driveways or something that lead to houses set back off the road, ones that can't be easily seen."

Though he knew what her answer would be, he had to ask the question. "You sure you don't want to sit this one out, given everything that's happened today?"

"You sure you want to keep breathing?"

"Okay, just had to ask."

"I know," she conceded.

Glancing at the dashboard clock, he said, "We're going to run out of daylight soon."

"So let's head out there now rather than going home."

"Forget it. You need a hot shower and a change of clothes. Plus, we're not going alone."

She tilted her head in curiosity, as if wondering who in this town would help them. Judging by what he'd seen at the game last night, he suspected Granville wasn't as devoid of decent people as she might have been thinking recently. But he had some far better assistants in mind.

"I called in a few friends to help with the investigation." He quickly told her about Julia and the others, not surprised she knew right away who they were.

"The eXtreme Investigations people? Their names came up in some articles about you."

"Yeah, well, don't judge them by those. They're good people. And excellent detectives."

"So they were the ones with you in the alley. Not just some Good Samaritans, huh?"

"Right. They're the reason I got to you in time."

She curled one leg up in the seat. "I'd meant to ask you about that. How on earth did you find me? I know you realized I was going to Berna Jackson's, but it wasn't even like you could drive around and search for my car since I didn't have it."

He shifted in the seat, focusing on the route, not on the additional questions an honest answer would raise. "Julia got a tip from a friend and drove me over."

"What friend?"

He flicked the turn signal as they reached her street, turned carefully, focusing on the road and hoping she'd forget the question since they were almost to her house.

Fat chance of that. As soon as he pulled into her driveway and cut the engine, she asked again. "Aidan? What friend tipped her off? Does she know someone else in Granville?"

"Not exactly." Opening the door, he got out and then walked around to the passenger's side, opening her door for her and extending a helping hand. She took it, let him help her to her feet, and leaned against him while he walked her to the door.

Again, he'd hoped she would be distracted, but the minute she turned the key in her lock and led him inside, she put a hand on his arm and looked up at him, her expression troubled. "What aren't you telling me? Something else happened. That's why you're being so secretive."

"No, it didn't, I swear. I just don't like to talk about Julia to people who don't know her."

Her mouth rounded into a shocked O and she immediately let go of his arm. Her lashes fluttering, she stepped away from him, as if he'd made her uncomfortable.

It didn't take a genius to figure out what had happened. She thought he was protecting some secret he shared with Julia. As in a personal relationship.

After the way he'd kissed her right in front of the other woman, and everyone else, back in that alley, she actually thought he was involved with someone else.

Having no other choice, he admitted, "Look, her partner told her. Morgan was scoping out the town, spotted you, and told her you were in some trouble."

She looked both relieved and more confused. "Well, you could have said that, couldn't you? How did he know me? Was he walking by the alley or something?"

Damn, she was relentless. Thrusting a frustrated hand through his hair, he spit out the truth, knowing she wouldn't believe it but unable to keep coming up with half answers to put her off. "He's a ghost, okay? Julia, my former boss, talks to a dead guy."

He had to hand it to her: She managed to refrain from laughing or rolling her eyes in disbelief. Instead, she merely shrugged. "Gee, why didn't you say so in the first place?"

He knew it sounded crazy. It had sounded nuts to him when he'd first met Julia, so for an in-your-face, truth-and-nothing-but reporter like Lexie, it had to seem even more ridiculous. But that didn't mean it wasn't absolutely true.

"Morgan Raines was Julia's partner on the Charleston Police Force. He was shot down by a scumbag druggie seven years ago. She says he showed up a few months later and saved her life when she was almost killed in the line of duty, too."

"Uh-huh," she said, nodding, that pleasant expression still on her face. He didn't have any trouble reading it—she was thinking about calling for the guys in the white coats and padded wagons. "I take it you've met this guy?"

"No. Only Julia can see him."

She snapped her fingers. "Wait, I think I saw this in a movie once. *Mystery Men.* This guy claims he can become invisible, but only if nobody's around to see."

Chuckling ruefully, he shook his head. "Julia's going to like you."

"That'll make my day, I'm sure—being liked by Casper's gal pal."

"Whatever. Believe it or don't. All I can say is, I've seen and done too much freaky stuff in my own life to question somebody hanging out with a ghost." Lowering his voice, he added, "Sharing someone's dreams isn't exactly normal, either."

Lexie's smile faded and she caught her bottom lip between her teeth. He'd made his point. She would at least open her mind to the possibility.

And once she met Julia . . . well, it was hard for anyone to resist Julia Harrington when she set her mind to being liked and trusted. The woman was almost as big a force of nature as Lexie.

Saturday, 4:45 p.m.

Surrounded by people who knew and cared about Aidan, Lexie had to wonder why he'd ever left Savannah. These people, his former coworkers at eXtreme Investigations, obviously missed him. She had no doubt they had been behind him all the way on that last publicity-tainted case. From the moment she'd gotten in Aidan's SUV, which his friends had driven over to her house, it had been painfully clear they all thought he was crazy to have moved to Granville.

Not that they were rude, God, no; they'd all been wonderful. More warm and considerate toward her than most people around here were these days—except for Walter and his family. But it was clear they thought he had wasted a year of his life on regret. Julia Harrington, who might talk to ghosts but was also incredibly charming and down-to-earth, seemed especially appreciative that Lexie had drawn Aidan back into the "land of the living" as she called it.

Huh. Guess she'd know.

"So have you found out what Chief Dudley Do-Wrong did with the bones?" asked Mick Tanner, the guy who'd had Aidan's back during the fight in the alley. With his broad grin, twinkling eyes, and flashing dimples, she suspected the sexy guy could be a wicked flirt. But he'd been nothing but cordial and professional with her.

Maybe because Aidan had given him a hard, warning look when he'd taken Lexie's hand to shake it. But she could have imagined that. After all, he'd known her less than three days. They weren't involved, had no claim on each other.

Except in their dreams.

"Lexie? The bones?" Mick prompted.

"Oh, sorry. No, I don't know what he did with them. That's something Aidan and I were going to get to work on. I was thinking it would be worth having Walter call the DA's office, filing a request for information. If Dunston gets some heat from them, he'll have to come up with some kind of answer."

"Sure," Mick replied, "as in, 'Bones? What bones?' "

Lexie shook her head thoughtfully, disagreeing. "Twenty-four hours ago, I might have believed that. But he's in the hot seat now. The spotlight is shining bright and he's going to play Mr. Good Cop at least as long as he thinks people in this town give a damn."

Olivia, who was as elegantly lovely as her boss, Julia, was flamboyantly sexy, cleared her throat. "Does your friend Walter know the medical examiner well? If he does get the remains, would he be open to allowing them to be . . . examined by anyone else?"

Lexie didn't know Olivia's background, if she was a psychic like Aidan, or saw ghosts like Julia. Come to think of it, she didn't know what kind of power Mick had, either. But she suspected Olivia was not asking because she had some kind of forensics background. The tension in her tight shoulders and the haunted shadow in her eyes said she didn't want to examine those remains but that she had to.

"Actually, yeah, they're old friends. If he can pry those remains away from Dunston, I imagine he'd be willing to let you examine them, as long as he knows you have the credentials and reason to do so."

Olivia nodded once, then looked away, focusing her attention out the window at the passing Georgia countryside. They had left town, heading west on Old Terrytown Road, with marshy flatlands and abandoned rice fields all around them. It wasn't a particularly pretty drive, nor a popular place to live these days. Which could explain the abandoned houses. Some of them had been empty shells for a year, some for a hundred. Either way, the remaining neighbors were few and far between.

She couldn't think of a better area to conduct meetings of a secretive club whose members had a predilection for teenage girls.

"Here's the mile marker," Aidan said, slowing as they drew close to the spot Walter had told her about.

They neared a mailbox that looked freshly painted and in use. Lexie studied the small name, and said, "Ah. Mr. McCurdy. He and Walter are old poker buddies. I'm sure he's the anonymous source."

"So this is the place," said Mick. "Why don't you pull over and let me get out, take a walk around? Obviously not many bones were found, and a single human body has a lot of them. Who knows? Maybe I'll get lucky."

Lucky enough to stumble over human remains on the side of a back country road. The thought was disturbing. But he was also right. "I should go, too. I know the area best."

Aidan met her eyes in the rearview mirror. "Yes to Mick; no to you. He can tromp around along the side of the road; you and I have a house to look for. We're going to drive up and back and see if we spot any old gravel roads, driveways, or paths, remember?" He shifted his attention to Julia, who sat beside her in the backseat. "Unless you have any other ideas, Julia?"

She shook her head slowly, gazing down at her own

lap. "I need to get out for a few minutes. Let me go with Mick." Lifting her head, she said, "I, um, might be able to narrow down the location of this mystery house."

Lexie saw the way everyone else in the vehicle nodded, and realized they all thought the woman might be able to get a ghost to tell her where they should search. She still couldn't wrap her head around it, but she also knew the other woman came across as competent, sharp, and, most important, sane.

And like Aidan had said, how normal was it to have shared sex dreams? She'd gone so far as to accept Aidan's psychic abilities as simple truth; it shouldn't be that difficult to accept what she was told about Julia.

Only, of course, it was. Psychic stuff, even dreams, had at least some kind of scientific possibility. She knew much of the brain was a mystery to researchers, so it didn't shock her to think it might be capable of a lot more than was accepted as fact. Someone who was able to tap into all that unused brainpower might indeed be able to see things others couldn't or even into other people's thoughts and dreams.

But ghosts? That was a whole other story. That was life and death, heaven and hell and earth in the middle stuff. She had her faith, and her beliefs; they didn't include wispy remnants of the dead hovering around the living.

Not that she was rude enough to say such a thing to Julia's face. Because, no matter what she thought, everyone else around her trusted and believed in the woman completely. Either that, or they just liked her enough to humor her.

Aidan pulled onto the shoulder, waiting while Julia and Mick climbed out. Olivia appeared undecided for a moment, then joined them. "No sense putting it off," she said with a stiff little smile. "If we find something suspicious, I'm the one who'll be able to figure out if it's part of a human body."

Okay, so maybe the woman did have a forensics background.

"Lexie, why don't you hop up front so you can get a better view?" Julia said as she stood outside the door. "You be the spotter." She glanced at Aidan. "When I get some information, I'll call you and try to narrow your search quadrant, okay?"

"Understood."

"It'll be dark soon," Julia added.

Lexie nodded in agreement. "We have no more than an hour of daylight left."

"Okay," Aidan replied, "so let's make the most of it."

Saturday, 6:30 p.m.

They started to arrive right on time.

Mayor Cunningham came first, then Harry Lawton. More followed.

Alone or in pairs, never in a group large enough to be noticed on the street, they'd smile at anyone passing by, then carefully make their way into a private side door of a building that was supposed to be closed for the weekend. The building, which provided office suites to a number of attorneys, investment types, and accountants, apparently also offered after-hours meeting space for some of its wealthy tenants.

Chief Jack Dunston watched them from his window-front table at the restaurant directly across the street. He'd specifically requested the spot, because of this view. Spending a long time looking at the menu and ordering slowly, he'd spread out his meal as long as he could.

No way did he want to give up his front-row seat, not yet anyway. Not until he'd figured out what to do.

Ignoring everyone else in the crowded place, which was popular with business lunch customers during the week and laughing young adults looking to hook up on Saturday nights, he took out a notepad and pencil and began jotting down names. He knew all of them by sight. Most he'd expected to be there. A few surprised him.

What he didn't know was how many more would

show up, how they might know each other, and, most important, why they were here. Why did these men gather at this building the second Saturday of every month? Were they the mysterious "club" his own officers sometimes talked about?

"So, Chief, will that be it for the night? Would you like me to bring you your check?" his waitress asked, startling him into covering up his notes with his arm.

"Uh, give me a little while, okay?" he said, offering her a big, aww-shucks smile. "I might want some dessert."

"You got it," she said before sauntering away.

He immediately peered out the window again, seeing two more men go through that door. *Young and Wilhelm*. He added their names to the list, which had grown to about twelve. Twelve men who he wouldn't think had much in common, beyond being respected around these parts. What the newspaper owner and the bank manager had in common with teachers and administrators, he had no idea.

One of them glanced around, his gaze falling on the front of this very place. Though he almost certainly couldn't be seen through the window, Jack pulled back instinctively, not wanting them to know he was spying on them. Not because he worried about their reaction, but because he felt a little unsure himself about what he was doing here.

Though he'd known about these meetings, he'd never given them a second thought. Jack had noticed the once-a-month pattern—no matter what anybody might think about him as a chief, he did pay attention. He'd seen some of the successful men of this town coming together at this place, on certain nights of the month, and then leaving together in a big rented van. He'd never questioned it, never asked them why. He'd certainly never spied on them before. No, sir, he knew how to mind his own business.

But he *had* noticed.

Just like he'd noticed how nervous and jittery they

sometimes got, especially back when those articles had been published in the paper.

Did he think some of the most respected men of Granville had anything to do with the disappearance of a bunch of Boro trash? Hell, no. Not a chance. But he didn't doubt they were up to something. He had the feeling they feared too much attention about those missing girls could cast a glimmer of light on whatever they were trying to hide in the shadows.

Until now, he hadn't really cared about being left out of the loop. Lately, though, it had started to bug him. Maybe because he'd been embarrassed, caught with his pants down in the paper and again at the game last night. Maybe because of the bruises on that reporter's throat—the woman might be a pain in the ass, but she was only doing her job. And he sure didn't want to think people were really getting attacked on the streets of Granville in broad daylight, no matter what neighborhood they were in. Nor did he like the threat from her pissed-off boyfriend, about a national spotlight being shone on this place. On him.

He was losing control of this town. And that he didn't like most of all.

No matter what anyone thought, and no matter how much he liked getting that wad of cash in his porch fridge, Jack Dunston would not stand for being made a fool of. Nor was he going to ignore actual murder.

That might not be related to this.

But he suspected it was. Something was going on with those secretive men across the street. Something dark and ugly going on here in Granville. The small bag of bones locked inside his desk at the station told him that much. He'd let himself believe they didn't—couldn't possibly—belong to a human being. But he'd since begun to wonder.

"So, have you decided on dessert, Chief? The carrot cake is awful good!"

Jack didn't respond at first, merely watching as the

big passenger van pulled into the parking lot across the street, just like always. He couldn't see who was driving, but was able to make out a couple of shapes in the passenger's seats, even before anyone from the building got in.

He wondered who those shapes belonged to.

The men began to emerge from the building, heading for the van. They were on the move, on schedule to leave right around seven p.m. Going to do whatever it was they did one Saturday a month.

He could stay here and eat a piece of cake. Maybe feel the mayor out tomorrow, hint that he'd seen activity in the building and wonder aloud what was going on. Or he could be a cop and follow them.

He thought of the cake. He thought of the cash.

He thought of the bruises. He thought of the bones.

Finally he said, "Tell you what, honey, why don't you wrap up a piece for me to take along. I just remembered, I have somewhere to be."

And, he thought, *some*one *to be.*

Granville's chief of police.

Chapter 11

It was full dark by the time they found the house.

Aidan had driven Lexie up and down Old Terrytown Road, pulling into a few overgrown, nearly forgotten driveways, checking out ruins that appeared to have been untouched by human hands for decades. There had been no recent tire tracks, no footprints, no signs of life. When they'd shone flashlights through the hanging doors or broken window frames, they'd seen rotting wood, half-fallen walls, nests left by wintering animals long since gone. The insides of the structures appeared far too flimsy and decayed to house any secret meetings.

They had been about to give up, ready to go back and pick up the others, who were still searching for human remains in the reeds and woods, when his phone had signaled he had a text message. It had been Julia, with some advice from Morgan: *Head back this way, go another quarter mile from where you are now. The drive-way is intentionally concealed by a downed tree.*

And they'd found it. Right where Julia's ghostly friend had said they would.

"I would never have even realized this place was back here," Lexie whispered, visibly shaken.

He had the feeling she hadn't quite accepted Morgan's existence. Now she was beginning to understand. The dead guy wasn't always reliable, sometimes disappearing when Julia seemed to need him most. But whenever he came back, he always had excellent information. He was already two-for-two today.

"The way that driveway is hidden, we never would have found it," she added.

"Which is exactly what they intended when they put that huge tree down."

It had been hollow. And easily moved, once he'd known to look for it.

There were no "Private Property" or "No Trespassing" signs. Nor did any kind of fence or chain try to keep people out. The men who used this place didn't want anyone thinking there was any property worth trespassing on deep in these woods, so they'd simply made all evidence of its existence disappear.

"Who would ever have imagined *this* was back here?"

This was an elegant old plantation house. The exterior almost fully intact, it stood about three hundred feet off the main road, behind a thick stand of thorny, dense trees, all decorated with tangles of Spanish moss as twisted and gray as an old terrorist's beard.

The two-storied structure, graced with columns and also with wide verandahs on both the bottom and top floors, had once been white. And it had once been beautiful.

Time and neglect had dulled the house to a mottled gray—the color most resembling a corpse's skin on this moonlit night. Moss and vines had encircled it in a thick, woodsy embrace. Runners clambered in all directions, climbing toward the sky, looking like veins pulsing with green blood.

Though no longer conventionally beautiful, the place remained darkly stunning. Mesmerizing, in fact. Unnatural and mysterious, the old plantation had seemed to become one with the woods at some point over the past century, as if the Georgia earth had reclaimed the land on which it stood, and the old house along with it.

Lexie said something else, but Aidan didn't answer; he couldn't. Because he had a hard time hearing her.

His mind had opened up as soon as they'd rounded a curve and spied the house. The tension had grown exponentially when they'd driven past several small, decrepit buildings that he suspected had once served as slave quarters.

Something in him had known, intuitively, that they'd found what they'd been seeking. The pounding in his head and the pressure in his chest couldn't be denied. He wasn't sure why yet, but already he felt this haunting place was tainted, so ripe with evil and ugliness, it might as well have come equipped with a poison sign.

Poisoned earth.

Knowing there was much to discover, he'd let the connection happen, anxious to learn any secrets hidden in this strange, desolate hideaway. Now, parked right outside the front door, he heard a cacophony of whispers that lingered here, hanging in the air like the remnants of a woman's perfume after she had passed through a room.

There were so many voices. Dozens. Hundreds. Each sharing thoughts, moments, memories, emotions.

None sounded like they were from today and he would bet anything not a single soul was currently inside that house. These thoughts and memories didn't feel immediate; they were weeks, months, years, and centuries old.

But they were still vivid. They hit him hard. Jerking back in the seat, he didn't fight it. He kept his body relaxed and flowed with the sensations, knowing they weren't his, weren't personal, and couldn't harm him physically. This wasn't his version of reality; it belonged to countless other people who'd come to this place before him.

His eyes dropping closed, his breathing became shallow and open-mouthed. He pushed back against the pressure, finally breaking free of it. Getting that flying sensation as his consciousness spewed up and over the entire area like a geyser, he began to search, seeking answers, or at least entrances into the past.

Beside him, Lexie's worry grew to something almost tangible, and he knew she was watching, fearful, wondering if she should do something. But he couldn't tell her he was all right, couldn't let her know this was his version of normal. He just had to ride it out.

Feeling like he was being pummeled by tiny pebbles, he tried to evade the impressions that wouldn't help him. He began to pick and choose the remnants, discarding the wispy, self-indulgent thoughts of Southern belles in their ball gowns, and the heartbreaking ones of the slaves who'd once worked the place. He ignored the smells of the fields and unwashed bodies, evaded the painful lash of the whip. Aidan didn't let himself think about it or acknowledge just how doomed to darkness and suffering this genteel, lovely estate had been from the moment it had been conceived.

He moved forward, swirling through time, pushing on into decay and silence, when the grand old dwelling had been abandoned and the trees had thickened and closed in around it. A little further—memories of curious children, vandals, thieves. Breaking glass and falling beams. And every so often, rough male voices, as if despite the abandonment, over the decades the place had often been used by men looking to abuse women.

Finally, he entered a recent time. Modern. He heard ugly, cruel laughter and loud, twangy music. Smelled sweat and sex.

And he burned. For an infinitesimal second, he felt like his feet were being held over an open flame, his skin melting off his bones, though he had noticed no burned remnants or other evidence of fire.

A man's voice, raucous and deafening, confirmed he had arrived in the present day. Aidan's instinctive reaction was to lift his hands to his ears. Of course, that wouldn't block out something that existed only as a memory inside his mind. Besides, he had to listen. He needed to.

Woo-ee, boys, would you look at that one? Look at those titties. Nothin' store-bought about 'em. No plastic surgeon ever made anything so fine. Girl, come on over here and show my son here what you got between your pretty little legs.

Other voices joined in, talking about their delight in their oh-so-special club. Laughter and brutal lust made animals of men the world probably saw as decent. They'd been here a hundred and fifty years later, but the words and tone sounded the same as the echoes from the slave quarters.

These monsters had passed along their warped tastes to their own sons, keeping the cruelty alive generation after generation.

He groaned, overwhelmed by a sense of fear that had consumed that nameless, faceless girl, knowing why she was afraid. She had been abused—slapped, pushed, and dragged. Rough hands had torn at her clothes and forced her down. Anguish overwhelmed her.

Someone else's tears burned Aidan's eyes; another person's screams wanted to erupt from his mouth.

He couldn't do this for much longer.

"Vonnie," he whispered, certain the key to her disappearance was here, needing to find it.

A new voice intruded, and suddenly it all became clear.

He'd *already* found her.

Mama, why? Why'd you do this to me? Please. No, please, don't touch me! I don't want to. Don't make me! That hurts, oh God, Mama!

His eyes flew open as Vonnie's voice—and everything else—disappeared. Aidan stared forward, unseeing. All the sounds, the words, and impressions settled into place in his mind, forming a picture, one he knew would never leave him. Just as the echoes of her tearful, girlish pleas would never leave him.

He understood now, saw the complete truth of this secret club and the men who came here. Saw what they wanted and what they did and who they did it to. They'd done it to Vonnie Jackson, long before she'd disappeared.

God, had that poor kid never had a happy day in her entire life?

"Aidan?" Lexie whispered. She reached for him, putting a hand on his arm, pulling back when she felt his undeniably tense body. He couldn't stop fisting and unfisting his hands, filled with anger he was desperate to release, as he'd released it against that thug in the alley earlier. Not at her, of course. God, no. But at the men whose voices he'd just heard.

"Are you all right?" she asked.

Taking a few deep, steady breaths, he nodded. His pounding heart slowed and he forced himself to relax, release his fingers, unclench his muscles. "Yeah."

"What happened?"

Huh. He couldn't explain it in a million years. Not to anyone, not even her, whose mind had melded with his the previous night. He didn't know that he could find the words to describe what it was like to have hundreds of voices all talking in his head at once. Especially when those voices had revealed some of the ugliest, most vicious memories of their lives, things that would confirm the worst pessimist's opinion of the vileness of the human race.

Sometimes he had to wonder if his parents had been right, and his ability was a punishment for some kind of original sin more than anything else. There were things he'd rather have gone to his grave not knowing. He desperately wanted to take a shower to wash clean the filth and corruption that seemed stuck to him now, as if he'd walked into a huge spiderweb and its stringy remnants clung to every inch of him.

Let it go. You know what to do.

He counted backward from a hundred, concentrating on the present, pushing all the rest away. There was only now, only this, only people to help, not sadness for those he couldn't.

The one sure way he was ever able to get past something so traumatic was to focus on the good he did with his ability. The lost people he'd found, the terrified families to whom he'd provided answers and given closure.

He knew he could do at least one more good thing with it—find out what had happened to Vonnie and all the other missing girls who, he now suspected, had been subjected to the same pain, degradation, and rape.

Finally, he was able to move completely past it, his mind clearing and his fury dissipating. He no longer had to fight for control, for peace. He simply attained it between one breath and the next, the promise of doing something about what he'd heard—attaining justice—bringing him completely back to himself.

Beside him, Lexie was staring out the window, gazing at the moon-brightened shadows of the wind-whipped trees dancing across the front of the house. "This is the place, isn't it?"

"Yes. We found the clubhouse."

"How can something intended to be so lovely," she whispered, "be so awful?"

"More awful than you can possibly imagine," he replied, shaking his head slowly. "We should go. We need to pick up the others and bring them back here."

She nodded, not asking any more questions, as if knowing he was simply incapable of answering them. "Good idea. That house is too big for just the two of us to explore."

True. But that hadn't been why he'd decided they needed to go get Julia, Mick, and Olivia.

He'd be willing to bet that old building contained an updated room—or several—probably lit by generator power, which contained all the modern conveniences sexual sadists would need. Bad enough for him, or Lexie, or anyone else to be exposed to any object in that room.

He couldn't imagine what it would be like for Mick, who, with a single touch, would see exactly how those objects had been used in the past. And who'd used them.

Hearing had been bad enough. Seeing it was more than he could stomach. But that was Mick's gig, the reason he'd come here.

Even more disturbing, though, would be if they did find any human remains, Jessie Leonard's or anybody else's. Because then it would be Olivia's turn to touch. Worse, it would be Olivia's turn to take the place of the victim and *feel* everything she'd felt, for the last one hundred and thirty seconds of her life.

God, what an awful, dark power.

Olivia Wainwright had died many deaths in the two years that he'd known her. The quiet woman had been stabbed, shot, strangled, drowned. Brutalized. He found it amazing she hadn't ended up in a psych ward. Or— considering he sometimes wondered if being completely drenched in so much pain and death wouldn't drive a weaker person to suicide—in the morgue.

Not Olivia. Instead, she kept coming to work every day, trying to solve those murders, help the people whose final two minutes and ten seconds she'd shared.

It shouldn't come to that tonight, however. He doubted they'd find any remains. Not because he didn't think any murders could have been committed in this place, but because he assumed anybody who'd committed them would have disposed of the evidence. There might be shallow graves on the property, but they wouldn't find them in the dark.

Tomorrow, hopefully, Derek, the other XI agent, would be able to come down and help them out. Because if anyone had endured a bad death here, Derek Monahan would know it. He'd see it, would be able to watch the victim reenacting his or her own murder, again and again, at the very spot where it had occurred. Not a ghost, really, merely the imprint—the photocopy—that had been made on the world through an act of explosive violence.

Aidan didn't doubt there would be something to see. This place, so coldly beautiful, but as wicked and corrupt as a prettily decorated chamber of hell, had definitely enjoyed its share of violence. Aidan knew that. He'd heard it and had felt its malevolence.

Funny, how all their abilities would be so important here. Mick could touch something and know it had been used in a killing. Aidan could hear death. Derek could see it, Olivia could feel it. And Julia interacted with it on a daily basis.

Every single one of those abilities would come into play. He'd found a place where each member of the eXtreme Investigations team would do what he or she did best.

Now he just had to get them all here.

Saturday, 7:35 p.m.

The area where they'd left Aidan's colleagues shortly before dusk wasn't far from the old house they'd found. Not in mileage, anyway. But as Lexie and Aidan drove down the hidden lane toward the main road, the tree limbs scraping the roof of his SUV like a dead man's fingernails out of some campfire horror story, she found herself wishing they had farther to go. A lot farther.

She didn't want to go back there. She definitely didn't want to go inside that house.

She had never once thought of herself as being any more perceptive than the average person. Smarter than some, yeah, though not as smart as others. But in terms of instinctively knowing something was bad just because of a sensation in her bones or a crawling on the back of her neck, no. At least, not until tonight.

"Somebody should have torn it down decades ago," she whispered, watching in the passenger's-side mirror as they rounded a bend and the house finally disappeared behind them.

He said nothing, merely reaching for her hand in the darkness, confirming what she already knew. Whatever he'd seen, or sensed about that place, it had been beyond awful.

"Is Vonnie in there?" she had to ask, her throat as thick and tight with emotion as it was because of the pain and bruises. "Are we going back to find her body?" *And the bodies of all those other girls?*

"No, Lex, she's not there, though I'm certain she was. At least a couple of years ago, I believe." A muscle in his jaw flexed, and she saw the anger that had seemed about to overwhelm him a few minutes ago when he'd been in that strange, frightening trance.

"The killer brought her here?"

He shook his head.

"The club," she said, at last understanding.

"Yeah."

"You know what it is?"

"I know." He sneered. "They call themselves the Hellfire Club. Good name for the bastards since I have no doubt they'll burn in hell."

He only hoped its flames were as painfully hot as they'd felt during those scant seconds when he'd felt them licking at his own feet.

"How do the girls come into it?" she asked, though she suspected she already knew.

"These club members are sexual deviants, or sadists, all with a taste for teenage girls. It looks as though they bring three, maybe four of them out here at a time every month or so. A dozen or more grown men spend the night sharing them, doing things to them that no decent person would ever do to another one." His profile, stark in the moonlight, appeared as hard and immoveable as a marble statue. "It's . . . depraved."

For a second, she thought she would vomit. Reaching

for the controls, she pushed a button to send the window gliding down, needing a rush of cool evening air on her face.

He had one more piece of information to share. "I can't say nobody has ever died in that house, but I didn't get any sense that murder is part of these men's repertoire. For them, it's all about rough, degrading sex with underage girls."

Lexie put her head back against the headrest, letting the ugly ramifications sink in.

She'd known more than ten teenagers had gone missing, had probably been killed. And she'd believed there was a killer at large. Now, though, the scope had just grown exponentially.

A dozen men. Three or four girls at a time. Every month. For years.

They could be talking about hundreds of rape or molestation victims here.

She pounded the side of one fist against her door, so overcome with anger and disgust, she just needed to hit something. "Oh, no, nothing bad could ever happen here in perfect little Granville," she snarled, mimicking the locals who'd been so angry about her articles. "I fucking hate small towns."

"Savannah's seeming more and more like heaven the longer I live here," he admitted.

"Or New York. You don't see people there throwing blankets over their heads, ignoring murder and abuse, pretending they live in a place that's much too nice for anything bad to ever take place."

Maybe she'd leave. Maybe when this was over, she'd say to hell with it and get outta Dodge. Her house was rented, so there was no property to worry about. She had only a few friends. And, other than getting to work with Walter, she couldn't say she loved anything about her job anymore. Picking up and taking off sounded better all the time.

It took a while in the darkness, but after a couple of

minutes, they reached the end of the dusty private drive-way. "Maybe I should pull the log back into position," he said, hesitating before pulling out onto the main road. "I should have done it before, just didn't think of it since I wasn't sure this would be the place."

"We're less than a mile from Julia and the others. You really think somebody's going to notice in the next five minutes that it's not where it's supposed to be?"

He hesitated, then shrugged in apology. "Sorry, I don't like to take chances." Pulling the vehicle out, and then onto the shoulder, he said, "Wait here."

Aidan exited and jogged back to the log, which looked massive and heavy but, he said, was easily moved. Shoving it across the lane, he was back in his seat within a minute. He'd just buckled up as a pair of headlights came into view, heading toward them, away from town.

"Close," he said. A few seconds earlier and those headlights would have spotlighted him shoving at a downed tree in the middle of nowhere.

Shifting the SUV into drive, he pulled out onto the road just as the oncoming vehicle, a large passenger van, blew past them going well above the speed limit.

"Hope Julia, Mick, and Olivia have been staying well off the road," Lexie said, frowning as she turned and watched the van's taillights disappear. "Even with their flashlights, some idiot going seventy on a country road might not spot them."

Glancing over, she realized Aidan wasn't listening. A dark, forbidding frown tugging at his brow, he appeared in the grip of another of those strange trances he'd been in a few minutes ago at the house.

"Aidan," she snapped. Realizing they were drifting into the oncoming lane, and another pair of headlights was heading for them, she raised her voice. "Pull over!"

He shook his head, hard, his hands jerking a little on the steering wheel, swerving the SUV back into their lane. "Damn," he muttered, sounding out of breath and shocked.

"Did it happen again?"

He nodded once. "I started hearing those voices all over again. I didn't go looking for them. I'd never do that while driving." He thrust a shaking hand through his hair. "I'm so sorry, Lex. I can usually control this. Guess touching the log again put me more in tune with the voices I'd heard, of the men who'd touched it before."

"It's okay. We're both fine."

He swallowed visibly, admitting in a low voice, "That house shook me up. It has some seriously bad karma."

"I know." Unable to help it, she had to admit, "I hate the thought of going inside."

"So maybe we shouldn't," he told her. As she started to protest, he held up a hand. "Not tonight, I mean. It's going to be pitch-black inside and even if there is a generator, as I suspect, we won't be able to fire it up and turn on any lights without potentially letting somebody know we're in there snooping around."

"What about flashlights?"

He hesitated, as if trying to figure out how to put what he was thinking into words.

"What we do, what everyone on the team does, is very precise," he finally said. "We all open ourselves up to some pretty intense situations every single day. Doing it in the dark, in a place like *that*, when we can't entirely control what we're touching, or what we might stumble over that could trigger a response . . . well, there are risks involved. Look at what happened just now, even after I thought I had shut it out."

She thought about that, the way the evil aura of the place had actually reached out and gripped him again, even when he was driving away from it. They could have been in an accident, and another trip to the local ER was not on her to-do list. Neither was getting killed.

"There they are," he said, nodding toward Julia, Mick, and Olivia, whose flashlights were visible just up ahead. "Let me run this by them and we'll decide as a group, okay?"

Fair enough. If Aidan had thought there was any chance Vonnie was in that house, or that going into it tonight might help them find her, she had no doubt he'd insist on doing it. That he didn't was both disappointing and a bit of a relief. Disappointing, because she had been hoping deep inside that they might actually find the missing girl at the whispered-about clubhouse.

Relieved because, as little as she wanted to go in that place at any time, doing it at night was something she just didn't want to contemplate. Not now, not after the day she'd had.

Within another few minutes, Aidan's three friends were back in the car. Insisting that Lexie remain where she was, Mick took a seat beside Julia in the back.

Aidan didn't turn the vehicle around, but he didn't head toward town right away, either. Instead, parked on the shoulder, he told them all that they'd discovered, and what he thought they should do about it.

Julia immediately agreed. "There's nobody alive in that house," she said, as if she'd already gotten an inside tip. "We'd go in looking for clues, not a missing person, and it's too easy to miss something in the dark."

"He's sure?" Aidan asked, obviously realizing Julia had been talking to her ghost.

The dark-haired woman nodded.

Lexie, who'd been wondering about something, had to ask, "If your, um, friend can find houses and know who is or isn't in them, why can't he just go find Vonnie?" She wasn't being snide, or disbelieving, she genuinely wanted to know.

"Like anyone else, Morgan needs a starting place, something to go on," Julia explained, earnest and serious. She hadn't taken offense at the question. "He found that house because he knew you were looking for one in this vicinity. Just like he found you because he knew roughly where you were. If we had a couple of possibilities where Vonnie might be, he could certainly check them out. But a whole town? Impossible."

"Okay," she said, feeling a little better about leaving without going deep into the creepy clubhouse for monsters tonight.

After hearing Julia's information, and everything Aidan had to share about the house—and how it had affected him—they all agreed to head back to town. Julia and the others would go back to Savannah and return in the morning, hopefully with someone named Derek.

"It's just as well we're waiting until the morning. It really wouldn't be a good thing for me to go stumbling around in the dark, touching things I don't need to touch," said Mick as they got underway. "I could get caught up in the history of an old broken teapot and get completely distracted from what we're supposed to be doing."

Lexie turned in her seat, looking back at the three psychic detectives. Aidan had told her nothing about what they did, or how they did it, and Mick's words were her first clue about his ability. "You can touch something and know how it's been used?" she asked, her curiosity getting the better of her.

Mick nodded. "And who used it, when, and where."

"That's pretty interesting."

"It's a good party trick," the man said with a grin. "Used to be a big hit on the carnival sideshow circuit." Closing his eyes, he lifted his hand, placing the back of it on his forehead. In a chanty, fortune-teller's voice, he added, "I see that this matchbook was used to light a cigarette for a woman in black. A woman you had dinner with when your wife thought you were at a business meeting." Dropping his hand, he added, "Unfortunately, I didn't get much repeat business."

She had to chuckle, surprised she was even capable of it after today, but incredibly relieved at how good it felt, even if her throat hurt a little every time she swallowed.

The others were smiling, too, including Aidan, who said, "Don't even try to tell us you didn't find some way to use your act to pick up women."

"Not at first," Mick replied with an innocent shrug, "considering I was only six."

Lexie took a second to be shocked by that, the knowledge that this man had been put in some kind of sideshow act as a child. Nobody else seemed fazed, so they'd already known.

"But once I hit high school age?" the man added. "Hell, yeah, groups of giggly girls would come in and I'd do everything I could to get their attention."

Julia smirked. "How many of them threw their underwear onstage so you could see where it had been?"

Mick's smile broadened, which caused Olivia, Julia, and Lexie to make, "Ew!" sounds.

"Only time I was ever able to touch something and see the future," Mick said, winking. "*My* future."

More groans from the women, though Aidan laughed, looking completely relaxed and at ease. If she hadn't already liked these friends of his, she would have just for that. She'd seen glimpses of the real man beneath the gruff, all-black-wearing exterior. That real man was especially in evidence when he let his guard down, as he did around these people. And, she had to admit, even around her. It was like they were all unified on some team, and she felt more a part of this group than she had with any other during the six years she'd lived in Granville.

"What about you, Olivia?" Lexie asked the quiet, red-haired woman, whose ability was the only one that remained a mystery. "What do you do?"

Olivia stared back at her, her smile remaining where it was—not widening, but not disappearing either. Still, there was something a little sad about her. Though not as forbidding as Aidan had been at first, she definitely didn't seem the type to invite people to ask questions.

Lexie was about to apologize for being nosy when the woman answered. As if admitting she occasionally forgot to take out the trash, Olivia said, "What Mick does with things, I do with humans. He touches objects and knows their history. I touch corpses and feel how they died."

Feel, as in experience? God.

Lexie snagged her bottom lip between her teeth, wishing she'd minded her own business. There was no laughter this time. How could there be?

"I'm sorry," she said. "That was none of my business."

"Thought people in your profession made everything their business," Julia said, staring at her, though more in an assessing way than a judgmental one. Considering the woman was Aidan's friend, and was therefore probably fully aware of what he'd gone through last year, Lexie didn't blame her. In fact, she liked her for her loyalty.

Aidan answered before she could say a word. "Lexie's not your average reporter."

"Oh, we're calling them reporters again?" Julie asked, her tone sharp but amused, as if she and Aidan were sharing some private joke. "Not 'lying, manipulative media cockroaches'?"

Gaping, Lexie stared at the man behind the wheel.

He shrugged uncomfortably, but she'd swear a hint of a grin was teasing those masculine lips. "That was before I met you. And to be fair, since we've known each other, you have called me cranky, callous, cowardly, and an asshole," he pointed out.

"Keep score much? Besides, I didn't call you an asshole. I said I was thinking about you as a bucketful of assholes when you slammed the door in my face."

The others in the back were silent for a second; then all three of them began to laugh, soft at first, then louder, desperately needing it after the tension of the day.

Mick seemed the most amused. "You'd better watch out, my friend. You are never going to get the last word with this one."

"I like her, Aidan!" Julia said.

Even Olivia's reserve seemed to have melted and

her eyes twinkled merrily in the dimly lit vehicle. "How long, exactly, have you two known each other?"

Lexie and Aidan answered in unison, exactly the same words, at exactly the same moment. "Fifty-two hours."

Julia gaped. "Not thinking about each other too much, huh?"

Which just made everyone laugh again. Embarrassment warming her cheeks, Lexie faced front, staring out the window as they came into town. For the entire evening, she'd been totally focused on the story, the case, and hadn't thought about everything else that had occurred between her and Aidan.

Now she did, unable to think of much else, since his well-meaning friends had pointed out that the two of them seemed to have become pretty well obsessed with each other in the short time since they'd met. There was a lot to dwell on: The dream. The embraces. The tender words. The connection that had started immediately, built in a heated, nightlong fantasy, and solidified with each and every hour they'd spent together.

Nothing like it had ever happened to her before. Like most women her age, she'd had the occasional one-night stand as well as the infrequent long-term relationship. Since she had those experiences to draw on, she was already able to determine that what was happening between them was not much like either, but a little like both.

Physically, in terms of pure sexual attraction, oh yes, she'd have wanted to go home with Aidan McConnell if they'd just met in a bar. Sparks had danced between them from the very first, and she'd been aware of his sexual appeal from the moment she'd laid eyes on him.

But it was more than that. They'd known each other for such a short time, but she already knew whatever was happening between them wouldn't be resolved with a simple one-night stand. The attraction wouldn't be extinguished once it was satisfied; it would only build.

More than all that, she knew she liked him. A lot.

It was too much to digest. Especially under the watchful eyes of his observant friends. Hardly fair, really, to get involved with a guy who palled around with psychics and mind readers and, well, whatever Olivia was.

Involved. Funny word. But it fit. They were involved, whether either of them had intended it that way or not. There was no if, no maybe, no could be. It was a done deal; even the three relative strangers in the backseat knew it.

The only thing she didn't know was how Aidan felt about it. Seventy-two hours ago he'd been a growling, semiretired loner. Now he was hip deep in a case, surrounded by people, and engaging in flirtatious banter with *her*, a woman who worked in a profession he hated and didn't have, as he called it, an off switch between brain and mouth.

They were nothing alike, completely mismatched, absolutely wrong for each other in every way. And yet . . .

And yet . . .

They were involved.

Saturday, 10:10 p.m.

Like most of the teenagers in Granville, the Kirby twins had spent a good bit of Saturday talking about the previous night's game. Or, at least, the half-time portion of it, when students from both schools had taken a stand in defiance of their coaches and teachers, demanding attention and justice for Vonnie.

It had been incredibly cool. It had also been Taylor's idea, and she was proud of herself for having thought of it. Jenny had participated, too. She was the one who'd written the speech the guys had delivered. Which had, quite simply, rocked.

So much for it being just her dad and Lexie trying to do something about all the recent disappearances that everybody knew were connected but nobody wanted to acknowledge. Now the whole town was talking about nothing else. She had heard from friends who said their parents were setting up neighborhood watch meetings, and others who were volunteering to do searches or go door-to-door passing out flyers. The usually-douchey principals of both schools were supposedly organizing a rally after school Monday, and she'd heard the phone lines at the police station had been jammed.

Everybody wanted to be involved. Finally.

Adults always accused kids her age of being spoiled, not caring for other people. Well, they were learning better now. It might take a while to get her generation moving in one unified direction, but once they had, they could be an unstoppable force. Chief Dunston and his skeevy friends couldn't tape closed thousands of angry mouths all screaming for justice.

The whole thing almost made Taylor feel better about the lie she and her twin were continuing to perpetuate about which of them had really been the last one to see Vonnie Jackson Monday night. Almost.

"You sure you're okay to drive?" Jenny asked. "Not too tired? I saw you falling asleep halfway through the movie."

"No kidding," she said as they left Granville's pathetic little two-screen theater, heading for Taylor's car in the dark parking lot. It was almost totally empty of other vehicles, the few remaining ones probably belonging to the workers who were inside cleaning up. All the normal, rational moviegoers, who'd gone to see a good film—the one Taylor had wanted to see—had gotten out forty minutes ago.

The movies had both started at seven. They'd just had the misfortune to see the excruciatingly long one, filled with scene after scene of sad-faced whiners crying about how miserable their lives were. If she could have climbed up into the screen, she would have gladly put them out of their misery.

"Come to think of it, I am exhausted. So you can drive," she said, tossing her keys to her sister and moving to Jenny's right, so she could head not toward the driver's side of her Beetle but the passenger's one. "If you're wondering why I'm sleepy, it's because that was the boringest flick ever made. You, Jenny Kirby, have the worst taste in movies. Geez, did you not notice that other than that couple who looked like they went to school with George Washington, we were the only people in the whole entire theater? And *they* had the good sense to get up and leave halfway through!"

"Everybody says it's going to win the Oscar," her sister replied, sounding lofty and prim in her oh-so-Jenny way.

"Okay, well, maybe it'll win the Oscar for putting the audience in a coma, but as for Best Picture? I've seen more exciting stuff growing in my gym locker."

"That's disgusting," Jenny said, playfully punching her upper arm.

"Next time, I pick. The preview for that 3-D slasher flick looked way cool," Taylor added. "You can't fall asleep when there's a knife aiming at . . ."

Her words were cut off by a sudden sharp, vicious blow to her head. She flew forward, crashing to her hands and knees, crying out in pain. She couldn't think for a second, couldn't process what had happened, what could have struck her, why she'd fallen.

Then she heard a scream. Jenny collapsed onto the ground a few feet away, landing hard on her stomach. Her twin's body was limp, her eyes closed. One pale hand was extended toward Taylor, as if she'd reached for her as she fell.

"Jenny?" she whispered, but another sharp pain sliced through her and she was unable to speak further. Tears of agony spilling from her eyes. Nothing made sense, nothing seemed real.

Jen?

She tried to reach out, tried to touch her sister, the person with whom she'd spent every day for the past seventeen years. But her hand felt heavy. So heavy. She couldn't hold it up, having to let it fall onto the blacktop close to Jenny's.

As it dropped, she realized she'd somehow managed it. She'd gotten so close, the very tips of their middle fingers touched.

It was one infinitesimal brush of skin on skin between two people who'd shared a womb. And it was what she most needed at that moment, just as she'd always needed to feel that unbreakable bond with Jenny at the most stressful times of her life.

Taylor stared at their hands, the seam where their skin met, and thought they must be lying like perfect mirror images, finger-to-finger, face-to-face. Tears filled her eyes, she stared so hard, and soon it became too hard to stare. Because for some reason her tears had turned red.

Not tears. No. She finally realized the red she was seeing was the pool of blood separating her from Jenny.

She just couldn't figure out, before blackness descended completely, whether that blood was hers, or her sister's.

Chapter 12

Aidan had fully intended to drive Lexie home the previous night. He really had. So why he'd cruised past her neighborhood and gone back to his place, rather than taking the simple detour down her street, he honestly couldn't say.

It was as if he'd been on autopilot. His mind was churning with everything he'd experienced at that house, not to mention all the rest of the day's events, and he'd zoned in on home and hadn't let anything else stop him from getting there.

Once they'd arrived, of course she'd stayed with the group. Everyone was tired, and he knew Lexie's throat was hurting her—she'd taken a couple of over-the-counter pain pills, not wanting to muddle her thinking with anything stronger. But hunger outweighed fatigue and he'd ordered some pizzas, not wanting Julia and the others to make the drive back to Savannah without having a bite to eat.

When they were leaving, at around ten, Julia had offered to drop Lexie off on her way out of town. Since the house wasn't on the way, though, Aidan had insisted it was no problem to take her home. And it wouldn't have been a problem—she lived a few minutes away. Only, when he'd gone into his living room to see if she was ready, he'd found her sound asleep on the couch.

Staring down at her, he just hadn't been able to bring

himself to wake her up, for two reasons. First, those bruises on her throat stood out like her assailant's fingers had been dipped in neon paint. The idea of taking Lexie home and dropping her off there, to spend the night alone, when they knew a psychotic killer was on the loose, had made him sick to his stomach.

Second, he liked having her here. Hard to believe, hard to know why. But it was true.

So he'd simply covered her up, turned off the light, then moved to a chair to watch over her, the illumination in the room growing, then dimming, as the moon moved across the sky during the night. He'd spent the night hours as he always did, drifting into short bouts of sleep; more often, drifting out of it.

There had been no shared dreams. He'd put up that mental wall to guard against them. The one they'd shared might have been hotter than hell, but it didn't mean the woman wanted him slipping into her sleep like a Peeping Tom.

Still, even without his front-row, center seat, he knew when Lexie started dreaming again. This time, judging by the sounds she was making, it wasn't a smooth, sultry interlude playing in her head. It was a horror movie.

"No, don't," she whispered, jerking on the couch. He'd been awake for about a half hour, lost in thought, focused on Vonnie and the other girls. On that house. On Lexie and the blast of energy she seemed to have brought back into his life.

Her tiny cries grabbed his attention; the pain and fear in her wounded, husky voice as she tried to stop some unknown assault, kept it.

"Please!"

He slid off the chair and knelt by the couch, brushing her hair off her brow. "Shh. It's okay, Lex. It's just a bad dream." He'd whispered the words, hoping to simply reassure her back into sleep. But instead, she awoke. Her eyes flickered, then opened, and she stared up at him.

Given her nightmare, he would have expected her

first reaction to be one of fear at finding a man kneeling above her in the shadowy, predawn darkness of the room. Lexie, though, slowly smiled, as if she'd seen exactly what she'd hoped to see the minute she opened her eyes.

"Hi."

"Hi." He didn't move away, liking the feel of her silky hair against his fingers, and the warmth of her body so close to his. There was intimacy in the moment and he didn't want to give it up right away, liking the soft look in her eyes and her languid, sleepy mood.

"I fell asleep here?" she asked with a yawn.

He nodded. "I wasn't crazy about the idea of you staying alone at your place, anyway, so I just let you be. I didn't want to wake you up, but you were having a nightmare."

"Don't remember it."

That was probably just as well.

She looked down, seeing he was still dressed, and asked, "Where were you?"

He nodded toward the chair.

"I'm sorry I kept you from your bed."

"You didn't. I never actually sleep in it."

"What *do* you do in it, Aidan?" she asked after the slightest hesitation.

Aidan's breath slowed, even though his heart rate kicked up a notch. There had been nothing subtle about the question, nor did her suddenly hot stare hold any coyness. They both knew what she was really asking, and what she wanted the answer to be. "Your throat . . ."

"Is fine." She didn't seem willing to risk him backing away. Lifting her arms, she twined her fingers in his hair, tugging him closer. "Please, Aidan. I want this. I want you. I want *us*."

So did he. Oh God, yes. But he didn't want to hurt her. He'd kissed her yesterday, then worried he could have caused her pain. Now the things he wanted to do to her—with her—well, he didn't know that he should even allow himself to start until she was one hundred percent well.

"I know it hasn't been very long since we met. But I've experienced things with you that I haven't shared with people I've known for years."

"Ditto," he said, thinking particularly of their dream. And of the instant desire he'd felt for her, which had almost immediately overcome his natural resistance to touching anyone.

"We could dance around this, keep dreaming and thinking about it and satisfy whatever convention that says nice people wait until they've known each other a month before having sex," she whispered. "But frankly, I just don't want to."

He let her pull him closer, until their lips were close enough to share a breath. Their stares met one more time, silently acknowledging how far they'd come and where this was going. What it meant, he couldn't say. He only knew he had to have her.

"You're absolutely certain?"

"*Yes*," she growled. "And if you ask me that again I'll have to hit you."

"I guess you are feeling better if you're threatening me with bodily injury," he teased.

But his laughter quickly faded. Unwilling to resist his overwhelming desire for her—and hers for him—Aidan didn't wait any longer before eliminating the sliver of air that separated them. He covered her mouth with his, gently at first, savoring the softness of her beautiful lips, the taste that was uniquely Lexie. She groaned, deep in her throat, twining her hands harder in his hair even as she tilted her head. Arching up toward him, she pressed against his body, her feminine curves the perfect complement to his hardness.

Aidan moved over her, onto the couch, holding his weight off her, but letting their legs tangle and their hips meet. She made no secret of what she wanted, thrusting her tongue against his, demanding the passion, the heat he'd worried she wasn't physically capable of handling.

She was handling it, all right. Taking every warm touch he offered, throwing accelerant on it, and turning it into an inferno.

"God, Lex," he muttered against her mouth before plunging his tongue deep. He ground against her, knowing that as good it felt to be between her clothed thighs, being between her naked ones was going to drive him out of his ever-loving mind.

Not content with devouring just her mouth, he tasted his way across to her jaw, then down the side of her neck. He slowed to press warm, tender kisses to the bruises on her throat, wishing he could take away the pain, determined to at least make her forget it for a while.

Any farther downward progress was halted by her clothes. He pulled away from her, wanting to see, feel, and taste every bare inch of her. Lexie sat up and wriggled to help him, tugging at the soft sweater. Aidan gently pushed her hands away, pulling it up himself, avoiding her bruises. He didn't want to risk even the scrape of fabric against her injured skin.

Once it was gone, he had to just drink her in, feeling hot blood rush through him, heat pulsing in his groin as the desire he'd already thought was overwhelming built to an even greater inferno. "Beautiful," he said, staring at her, now clad in only her jeans and a pretty, pale pink bra that wasn't nearly as attractive as the curves it contained.

Lexie pushed at him, until he was sitting up on the couch. Then she rose to her feet, standing right in front of him.

It was still a few minutes before sunrise, but the light coming in through the slotted blinds on the front windows had already begun to take on that purplish hue that came whenever midnight melted into morning. Lexie seemed a part of both—as darkly sensual as the night, but as beautiful and breathtaking as the dawn.

He wanted her with every ounce of his soul.

Standing before him, Lexie saw the intense, covetous look on Aidan's face. And, in that moment, she realized what she'd been missing all her adult life. She'd had sex before. She'd had relationships before. But she'd never been absolutely devoured by the ravenous stare of a man desperate to have her or die trying. Not once.

"I want you, too," she admitted, though he had said nothing. He hadn't needed to. She got it.

Never taking her eyes off him, she reached around and unclasped her bra. She dipped one shoulder, letting the strap fall. Then the other, and the lacy fabric dropped onto the floor.

He stared, hissed, and the tension rose.

When he reached for her, she shook her head, backing up a step. Once she was back in his arms, she wanted absolutely no impediment, nothing to stop him from thrusting into her and taking her until his body became an extension of her own.

She reached for her waistband, unbuttoned and unzipped her jeans, then pushed them down. Kicking them off, she remained there, nearly naked, wearing only the skimpiest of underwear, letting him look the way she knew he wanted to.

"Ask me that question again—the one you asked at the game. About whether you're sexy," he growled.

When she moved her fingers to the elastic edge of her panties, he stopped her. Putting his big, warm hands on her hips, his fingers squeezing her bottom, he drew her closer, until his mouth was an inch from her stomach. His warm exhalations flowed over her skin, bringing goose bumps and the most delicious sense of anticipation.

"There it is," he murmured.

She didn't know what he meant until he pressed his hot mouth to her hip, kissing her birthmark, which was shaped as if it had been formed solely for this man to taste.

And suddenly she recalled their shared dream, where

that wicked mouth had moved when it had left her hip. "Oh God," she whispered, every inch of her remembering at once. Remembering—and wanting to do everything they'd done then, for real this time.

Every single thing.

Aidan rose from the couch, his hands and mouth brushing against her every inch of the way until he stood right in front of her. His thick, muscular arms flexed as he pulled his shirt up and off. And it was her turn to stare, stunned that he truly was as perfectly formed, as utterly magnificent, as she'd dreamed him to be. Thick shouldered, broad chested, with a flat, muscled stomach and lean hips, the man should star in every woman's most erotic dreams.

But only in her reality. At least for now.

He drew her closer, until her hard nipples scraped in the wiry hair on his chest. She quivered, even that tiny contact sending spasms of delight through her.

Knowing, already, just how to touch her, just how she liked it, Aidan lifted a big hand to her breast. She arched back, wanting more, and he gave it to her, bending to cover her incredibly sensitive nipple with his mouth. He licked lightly, then sucked hard and both sensations competed to be the one that would make her legs give out first.

She didn't know which won. She just knew that suddenly he was supporting her weight, his strong arm around her waist as he bent her back so he could lavish attention on her breasts, her throat, her neck. Feeling like she was on fire, she ran her hands over as much of him as she could reach, marveling at the coiled strength of the man. He let her, until she touched the front of his jeans. Then he stood her upright and backed up a bit. "Uh-uh."

She frowned. "You still have way too many clothes on."

"Not for long, angel." He unfastened his pants, let them gape open, but didn't take them off right away.

Instead, he pulled her back into his arms, pushing at her underwear, sending them to the floor. "Are you on something?"

She nodded, knowing what he meant.

"Good."

Oh, it was going to be very good. So very good. She had no doubt of that.

Aidan shoved his pants and boxer briefs down, and Lexie smiled, seeing all that male power, knowing it was going to feel amazing when buried inside her.

He continued to stroke her, all sizzling heat but also sweet, erotic tension. When he moved a hand between her legs, she quivered, a tiny cry emerging from her throat as he slid his fingers into her damp core.

That helpless, desperate cry seemed to finally drive him over the edge. "Come here," he ordered, backing up and again sitting on the couch. He pulled her down, too, so she straddled him.

She didn't hesitate, didn't tease or build this any more because, honestly, she was just too desperate. Instead, Lexie eased down onto his shaft, taking him into herself inch by inch until the man had utterly and completely filled her.

Nothing had ever felt this good. Not. One. Thing.

Throwing her head back and closing her eyes, she savored every sensation, took his every upward thrust, answering it, meeting him, rocking with him as wave after wave of delight rolled over her. It seemed to go on forever, and, in fact, their bodies were sweaty, bathed with bright sunlight when she finally heard his breaths grow choppy and a little hoarse.

"Yes," she whispered, pressing her mouth to his for a deep, warm kiss.

He twined his hands in her hair, stroking her, cupping her head, just like he had in the dream. Just like then, the sweet tenderness of it made her feel utterly cherished and wanted.

There was one more thing that happened just like in

the dream. Aidan wouldn't let himself finish until she had. It wasn't until she cried out in delight, shaking as waves of her orgasm threw her into an ocean of physical pleasure, that his thrusts grew frenzied and he let himself go to the deep end, too.

Afterward, she sagged down onto him, her arms draped around his shoulders. Without leaving her, Aidan shifted and pulled her down to lay on top of him on the couch. And together, still joined, they fell back to sleep.

Sunday, 9:25 a.m.

Aidan awoke with a start, unsure for a second where he was, or why he felt a weight on his chest. Seeing Lexie curled up on top of him, memory instantly flooded back.

Hot, steamy memory.

He smiled, stroking her naked hip, careful to avoid the bandaged spots where she'd been scraped against the bricks yesterday. She had to be sore, but the cries coming out of her mouth a few hours ago had sounded like anything but pain. The woman sleeping so peacefully against his chest had been wild and sensual, wanting everything, and then wanting it again.

He wished he had the whole day to give it to her. Wished this dark cloud hanging over the town, and them, would disappear so they could maybe try to act like a normal couple at the start of something pretty intense, as they both knew they were. How, he couldn't say. But they both knew.

He glanced at the clock, realizing they had only about an hour and a half until the world intruded. About to slide out from under her, pick her up and go find that bed he so seldom used, he flinched when a knock sounded on the front door. And he suddenly realized that sound was what had awoken him in the first place.

Julia and the others had promised to be back at around eleven, and he couldn't imagine them showing up this early without calling. But a quick glance through the sheers on the window right behind the couch confirmed Julia's silver car was parked out front, exactly where it had been last night.

"Hell!" He bent to kiss the top of Lexie's head, whispering, "Hey, wake up. Your parents got home from the movies early and they're about to catch us naked on the couch."

"Rats, busted," she mumbled sleepily. Then the doorbell rang, and her eyes flew open. She jerked her head up, looked around, and said, "What time is it?"

"Ninety minutes before they were supposed to be here," he said with an annoyed frown.

"Oh my God!" She leapt to her feet, looking frantically around the room for their clothes, as if she really were that busted teen or a cheating spouse.

"Calm down. Take your time," he said, amused by her un-Lexie-like panic. "I was kidding about getting caught—they can't come in; they don't have a key."

The words had no sooner left his mouth than he heard the distinctive squeak his front door made when it was slowly opened. Julia called, "Knock-knock! Aidan? We've been standing out here forever. Where are you?"

Lexie's mouth fell open in shock. "You forgot to lock the door?" Diving on her clothes, she started yanking them on, not even glancing at tags or attempting to make sure things weren't inside out.

"Hold on; I'll be right out," he called, trying to remember where the hell he'd thrown his pants. "Just a second."

"What are you . . . Oh, hell, sorry!" Julia said.

She hadn't waited. Right now, she stood in the arched doorway, apparently having gotten quite an eyeful. Throwing her hands over those eyes—a little too late—she began to back away. Somebody was apparently behind her because she said, "Back up. He needs a minute."

"What, did you catch him sleeping in his shorts?"

asked Mick, who, ignoring all boundaries, came walking into the room anyway.

Fortunately, Lexie had managed to find her skimpy underwear and her sweater and had pulled both on. Having stuck only one leg into her jeans as the other man intruded, though, she quickly leapt behind a chair with an embarrassed squeal.

"Would you please get out?" Aidan snapped.

"Whoa! Sorry, dude." The other man made that same dramatic cover-the-eyes move as Julia, then backed out, his amusement a little more obvious than his boss's had been.

Huh. And to think, yesterday he'd actually started to like being around these people again.

"Oh my God, I can't believe this. Literally caught with our pants down." Lexie looked like she wanted to sink through the floor.

Considering he wanted to pound Mick right through it, he thought he might be able to make a big enough hole.

She muttered something under her breath. "Fifty-two hours."

"What?"

She didn't repeat herself, instead saying, "They're going to think I'm a skank."

As ridiculous as that was, he didn't laugh at her, hearing her genuine concern. "Actually, I believe they're going to think you're a miracle worker. As far as I can recall, none of them have ever seen me with a woman in all the time they've known me. I'm a little private that way." Unable to resist, he lifted a hand to her cheek, rubbing his thumb across her full lips. "Today, I don't mind so much."

Other than Mick having seen her in her skimpy underwear.

Her stormy green eyes softened, and she tilted her head a little, curving into his touch, probably not even realizing she was doing it. Like they'd spent a whole lot more nights together than just the last one and were utterly familiar with one another.

But the mellow mood didn't last very long. Julia interrupted it, calling, "Hurry up—we need to talk to you."

Lexie pulled away and finished buttoning and zipping as she whispered, "I still can't believe you forgot to lock the door."

"I'm sorry," he said, pulling his clothes on. "I didn't lock it when they left last night. I thought we'd be leaving right away. Just zoned out about it."

She'd managed to work her way into her jeans, and appeared as presentable as a thoroughly made-love-to woman could look. The bare feet, tangled hair, and well-kissed lips were acceptable, but he quickly realized she had not been able to find her bra, and that soft sweater now looked utterly sinful.

"I'll go talk to them," he said, bending over to pick up the scrap of pink lace she'd apparently overlooked. Dangling it by the strap from his fingertip, he handed it to her, trying not to laugh as she snatched it away.

"Go ahead and laugh—ha-ha, very funny," she said. Then, smirking, added, "Just remember to zip up your fly before you go out there. Oh, but be careful with that zipper. I see I'm not the only one who didn't have any luck finding all of my underclothes."

He glanced down, realized she was right, that his fly was down, and actually did laugh. Even as he did so, he had to think how strange that laughter tasted in his mouth. It had been such a long time since he'd felt like this. Normal, a little goofy. Easily able to tease and play with a woman, to laugh at himself and at others.

Honestly, when he thought about it, he knew it had been longer than a year. Well before he'd decided to turn off and drop out of his life. In fact, he wasn't sure he ever had been like this. His earliest memories didn't include laughter—far from it. And his more recent ones, involving women, included sex but definitely not banter, flirtation, and good humor. Something about Lexie simply brought out an unexpected side to him.

Tucking his shirt into his pants, he walked out of the living room to the foyer, where Julia and Mick stood together. He opened his mouth to harass them for what they'd walked in on, then realized they weren't smiling, and in fact looked very serious. Aidan suddenly realized their early arrival might not have been a mere accident or miscalculation. "What is it?"

"I guess you haven't turned on the news today," Julia replied. "We heard it on the radio this morning and decided to head down early. I tried to call your cell phone."

Which was on his desk in the other room, out of earshot.

"Olivia and Derek are coming down later," she added.

He ran a hand through his tangled hair, trying to follow. "What, exactly, did you hear on the radio?"

"Something on the radio?" Lexie asked as she joined them from the other room, now fully dressed and trying to act like the whole embarrassing scene hadn't just taken place. "Was it about Vonnie?"

Crossing his arms and shaking his head, Mick answered, "There was an attack last night, here in Granville."

"Oh, no," Lexie whispered.

"We can't be sure it's related to the other kidnappings. It has similarities, but doesn't sound like this guy's MO."

"How so?" Aidan asked.

"Well, he stalked two girls together, stabbing one, taking the other. And it wasn't down in the bad area where you were attacked, Lexie, but at a movie theater in North Granville."

"Oh my God," Lexie whispered. "Who? Who are the girls?"

"They aren't releasing the identities of the victims," Julia said. She appeared sympathetic, as if knowing Lexie was already running down the names of every teenager she knew in town. Considering he'd seen a number of them Friday night, himself, he completely empathized.

"Apparently they can't make a positive ID yet. The news is saying there's a complication identifying which girl was taken and which one was left bleeding on the ground outside the theater," Mick explained.

Aidan didn't follow. "Why? What kind of complication?"

The other man shook his head in sadness and disgust. "I guess they were sisters."

Behind him, Lexie stiffened, and he knew her mind had immediately gone to the worst possible scenario. Aidan said, "There are a lot of families in this town, Lex. I'm sure it's not Walter's."

"Tell me everything," she told Mick. "What other details have they released?"

"That's . . . that's all, I think," he explained. "I'm sorry."

Lexie still wasn't satisfied. Her jaw shaking, her eyes enormous, she grabbed two fistfuls of Mick's shirt and physically shook him. "What else?"

Julia put a hand out, covering one of Lexie's. "Wait, I do know a little more."

Spinning around to look at the other woman, Lexie snapped, "Your ghost?"

Julia nodded, not taking offense at Lexie's tone, obviously knowing she was distraught. Not sure whether she was about to deliver good news, or bad, she hesitated.

"Well?" Lexie demanded.

Julia cleared her throat. "The problem isn't just that they're sisters. They actually can't tell for sure which one was taken and which was left because they are identical twins."

"Oh God," Lexie moaned. Aidan reached out to steady her, but Lexie, exhibiting the strength he already so admired, instead stiffened in resolve and simply said two words.

"Let's go."

Chapter 13

Last night, when he'd dragged a limp, lifeless form into her cell, Vonnie had begged her captor to unchain her. The girl, whom she'd immediately recognized from school as one of the Kirby twins, looked half dead. She crumpled to a heap on her stomach, her face turned toward Vonnie, her dark hair made darker with blood, her clothes drenched in it.

Worst, she was utterly quiet. Deathly still.

Refusing to let Vonnie help her, the monster hadn't spared a glance for his other victim on the hard floor before departing, saying he'd see them both—or maybe just one of them—in the morning. He'd slammed the metal door closed with a clang, cutting off their only source of light. She was left to lie here all through the dark night, not knowing if the person lying a few feet away from her was dying. Or already dead.

Vonnie had tried begging the girl to wake up—so she could unchain Vonnie, who could then save them both. She'd also, at times, held her breath in an effort to hear if Taylor or Jenny was taking any breaths of her own. She heard the creaking of the building and the groaning of old pipes and the scurry of creatures in the walls and her own heart beating. But from the unconscious girl, absolutely nothing.

Hour after hour, she peered into the darkness, straining her eyes, needing to know if she was talking to an injured friend, or a corpse.

At dawn, when sunshine had begun to slant in through the tiny barred window in the cell, she'd turned her head and watched. It had taken a long time, until that rectangle of light had created a solid shape on the cement, before she'd finally seen something.

A pale hand, moving ever so slightly against the filthy, blood-stained floor.

Thank you, Jesus.

Once she'd known the other teen was alive, Vonnie had begun talking to her in earnest, whispering reassurances that they were going to survive, that they had each other. She got no response, yet she still whispered, talking about how she'd ended up here, the things he'd done to her, the way she'd been feeling stronger hour by hour. She vowed retribution and she swore out a need for blood and released some of the rage she'd been hearing only in her head for days.

For some reason, no matter which twin was actually here, the girl next to her had become Jenny, because Jenny was the one she knew best. Jenny had been one of her first new friends at school. Jenny had been the one who'd walked her out Monday night and offered her a ride.

"I'm sorry," she said, starting to cry softly, then harder, wishing, for both their sakes, she'd taken that ride.

Vonnie tried to suck it up, tried to force herself to stop since she had no way to wipe away the tears or the snot. She hadn't really lost herself to weeping since she'd been brought in here—other than tears she'd shed when asking the monster not to kidnap somebody else. But the long, desperate hours of waiting for any kind of sign, and the continuing silence after that one small hand movement, appeared to have finally cracked her spirit.

"It's my fault," she said, her voice shaking with emotion and fatigue. "My fault he took you and I'm so sorry."

She didn't know if Jenny heard or was just coming out of whatever their attacker had done to her, but at last the girl let out a low groan. It was the first sound she'd made in hours.

"Jenny?" She bent her head as much as she could, peering down over the cot. "Oh God, please wake up. Come on. It's daytime; we haven't got much time."

Another groan.

"Oh, please, girl, please," she hissed. "He could come back at any time. You're not tied up; you can move if you only wake up. You need to snap out of it, come over here, and help unchain me so we can both get the hell out of here."

She knew even as she said the words that it was wishful thinking. Jenny wasn't even conscious, so the idea that she might be able to aid in their escape was crazy.

Still, the girl tried. As Vonnie watched, one of Jenny's bloody arms began to slide upward, the fingers inching on the rough cement. Making no sound, still flat on the cold floor, she kept trying, extending her arm outward, like she was trying to grab something. Her eyes remained closed, her bruised face expressionless. No other part of her moved except that arm, that hand, which she pushed and pushed.

"Come on, girl," Vonnie whispered. "You're okay; wake up, now."

Jenny's arm made a faint scratching sound as she strove on, until her fingertips emerged into the bright rectangle of sunshine on the floor. Vonnie wanted to cheer for her, watching as her hand pressed on, an inch at a time, into the light. It broke her heart to see how her friend was trying, how she reached for her, though she obviously had no strength to do more.

Finally, when the arm was fully extended, that pale, scratched hand slowly lifted a few inches off the floor, the fingers flexing, reaching . . . reaching. The tip of her index finger quivered with the effort to stay straight as the others curled down toward her palm.

Vonnie had taken an art history class, and she was instantly reminded of the ceiling on the Sistine Chapel. That extended arm, the fingertip touching God, all hope and prayer and faith expressed in the slightest of touches. It made her gasp, stopped her heart.

Then the hand crumpled to the floor. All movement ceased. And Vonnie's cellmate succumbed again to whatever blackness had kept her still throughout the long night hours.

"Thank you," she whispered, not sure she'd ever seen anything so heartbreaking as that poor, pathetic girl reaching to her from the shadows. "Thank you for trying."

Full of rage now, Vonnie strained against the chains, arching her back, tugging until her shoulders ached. She wished that bastard would come in here now; she felt fully capable of murdering him with her bare hands. She only needed one free and she'd kill the motherfucker for everything he'd done—most recently for causing the sad desperation of the girl lying on the floor.

"Gonna get you," she muttered. "You're gonna pay for this." She worked on her hands, flexing and excrcising them as she had since they'd fallen asleep yesterday, wanting to keep them limber. She pulled her hands apart, working that drying, tired tape, stretching it just a little farther.

She'd have a chance; she had to believe that, simply had to, and she wanted to be ready when it came. Because she was going to survive this.

"And you're going to survive it, too," she told her friend. "I'm going to get us out of here. I swear to you, I'll get us out."

*   *   *

Sunday, 9:45 a.m.

Lexie couldn't stop shaking. Her whole body was racked by tremors as she sat in the passenger's seat, craning forward to peer out the windshield as if doing so would get her to the hospital that much sooner. Beside her, Aidan gripped the steering wheel in tight fists, his back ramrod straight, every muscle straining.

She knew he wanted to tell her everything would be all right.

They both knew that would be a lie.

Using Aidan's phone, she'd tried calling Walter and had gotten no answer. Cursing the fact that she'd lost her own phone, wondering if he'd been trying to call her all night, she'd asked Aidan to take her to the hospital she herself had left less than twenty-four hours ago. The radio newscaster had reported that one of the girls had been taken there.

Of the other, there was absolutely no sign.

The few other reported details were sketchy. After they'd closed up for the night, movie theater employees had discovered a bloody teenage girl lying in the parking lot. They told police she'd left the building fifteen minutes earlier with another girl, who was nowhere to be seen.

Something deep inside her already knew, without a doubt, who the girls had been.

Identical twins. How many sets of identical girls, teenagers, lived in Granville? She had spent a lot of time with the Kirby girls and their friends over the years and knew a lot of the families. Plus she'd been talking to teachers, students, and administrators from both local high schools in recent weeks. And she could not recall one other pair of identical girls of driving age.

Walter's daughters *had* to have been the ones who were attacked. The question was, why?

So far she'd been able to think of only one possible answer.

"Do you think he stalked them because of my articles?" she whispered, voicing the awful theory that had gripped her almost immediately—that she could be at fault.

He didn't try to calm her with some kind of assurances that she couldn't know it was the Kirby twins. They were both well beyond that. Instead, Aidan said, "Lexie, I know you're upset, and you have reason to be, but think about it. If this guy got angry about your articles and wanted to get back at you, and at Walter, the editor of the paper, wouldn't he have done it a month ago when you first exposed him?"

She hesitated, thinking about it, then slowly nodded. "You'd think so. But maybe he heard I was digging into it again and wanted to scare us off."

"By attacking the beautiful, vivacious twin daughters of a prominent, well-known, well-loved family? Not only will that *not* get the local press to back off, it's going to bring the eyes of the national media onto this town," he said, so reasonable and thoughtful.

Unable to prevent a note of bitterness, she replied, "They sure weren't flying in here to cover the story when it was a bunch of missing girls from the wrong side of the tracks."

"I know," he replied, sounding as bothered by that as she was. "But to be fair, this is the first time there's an actual victim to prove a crime occurred. Nobody can say the Kirby girls weren't really attacked when one of them is lying in the hospital."

"I suppose," she admitted.

"The point is, this guy is not stupid. If he wanted to get you to back off, victims as high profile as the Kirby twins are the last ones he would target. Something else happened; something else drove him to do this." He reached over and grabbed her hand, squeezing it. "This is not your fault."

He made perfect sense, and logically, she knew he was right. But deep down that guilt still clawed at her. Even worse than the guilt, though, was her fear for the girls. Having met them as soon as she'd moved here, Lexie had watched them grow up from gawky tweens to the young women they were today. She had treated them like the kid sisters she'd never had. She had spent nights in their house, braiding their hair, playing board games. Walter's family had become closer to her than the few remaining members of her real one.

As if that weren't bad enough, her heart was also breaking for Walter and Ann-Marie, who'd already been through so much. They'd thought they had emerged from their long, dark tunnel, with only good days to look forward to. Now they'd been thrust into every parent's worst nightmare.

One stabbed. One taken. Two lives at stake.

They had to do something, soon. "Aidan, is there anything you can . . ."

"I'm going over to the crime scene after I drop you off," he told her, anticipating the request. His words low, he wouldn't look over at her as he said, "I can't imagine the locals have covered every single thing, so I'll start there. If I don't get anything, and if I can't find something I can touch, you can get me into the Kirby house, all right?"

Something to touch. A hair clip, a key, a torn scrap of clothing.

A drop of blood.

Anything to connect him with the girls.

"My God," she muttered, "I still can't wrap my mind around it."

"Everyone's going to be working on this, Lex," he told her as they drew within a few blocks of the hospital. "I guarantee you, Dunston won't be able to impede this investigation. State and probably even federal officials are going to get involved, since this is a forcible kidnapping."

"Yes, but will they do it in time to save her?" Thinking of Vonnie, she clarified. "To save them?"

"I don't know."

Glancing over at him, seeing the stubborn set of his jaw, the fierce look of determination in his eyes, she felt sure of one thing. Whether anybody else got involved in time to help those girls, Aidan wasn't going to give up.

He was in this now, part of this. Even if they hadn't spent this morning making amazing love, he would still be here, committed and by her side until the very end. Whatever demons had kept him from doing what he was born to do had either been exorcised or at least shoved away while he focused on this case, these missing teenagers.

"My whole team will focus on nothing else, twenty-four/seven, until it's done," he promised her. "Julia and Mick are already heading out to that old plantation house and Olivia and Derek are meeting them on site. They should know within a couple of hours if Jessie Leonard really died there, and how she died."

She wanted to know that, wanted the girl's mother to know the truth. But right now, that wasn't as important as helping the girls who were still—please God—alive.

"Plus, Julia told me she intended to go look into county property records and see who owns that place. I can't see a bunch of men using it month after month without knowing the rightful owner isn't going to stumble out there and catch them at their dirty games."

"I'd actually thought of that last night right before I fell asleep on the couch," Lexie admitted, just now remembering. "I'm good at doing grunt research. I had intended to offer to do it today, while you all did your thing." She didn't add that she'd wanted to do it specifically because she did not want to go into that evil old house. "I, uh, might still be able to. I honestly don't know what I'll be doing all day."

What if Walter and Ann-Marie didn't want her there, keeping vigil with them for their daughters? For all that Aidan could logically say it wasn't her fault, would the grieving parents see it the same way?

As they pulled into the hospital entrance, she could

only hope they would know she would never have intentionally done anything to put their children in danger. She would give anything to be able to go back and change it if it would prevent this from ever happening.

And if she ever discovered she had somehow triggered that monster into targeting Walter's daughters, Lexie would never forgive herself, not for all the days of her life.

"I'll park and come in with you for a minute before going over to the crime scene," he said, obviously not wanting to drop her off at the hospital entrance.

Suddenly thinking of something, she realized there was a better way for Aidan to build a connection between himself and the Kirby twins. "I have to ask—isn't a real, physical touch between you and another person better than touching an object?"

He nodded.

"So instead of going over to the scene, why don't you stay here and get the touch you really need? It's better than trying to find some random drop of blood on the ground."

"It would be, but how would the parents feel about that?"

"Walter knows who you are and what you can do. I'm sure he can get you in to see her."

She swallowed, thinking about her own words.

Her.

Jenny or Taylor? The sweet academic or the fiery bad girl?

Which twin was fighting for her life in the hospital? Which was in the clutches of a brutal psychopath?

And which was worse?

Sunday, 10:00 a.m.

Jack Dunston had spent a lot of years being a yes-man, and he knew it. It hadn't really seemed to matter. In a town like this, was turning a blind eye to the occasional parking ticket or speeding charge leveled against one of the more important residents really so bad? Had anybody ever been hurt because he sometimes leaned on kids for riding skateboards too close to the bank, or because he arranged for a tow-away of a car parked once too often in front of the mayor's trash cans? Did anybody really care?

Probably not.

But everything had changed. His days of not caring, of being the yes-man, had come to an end. Some would say not a moment too soon.

It had started last evening, when he'd gotten in his truck and followed that van on a long, fruitless drive all over the county. It had been completely confirmed later in the night, when he'd received the call about the bloody attack against two good kids whose father was one of the few people in this town Jack would actually like to have for a friend. For all that the newsman had given him shit over the years, and seen him for exactly what he was, Jack had always respected Walter Kirby. It pained him now to see the grieving father about as close to breaking as any human being he had ever known.

Having just finished interviewing both the girls' parents, he intended to head back over to the crime scene, to make sure it was being processed correctly. His technicians were young and pretty inexperienced, certainly not used to dealing with the kind of violence that had taken place outside that theater last night.

This wasn't a drug deal or a simple burglary. There was innocent blood on the streets of Granville. He'd never have believed it possible and had to wonder if he'd been wrong about everything. Certainly he'd been stupid. He'd been lazy and a little too quick to listen to folks who didn't believe the crazy, wild theories that turned up in the newspaper.

Only now they didn't seem so crazy and wild.

What if there really was a serial killer lurking in Granville? What if he really had been picking off its residents one by one for the past three years while Jack Dunston kept opening up his fridge and pulling out beers and twenties?

If that was true, he'd honestly deserve whatever scorn and hatred got heaped on his head by all those angry families.

Well, that was over now. There could be no more sitting on the sidelines, letting things play out. He was in this. No more laid-back, good old boy, he was the chief of police. From here on out, he would do everything he could to find out what in the hell was going on here, and bring those responsible for it to justice.

"Can you even imagine such a thing?" a voice said, surprising Jack as he stood in a private alcove just inside the hospital entrance, finishing up his notes from the interview before heading out to his squad car.

"I just heard the news," added Mayor Cunningham, *tsk*ing a little as he joined him. Though the man was, as always, well dressed and groomed, he didn't look his normal, happy self. Dark circles under his heavy-lidded eyes said he hadn't slept well last night and his jaw twitched, as if he were gritting his teeth.

Nerves working on him. The easygoing mayor was worried about something.

"Dark day for this town," Jack replied.

"How's Kirby holdin' up?"

"About like you'd expect."

"Bet it was some tramp passin' through," the mayor said, the weakness of his tone saying even he didn't believe the bullshit excuse. "Nobody from 'round here would evah do such a thing."

A few days ago, Jack would probably have agreed with him. Not anymore. The blinders were completely off.

Pasting on that fake-caring expression that had put him into office election after election, for the past twenty years, the mayor patted Jack's shoulder. "Well, now, you be sure to let me know if there's anything I can do to . . ."

"There is."

"Excuse me?"

"We need to talk."

Cunningham's smile faded. " 'Bout what?"

Staring directly into the man's slightly bloodshot eyes, Jack replied, "About where you and all your friends were heading last night."

Cunningham's normally pink-cheeked face went a bit pale and his deep-set, beady eyes darted back and forth. Used to having his posse around him most times—Lawton, Underwood, and the others—he looked a little like a cornered rat. "I don't know what you're talkin' about. We had a financial plannin' meeting, just like every month." He let out one of his hearty laughs, only it came out weak and phony. "Stock market isn't bein' too kind, lately."

"I saw you," Jack replied flatly. "Saw you get in that white van. I followed you all the way down Old Terrytown Road."

Pale? No. Now the mayor's face looked about the color of wet flour. He opened his mouth, snapped it closed, looking around more frantically this time. The man didn't know what to say if his words hadn't been put in his mouth by someone a whole lot smarter or written by a speech writer.

"Why'd you just drive around and come back to town?" Jack asked. "You slowed down once, like you were gonna turn, then sped up like y'all were being chased by demons. And I somehow doubt it was because you suddenly spotted me a quarter-mile behind you."

The mayor started shaking his head, mumbling, "No, I can't talk right now. I have places to go."

"Heading to church to sing nice and loud with all your friends?" Jack inched closer, staring down at the mayor, his spine a mite straighter than it had been in a whole lotta years. "I am going to find out what you're all up to. And I'll tell you this: If any of you had anything to do with those missing girls, I will make sure you pay for it."

"No!" the other man insisted, his eyes as round as tennis balls. "No, they're just trashy little sluts, runaways, like you thought."

"Including the Kirby girls?" he snapped.

"They're not connected; they got nothin' to do with us, don'tcha see? We never had them out t' the club—wouldn't do that. What kind of man would do that?" He was babbling now, scared and almost weepy. "The other ones, they're just runaways, Jack. You gotta believe me!"

"The club?" he asked, zoning in on the words that most interested him. "What club would that be? And where? Is it someplace on Terrytown Road?"

"No, no, forget I said anything!"

"Too late." He reached out and put a steadying hand on the other man's shoulder, sensing he wanted to bolt. Certain Cunningham knew a lot more than he was ready to say, he decided to try another tactic. "Look, Mayor, we both know something bad is happening here in our town. People are being hurt. We don't want that, do we? Neither of us."

The older man's chest puffed out. "No, of course we don't!" He wagged an index finger in Jack's face. "You find the awful man who did that to those beautiful Kirby girls last night."

"When I do," Jack murmured, "am I going to find out he spent the earlier part of the evening with you in that van? As I recall, you were all back in town by eight thirty. Plenty of time for anybody to stalk the twins."

The mayor hesitated, his jowly chin trembling. "You can't think . . ."

"I don't know what to think," he admitted. "But I do know there are a whole lot of people with some ugly secrets around here. If any of those secrets can help me figure out what's been happening to all those girls, believe me, I will not stop digging until I uncover them."

The mayor's bushy brow drew down over his eyes as he tried to reassert some kind of authority. "You're not paid to dig into people's private business."

Jack stepped closer until their faces were mere inches apart and his hand tightened on the other man's shoulder. His voice not much more than a whisper, he said, "And neither one of us is paid to let anybody get away with murder."

Their stares locked. Looking at the mayor's face, he'd swear he saw fear and cowardice. But murder? Serial murder? It seemed impossible.

"You do some thinking," he said, stepping away, speaking in a normal tone of voice. "And I'll be by later so we can talk some more."

That seemed to be enough for Mayor Bobby Cunningham. Without another word, he spun around and left the alcove. Hearing the *whoosh* of the sliding-glass doors, he didn't suppose the man had even waited for them to open all the way before he'd stormed out into the sunshine, probably beelining for his cronies to ask them what he should say.

Hopefully, the mayor's panic would spread and one of the members of their so-called club would get nervous enough to talk.

Tucking his notebook into his pocket, Jack headed out, too, but he didn't make it quite as far as the mayor had. Because as he turned the corner of the alcove, he saw two people standing behind a nearby column, eyeing him.

The reporter, Lexie Nolan, and her moody boyfriend. Christ Almighty, just what he needed. If they hadn't eavesdropped on his conversation with the mayor, he'd eat his own shoe.

He put a hand up, ready to tell her he had no comment, but before he could do so, the dark-haired man with those fierce, gray eyes spoke. "Chief, if you really want to get to the bottom of what's happening around here, maybe you and I should go somewhere and talk."

Jack hesitated.

"We heard some of what you said," Lexie admitted. Though frowning, her eyes were perhaps not quite as hard as he was used to. "I have to admit, I've been wondering if you were one of *them*. But I guess not."

Stung, he shot back, "I'm a member of the Granville Police Department, young lady. That's the only group I'm a member of."

She and the man exchanged a look, as if they weren't sure whether they could trust an officer of the law. Jack bristled for a moment, then forced himself to calm down, knowing he hadn't given this woman much reason to trust him. He regretted that now, not that this was the time or place to talk about that.

"If you have information that can help me solve this case, I'd like to hear it, Mr ...?"

"McConnell. Aidan McConnell."

He thought for a second, then placed the name. An angry sigh left his mouth and he prepared to push past them. "Oh, for God's sake, I don't have time to deal with phony psychics who play on people's fears and superstitions."

"We were at their clubhouse," Lexie said. She stepped closer, putting a hand on his arm. "We know what they do there; we know who they bring there. We also think we know which girl actually died there." Her stare unwavering, she added, "I suspect some of her bones are probably locked up in your office right this minute."

Hesitating, wondering if she was going to accuse him of something, he looked back and forth between the couple. They said nothing, merely waiting, leaving the ball in his court.

He considered it. The psychic stuff might be all hooey, but if they really had been out snooping around and had found something, he wanted to know about it.

"All right," he told them. "Let's go talk. But fast—I want to get back out to the crime scene."

The stranger bent to kiss Lexie's temple. "I know you're anxious to go find Walter and his wife. Let me do this and I'll join you in a few minutes."

Turning her face up to him, she nodded, which enabled Jack to get a better look at those bruises on her neck. He cleared his throat, mumbling, "Sorry if I was a little gruff with you yesterday."

She waved off the apology. "Now that I know you're not completely corrupt, I can forgive and forget."

Corrupt. Damn the woman was mouthy. But she was also injured, frightened, and visibly exhausted. So he let it slide.

"I'll see you soon," she told her friend. "I imagine Walter and Ann-Marie are up in ICU."

Confused, Jack tilted his head. "Why would you think that?"

"I just figured, since she's been here all night . . . Oh God, is she still in surgery?"

The woman hadn't heard. She'd come here thinking she would be helping a friend watch over his hospitalized child.

He didn't know Lexie Nolan well, but he did know she was very close to the Kirbys. She must have been out of touch; otherwise he felt pretty damn sure Walter would have called her and told her the whole story.

"Well? Where is she? They didn't transfer her, did they?" she asked.

Jack couldn't hide his sympathetic frown.

Seeing it, the boyfriend made a small sound, grasping the truth, then put a hand on Lexie's shoulder. "Lex?" he murmured.

Her mouth trembled, and Jack could hear the quick, deep breaths the feisty young reporter was sucking in through her mouth as the possibilities began to flood her mind.

He doubted any of them were as bad as the real thing.

"Where *is* she?"

With genuine regret, he told her the truth. "I'm sorry, Ms. Nolan. But the little Kirby girl isn't in ICU, or in surgery. She's downstairs. In the morgue."

Chapter 14

Aidan couldn't leave her.

He wanted to talk to Chief Dunston, but there was no way he was going to send Lexie to the morgue by herself to console her friends, whose daughter had just been murdered.

Murder. It didn't touch many lives, but when it touched yours, you never got over it. This day would never leave Lexie's memory.

After they'd heard the awful news, she had nearly collapsed. He'd taken her into his arms and held her while she sobbed, feeling her tears soak his shoulder and her body quake with to-the-bone grief. Asking Dunston if he could come to the crime scene later, he'd pulled Lexie to a bench in the alcove and stayed there with her for the past twenty minutes, offering his support, which was all he could do.

"She was just a girl," she kept repeating, "just a sweet, wonderful girl."

Several times she'd added, "Goddamn it, I don't even know *which* girl."

According to Dunston, nobody did. Before he'd left, he'd told them the Kirbys had been downstairs all night, refusing to leave, even after admitting they couldn't identify the body. He didn't know that he'd ever heard anything more brutal. A father and mother could not even tell which of their daughters was lying dead on a slab in the morgue.

Lexie had mumbled something about a birthmark, but Aidan had to assume there was some kind of problem with that, otherwise the victim would surely have been ID'd. He hadn't questioned her about it, though, knowing Lexie needed to accept the truth of it before getting lost in the ugly, minute details. Dunston had told him a state expert was coming down later today to conduct an autopsy; perhaps that would resolve the issue.

Finally, when she seemed able to stand again, she said, "Okay. Let's go find Walter and Ann-Marie."

"You're sure?" he asked.

She nodded, then pushed herself to her feet. When he did the same, she leaned in to him for a moment, taking a deep breath. Also, he knew, taking a little strength for the ordeal to come.

Putting an arm around her shoulders, he walked with her down the quiet corridors of Granville Memorial Hospital. She moved slowly, trudging, as if already in a funeral march. Her eyes were still moist, but mingled with her obvious grief was worry—for the parents, for the younger sisters. And still that hint of guilt she couldn't push away, the fear that she had brought this hellish punishment down on her boss's family.

He couldn't make her believe that wasn't true; she was smart enough that she'd accept it herself eventually. Aidan also had to wonder, though, if her boss ever would. The man was likely carrying that same cross. He'd made the decision to run Lexie's articles in the first place. Plus, he had been the one to push Lexie into going back to the story she'd already abandoned.

Steeling himself for his meeting with a man who'd just lost his child, he reminded himself that this was far different than the last time. Walter Kirby was, according to everything he'd heard, a wonderful, loving man. Nothing like Ted Remington. Still, he couldn't prevent himself from keeping a protective arm across Lexie's shoulders when they reached the entrance to the morgue. He didn't think Kirby would be the type to lash out and blame anybody else he could, but he wasn't taking any chances and wanted to be able to hustle Lexie out of there if necessary.

When they pushed open the swinging doors into the small, stark waiting area, and a red-faced, middle-aged man looked up and saw them there, he realized it wasn't going to be necessary. Because the man—Walter Kirby—slowly rose, tears streaming down his face, and opened his arms to her.

Lexie flew into them. "Oh God, I'm so sorry." When Mrs. Kirby rose from where she'd been sitting and embraced Lexie as well, she said them again.

"Our baby girl, Lex, she's gone. He hurt her . . . he hurt her so much," Walter said, every word stumbling on a tiny sob.

Aidan remained away from them, not wanting to intrude, but he listened to the conversation, all his focus on finding out who had done this. Not having known the family, he was the only one able to separate himself from the grief of this awful thing enough to think only about the case. And on finding the other teenage girls whose lives were still at stake.

"We don't know her; we can't tell. Our baby, and we can't tell," Kirby said, his voice breaking as he buried his face in a handkerchief.

Lexie, her face wet with fresh tears, asked, "Why? I don't understand." Her voice tentative, as if she feared upsetting them, she asked, "Taylor's birthmark?"

Walter turned away, his big body racked with fresh sobs. It was the pale, quiet wife who explained, her voice as brittle as chipped ice. "He cut her throat, gouged at her. More than once. If there was a birthmark there, well, it isn't there anymore."

Lexie swayed a little and the last bit of color dropped out of her face. "Oh no."

Mrs. Kirby wrapped her arms around herself, shaking. "I could always tell them apart, even without that birthmark. Always, from the time they were young." A sound that was half laugh, half sob emerged from her mouth. "By their smiles, their moods, the way they talked, the way they carried themselves." She shook her head back and forth, again and again, muttering, "But not now. Not now. My beautiful girl, everything that made her who she was is gone and I see just a shell of my child. And I don't even know which one."

"It's wrong," Walter said, his back still to all of them. "Wrong on every level to not know which daughter to mourn and which one to hope might still have a chance to come home." Leaning over, he put a hand on the wall, flat, his fingers spread, as if needing to hold himself up. "I can't even go into the chapel and pray because I don't know which one I'm praying for."

Lexie walked over to her friend and put a hand on his shoulder. "Taylor and Jenny were part of each other. Two halves of a whole. No matter which name you use, you're praying for *both* of them."

The man turned to look at her, his shoulders relaxing a little, though he remained unable to speak. His wife, who had lowered herself into a chair a foot from where Aidan stood, looked up at him and raised a curious eyebrow. Aidan squatted down in front of her and introduced himself, adding, "I'm so sorry for your loss."

She nodded slowly. "You're the psychic who has been working to find this evil man."

"Yes," he replied.

She reached for one of his hands, slipping her cold one into it, and squeezed. "You'll find our other daughter."

His breath caught in his throat and his heart seemed to pause midbeat. The room, which had felt cold when he'd entered, suddenly grew hot, stifling. *Suffocating.* He had the urge to tug his constricting shirt away from his throat just to get some much-needed air.

Her husband overheard and turned around, finally

noticing Aidan was in the room. His eyes lit up for the first time since they'd walked through the door. And, though they didn't say a word, Aidan knew both parents had focused every bit of their hope, every emotion they possessed, on him and his ability to save their other child.

Staying there and letting them was one of the hardest things he had ever done.

Because his first instinct was to go. To get up and walk out before he could do something insane like promise he'd find the other girl before it was too late.

Oh, he had no intention of giving up on this case, and he intended to find out who was behind this awful string of crimes. But he did not want all hopes pinned on him, couldn't offer promises of salvation that he knew from horrible past experiences were impossible to keep.

"Mr. McConnell?" Kirby asked.

He steeled himself for it, for the request. The demand. *Promise you'll find my child.*

"Will you do something for us? Please?"

Rising, he turned to face the man, seeing Lexie watching from a few feet away, stricken, as if knowing what was about to happen. The word *No* came to his mouth, came close to spilling out, but before they could, Walter made his request with quiet dignity and grief.

"Will you please use whatever powers you have to tell us which of our daughters we're going to be burying this week?"

He remained very still, surprised, yes, but also angry at himself. He'd let his past fears and hang-ups dictate his present actions, and had almost done something heartless. Lexie had once accused him of being cowardly and in the moment that just passed he'd come about as close to it as he ever wanted to be in his life.

"I'm not sure I'll be able to," he told the man, "but I will try." Realizing he could do more than try, he added, "If I can't, I do know someone who can help."

Olivia Wainwright would hate it. She used her abilities only in extreme cases, and then only because a cause of death couldn't be determined due to the age or condition of whatever remains had been found.

In this case, they knew the cause of death. And it was an awful, brutally painful one.

If she came here and she touched that body, it would mean she would have to suffer that pain for herself. She'd have to endure whatever that teenage girl had endured in her final two minutes and ten seconds in order to allay these parents' suffering.

Honestly, he didn't know if she would. He didn't know that *he* would, in her place.

Hopefully, though, it wouldn't come to that. He had never tried actively tapping into the thoughts of someone he already knew was dead, though he'd certainly caught remnants and emotions they'd left behind. But it could work.

And if it helped to end the suffering of the grieving people in this room—including Lexie—he was more than willing to try his damnedest.

Sunday, 12:25 p.m.

The new girl had apparently survived the night.

He kept his eyes on the monitor, sitting in the kitchen where his mother had once busied herself baking nothing and drinking away her humanity. Having watched all morning, he'd noticed right away when the crumpled form on the basement floor began to move.

The surveillance system had video only, no sound, so he couldn't hear what she said, but Vonnie obviously became very excited and spoke to her companion. The newcomer fidgeted, moving an arm, then a leg, but didn't try to roll over. Probably because of the small knife sticking out of her back.

It certainly hadn't been a death strike, just something quick and shallow to shock her. Nor had he intended for her to be unconscious for quite so long when he struck her in the head with an old wooden baseball bat. Well, he never had been much of a baseball player; sports had been Jed's purview. Guess he didn't know when to pull his swing.

But no matter. She'd survived.

The new one wouldn't need to eat or drink yet, and should be kept hungry and thirsty to better break her and keep her docile. Vonnie, however, probably did require some nourishment, so he prepared her a liquid meal. And because he didn't like the energy with which she'd been moving lately, and the quick responses during their last conversation, he opened a handful of capsules and dumped their contents into the drink before he stirred it up.

"Ready for me, ladies?" he asked, glancing again at the monitor, seeing that Vonnie was still leaning down as much as she could, talking to her unmoving companion.

Carrying the drink, he turned to leave the kitchen, then remembered his disguise. The mask lay on the counter, its jolly smile looking evil even before he put it on. He had enjoyed wearing the thing for the past week, but had also been looking forward to taking it off and revealing himself to Vonnie. She would undoubtedly lose what little sanity she had left when she realized who had taken her.

"No, not yet," he told himself. He didn't want to give up the game completely while the Kirby girl had yet to be played with.

"The Kirby girl," he mused, realizing he never had found out which one he'd grabbed and which one he'd hacked the throat out of.

Of course, he had intended to take Taylor, the one who drove the VW Beetle he'd seen last Monday night. Finding out which GHS student drove the car had taken almost no effort at all; he'd simply watched her get into it after the game Friday, hearing one of her friends call her by name just before she drove away.

Problem was, when he'd tracked her down late last

night, she hadn't been alone. She'd had her twin sister with her and though he'd stalked them through the parking lot, and heard snatches of their conversation, he hadn't heard enough to identify them. Some keys had been tossed between them, so he wasn't even sure who usually drove the damned car.

In the end, it hadn't mattered. One was dead, one in his basement, so neither could say a word to anyone about having seen him last Monday night. Nor, he suspected, had they told anyone before now.

"Definitely not," he told himself. Vonnie—clever little Vonnie—had been right about that. If he'd been spotted, somebody would almost surely have come to talk to him by now.

Still, better safe than sorry. He had learned at a young age to do whatever he had to in order to keep his secrets. As boys, he and Jed had gotten quite good at concealing what happened behind the closed doors of this house. Lying, hiding bruises, never letting on about the sadistic games their parents had liked to play with them in the basement.

Jed's father's abuse had been raw and brutal.

Hers—his own mother's—had somehow been worse. To sit there and laugh, drunkenly reading them bedtime stories, even while the beatings and the rapes were going on . . . God, how he'd hated her. But they'd never told anyone.

"Never let outsiders know your business."

Jed had shared his deep need for privacy, which was one reason they had kept their past relationship secret once he'd come back here to Granville. Nobody else needed to know his mother had once been married to Jed's father. Like two soldiers who'd come through the same bloody battle, they had kept their horrific history just between them.

Horrific. Yes, that was the word. He sometimes wondered how his stepbrother had survived, stayed sane, once it had been just him and his father in this house.

He didn't want to think about that. Jed was long past being hurt now.

Enough. Time to visit the little women.

Young Miss Kirby—Taylor or Jenny—may have moved, but she wasn't back to normal yet. He needed to get down there and restrain her before she got to that point. So he donned the mask he'd been holding.

He thought about wearing a hood, instead, but decided against it. It probably wasn't necessary, not on this visit, since his new visitor was as weak as a kitten. But next time, when she was more clearheaded, he might need to make other arrangements. He'd taken care to never turn his back on Vonnie, fearing even the color of his hair might give her a clue to his identity before he was ready for her to figure it out. Once the other one was fully conscious, he'd have to be especially cautious. For now, though, he should be all right with just the plastic mask.

Making his way down the steep stairs, he stopped to unlock the first metal door. He stepped inside, turned, relocked it, then proceeded down the narrow hallway, lit only by one bare bulb above his head. He had another small light he used when reading to his visitors, but it wasn't on. It sat right outside the next heavy door, beside the stool on which he usually sat during his story-time visits.

Hmm. He wondered what kinds of stories Miss Kirby liked to hear.

Perhaps *Arabian Nights*. Oh, how he had loved that book as a child, partly because *she* had never read it aloud to them. He'd read it on his own, pretending he and Jed could fly away on a magic carpet, far from Jed's father and his own whore of a mother. Never to return to this awful town.

He had returned, though. And poor Jed had never gotten to leave.

Slipping the key into the large, old-fashioned lock, he

entered the cell. "Good morning, ladies," he said in his most cheery voice. "Sleep well?"

"She's in a bad way," Vonnie said, not even attempting to be pleasant.

"But she's alive, right?" he asked. "She's been moving, fidgeting all morning, so she can't be too badly hurt."

"Please, you gotta let me help her."

He lowered Vonnie's drink to a rickety old table that stood by the door. "Really? Do you think we should *do* something with her?"

Vonnie watched him suspiciously from her cot. "I'll do it. Just unchain me and I'll take care of her." Even from here he saw the way her throat worked as she swallowed. "I won't try to run away, I swear. I just want to make sure she's okay."

"Oh, how sweet! You helping a snotty bitch who would never even have spoken to you if you hadn't transferred to her school. Nice little white girls from the suburbs don't usually associate with *your* kind, you know."

"You're wrong."

Oooh, kitten had her claws out. It was a good thing he'd spiked that drink, because Vonnie appeared to have regained some of her fighting spirit.

"She's my friend. She offered to drive me home last Monday night."

He *tsk*ed. "You probably should have taken her up on that offer, dear." Then, thinking about it, he asked, "Do you happen to know which twin this is?"

Her eyes grew rounder. "You don't?"

"No, I haven't got a clue."

She appeared astonished by that, which disappointed him. Usually Vonnie wasn't so lacking in vision. How could she not have immediately seen what he'd done to cover all the bases?

"Well, then, how do you know you got the right one, the one who might have seen you following me last week?"

He laughed wickedly. *That's for me to know and you to find out*.

But why not let her find out now? If Miss Kirby here was playing possum and was a little more conscious than she appeared, he couldn't think of a better way to coax a reaction out of her.

"I don't," he told Vonnie, though his eyes remained on his other young friend. "But you see, it doesn't matter. Because before I took this one, I slit her sister open and left her stone-cold dead on the ground. She won't ever be talking to anyone again."

There might have been a twitch, maybe a tiny sound, but the unconscious girl did not cry out or scream or well up in tears.

Okay. She was really still unconscious. Little weakling.

Tempted to say more, he thought how it would both upset Vonnie, and amuse him. He wanted to describe how he'd hacked at the other one's throat, and why. It hadn't been entirely necessary, it had just given him a kick to think that, just as he didn't know which girl he'd killed—since it had been dark and he'd had to work fast—the police might not be able to figure it out, either.

He could easily find out which girl was lying on the floor by lifting her head and looking at her throat, but something about not knowing made it all the more delicious. Because, like all the other girls, it really didn't *matter* who they were once they arrived in his basement. They were toys for him to play with—anonymous, nameless, mere instruments of his amusement.

Vonnie was the only one who'd ever been more than that. Which would make the eventual breaking of her psyche all the more wonderful when it finally happened.

Almost as wonderful was thinking how the Kirbys must be feeling.

He'd originally considered taking both twins, but kidnapping two girls would have doubled the risk. Besides, he loved the idea of the Kirbys having to grieve for one daughter they knew was dead while at the same time holding out vain hope that the other might escape her sister's fate. All the while not knowing which was which.

It would be agonizing.

And that simply delighted him.

There was one more benefit: Making the identification more difficult might keep people from wondering too much about a motive, trying to figure out if the dead girl had any connection to him.

Which she did. All the girls did, of course. He never did anything without knowing exactly why he was doing it.

He didn't elaborate on any of that, though. Vonnie was a little too focused to waste any more time. He needed her drugged.

"Now," he said, picking up the drink and carrying it over to the restrained teenager. "Drink up. You must be hungry, so I went ahead and made you one of those instant meals. It's very nutritious."

She said nothing, still visibly stunned by what he'd just said about the other girl's sister. Funny, he wouldn't have expected Vonnie to care so much. She was so smart, had been so determined all her life to get out of the awful nightmare in which she lived, he would never have imagined that looking-out-for-number-one gene hadn't been clawed into her genetic code.

"Lift your head," he told her, guiding the flexible straw toward her mouth.

She watched him closely, hesitating for an instant.

"Come on, now, you have to drink or you'll never be able to help your friend over there."

"Please don't hurt her any more," she whispered.

"Do what you're told and maybe I won't."

That got her attention and she carefully sucked up a mouthful—a small one, like always, as if each time she knew he might have filled the glass with bug spray.

"See? Nice and nutritious. Milk and vitamins," he told her.

She swallowed a mouthful, then sucked again, slowly, smart enough to know if she slurped she'd throw everything back up.

He watched her down every drop, then, once she was finished, straightened and backed toward the door. "I guess our friend can stay where she is there for a little longer while I put together something for her to lie down on. Can't very well chain her to the floor."

"I'm surprised you didn't think ahead and have something made."

Sneering beneath the mask, he snapped, "Well, I'm surprised you were a stupid enough little bitch to let your mother trade you to a bunch of old men for drug money."

And with that, he left the room, slamming the metal door hard, the keys shaking in his hands. He hadn't liked the reminder that he had forgotten to make up a place for his new guest.

"Know-it-all slut," he mumbled as he pulled off the mask and trudged toward the steps. "Damned teenagers today, nothing but lip." Sometimes the girl was a little too smart for her own good.

Maybe he wouldn't bring Vonnie anything to drink again tomorrow. Or the next day. See if she was quite so sassy when her tongue was so swollen and dry it would choke her if she didn't turn her head to the side.

"See how you like that!" he yelled before exiting the second door.

Vonnie heard the echo of his angry yell, knew she had enraged him, but she didn't respond. She was too busy listening, waiting for the sound of his footsteps to die away, wanting to be sure he wasn't going to pop back in and surprise her.

Think fast, girl; move quick. She had only a few minutes before the drugs he'd given her hit her bloodstream. She wasn't stupid enough to think he had forgotten this time. His insistence that she drink every drop, and the faintly bitter taste of the last couple of sips, had convinced her he'd packed a massive dose in this latest cup.

"Not gonna work, psycho-prick. You're not gonna drug me again," she muttered, twisting her head around to face the rough cement wall. She wished her hands were free, would give anything to be able to stick her fingers down her throat, but she didn't have that luxury. Nor did she have time to waste continuing to try to work her hands out of the bindings.

She had to get the drugs out of her system now, before she digested them. Because once she had, she would be useless, both to herself and to the girl lying helpless on the floor.

Thinking of the awful things he'd done was enough to make the milk in her stomach churn, but no more. There was, however, one way to get rid of it for sure. She leaned close to the wall, and began to lick at the crumbling cement, tasting dirt and mold, thinking she probably wasn't the first desperate girl who'd puked on this very spot.

That did it. She started to gag, dry heaves racking her body, trying to bring up the small amount of nourishment in her stomach. But before she leaned over the bed to be sick on the floor, she heard a voice rising from the other side of the room.

"Turn your face to the wall and do it into your pillow."

Shocked, she froze. "What?"

"Hurry! He's watching us."

It was Jenny . . . Taylor? Sounding not at all woozy and unconscious, but alert and aware, though she hadn't moved a single muscle, still just that lump of clothes and bones on the floor.

"He's got a camera on us, but I don't think he has audio. If he did, he would have heard you talking earlier and would have known you aren't sure who I am."

She opened her mouth to ask that very question—who was she?—but before she could, the other girl spoke again.

"Now, unless you want him to know you puked up whatever he just made you drink, turn your head into the pillow and do it as carefully as you can."

Vonnie didn't ask stupid questions, didn't waste time telling the other girl how glad she was that she'd come to. She thought clearly, focusing only on the goal: getting out of there.

Now, knowing she had a conscious ally—who wasn't restrained in any way—hope bloomed in her heart and made her feel truly alive again for the first time in days.

She might survive this. Might really make it out of here alive. Might live to see justice and gain vengeance and salvage the life she'd been so sure was already lost to her.

With that goal in mind, Vonnie turned her head and forced herself to be sick right on her cot, hoping the violent convulsions of her body would be mistaken for shivers of cold.

She also hoped she hadn't waited too long.

Sunday, 1:40 p.m.

Olivia refused to allow anyone into the room with her when she went to see the body.

Lexie, who understood the woman's reluctance, based on the little she knew of her abilities, had offered, even though she wasn't really ready to see that sweet girl in death. So, of course, had Aidan. Not to mention Walter and his wife, who seemed to have taken the woman's abilities in stride. Maybe simply because they were so desperate for answers.

But the pale redhead had insisted on going in by herself.

God, how Lexie wished Aidan had been successful when he'd tried to find the answers they sought. He'd spent a long time sitting beside the body, trying as hard as he could, but had simply been unable to come up with anything. Not about who was lying dead in the next room, or anything about her twin sister, wherever she might be. So, as much as he'd hated to do it, he had contacted Olivia, then had gone out to the old plantation house to get her and bring her back here.

Lexie had the feeling this effort Olivia Wainwright was about to make would cost her greatly. Whatever demons Aidan battled, he seemed much more able to bounce back after one of his psychic episodes. And while he obviously was affected by the plight of the people he looked for, he never seemed to be personally devastated when his strange connections took place.

Olivia looked devastated even before she pushed into the room where the draped body still lay on a cold, metal gurney.

"You're sure?" Aidan asked. "I can go with you. I've already been in once."

The woman shook her head. "No. I need to be alone with her."

Walter and Ann-Marie exchanged a look.

"I'll try to find out as much as I can," Olivia promised them. "But honestly, there's only so much I can do. I won't be able to experience more than the last 130 seconds of her life. If she was already unconscious . . ."

"Thank you for trying," Walter said, lifting a shaky hand to stop her from saying anything more. "Whatever you can do."

Then, with one more steady, reassuring stare from the parents, Olivia turned and walked into the other room.

Nobody sat; they all gathered near the door, and Lexie would bet every one of them cast a look at the large wall clock, measuring the seconds as they ticked by.

Fifteen seconds felt long.

Thirty interminable.

By the time they reached one minute, she realized she was holding her breath, listening for any sound, however minute, from the other room.

Aidan reached for her hand, holding tight, equally as tense and anxious.

The clock ticked on, seconds sweeping by. It was more than two minutes, well over four, in fact, before they finally heard Olivia's shoes tapping on the linoleum floor as she walked toward them. The door swung open, and she emerged through it. Seeing her, Lexie instinctively reached out and grabbed her arm, sure the woman would fall.

She looked like she had aged a decade.

The pretty, delicate redhead was now gaunt, her mouth hanging open, lines of pain carved into her face as if she'd emitted a long, silent scream that had left its permanent mark on her. Her whole body quivered and shook, and her breath came in short, raspy bursts.

"Come on, Liv, sit down," Aidan said, taking one of her arms. Lexie still had the other, and together they guided her into the closest chair.

"Is she all right?" Ann-Marie asked.

Walter also appeared worried, but he was still enough of a frightened father to ask what they were all wondering. "Did it work? Were you able to . . . discover anything?"

Olivia's head dropped back, and she flinched, jerking once, twice, as if she were being struck, or in the grips of deep, violent chills. Finally, though, the spasms stopped ravaging her body. Her breaths slowed, the color began to return to her ghostly white cheeks.

"Olivia?" Aidan asked, his tone gentle.

The other woman licked her lips and nodded weakly. "I'm all right." Her teeth chattering a little, she added, "Just cold. So cold."

Then, with one final deep sigh, she straightened and looked at Walter and his wife. Her tear-filled eyes held such pain, such unimaginable anguish, Lexie wanted to beg her forgiveness for ever asking her to do this.

Walter and Ann-Marie grabbed each other's hands, obviously just as overcome by the momentous thing this stranger had done for them. Their remorse had to be tempered by hope, however, that Olivia might have learned something.

Finally, the brave woman opened her mouth and told them. "I heard them talking. Their last conversation, the twins. Funny. Joking." Her voice broke. "Then it happened. Came at them from behind."

Ann-Marie made the sign of the cross, but said nothing.

"It was quick; she didn't suffer long before she died," Olivia said, her voice clipped, her lips still trembling with cold, and, Lexie suspected, pain.

The shared death might not have taken too long, but, she suspected, the agony of it would endure Olivia's entire life.

"She didn't know," Olivia added. "Talking with her sister one minute, gone the next."

Tears streamed down Walter's face, but she imagined they would have been much harder had he found out his little girl had suffered for a long time.

Olivia cleared her throat. "Your daughter, the girl lying in that room?"

Walter tensed, putting an arm across his wife's shoulders, both of them readying themselves. "Yes?"

"Her name was Jenny."

Chapter 15

Though Olivia swore she was all right, and wanted to get back out to the plantation, where Aidan had picked her up earlier, he and Lexie instead took the woman back to his house and ordered her to lie down. If they'd had the time to spare, he would have insisted on driving her all the way back to Savannah. Liv promised she would rest and wait for the others to return so she could head back home with them.

He'd seen her work before, but he didn't know that he'd ever seen her so affected by what she did. But he suspected, given the gratitude of Walter Kirby and his wife, Olivia didn't have any regrets about it, despite how long the memories might live in her mind.

Having talked to Julia about what was going on there, he considered going out to the plantation house himself. Two things stopped him, though. First, he still hadn't talked to Chief Dunston. He'd been sidetracked by the request the Kirbys had made and had never made it out to the crime scene.

Second, he didn't want to leave Lexie alone.

Walter and his wife had finally agreed to go home. They not only had decisions to make, they also had two other daughters in the care of relatives, waiting to find out what had happened to their older sisters. He didn't envy them that conversation.

Knowing there was nothing she could do to help them

now, beyond fighting to bring Taylor home, Lexie had insisted on getting back to work. With that obviously foremost in her mind, as soon as they left his place again, she said, "Can you take me downtown? I want to go to the county office building, start searching the records on that property. I don't have the actual address, so I'm going to have to check some survey maps."

"It's Sunday; won't they be closed?"

With a grim smile, she said, "One of the few benefits of living in small-town hell. The town clerk is another one of Walter's poker buddies. I called him while you were talking to Julia, and he agreed to meet me over there."

"All right. While you do that, I'll track down Dunston."

"Chief Dunce," she murmured, slowly shaking her head. "I still can't quite accept that he might not be the douche bag I've always thought he was. I never would have believed the way he talked to the mayor if I hadn't heard it for myself."

"I don't think he's bad. Just lazy. He started believing his own stories about how quaint and peaceful this place is and turned a blind eye to anything that didn't fit that picture."

She sneered, staring out the window. "It's as quaint and peaceful as a slaughterhouse. I am so outta here when this is over."

He understood the sentiment. A year ago, when he'd come here to escape everything about his past life, he hadn't imagined ever wanting to go back. Now that he'd been so forcibly reminded that ugliness and evil were in no way exclusive to any one place, he had to admit, he wouldn't mind getting out of here, too. The sooner the better.

Especially now that the only thing he liked about Granville had just told him she intended to leave it.

"Where will you go?" he asked.

"I don't know. Savannah. Atlanta. Maybe Jacksonville."

Though he knew he probably didn't have to remind her, he still said, "You do know there's no place you can go that won't have its own brand of tragedy and ugliness."

She turned to look at him, her pretty face still marked with the tracks of her tears. "Says the man who moved here just to escape?"

"True enough," he admitted, "which is how I've come to realize it doesn't matter where you are. Humans will be humans. As capable of brutality as they are of love, and it really doesn't make any difference where they go to sleep at night."

"Does that mean you're actually going to stay here?"

"Fuck no," he snapped, the words flying out of his mouth. "I hate this town." He'd always hated it; he had just thought hating his home was fine when he had spent the past year pretty much hating himself.

Lexie laughed briefly, though the sound quickly died, humor unable to be sustained on a day this bleak. "Ditto."

"You'll have to be sure to leave me your forwarding address when you go," he said, trying to keep his tone light, though the thought bothered him. A lot.

But after knowing her such a short time, he had absolutely no claim on her. She could go wherever she wanted; the fact that they'd had sex this morning didn't change anything.

"You planning to come visit me?"

"Would you want me to?"

She didn't respond right away, instead shifting a little and reaching for his hand. He took it, lifting her cold, trembling fingers to his mouth and brushing a kiss on her knuckles.

"Actually," she admitted, "I'm counting on it, Aidan. When this is all over, no matter where I go, or where you go, I'm depending on you still being around, even if you live in the next state." She brushed her fingertips against his jaw, adding, "I think you could be someone I want in my life for a long time."

He hesitated, realizing she was admitting she had feelings for him that went beyond this week, this story, this immediate sexual attraction.

That admission scared the hell out of him. He had a hard enough time maintaining his own sanity without bearing the burden of someone else's emotions, which is why he'd never let himself really care about anyone beyond the most basic friendships.

Funny, though. He had the feeling it had happened anyway.

He and Lexie had known each other only a few days, but they were already far beyond anything he'd let himself feel before. Basic friendship would not have filled him with the driving desire he felt for her. Nor with the tenderness he'd felt when watching her sleep in his arms. It wouldn't have him ready to rip someone apart for putting his beefy hands on her in that alley, or made him feel helpless against those tears in her eyes. It wouldn't have landed him in a room with a set of grieving parents who he knew wanted him to be their child's savior. He most definitely wouldn't have already begun to trust her—especially given her profession, if he felt only the most simple, casual friendship for the woman.

She'd worked her way in. Quietly, quickly. Thoroughly.

She'd inserted herself into his life.

Lexie changed the subject before he could come up with any kind of a reply. "There it is," she said, pointing to a pretty, three-story brick structure that dominated the square at the center of downtown Granville. Few cars were parked on the nearby street, with most of the shops closed on Sunday, so he was easily able to find a spot at the side of the building.

He had already decided to walk her inside, not about to let her out of his sight given what was going on in Granville, when he realized he was probably going to end up sticking around a little longer, anyway. Because pulling into the parking space directly behind him was a squad car. And behind the wheel of that car was just the man he wanted to see.

"Think that's a coincidence?" he asked, eyeing the chief in his rearview mirror.

Lexie turned around in her seat and raised a speculative brow. "I somehow doubt it."

They got out of the SUV just as Dunston reached the driver's-side door.

"Chief Dunston," Aidan said, "I'm sorry I wasn't able to get over to see you sooner. We got tied up at the hospital."

"I heard," the man said, his tone hard, but his expression at least a bit interested. "You tellin' me some friend of yours really knows for sure which Kirby girl is lying in that morgue?"

Lexie joined in the conversation from the sidewalk. "There's no doubt about it, Chief. I've never been much of a believer in this stuff, and I know Walter and Ann-Marie haven't, either. But we were all entirely convinced."

That was true. When Olivia had related how she knew it was Jenny who had died last night, including repeating the words she'd heard between the girls, Lexie, Walter, and his wife had all started crying all over again. Lexie had told him afterward that it was because Olivia, who had never met either of the twins, had relayed exactly the kind of conversation they would normally have, nailing each girl's personality, right down to the cadence, the words they'd used and the way they'd spoken to each other.

"So, did you just happen to see us pull up?" Aidan asked, suspecting that wasn't the case.

Dunston shook his head. "Got a call from Frank. He wanted to know if it was true, what Ms. Nolan here told him."

Raising a questioning brow, he asked, "Frank?"

"The county clerk," Lexie explained.

"He seems to think you are on the trail of some important clue," Dunston said, staring hard at Lexie. "You aren't running around trying to play detective, are you?"

She lifted a shoulder and responded, "Old habits. You've got to give me a chance to get used to the idea that you might be on my side all of a sudden."

The man pushed his sunglasses onto the top of his head, his gaze clear and unwavering. Any blinders he'd been wearing up until now had definitely been torn off. "I am on the side of this town," he told her, "and every person who lives here, both north of Woodsboro Avenue and south of it."

"Fair enough." Lexie stuck out her hand to the man, and Dunston took it. "Let's go talk inside. Aidan can fill you in on what we know and I'll tell you exactly what we're looking for here."

The chief nodded his agreement, and the three of them walked together up the tree-lined sidewalk. A thin, nervous-looking man of around sixty stood outside a door marked "Employees Only." As they approached, he saw Lexie and the chief together, and suddenly appeared worried.

"It's all right, Frank," said Lexie, waving a hand, letting him know she wasn't angry that he'd called the chief on her. "We're all in this together."

"I was so sorry to hear about Walter's daughters." The man's voice wavered, as if he'd done some crying himself today. "Anything I can do to help, I'll do it."

"That's good," said the chief, clapping the other man on the shoulder. "Actually, I'm waiting to find out what we're doing here, too."

Once they got inside, the clerk led them to a conference room. "If you'll wait here, I'll go get the information you asked for, Lexie. I already started looking for the file on that property and should have it within a couple of minutes."

"Thank you," she said, leaning against the large block

table that dominated the room. She didn't sit down, looking too keyed up, desperate for this to work, for them to find something.

As soon as they were alone again, Aidan began to explain everything to Chief Dunston. He did it as quickly and concisely as he could, and Lexie jumped in to add details he neglected to mention, including the fact that they'd first heard about the mysterious Hellfire Club from some teen prostitutes.

"Out in the country, according to these girls," the man said, rubbing his jaw thoughtfully. "And what led you to decide that meant Terrytown Road?"

When Lexie fixed a pointed stare at him, Dunston's face reddened. "I turned those bone fragments over to the medical examiner this morning," he said. "Didn't fully believe it myself, but he confirmed they're human soon's he saw 'em."

"Jessie Leonard," Lexie murmured.

"The first girl? How do you know it's her?"

Telling the man what the prostitutes had said, about how Jessie had gone to one of those club parties and had never been seen or heard from again, Lexie made a pretty convincing case.

They might get even further confirmation soon. Derek, Julia, and Mick were still out at the plantation, and if they found the actual spot where Jessie died, Derek would probably know it. At least, as long as the death had been a violent one. Peaceful passings didn't usually leave an imprint on this world—but he didn't imagine any death that took place at that club could ever be assumed to be nonviolent.

God, did he hope it played out that way, and they didn't have to ask Olivia to touch the remains Dunston had turned over to the ME. He didn't know if the woman would be up to going through that twice in one day, especially since she usually resisted doing it at all.

Dunston, who listened to Lexie's explanation about

what had led them to that house without interrupting, hesitated when she finished. Then he made a surprising admission of his own. "I was out on Old Terrytown Road myself last night. Following a van full of local men. Guess you didn't hear that part of my conversation with the mayor."

"No, we didn't. Why were you out there?" asked Lexie.

He told them what he'd been up to, and Aidan and Lexie could only exchange looks of shock as they realized they had seriously underestimated this "local yokel" police chief.

Aidan had a hard time believing it, but it sounded as though they had come close to running into the members of the club last night. "What time was this?"

"About seven thirty or so."

"Right around the same time we were there." As the truth suddenly hit him, Aidan smacked his hand on his own forehead, wanting to hit himself again for having been too stupid to see it. "Damn it, that van!"

Lexie sucked in a shocked breath, understanding, too.

"A white passenger van flew by us when we were leaving the estate," Aidan admitted. His muscles tensed and his hands fisted. "I heard them. Sons of bitches, I *heard* their sick, twisted voices and attributed it to moving the log back into place."

Dunston appeared dubious. "Heard them, from inside the van?"

Lexie crossed the room and put a hand on Aidan's shoulder. "Considering how that place affected you, you couldn't possibly have realized they were passing by us at exactly that minute." She glanced at the chief. "You know who Mr. McConnell is, so you must have some idea of what he does. The feelings he got off that house confirmed every one of our theories, and the girls' stories. Some local men—the ones in that van you were following, I suspect—have been doing some pretty sick things to young women from this community."

Dunston's jaw thrust out and he hunched forward. "Killing?"

She shook her head, telling him the rest, everything they hadn't shared thus far. Including Aidan's own certainty that Vonnie Jackson had been to that club, but that she wasn't there now.

When she was finished, Dunston shook his head, appearing confused. "So if you already know she's not there, why are we here, trying to find out who owns the place?"

Aidan explained. "We know two of the missing girls were at that house, both wrapped up with that club. A lot of other girls—girls whose backgrounds and descriptions fit the type these men like—are also missing. Right now it's the only solid link we can find between them, and it has to mean something. We need to find out who the members are and what else they know."

Dunston rolled his eyes and shook his head, "Well, I can tell ya who the members are. I watched most of them from across the street last night."

"We didn't exactly know that that before we came down here," Lexie replied, her eyes narrowing.

Sensing the rising tension between them, Aidan interjected. "We're here. We're close to getting the property records. Let's find out who owns it and see if we can use that information to get one of those men to start talking."

"Good point," Dunston said with a nod. "If one of 'em thinks he might take the fall for all of it, he might start spilling his guts a little faster. Just depends on who it is."

"What about getting a warrant?" Lexie asked.

"You mean the document your friends think they don't need to have in order to trespass on private property?" Dunston asked, visibly irritated. "Yes, I do need one before I can set foot on that place. But I won't get it now, not with what I have—the say-so of a psychic who practically got run out of his last town." He looked at Aidan. "No offense."

"None taken."

Lexie wasn't giving up. "What about the bone fragments?"

"Think a judge is going to give me a warrant to search every house on that road? There are dozens of 'em, some occupied, some not. I still don't know how you found the right one."

Neither of them answered that question. The chief probably wasn't quite ready to hear about Morgan.

As if knowing they weren't going to explain, Dunston continued. "Nah, we need more before I even try it." The man's lip curled up on one side. "Especially because I saw a judge climbing onboard that van last night."

"Good Lord," Lexie groaned, rubbing at her temples.

Frank, the clerk, suddenly returned, pushing into the conference room, his arms loaded with photocopied documents. "Here we go, everything I've got. This has to be the place, Lexie. I looked up all the survey maps based on the mile markers you told me about." He put the files and loose pages on the table—lien records, property transfers, wills. It looked like he'd gone all the way back to the construction of the house in the early eighteen hundreds.

But the piece of paper they were looking for was much more recent than that. And Lexie, with her cold, researcher's eye, found it first, within just a minute or two.

"Here!" she exclaimed, holding up a sheet of paper he recognized as a recent tax bill. She read it, sucked in a surprised breath, then mumbled, "Oh boy."

Dunston plucked it out of her fingers and read it. "Ahh."

"What?" Aidan asked, not caring so much about the name—since he knew barely anybody in this town—but why the others were so surprised by it.

"The man who owns that place is pretty well known around these parts," Dunston explained. He cast a look at Lexie that could have been apologetic, or at the very least sheepish. "I think I can see what happened last month a little more clearly now."

Lexie ignored him, flipping through the pages as she told Aidan, "It's Ed Underwood. He owns the estate, looks like it's been in his family for generations, since just after the Civil War."

"Damned carpetbaggers," the chief muttered.

"Underwood . . . why do I know that name?"

"Because," she said, "he's majority owner of the paper. No wonder he was so anxious to shut me up. You know if I had kept digging into those missing girls, I would have found out about this dirty club."

This time, Dunston didn't convey his feelings with only a look. He cleared his throat, saying, "I apologize, Ms. Nolan. I regret not believing you."

"Thank you," she replied absently, as if she'd moved past the painful episode. Maybe now, with so much at stake, she had been able to.

Dunston looked at Frank and waved the tax record. "Mind if I hold on to this?"

"If it'd help you find Taylor Kirby, you could have the original," the clerk said.

"That's another thing," Dunston muttered. "How do the Kirby girls tie in to everything? I sure can't see the members of this club playing those kinds of games with girls who are close enough to their parents that they'd tell 'em what was going on."

Lexie turned away, wrapping her arms around herself. She hadn't said anything, but Aidan imagined her guilt had only grown more weighty with the discovery that Jenny was actually dead.

"I've been thinking about that," he told them both.

Turning her head to look over her shoulder, Lexie waited. Hoping she'd see the reason in his theory, he said, "Look, Taylor was one of the students who got up and spoke at the game Friday night."

Dunston crossed his arms over his chest, looking belligerent. That memory was obviously a raw one.

"Maybe the killer was there. He was angry, challenged, and decided to grab one of those two girls, as payback or something. Taylor was who he found first, and poor Jenny was just in the way." Expounding on the thoughts that had been nagging in his brain, he added, "Or hell, maybe he liked the attention and decided to get even more of it by taking someone he knew would cause an uproar."

Aidan honestly didn't know. None of them could, not until they found the monster responsible.

"All that makes sense, but there's no point wonderin' about it now," Chief Dunston said. "Not when we got somebody to talk to." He looked at his watch, then at Lexie. "Do you happen to know where Ed Underwood spends most of his Sunday afternoons?"

She shook her head.

"Well, I do. He likes to sit in Walter's office and go over every bit of the business, make sure each nickel is accounted for and everything is being done just the way he wants it. He's the type who thinks everyone's out to rob him blind."

"Do you think he'd do that today, with what's going on with Walter?"

"Ayuh. Even more reason for him to if he thinks Walter won't be around for a while. Too worried about being cheated to think about his partner's kids."

Lexie sneered. "Asshole."

"Maybe so. But at least he's a predictable one." Pulling his sunglasses off his head and wiping them with a corner of his shirt, he added, "You wouldn't happen to have a key to your office, in case you need to get in there after hours, would you?"

A slow smile creased her face as she nodded. "As it

just so happens, I do, Chief Dunston. But if you want to use it, you're going to have to let me—us—come with you."

The chief sighed. "Christ Almighty, what am I doing?" Then, almost resigned, he agreed to her demands. "Considering my own men don't even know any of this is goin' on, I'll consider you my backup." When Lexie's smile widened, the chief pointed a finger at her. "However, you're a silent, invisible backup. You two stay out of sight, and let me do all the talking. I know this man. I know he's not going to want to say a thing, and he won't if he thinks there's anybody else around to hear. And if I think he's involved in a crime and he might incriminate himself, I'm going to have to read him his rights and take him in."

"I can't see Ed Underwood being smart enough to be behind these killings," Lexie said. "He doesn't care about anything except money."

"And having sex with teenage girls," Aidan pointed out.

Lexie and the chief both fell silent, acknowledging that bitter truth.

Nobody really knew what anyone else was capable of. They had been neighbors with all these "good" people. They'd been friends with them, worked with them. Before now, he didn't suppose Lexie or Chief Dunston had ever imagined those men capable of the things they'd done. So how much of a stretch was it to think they might have done even worse?

Maybe a lot worse.

Sunday, 4:50 p.m.

Jenny. Her sister, her other half.

"Gone," she whispered.

He killed my sister. He killed her. She's dead.

Taylor knew the words repeating over and over in her brain would eventually sink in. They'd stab her through the heart and she'd believe them and then she'd lose her mind. So she did everything she could not to go down that path. In her brain, she accepted it, but she refused to allow the awful truth of it to overwhelm her emotions and crush her heart completely.

She couldn't, not yet. Couldn't cry for the twin who she would grieve for as long as she lived—whether that was another hour, or another century.

Taylor had known Jenny was gone from the moment she'd woken up in this hole. Everything had felt different right away and she'd noticed that difference as soon as she'd fully regained consciousness. Not because she was in so much pain—her head throbbing, her back feeling seared—and scared and lost in the darkness. It had been more subtle, infinitely more awful.

Her world had been solid and secure every day of her life. Until now. Now there was some intrinsic, vitally important piece missing. Just like she always knew when Jenny was sad or hurt, the very emptiness, that lack of connection, had made it clear her sister was no longer alive.

She hadn't needed the filthy, murdering bastard—whose voice she would swear she knew from somewhere—to say it. She'd already known.

Tears tried to rise, but she blinked hard, knowing her sister would be angry with her if she gave in to them. *You're the strong one, Taylor, so be strong!* Jenny would say.

She'd already had to exhibit more strength than she'd ever have believed she possessed. Just by doing absolutely nothing. If that psycho had shared that awful truth when she hadn't been prepared for it, Taylor would likely have done exactly what he'd expected her to do: Break down. Scream. Sob.

But she hadn't. She'd lain on that cold, hard floor, listening to him describe the awful things he'd done to the person she'd loved most in the world, and she had controlled herself. She'd stayed still. Let him think she was unconscious, in a coma, or almost dead.

At first, she'd wished she were. She didn't want to fight, didn't want to survive at all.

Her sister wouldn't let her give up. *Don't you dare, Taylor Kirby. Don't you let him win. He can't have us both! You have to fight. Mom and Dad need you to. They can't survive losing both of us; you know that.*

Jenny had been right. And Taylor had listened, and obeyed.

Even while he walked around the room, mere feet away, the image of her sister had kept Taylor's entire focus. Her eyes had been closed, and yet she'd *seen* Jenny there, exactly as she'd been on that parking lot, lying on her stomach, a few feet away, her arm outstretched. Their fingers had touched again, their bodies mirroring each other. Only this time, Jenny's eyes were open, her lips pursed as she silently whispered, "Shh!"

Her sister's voice had ordered her to be still. Jenny's hand had held her down, kept her from swinging out in fury, despite the pain of hearing the truth put into words. And once the murderer was gone, Jenny had told her what to tell poor, beaten Vonnie to do before she got sick all over the floor.

Unfortunately, though, Jenny now seemed to have fallen silent.

So had Vonnie.

Believing Taylor's claim that they were being watched, Vonnie hadn't spoken much once they were alone. She'd tried a few words, which sounded as though they'd come from a mostly closed mouth. After confirming Taylor's identity, she'd repeated the same phrase that had awakened Taylor this morning. *I'm sorry. I'm so sorry.*

As if any of this were her fault.

Then the other girl had grown quiet again. Waiting for the dark, as Taylor was.

Holding out for the dark.

She only hoped that when the dark came—as the late-afternoon shadows seemed to say it soon would—Vonnie would be able to speak. She had fallen asleep, or else she hadn't gotten the drugs out of her system soon enough. She was still over there on that cot, her deep, even breaths telling Taylor she was completely dead to the world.

Taylor wondered if the other girl was dreaming. If she was even capable of dreaming anymore, after being locked down here for almost a week, enduring whatever she'd endured that had left her so bruised and bloody.

The shadows grew longer, the cell dimmer. But Taylor remained patient. Partially because she knew she had to, due to the cameras he must have hidden down here. And partially because she was so overcome with terror, she didn't know if she was capable of movement.

Yes, you are.

"Yes," she mumbled, glad to be hearing Jenny's voice again, even if she couldn't see her right now. She'd swear she'd felt the warmth of her sister's breath on her cheek as she'd whispered in her ear. Taylor remained calm, knowing that, no matter what happened, her sister would be here with her.

The last bit of daylight coming in from the window over Vonnie's cot went out, like a candle being extinguished. Darkness descended, full and thick. And while she certainly didn't think it would be safe to get up and move around, she at least felt confident he wasn't going to be able to see her lips move, especially not with her tangled hair still lying across her face.

"Vonnie?"

She'd thought the other girl was asleep. But the response was immediate. "I'm here, Taylor."

"I was afraid you had passed out."

"No. Just wanted him to think I had."

Smart girl.

"I'm sorry, I didn't mean to scare you," she added.

Taylor couldn't help letting out a small laugh, thinking of all the other reasons she had to be scared.

Vonnie chuckled, too. "Okay, forget I said that. Are you okay?"

The pain in her back was bad. So bad. And lying the way she was for so many hours had made it worse. Though she didn't like the idea of him knowing she was mobile, she had to shift. "I think he stabbed me."

"Considering there's a knife sticking out of your back, I'd say that's a good bet."

A sob rose in her throat. She swallowed it. Now it wasn't Jenny's voice she heard telling her to hold it together, it was Vonnie's matter-of-fact one. "It's tiny, like a penknife. It's closer to your side, and if he'd hit any vital organs or major vessels you'd already be dead. So we'll deal with it when we can. Until then, try not to move."

They'd deal with it. Okay. But not moving seemed even more impossible than the idea that they could actually escape from here.

Vonnie's chains clinked, as if she were rolling around. Taylor suspected the girl was trying to turn enough to see her, probably desperate for a familiar face.

"Everybody's been so worried about you. There was a big protest at the game Friday night. Kids from both schools."

"I can't believe it," Vonnie whispered.

"Believe it. People care. Everyone was devastated, afraid you were dead."

"I thought I was, at first. Wish I'd taken that ride home from your sister." The girl sniffled. "I'm so sorry, Taylor." Then, her voice sounding a little stronger, she added, "But, you know, maybe it's not true. You can't believe everything he says. He lies. I know he lies."

Jenny. She squeezed her eyes tight, forcing the tears away. *Not now. Can't think about that now.*

"He's not lying," she said, not wanting to explain how she knew. Most people wouldn't understand. "And you should know, my sister isn't the one who offered you a ride."

She told Vonnie what had happened, how she and Jenny had switched places—never again. Oh God, never again.

Stop it, Taylor.

"Okay, Jenny," she whispered.

Hearing that story, Vonnie, in turn, told Taylor why the monster had targeted her—them.

Hearing the true reason, that all of this might have happened because she'd driven her car across the parking lot without the headlights so they wouldn't get busted for trading places, she thought she'd be sick. "Jenny died because of that?"

"Jenny died because a fucking psycho decided to kill her," Vonnie declared. "That's all. You were awake—you heard him talking. It could just as easily have been you. He didn't know, and he didn't care, and it's definitely not your fault."

It could have been her? It *should* have been her. She wished it had been her. Because of the two of them, Jenny was the good one, the nice one, the smart one. The one who would have done something amazing for this world, if only by being a part of it for the next eighty years.

"Stop it."

She thought for a second she'd heard Jenny's voice again. But it was Vonnie's.

"I knew your sister. I know everything going through your mind right now would be going through hers if the situations were reversed."

Maybe. Probably. But that didn't make the pain of it go away.

She still found it hard to believe all of this had come about because of this monster's crazy paranoia. "He thought I *might* have seen him driving after you so he killed my sister and intends to kill me."

Vonnie didn't sugarcoat it. "Yeah."

"I don't remember seeing anyone out of place," Taylor insisted. "Nobody I wouldn't expect to see leaving the school at that time of night."

"What can I say? Neither did I. Didn't know a thing was wrong until he took me. Never felt like anybody was watching me, had no warning whatsoever."

Neither had she and Jenny. Not a single goose bump, despite what happened in books or movies. The man who had done this had not given them even a faint psychological hint of what he intended to do.

The man who'd done this.

Who was he? Who could be so vicious?

The voice might have sounded vaguely familiar, even though he'd disguised it. But trying to connect that voice to someone she knew who was capable of doing what this man had done was simply impossible. Her mind wasn't wired to spot something so utterly evil. And Jenny's definitely hadn't been.

She fell silent, lost in her thoughts. So did her cellmate. Until finally, after a long moment, Taylor asked the question that was probably most on both of their minds.

"Vonnie, how are we gonna get out of here?"

Chapter 16

As the chief had predicted, when they arrived at Lexie's office, they found Ed Underwood. He sat in Walter's office, going through his files and his paperwork. The fact that the man whose desk he was rifling through had lost a child last night didn't seem to matter much.

She wanted to slap him. Instead, she'd been forced to hover outside in the hall, lurking and listening, just like Stan had the other day. This time, though, the door was slightly open; Dunston had left it that way so she and Aidan could hear what was happening.

At first, Underwood tried to bluster his way out of it, until the chief had slapped down a copy of the tax record and told the man he'd followed them the previous night.

"Look, Jack, there's nothing mysterious about it. We got a financial club, that's all," Underwood said. "Me and some of the other guys get together and pool our money in the stock market. That's all there is to it."

Even from out here, she heard the lie in his shaky, weak voice. She suspected members of the Hellfire Club had come up with that story and any one of them would repeat it if pressed.

"Okay, then, if that's all there is to it, you won't mind giving me a list of the names of the club members. Every one of them. I know not all of them were around last night. Some months there's as many as twenty men."

"Have you been spying on us?" Underwood sounded indignant.

"The list," Dunston said, not distracted.

"I can't. Don't you understand?" The man's voice went softer, as if he was afraid. "They're not all like you and me, Jack. Some of them are dangerous."

"I'm nothing like you," Dunston snapped. "Now, the names. I already know Mayor Cunningham's involved. Plus Harry Lawton. I saw them both last night."

"Yes, yes," the man said, sounding weary.

"And Wilhelm, that teacher from the high school. Vice Principal Young, too. Is Principal Ziegler part of it?"

"No, but Principal Steele is."

The chief rattled off a few more names, most of which shocked Lexie. She shook her head in disgust, thinking of how proudly those men wore their piety and touted their nice, wholesome family values. God, to think high school teachers and principals were involved—abusing girls they were supposed to be educating, protecting. It made her want to throw up.

Beside her, Aidan suddenly stiffened. He pulled his phone out of his pocket. It had apparently been vibrating. Mouthing, "I'll be right back," he headed down the hall so he could answer the call out of earshot of the other two men.

When he returned a few minutes later, tension rolled off him. Beckoning her over, he whispered, "We need to get Dunston out here. I've got a name to feed him."

"From?"

"Derek." He sighed. "He found the spot where Jessie Leonard was killed."

"Oh God."

"He also knows something about the man who killed her. I think Dunston could use that information to work on Underwood."

She considered, knowing they couldn't do anything to arouse Underwood's suspicions. "We should have gotten his cell phone number. Maybe I could. . . ." Her words trailed off, however, when she saw a shape move across the inset glass panel on a door that led to another set of offices. The figure wore a ball cap and was bent over, as if pushing something. Like a mop.

"Wait here," she whispered, suddenly having an idea. Not wasting time to explain, she tiptoed over, slipped into the other area, and called to the man, who was mopping his way down the corridor. "Hi, Kenny."

The scarred maintenance man spun around, startled, his mop handle clutched tightly against his chest. "Miz Alexa?"

"I'm sorry I startled you," she said, holding her hands out in supplication. "I was just wondering if you could do me a favor."

"I came in to work. Didn't have anywhere else to go and wanted to be here, in case Mr. Walter needed anything." Tears formed in the man's eyes. "Did you hear about his girls?"

She nodded and stepped closer. "Yes, I did. I'm trying to help find out who did this awful thing to them."

"They're beautiful girls," he said, as if not hearing her. "So pretty and nice. Not mean like some of them at the high school. They always said hello to me, even if they was with a bunch of their friends, always had time to stop and say hello just 'cause that's how nice they were. And because Mr. Walter's been so good to me, I always kept an eye out for 'em. Looked after those girls without them ever knowing it."

She reached for Kenny's arm, needing him to focus, and needing to do the same, too. "Kenny, there's still a chance to help Taylor come home."

"Really?"

"That's why I'm here. Now I need to ask you a favor. Could you please go into Walter's office and tell Chief Dunston he has a phone call and needs to come out here?"

Kenny's eyes rounded. "The chief's in there? With Mr. Underwood?"

"Yes, exactly! And I don't want Mr. Underwood to know my friend and I are out here waiting. So will you please do as I asked?"

"Yes, ma'am, I will."

Without another word, he leaned his mop against a wall and went back through to the other offices. He hesitated for a second when he spotted Aidan, offered him a brief nod, and went right to Walter's door. Knocking once, he pushed inside.

Lexie beckoned for Aidan to join her, and he did, the two of them waiting at the other end of the hall while Kenny coaxed the chief out. While they stood there, Lexie noticed Aidan had lost some of his color. Leaning a shoulder against the wall, he swallowed visibly a couple of times. Then he looked around, sniffed, and wrinkled his nose as if he had noticed a bad odor.

"What's wrong?" she whispered.

"I don't know. Smells like sour milk or something."

She sniffed, but didn't notice anything. Before she could say so, Dunston emerged, heading straight toward them. "What's going on?"

Aidan explained he'd gotten a tip from a friend, adding, "Do you know anyone named White? First name is short and begins with a J—maybe James or Jim?"

Dunston considered, then asked, "You mean Jed White? The old football coach?"

Lexie recognized the name, too. "He died three years ago."

"Exactly three years ago?" Aidan asked.

"This month," Dunston said. "They were going to dedicate the game to him the other night. He died in a single-car crash out on . . ."

"Old Terrytown Road," Lexie whispered. The pieces continued to click together in her mind. "Jessie disappeared right around Halloween, a few weeks earlier than the coach. Aidan, are you saying White had something to do with Jessie's death?"

He nodded once. "I'm saying he caused it. He was a

member of the club, and apparently he liked things especially rough. He killed Jessie that night and the others helped cover it up. She's buried in the ruins of an old barn on the property. Well, most of her is. I think some animal got in there, which is how those fragments were found up the road."

"Son of a bitch," Dunston muttered. "How do you know all that?"

"You wouldn't believe me if I told you," Aidan replied, "and it doesn't really matter now. The only thing that matters is using that information to startle Underwood into talking."

Dunston hesitated. This was so far out of the straightforward lawman's realm, she actually couldn't believe he'd gone along with them this far. A voice inside him had to be telling him to get out now before they got him completely wrapped up in their insanity.

But another one, the voice of the decent man who she had so recently discovered lurking beneath his brusque exterior, wouldn't allow him to. Not if there was a chance to find out what had been going on here in Granville. He was like a big bear who'd been awakened from a long winter's nap and now found himself having to clean out the forest that had been overrun with vermin while he hibernated.

"All right," he said, growling the words like that newly awakened grizzly. "Let me go see what I can get out of that scumbag."

Sunday, 5:40 p.m.

Aidan wanted to stick around while Dunston finished his interview, but he suddenly felt the need to get outside. The air in the building had become not only stale and stifling, but a little rank. At least, that's what he'd thought at first. But when he realized Lexie hadn't noticed a thing wrong while he'd been inhaling sour milk for the past several minutes, he figured something else was going on. Something powerful.

Making an excuse, he quickly left the building. He needed privacy, and he needed to sit down, so he went to his SUV and got in the driver's seat. Though he lowered the window to keep the air moving, he didn't leave the car running or buckle up. Instead, taking slow, even breaths, he cleared his mind and invited it in. Invited the connection.

It wasn't gingerbread this time, yet he felt sure what was happening now was related to what had happened Thursday morning. He was just conscious and aware now, could control it, either protect himself from it or strengthen it.

He closed his eyes, dropped his head back. Felt the pressure, felt the weight. Then no longer felt either one as he had the sensation of being lifted high in the air.

Vonnie. Where are you?

Floating, spinning, flying. The same snippets of conversation—the entire town talking about the tragedy that had befallen that nice Kirby family. *Who could have done it? Who could be next? What if the police find out about our meetings?*

That last one distracted him momentarily, but he shoved it aside, needing to focus now only on finding her, not on the thoughts of any sadistic member of Underwood's club.

We can do this, Taylor. We'll make it out of here.

Found her! Oh God, had he actually found *them*? Together? Alive?

And if he'd heard them a few hours ago—heard Vonnie call Taylor by name—might he have saved Olivia the torment of having to live through Jenny's final minutes?

He threw off that thought, knowing he couldn't let himself be distracted. Focusing harder, he pictured Vonnie's face, imagined her voice as the only sound in an entire universe of nothingness and forced himself to drift closer to it.

That's it. I'm almost free. Just peel away the last layer.

His hands clenched, flexed. Then a tearing sensation, like tape being pulled off skin. It stung, burned, and his fingers tingled with a pins-and-needles sensation.

It wasn't enough. He needed more. Needed to see where she was.

He pushed on, flew farther, feeling like he was flying into the sun, like the character from that ancient Greek myth. Too close and his wings would burn up and he'd tumble down to earth. But he needed more, needed to find out anything he could.

Vonnie.

Something appeared in his mind. A chipped wall. A filthy cot. He caught that rancid smell again, only now it seemed to be all over him, his head, his face.

Then he heard her voice again, clear as a bell.

He's going to be back soon.

"Who?" he whispered, needing a name, some clue to the identity of their kidnapper.

But he didn't get it, and when he tried to picture the face of the man, he could see nothing except a hard, plastic-looking smile.

You're going to have to hit him as soon as he turns his back on you. Then get the keys off his belt. Hit him hard, take him down. If he stays up, we're both dead.

They had a plan.

Those incredibly brave girls . . . He wanted to help them, to be there with them, wanted to pick them up and fly them away. But he pushed too hard, got too near the heat and like that old myth, his wings melted and he felt himself free-falling. Down, down, seeing his own hands trying to grab them, take them with him, but grasping at nothing but air.

He hit his own body, jerked in the seat. Back where he'd started.

But he was no longer alone.

Lexie stood right outside the car, watching him through the open window. She'd apparently been watching him for quite some time. There were tears in her eyes, and he imaged it wasn't easy for her, seeing him like that. So lost. Just the shell of his body here, while his psyche, everything that made him who he was, had been somewhere . . . else.

"Are you all right?" she whispered, her first concern being for him, rather than what he might have seen.

He reached for her hand. "I saw them."

"Them?"

"Both of them. And I don't think this was in the past, Lexie, it was now. Vonnie and Taylor, together, making their plan to escape."

Though her first reaction, like his, was joy at knowing they were alive, her mouth fell open on a gasp as the same instinctive fear hit her. Two weak, abused teenage girls going up against a monster who had killed more than a dozen others?

"God help them," she whispered. "Where? Do you know?"

"It looks like they're locked in a basement somewhere."

"So they're probably not east of here—the closer you get to the coast, the less likely you are to see real basements."

"I never had one in Savannah," he admitted, again noting how quickly her mind worked.

"What else?" she asked.

"When he comes back, Taylor's going to hit him and take his keys so they can get away."

That was all he had, all he'd gotten. But the joy in her face in just knowing that they weren't too late, and the missing girls still lived, said it was enough for this moment, anyway.

He reached for the door handle, opened the door, and stepped out into the evening air, breathing deeply of it, needing to clear his head and fill his lungs, which had seemed to inhale nothing but mildew and filth.

That's what they're breathing.

He forced the thought away. "What happened in there?"

"Underwood cracked," she told him, her pretty face grimacing with distaste under the overhead streetlight. "When Dunston confronted him about Coach White, he completely broke down, admitted the man was a little crazy, had an awful violent streak, and killed one of the girls before they could stop him. They knew they'd all be blamed, so they helped him cover it up."

Aidan had a suspicion about what had happened next. "Then they got rid of White."

One brow shot up. "Seriously? You really believe they killed him?"

He definitely thought so. "Pretty big coincidence, don't you think? Their biggest liability dies in a single-car accident right after they help him hide his mess?"

"Maybe."

"I doubt all twenty or so men in that club were in on it, but I wouldn't be surprised if a few of them—the ones Underwood sounded afraid of, who he called 'dangerous'—took it upon themselves to make sure something like that didn't happen again."

"Not to protect the girls, I'm sure," she said in disgust, "but to protect their precious club."

Crossing his arms, he leaned his back against his SUV. "The question is, if White killed Jessie, and then White died, who started killing the other girls six months later?"

"That's what Underwood wants to know," she told him, leaning beside him. "He gave Chief Dunston the list of members, and said they've been living in fear ever since they read my articles last month and realized how the girls were connected." She sighed heavily, shaking her head. "And the bastard admitted there have been some strange things going on at their club for a while. Items left onsite, between their regular get-togethers—underclothes, a backpack with one of the girls' names in it. Things like that."

He wanted to go find Underwood and throttle the man. "So they *knew*. They've known for a long time these murders were connected to what they've been doing and they didn't do a damn thing to stop it."

"Not only that, they still went out there intending to have one of their parties last night," she said, sounding as anxious to hurt someone as he felt.

"And it all comes back to White. He's the link."

"Exactly," she said. She wrapped her arms around herself as the evening air grew chilly. "Underwood thinks somebody found out about him and decided to play some mind games."

"Which essentially confirms that they killed him."

She thought about it, then slowly nodded. "Yeah. I guess it probably does."

If that was what they were dealing with here, the killer had to be someone close to White, someone who had taken his death personally. Someone with a dark enough soul to take his revenge by committing atrocities against innocent girls, just to make his enemies squirm.

"But who would it be?" she asked. "From what Dunston just told me, White was a bachelor, never married, no kids, no siblings, parents both dead. He lived alone in an old farmhouse just outside of town, the same house where he grew up. He was born and raised here, but he didn't seem to have many friends. So who would commit murder to avenge him?"

Excellent question. Who would care?

They fell silent for a moment. Sensing her shiver again, Aidan reached for her, dropping an arm over her shoulders and pulling her tight to suck up some of his warmth. Both physically and emotionally.

She felt good there. Damn good. Not for the first time, he realized how glad he was to have her beside him, with him on this. Lexie was smart and quick; every idea he raised she bounced back with a new element added to it.

They made a hell of a good team.

"Okay. So we need to learn everything we can about White," Aidan said. "Immediately."

She nodded. "Dunston took Underwood over to the station. I guess he's finished playing around with us and is going to make this official. Let's go inside and see what we can discover online about the late coach."

Agreeing, he walked with her, his arm still across her shoulders. But before going in, he paused to pull his phone out of his pocket. "Let me give Julia a call and let her know what's going on."

Reaching Julia on the second ring, he filled her in on what had happened with Dunston, and with his own vision. He told her they could stop what they'd been doing out at the old house, adding, "I don't think there's any more we can learn from that place tonight. The chief knows the truth about Jessie, and hopefully tomorrow he'll be out there bringing that poor girl's remains up into the light."

"It's about time," Julia murmured, sounding relieved.

She also sounded tired—and, after a little prodding, admitted Derek and Mick were wiped out, too.

"Why don't you swing by my place, get Olivia, and head home? You're less than an hour away. If we turn anything up, we'll call you back down," he told her.

"You're sure?"

"I'm sure. It might be hours before we know more. Go get some sleep while you can. We might need you later."

"Okay," she said. "But call the minute you find anything. We'll be ready to come back as soon as we hear from you."

"Thanks."

He disconnected and they went inside. Kenny, the maintenance man, was obviously still around; the men's room door stood open, propped by a mop cart. Otherwise, they had the building to themselves.

"Walter's got the only decent computer," Lexie said, heading straight for that office.

Once there, she took a seat behind the man's desk. Aidan saw her close her eyes briefly and clasp the chair's armrests. Seeing the family photo on the desk, Walter and his beautiful wife and daughters, he understood why.

Squaring her shoulders, focusing on the task of now rather than the grief of tomorrow, Lexie got to work. Her fingers flew over the keys as she got online, pulling up the archives of her own newspaper. "Here's his obituary." She didn't waste time having him read it over her shoulder, sending the page to a printer instead. Once it had started, she moved on, letting Aidan grab the printout and read it for himself.

Everything was as she'd already said, at least some of the story printed in black and white. A tragic, fiery accident had ended the life of a local man. What it didn't say was that he was a brutal one who'd raped and murdered a young girl.

Justice, some would say. In any case, who would mourn him? Who would avenge him? An angry student he'd once coached? A best friend who shared his sick tastes? "I can't figure out whether the killer is someone who was in the club or not."

Lexie looked up in surprise. "You think he could be one of them? Why would he plan this elaborate revenge that would bring attention and exposure to himself, as well as everyone else? If he's in the club, and knows who took White out, why not just kill the men responsible?"

"I'm not saying that's the case, but if he's not a member, how else would he know exactly which girls to go after?"

"He waited six months. Maybe he did some research."

"Or," Aidan mused, "maybe it took him that long to realize White's death wasn't an accident."

She pursed her lips, thinking about it, nodding. There really was no way to be sure yet.

"What else have you got?" he asked her, knowing they needed to focus on what they could find out. "Anything on his family?"

"Jed White's obituary listed his parents' names—I found a death notice on his mother, who died when he was only a year old. There's a full obit on the father, who was killed in some kind of accident right after the son turned twenty-one. That was two decades ago. County property records show White inherited the father's house and lived there until his own death."

"Then what happened to it? Did he leave it to anyone else?"

She checked the screen. "Sold at auction. Guess the perv wasn't big on paying his taxes."

Damn. "The man had to have friends, someone he was close to outside of the Hellfire Club. We need to talk to people who worked with him, his students."

"Why don't you talk to his brother?"

Aidan and Lexie both swung around, shocked as a strange voice intruded. They were equally shocked by the words he'd said.

Kenny stood in the doorway, his mop in his hands. Though the scars made his expressions hard to read, there was no hiding the tension in his pose.

"What do you mean?" Lexie asked, rising from the desk. "Coach White didn't have a brother."

"Sure he did." Kenny frowned, then scrunched his eyes closed. "Uhh . . . oh, boy, my brain just doesn't wanna work right. Can't recall his name."

Walking over, Lexie put a hand on the man's shoulder and led him to a chair. "Did you know Mr. White, Kenny?"

He nodded as he took a seat. "Went to school with 'im. Jed was quiet, cried a lot, and got picked on. But his big brother was a real bully."

"We can't find any mention of a brother anywhere."

"Are you sure?" Kenny's face scrunched up as he thought. "I coulda *swore* he had one. But I guess maybe

I could be wrong. I get confused sometimes. It was a long time ago."

A brother, not mentioned anywhere? Was that possible?

Kenny's frown deepened as his frustration grew. "Maybe it was a cousin? I'm so stupid, I never get anything right!"

"Give it a minute." Aidan walked over to stand on the other side of Kenny's chair. "Don't concentrate too hard, just let it come."

The maintenance man sniffled. "Been thinking hard all day, 'bout Miss Taylor and Miss Jenny."

"I'm sure you have."

"Rascals, the two of 'em," he whispered. "The way they'd switch places. I knew right away Miss Taylor swapped with Miss Jenny last Monday. Lordy, was I thankful to hear she was okay after I heard the one she walked out with got grabbed by the Ghoul." He wiped his nose with his sleeve. "Never dreamed he'd get her a few days later."

Lexie tilted her head in confusion. "Wait, you're saying you saw *Taylor* at school Monday night? With Vonnie Jackson?"

"Yeah. Swapped places, they did. I was cleaning up after the meeting and saw her. No mistakin' Miss Taylor's smile, even if she was calling herself Jenny."

Shocked, Aidan had to wonder what this could mean.

Kenny continued. "When I heard what happened to them girls, I got to thinking about it. Wondering if maybe the Ghoul was afraid Miss Taylor'd seen him and that's why he took her."

Aidan could only stare at the man, so often ignored and overlooked by those around him. His ears and eyes were always open, though, picking up truths and tidbits others would never notice. Because, of course, what he said was a possibility. They'd all been focused on where Vonnie had been grabbed—in the Boro, where her books had been found—they hadn't considered that she might have been stalked while still at her own school.

What if Taylor had seen something? Or if the killer *thought* she had?

Kenny lifted both his hands to his head and pressed them there, tangling his fingers in his hair. "Think, dummy, think," he told himself, looking on the verge of tears.

Lexie bit her lip, obviously, hating to see the man torment himself. But she knew as well as Aidan that he might have information that could be the key to solving this. To saving the girls.

Unfortunately, it appeared that the harder he pushed, the more elusive the memory became. Finally, grunting in frustration, the poor man threw himself into a chair, pounding his fists on his own thighs.

"It's okay," Aidan said, soothing and calm. "It's all right. Just sit quietly for a minute, okay? Don't try to talk; don't tell us what you're seeing. Just try to let the memories of those younger days when you knew Jed and his *brother* float free. Don't try to catch them; just let them go."

He glanced at Lexie, who apparently realized what he was doing. She didn't hesitate, she merely nodded, agreeing that he should do whatever he could to share in this poor, wrecked man's memories.

Kenny did as Aidan asked, remaining quiet, his eyes falling closed. Sitting opposite him, Aidan breathed deeply, allowing his body to fall into a familiar, relaxed state. He stared at Kenny's poor face, not allowing himself to wonder how it had become that way, then focused, hard, on what the other man had looked like when he was younger. Before his accident. When he was twenty. Fifteen. Ten.

Finally, he closed his eyes as well, falling into Kenny's past.

The man held nothing back. He might not be able to grab the hints of memory from the deep recesses of his brain, but that didn't mean they weren't there. Aidan watched as they emerged, taking shape in the foggy mist that appeared behind his closed eyelids.

Kenny might not be able to verbalize them, but Aidan saw them. Heard them.

Why don't you watch where you're goin', retard? A cruel voice. A youngster's voice.

Kenny, crying. Asking the other boys not to take his lunch money. Not to hide his books. Not to laugh at him in gym class.

Aidan's heart twisted, but he didn't let himself dwell on the wrongs done to this poor man in his childhood, or how unjust it was that he now bore a scarred face inviting even more ridicule. Because through it all, Kenny's kindheartedness remained clear.

That kindness included his worry over a classmate who always came to school bruised and sad. Jed, who sat beside Kenny in Mrs. Finkelstein's first-grade class.

Stop crying, Jed! The bully's voice again. Only this time, it wasn't sneering or vicious; it sounded almost . . . tender. *Don't let anybody see you cry. Not ever. I'll take care of you.*

He saw the two boys, huddled in a corner near a water fountain in what looked like an old school building. They didn't know Kenny was lurking nearby, overlooked, ignored, like always.

Then he heard another voice, softer, weak, from the small, thin child. Jed. *You promise, Markie? You won't ever leave me, will you? You won't leave me alone with him, down in the dark?*

I won't. You're my little brother. Brothers are always there for each other. You believe me, right?

I believe you, Markie. But what if they make you? If they get a divorce and your mom goes away, you'll have to go, too, right?

If they force me, I'll find a way to come back for you, I swear. Nobody's gonna hurt you, Jed. If they do, I'll make them pay.

I'll make them pay.

The memories shifted, more children, loud and cruel,

more of Kenny's quiet stoicism. He was losing himself in more personal memories. Heartbreaking ones.

Aidan drew back, pulling away from the mist, erecting the wall between his mind and Kenny's memories. He had what he needed.

There had been a brother—a stepbrother. His mother had been married to Jed's father. All they needed to find was a marriage certificate, and then they'd have a name.

Aidan rubbed a hand over his eyes, then lifted his gaze to Lexie. "Look for marriage and divorce records on Jed's father. He remarried sometime after his first wife's death. And his second wife had a son, called Markie."

Kenny's eyes flew open and he snapped his fingers. "Markie! That's it, Jed's big brother was named Markie."

"Are you sure?" Lexie asked.

Kenny answered even before Aidan could, as if the memories had solidified in his mind with Aidan's words. "Sure I'm sure! Jed was my age, we was in the same class. Markie was older, grade three, I think. Him and Jed didn't have the same last name, though, 'cause he was already born when his mama got married to Jed's daddy."

Aidan nodded once, confirming what Kenny had said.

Lexie hurried back to the desk, obviously intending to look up more information on Jed White's mother. Aidan focused on the maintenance man, who was proving to be so vitally important to this case. "Kenny, what happened to Markie, do you remember?"

He nodded eagerly. "Yeah! Markie's mama divorced Jed's daddy and they moved away. Jed was sad, I can tell you. Talked about his brother for years. Anybody was botherin' him, he'd say, 'My brother Markie's gonna come back one day and make you sorry you were ever mean to me!'"

Everything clicked into place with that one sentence, a few words whispered by a little boy over thirty years ago.

He'll make you sorry you were ever mean to me.

Markie had promised to make them pay. And it appeared he had made good on that promise. If Aidan's suspicions were correct, Jed White's long-lost stepbrother had been playing a game of cat-and-mouse with the men he held responsible for Jed's death.

It was all supposition, guesswork at this point. But somehow, deep inside, Aidan knew he was right.

"Oh my God," Lexie whispered. "Is this possible?"

Aidan jerked his head to look at her, seeing Lexie literally shaking in her chair. Her face was pale, her mouth open in an O, short, tiny gasps coming out of it.

"What is it?"

She couldn't speak, merely pointing to the screen. Aidan rose from his chair and hurried to her, bending over her shoulder to look at the monitor for himself.

It was a marriage record, detailing the marriage of Jed White's father, Jedediah, to a woman named Alice, when Jed was about two years old.

Lexie's trembling finger was pointed directly at the mother's name. Her last name.

Young. Alice Young, who had apparently had a son from a previous marriage. Markie.

"Markie would be a nickname, of course," she whispered. "For Mark."

He now remembered where he'd heard the name. It had been at the football game, when she'd been pointing out who was who in this town.

One of whom had been vice principal Mark Young.

Chapter 17

"I hear a car. He's coming back."

Though they had been lying in the dark, waiting for this moment, ready for their chance to put their plan in motion and escape from here, Taylor couldn't deny a shiver of raw terror ripped through her body at Vonnie's whispered words.

The monster was coming. And they thought they could escape him?

She couldn't do this. Just couldn't. "Oh my God."

"Calm down," the other girl ordered. "I can smell your fear from over here. If he knows you're conscious and waiting for your chance, he'll come in here ready to put you down like a dog. Just get back over there where you were, and stick to the plan. You hit him, you take his keys, and you run like hell. Get help, and come back for me."

"I can't just leave you . . ."

"We have one shot," Vonnie insisted. "You can't waste time trying to find the keys to the lock on these chains, as well as the one to the door, unless you kill the sonofabitch, which would be just fine by me."

"Me, too."

"Barring that, the second he goes down, you get outta here and find help. I've held out this long, I'll survive till you get back, and if he gets close enough, I'll hold him to give you more of a head start."

Taylor couldn't help it, she began to cry. She tried to blink away the tears, then did as Vonnie had told her, getting back into her position on the floor, the damn knife still sticking out of her back. Vonnie hadn't let her pull it out, saying it could be keeping a wound plugged up and if it came out she could bleed to death. Even if that didn't happen, it wasn't worth the risk that their captor would see it was out as soon as he returned. No way would he think it had fallen out on its own, not when it had stuck tight throughout the rest of the ordeal. He'd know she had regained consciousness and would be more wary when he entered.

"You back where you were?"

"I think so," she said, unable to be totally sure in this pitch darkness.

"Good. Stay still. Remember, don't listen to him; no matter what he says, try not to react."

A car door slammed. Taylor closed her eyes. *Jenny, help me. Please help me stay calm.*

You can do this.

Thinking of how rational and smart her twin had always been, she forced herself to take deep breaths, to try to still her racing heart.

Breathe. Just breathe. He's not a monster; he's only a man.

The man who had destroyed her family. The man who had killed her sister. The man who intended to torture her to death.

Her body relaxed, but her mind hardened with resolve.

Maybe she couldn't do this. Maybe she wouldn't escape.

But she could try.

Hearing a clink, she figured Vonnie was still frantically trying to work her way out from under the chains. Now that her hands were free of the tape, which Taylor had pulled off bit by bit, working blind in the dark, Vonnie seemed to think she might be able to get herself up without having to wait for someone to rescue her with the key.

Over the past hour, she'd heard the other girl grunt, then whimper as she maneuvered her arms and shoulders into impossible positions. Vonnie was trying to flatten herself, to twist out from between the cot and the restraining chain looped around her.

That would be a miracle. With two of them able to leap on the man, surprising him as soon as he came through the door, they might be able to actually do this.

But Taylor didn't believe in miracles, not anymore. Not after last night.

She couldn't rely on Vonnie's help, not unless she was lucky enough to knock their attacker out and had time to look for all his keys. Until then, she was entirely on her own.

No, you're not.

Taylor breathed out, slowly, calm again. She couldn't see Vonnie in the darkness, but she could see Jenny, still lying there on her stomach, just a few feet away. Reaching for her. Smiling.

Taylor reached, too, pressed the tip of her finger to her sister's, absorbing her strength and her love.

Ready?

"Ready," she breathed.

A sound from above made her stiffen. Jenny disappeared, but still, Taylor felt her touch.

From nearby came a heavy footfall. A clang of metal— the outer door.

"Stop moving," she ordered Vonnie. "He's here."

Oh God, help me, he's here.

Sunday, 7:15 p.m.

"I still can't reach him," Lexie said as she slammed her cell phone down onto her lap. She leaned forward in her seat, staring out the windshield, silently urging Aidan to drive faster. "Damned dispatcher says he's interrogating a prisoner and refuses to be disturbed."

"Did you tell her why you were calling?"

"I told her it was about Jenny Kirby's murder, but she didn't seem to believe me. The chief might have started taking my side, but to everyone else, I'm still the girl who cried wolf."

She should have made the call anonymously. Better yet, they should have just driven to the police station and raised hell until they got into the chief's office. But once they'd done a bit more research—enough to convince them Mark Young was, indeed, the Granville Ghoul, they'd both been too fearful for the girls and had driven out to the house, not suspecting they wouldn't even get their calls put through to Dunston.

"Hell," Aidan muttered. "We shouldn't be doing this alone. It's insane."

He was right. They had absolutely no business going to find Young themselves. But who else was there? His friends had gone back to Savannah—though he'd called Julia, they were all still an hour away. The other members of the local police wouldn't listen to a word Lexie said.

Aidan had seen in his vision that the girls were going to try to make a break for it the next time their psychopathic captor came into their cell. And what chance did they have? They would probably both die in the effort.

No, there was no time to wait. They couldn't just hang around for Chief Dunston to call them back, nor could they call 911 and have them go to the house where they were now headed, without even knowing if it was the place. For all they knew, Young could be at his own home, which was, revoltingly, in the same neighborhood as the Kirbys'.

But she didn't think so. She had the feeling he was at the place in the country, far from any neighbors. The house where Markie Young had lived as a boy, with his mother, his stepfather, and his stepbrother, Jed White.

The house he now owned.

She'd gone back to the county tax records site before they'd left the office. Young had been the one who'd bought White's house at auction almost three years ago, right after Jed's death. That was only a few months after Young had arrived in Granville to take the job as high school vice principal.

Before then, he'd been doing the same job at a school in northwest Georgia. Funny, the minute she read the name of the town he'd lived in before, she'd thought of those other missing persons cases, the ones she'd flagged when researching the story. Something told her Mark Young had not developed his taste for killing after he'd arrived here in Granville. He'd simply indulged it more— and enjoyed the side benefit of psychologically tormenting his enemies.

The urge to return to Granville, to be near his "brother," must have been a strong one. How the two must have enjoyed the few months of their reunion, when they'd worked together at the same school, no one ever knowing of their decades-old connection. Or their shared tastes.

But their reunion had been short-lived. Jed had died—sometime after introducing his stepbrother into the Hellfire Club.

How long had it taken Mark to find out Jed had been murdered by the other club members wanting to cover up his crime?

That wasn't hard to figure out—it had probably been around six months. About the same amount of time between Jessie Leonard's murder and the next one.

Judging by the little they knew of Young, she could only think he was the type of man who liked to pull the wings off flies and watch them suffer. Killing the girls, then leaving clues behind at the clubhouse to mess with the minds of the others in the Hellfire Club, had been his own way of torturing them for what they'd done. His revenge had continued, girl by girl, murder by murder. How easy it must have been. Who would ever suspect him? He probably had been able to lure some of the girls by virtue of his position in the community.

"I wish the sick bastard had just taken the rapists rather than the poor victims," she said, snarling.

Aidan reached for her hand in the darkness. "Given what Kenny heard the boys say, I suspect there was something very wrong in that house when they were little. They grew up to be two violent, angry men who lash out and brutalize women."

"Abuse?"

"Almost certainly. So I don't think killing men would have satisfied Young."

"You don't seem to have any doubt it's him."

"No," he said, "I don't. Do you?"

"No. We got a teensy glimpse of the real man behind the mask Friday night. Do you remember? The way he talked to Kenny?"

"I remember."

"He's got a temper. He has the motive, the means. He's smart enough to have done it. This took a lot of planning," she said. "I know in my heart that it's him."

"Me, too."

Reaching for her phone again, she dialed the police station, cursing herself for not getting Dunston's direct number.

"Give it to me," Aidan ordered.

She passed it over in silence, listening as he handled the call a whole lot more calmly than she'd been about to. Giving the dispatcher his name, he'd gone on to say, "I just left Chief Dunston a short time ago, we were talking to Ed Underwood, whom I assume he is currently interviewing at the station."

Smart, pointing out something he couldn't know unless he was telling the truth.

"I need you to interrupt the chief and give him this message. It is vitally important. Tell him we know Coach White had a stepbrother and we're on our way to see him now."

Lexie noticed that he didn't name names, or accuse anyone of being a psychopathic killer. Though surprised at first, she realized he was being smart. As sure as she was that Young was her man, there was the whole innocent-until-proven-guilty issue. If there was any chance they were wrong, and some yahoo local cop went in there guns blazing and killed an innocent man, they'd live to regret it.

Though, not as much as they'd regret it if they were right and they didn't get there in time to save Taylor and Vonnie.

Aidan lowered the phone to his chest, saying, "She's getting him."

When the chief came on the line a moment later, she could hear his gruff voice from the other seat. Aidan explained what they'd learned, and the chief's response was loud enough for Lexie to hear from the other seat. "Son of a bitch! It all fits. Underwood told me Mark Young was the last new member of the club—that Jed White brought him into the group a couple of months before he died."

"Just as we thought," Aidan replied.

"You stay put!" the man ordered. "Don't go any farther. I'm going out there myself."

"You're twenty minutes away," Aidan replied, staying calm, "and we're almost to White's old house."

Lexie looked up, saw the mailbox, and realized he was right.

"I mean it, now. Don't you do anything. Pull over and stay right where you are."

"As you wish, Chief," Aidan said, pulling over right past the mailbox. He cut the engine. "We've stopped."

"Where?"

"About ten feet from his driveway."

"Damn it, don't do anything! You'll get yourself killed, and that other one with you."

That other one. Hmm. So nice to know he cared.

"Gotta go, Chief. You'd better hurry." Dunston sputtered, but Aidan cut him off. "I will promise you we won't do anything other than look around until you get here. Unless we see something that convinces us the girls are here and are in imminent danger." He and Lexie exchanged a look. "If that happens, all bets are off."

Sunday, 7:20 p.m.

Vonnie had almost been there. She couldn't believe it, but was so close to escaping her chains, that if she'd had another ten minutes, she felt sure she could have done it.

Her hands were unbound, one arm completely free, but that wasn't good enough. She couldn't get up and fight with Taylor. The only way she'd be of any use was if he came close enough for her to swing.

She'd like that. In fact, she had a fistful of loose chain, just in case, and had been flexing and unflexing her hand and arm, counting on her muscles to be there for her when she needed them. She'd like to whip that long, hard strand of metal links across his face, strip that mask off blow by blow.

A key turned in the lock and Vonnie sent up a silent prayer, both for herself, and for Taylor. They'd have one chance at this, only one. Because if they failed, he would kill them both, in the most brutal way he could devise. Of that she had no doubt.

"Hello, my pretties," he said as he pushed the door open. He didn't come in right away, pausing for a second to flip on the light switch that was just outside their door.

A weak, dirty bulb flicked on overhead, sending a

pool of light straight down onto the floor. Enough to spotlight Taylor's pale hand, her leg, a few strands of her hair.

"Have you missed me?" he asked, stepping all the way inside. He stepped over, then pushed the door closed and locked it behind him, never fully turning his back. Putting the keys in his pocket, he added, "How's our new friend doing?"

"I keep thinking maybe she's dead," Vonnie said. She tried to sound weary, rather than enraged, knowing he expected her to be drugged.

"Do you, now?"

She forced herself to giggle, as if high. "She kept twitching and drooling all day and she threw up. Gross."

He hesitated, watching her from across the room, not bending down to check Taylor, not coming over to her, either. He was like an animal, tentative, sniffing the air to see if it was safe to proceed. "And how are you feeling, sweet little girl?"

Vonnie sighed deeply, letting her eyes fall closed as she yawned. "Okay." Behind her back, her hand tightened on the chain, gripping it as hard as she hoped Taylor was gripping that long, thin piece of wood—one of the chair legs.

If he noticed the chair was broken, they were done for. If he tried to use it, pulled it over to talk to her close-up, for some reason—which he'd only done once or twice, preferring to torment her and read to her from outside the room—he'd know right away.

Please, let us be lucky. For once, let me have some good luck.

She watched through mostly lowered lashes, seeing him move a step closer. But then he stopped, inches away from Taylor, who lay still, almost exactly where she'd been before.

The monster gave no hint of what he intended to do before he attacked.

He kicked brutally, his big foot hitting Taylor in the

side, not far from where the knife still stuck out of her back.

Vonnie flinched, feeling the blow from across the room, certain Taylor would cry out in pain, curl up, react somehow.

She didn't. She did absolutely nothing. Taylor just lay there and took it.

Vonnie had never seen anything more courageous. She didn't think she could have done it. And she was so overwhelmed with love for that girl, she wanted to wrap her arms around her and take away her pain.

Knowing any tears would give them away, she forced herself not to cry, picturing the tears that had to be gathering in Taylor's eyes, but were hidden by the thick tangle of hair lying across her face. She remained still, breathing evenly, as if she were drifting in and out of sleep, the way she had when she'd been sedated last week.

And finally, he let his guard down. "Well, I suppose you might be right. She's still breathing, so she's not dead yet. But I think her brains are a little bit scrambled up." He chuckled evilly. "Maybe I should have used a plastic bat instead of a real one, huh?

"Guess we never will know which Kirby girl you are, will we? Wonder if your parents will bury your sister under a headstone that has your name on it. I saw them today, you know, coming home from the hospital, looking like someone had just ripped their hearts out." He laughed again. "Guess that'd be me!"

Don't do it, girl. Don't listen. Don't.

He hadn't gotten a reaction out of her with a brutal blow. God, how she hoped he wasn't able to do it with some hateful words.

"So pretty, you really are so pretty," the man said.

Vonnie heard a note in his voice. An ugly one. One she recognized from the night she'd met a bunch of other men just like him.

No. He couldn't be thinking of this. Couldn't intend to rape a comatose girl.

She opened her eyes all the way, peering across the room, biting her bottom lip as he squatted down in front of Taylor. He reached out a hand and brushed her hair back from her face, his fingers moving against her lips.

Vonnie's own teeth clenched with the desire to bite at him. She didn't know if she could have resisted.

"And you're not all used up like Vonnie is, are you? You never got invited to one of our parties. Never had all those old men stick it to you."

Vonnie wondered if that was why he hadn't touched her sexually. Did he prefer his girls more innocent, less broken in? Like she had been before she'd been initiated into his sick club?

"Think I might have to try you out before you kick off," he said. "Sweet little thing like you, it'd be a shame for you to die a virgin, which I bet you are, you being such a good girl."

She had to do something.

"That's gross," Vonnie said, trying to retain that amused-yet-disgusted tone she'd managed before.

He ignored her, didn't even look at her. He was totally focused on Taylor.

He ran his hand down her neck, over her shoulder, then her back. "Whoops, might want to get that out of the way," he said, his fingers tracing around the knife, not pulling it out. "Or maybe not. You don't have to roll over onto your back for this, do you, sweetheart? We can do it another way."

The hand moved on, to her hip, her butt, until he slipped it between her legs.

Taylor flinched.

"Ahh . . ."

And that was it. They were done. It was over.

Only Taylor hadn't gotten the message. Because moving with a suddenness Vonnie couldn't even imagine, the girl rolled up onto her side. At the same time, she thrust up the long wooden chair leg, which had been underneath her, aiming directly at their attacker's throat.

"Yes!" Vonnie shouted.

If Taylor had hit her target, the blow could have killed him. Could have crushed his windpipe. But he jerked away at just the right moment. Still, the hard wood struck him in the face and he flew backward, sliding across the floor, crying out in pain. Grabbing at his mask, he ripped it off. Taylor launched herself to her feet, gasping in shock when she saw his face.

"Bitch!" he snapped.

He was close. So close Vonnie could almost feel him. *Give me two inches, come on.*

"I'll kill you!" he said, trying to lurch to his feet even as Taylor edged toward the door, panicking, knowing she needed the key to get out but too terrified to come and get it.

Blood dripped on the floor. The monster rose to one knee. But he was wobbly, disoriented, and he leaned back.

Close enough.

Vonnie leapt. Using her free arm, she looped the chain around his neck and pulled with every ounce of her strength.

"The keys!" she screamed, knowing she wouldn't be able to hold the man for long.

Taylor ran over, slapping his hands away as he tried to grab her, shoving him down when he tried to rise to his feet. One strong kick to his groin caused him to grunt in pain and stop struggling long enough for Taylor to reach into his pocket and pull out the key ring.

"Now go," Vonnie ordered, feeling her strength wane. She was strong, always had been, but she'd had no food and had been chained flat on her back for almost a week. They were almost out of time. She couldn't keep this up.

"The key to the chains could be on here . . ."

"Get the hell out!"

Taylor went. Sobbing, slipping, she ran to the door, trying first one key, then another.

The monster had stopped struggling as much, and Vonnie hoped it was because he was choking to death, but she doubted it. Taylor had been playing possum. She had no doubt he'd do the same thing. She didn't intend to let up until she had not one bit of strength left.

Taylor finally got the door open. She cast one anguished, wide-eyed stare at Vonnie. "I'll be back for you. I swear I'll be back."

"Go!"

She didn't hesitate. Taylor simply went.

Sunday, 7:30 p.m.

Aidan saw her first, a pale figure emerging from the front door of Young's house. For a second, she was silhouetted by the light from within, and he saw the blood on her torn clothes, the hysteria in her face.

Her scream split the night in half.

"Oh my God, Taylor!" Lexie immediately started to run. They were a good distance away, having been lurking in some trees along the front of the property, trying to decide the best way to approach the house without being seen.

The girl heard, looked into the darkness toward them, then stumbled across the porch and down the steps of the old farmhouse. She limped, and was bent over, clutching her side, yet still managed a hitching run. "Vonnie, help Vonnie," she called as she got closer.

Reaching her, Lexie caught Taylor in her arms, holding her carefully, spotting the knife sticking out of her at the same time Aidan did.

"Don't touch it," he snapped. "Taylor, where is Vonnie?"

"Basement," she whispered. "Kitchen's to the left, stairs hidden in the back of the pantry. Two doors . . . I dropped the keys. He's with her!"

He nodded. Catching Lexie's eye, he tried to communicate a lot with one look. That he cared about her, that he would be back. That he would save Vonnie.

He merely said, "Get her out to my car and call Dunston."

She nodded, but before he could run into the house, she grabbed his arm. "Please be careful."

"I will."

Hold on, Vonnie.

He ran to the house, up the steps, and inside. As soon as he hit the threshold, he got that strong smell of gingerbread again, just as rotten, just as filthy. It smelled like death. This whole house smelled like death and utter corruption of the spirit.

The kitchen was to his left, and as he ran through it, he saw a surveillance monitor. The picture on it chilled his blood.

Vonnie was lying on a cot and a man knelt on top of her, choking the life out of her.

Aidan didn't even waste the time looking for a weapon; he leapt for the stairs and took them three or four at a time. He found the keys at the base of them, scooped them up midstride just in case, and ran through an open door and down a short hallway.

A second door, ahead of him, was closed. Gripping the keys, he ran to it, tested it, and realized it was locked. Doubting Taylor had stopped to lock Vonnie in with the madman, he figured it had to lock automatically from the outside.

"Damn it," he snarled, shifting frantically through the keys. Luck was with him, and he found the right one almost immediately.

The man kneeling on the bed was so busy trying to murder Vonnie Jackson that he didn't even hear Aidan push the door open and burst into the room. Running to build up speed, he launched himself at Mark Young, sending both of them flying right over Vonnie's head into a hard cement wall.

Young, whose face was dripping blood, tried to fight.

But it wasn't so easy when he didn't have a young girl's throat between his hands.

Still, he was cornered and he knew it, so he gave it his all. Shoving the heavy metal cot out of the way, he tipped it over, trapping Vonnie beneath it, and tried to make a break for it.

"No, you don't," Aidan snarled.

He couldn't stop to help Vonnie, who was squirming under the bed. He had to stop Young.

Aidan attacked again, certain he'd never in his life been so overcome with rage. He pounded the man, throwing every ounce of himself behind every punch that landed on the killer's face. His knuckles grew bloody and he knew he was probably breaking some fingers, but he couldn't stop, not while Young fought back, kicking and scratching like an animal.

Suddenly, the other man bent over and managed to wrap his hands around a length of chain. He swung it brutally, cracking it against Aidan's face, splitting his cheek open. Roaring, Aidan wiped off the blood with the back of his arm and charged again. But Young still had the chain, and this time when he cracked it, it caught Aidan in the throat.

He gasped for breath, hesitating for a moment. Young took advantage and darted toward the door.

But the former high school vice principal had made a basic mistake. He had neglected to kill his very angry victim.

Somehow, Vonnie had wriggled free of her chains and escaped the cot. She'd crawled out of the way, and, apparently seeing Young trying to get away, grabbed a long, thin piece of wood that had been lying nearby.

Aidan saw her step out of the shadows as Young tried to run past her.

He saw her plunge the pointy, broken end of the stake into the man's chest like Van Helsing taking out a vicious vampire.

He heard the killer scream, then watched him fall.

Young clutched his chest, blood gushed up around the stake, more pumping out with every beat of his black heart. And above him stood Vonnie. She stared down, shell-shocked, like a prisoner of war. Yet her eyes were filled with fire—hatred and rage—as she watched her tormentor bleed out.

As Aidan regained his breath and made his way toward her, Vonnie whispered something to Young, who lay dying at her feet.

"Fuck you. And fuck your bedtime stories."

Chapter 18

Lexie made her way out of the hospital that morning, after spending a half hour with Taylor and Vonnie. Minor celebrities now—the girls who had survived the Granville Ghoul—they were sharing a room, surrounded by well-wishers. Not to mention the police and the media. National news trucks were parked outside and everybody from Greta Van Susteren to Larry King wanted to talk to the girls. And to Chief Dunston.

That made her smile. At least, what little she could smile lately.

Taylor's parents, heartbroken and joyful at the same time, were at the hospital nonstop, too. They spent their time nursing one daughter back to health while planning the other one's funeral.

Sunday night, when they'd arrived at the hospital and Walter and Ann-Marie had learned Lexie had been the one who'd gotten Taylor to safety and stayed there, guarding over her until the police arrived, they had been unable to stop thanking her. As she'd told them, she didn't deserve the thanks. She'd just been a babysitter, like she had when Taylor and her beautiful, lost twin had been sassy little girls.

Aidan deserved thanks, yes.

In truth, though, Taylor had saved herself, and her friend, by being strong enough to break free and get help. But only after Vonnie had saved her, too, holding Young back so Taylor could get away.

The brutalized teenagers had saved each other. It was movie-of-the-week stuff. Which was already being discussed, or so she'd heard.

Fortunately, since Vonnie had turned eighteen during her ordeal, and therefore had the right to determine who could come in and who couldn't, her mother was not among the well-wishers. Last she'd heard, Berna Jackson was at a bar, wailing to anyone who would listen that her precious daughter had been brainwashed by that monster into not wanting to be near her own loving mama.

"Good riddance," she muttered, knowing when the police went to tell her Vonnie had been found alive, her first comment was that her daughter would be getting a lawyer so they could sue somebody.

Heading outside, she paused to appreciate the beautiful November morning, warm and sunny. The town of Granville, with its church spires and its quaint downtown probably looked like a picture postcard on the daily news being broadcast all over the country.

God, she could not wait to get out of here. Ever since she and Aidan had discussed it the other day, she'd known it was going to happen. She loved Walter, and she'd stay around for as long as he needed her. But once that was done, she was picking up stakes and moving on.

The only question was where.

The answer to that question kind of depended on a man she hadn't even known one week ago.

"And what are you going to think about that?" she muttered as she crossed the hospital parking lot.

He'd probably think she was crazy. But over the past few days, reality had not only slapped her in the face, it had also kicked her in the gut. She'd always known life was short, but had never really acknowledged just how easily your entire world could turn upside down. How the people who were part of it could feature prominently in your morning and be dead that night.

If she'd learned anything at all, it was to not waste what time you had. Not in a job that sucked, or in a town she hated, or in an empty bed when she could share a wonderful, sexy man's. At least, as long as he wanted her to.

After this morning, he might not want her to.

Reaching the rental car—she'd finally remembered her own, and had it towed from the school parking lot yesterday—she drove away from the hospital. Her car would be undergoing repairs for a week. Thankfully, Dunston had offered to help with the insurance issues, especially since a member of the Hellfire Club had admitted to vandalizing the car in an effort to get Lexie to back off the story.

Though she had a lot of work to do, since she and el-creepo Stan would be handling the paper while Walter was out, helping his family recover from their tragedy, she knew there was one stop she had to make before she went back to the office.

Part of her couldn't wait, needing to see Aidan, to touch him and suck up some of the strength and warmth—the calmness—he brought to her. She also wanted to see for herself that he was okay, that his bruises were healing and he was taking care of his bandaged hands and stitched cuts. She'd slept at her own place last night, after having spent the previous two in his arms, and had felt his absence so keenly it was like they'd shared a bed—or a couch—for years.

How she could so desperately miss something she'd had so very briefly, she didn't know. But she knew what she felt and she wanted to be near him.

Mostly.

Yeah. Mostly. A tiny part of her wasn't looking forward to going over to his place this morning one little bit. She glanced at the passenger's seat, seeing that reason sitting starkly against the gray fabric. The paper-clipped pages were an eight-by-eleven accusation that had taunted her since the minute it had come off her printer late the previous night.

It was the article she'd written for tomorrow's *Sun*. A firsthand account of everything that had happened, her own involvement with it, from start to finish. She'd needed to get it all out and had spoken to no one before committing the story to paper.

Aidan was going to hate it. And maybe her.

"No," she whispered as she reached his street, "he'll understand. He'll have to."

Parking in front of his house, she took a deep breath, stuck the article in her purse, and walked to his front door. This time when she knocked, he opened it with a smile.

"Hey."

"Hey yourself," he said.

"Can I come in?"

"Unless you want me to kiss you on the front step."

She smiled. "Actually, that would be fine."

So he did. Stepping out of his door, Aidan joined her on the porch and cupped her check in his hand. He tilted her head back, then bent to press his lips against hers, kissing her slowly, thoroughly.

Lexie's eyes drifted closed. She parted her lips, welcoming him, knowing his taste and his scent. Their tongues slid together, easy and soft, and she melted against him, every feminine bit of her reacting to his touch.

They'd shared sultry passion the first time they'd made love Sunday morning. Yesterday, after all they'd gone through the night before, it had been desperate and wild, as if they both needed to feel alive by giving themselves over to sensation and instinct.

This, though, was different. Sweet and sexy, tender and familiar. He knew how to kiss her now, knew she loved the way he teased her a little with his tongue before plunging for a deeper taste. She'd dated men for months who'd never realized how much she loved deep, slow, wet kisses that went on for hours. But Aidan already knew. Just like he knew when she needed a slow, steady possession, or when she wanted to be taken so hard she lost her mind.

He knew every inch of her. Because he'd shared her dreams. And he'd shared her reality.

They had been allies. Now they were lovers.

It was what came next that worried her.

So, with a low sigh, she ended the kiss. "I needed that," she admitted.

"Me, too."

Dropping an arm over her shoulder, he led her inside, shutting the door behind them. She watched, unable to prevent a smile when she saw what he was wearing.

"What's funny?"

"Yellow? Seriously, you're wearing yellow?"

"Hey, it's not black," he said with a shrug, pulling at the neckline of his pale yellow sweatshirt, which he wore with a pair of black pants.

"You look like a freaking bumblebee," she had to say, shaking her head as she laughed.

That was enough. Aidan grabbed the bottom of the sweatshirt and pulled it off, tossing it to the floor. "That's why I always wear black," he snapped. "I'm lousy with colors."

She couldn't laugh at that; she was too busy staring at the bare chest, the strong arms. *Bad move, Nolan.*

Clothed, Aidan took her breath away. Shirtless, with that broad male chest rippling and hard, he almost stopped her heart. And he knew it, too. His hot stare narrowed in on her mouth as he stepped forward, reaching for her.

Lexie stepped back, holding up a hand. "Wait."

"Are you kidding?"

Swallowing hard, she said, "I need to talk to you about something." She gestured toward his office. "Can we go sit down?"

Aidan's sexy mood faded. He could obviously tell by her tone that he wasn't going to like whatever she had to say.

Definitely no kidding about that.

She led him into the office, taking a seat on the sofa, waiting for him to sit beside her. But he didn't. He stayed over by his desk, leaning against it, his big arms crossed over his bare chest.

Oh, how she wanted to feel those arms around her again. Hopefully, after this conversation, she would still have the chance to.

"What is it?"

Lexie reached into her bag and pulled out the article, setting it on the table.

"I know I promised you not to mention—"

"Hell!"

"Hear me out."

His mouth stayed shut, his jaw clenching.

"Aidan, if you had been a source, a tip, I would absolutely have left you out of it. Period. End of story. But you became part of the news. Don't you understand? You saved those girls' lives. You were there every step of the way. How can I leave you out of the story?"

"Why does there have to be a story?" he asked, grinding the words out like he had the first time she'd come here to see him. "Why do you have to be the one to tell it?"

"Because it's my job, for one thing," she said, knowing as soon as the words left her mouth that it wasn't enough, and she hadn't put that right.

"Yeah. Your job. You're a reporter; it's what you do," he spat.

Lexie rose from her seat and walked toward the desk, stopping a few inches away from him. "I know you hate everything about my profession, okay? I get that. But can't you acknowledge that maybe—just maybe—the reporters weren't the bad guys in this? If I hadn't gotten shut down a month ago, maybe that bastard would have been caught sooner." Her breath hitched in her throat. "Maybe Jenny wouldn't have died."

He closed his eyes for a second, breathing deeply. "I know. I'm sorry."

Lexie hadn't been after his sympathy, only his understanding. "I came here to show you the article, to see if there's anything you want me to change."

"Not to ask me if you can go ahead with it?"

She could have lied, could have tried to ease him into agreeing, but she wasn't that person. She just couldn't be. "No. I'm going ahead with it."

He nodded once. "At least you're honest."

"Always," she promised him. "Being totally honest, let me add, I did the best I could to keep my word to you. There's not a single sentence in there about visions or psychic phenomenon or anything else. Just the facts, not interpretations. You're mentioned as a local resident who helped rescue the girls. Which will come as no big surprise to anyone, considering Taylor and Vonnie, and Chief Dunston, have already mentioned you in interviews. I'm just expounding on it, filling in the black-and-white details."

His stance relaxed a little; she saw the stiff shoulders loosen. "I don't understand," he told her. "The way you walked in here, I thought . . ."

"You thought I wrote a big article about the Savannah psychic who used his woo-woo mystic powers to save the day?"

He shrugged, looking uncomfortable.

"I didn't. I wouldn't. I'm a reporter and I report the facts. I don't share impressions or feelings or my thoughts about what you were doing whenever you tried to reach out to those missing girls." Reaching up, she put a hand on his chest, unable to resist digging her fingers into that ridge of muscle. "I cannot change what I do—because I don't want to. But I can tell you I am someone who does it with integrity and honesty."

After a long hesitation, he admitted, "I know you do."

Lexie inched closer. Now was when it got important. So terribly important.

"Aidan, I have never believed in love at first sight, and yet I already know I have feelings for you. They get stronger every time I'm with you."

He licked his lips, considered, then admitted, "It's the same for me."

"I think we can have something. But to be blunt, I don't even want to try until I know you're going into this with eyes wide open, seeing me for who I really am, and accepting what I do, and still able to like me at the end of the day, as well as fall in love with me." She leaned closer, brushing her mouth against his cheek. "Just like I see you for who you really are. Like you. And am probably falling in love with you."

"You think so?"

She nodded. "You're deep, and you're calm. You're wounded, and you're strong. You're brave and you're loving. You have a gift you've been afraid to use and you haven't ever let yourself truly fall in love with anyone because you know when that happens, you're going to fall so hard it will affect you heart, mind, and soul. Forever. Am I right?"

She held her breath, waiting for what seemed the longest time.

Then he slid his hands around her waist, and she got her answer.

"You're mostly right," he whispered, drawing her closer so that she rested against his warm body.

Lexie was so relieved, so utterly happy, she didn't say anything, she merely wrapped her arms around him, rested her cheek on his chest, and let him hold her.

"I do like you," he admitted, brushing his lips against her hair, then her temple. "Everything about you, including the fact that you're a pain-in-the-ass, but still a very noble, reporter."

She smiled. "Thought we weren't going to use P words."

"That didn't end in a Y," he replied with a soft laugh. Then the laughter faded. Tilting her head back, he lightly pressed his lips on one closed eyelid, then the other, then moved toward her mouth. But before he kissed her again, he said, "You know, you are wrong about one thing."

She gazed up at him, looking up at his handsome face, losing herself in the deep blue of those mesmerizing eyes, which held not a trace of gray. "What's that?"

His lips moved toward hers, hovering no more than a whisper away. Right before he eliminated that tiny bit of space, he breathed an answer so soft, she almost didn't hear it.

"I do believe in love at first sight."

Epilogue

May 4, 8:05 p.m.

As they walked down one of Savannah's quaint, elegant squares, heading for a local restaurant that had become Lexie's favorite, Aidan couldn't help thinking about where he'd been a year ago. Alone, first of all. In Granville—a town he'd happily never lay eyes on again, if he had his choice. Without friends or a job. Worst of all, without Lexie.

Now, though, everything had changed. Life couldn't possibly have gotten much better.

"What?" she asked, slipping her arm in his as they walked. "What are you thinking?"

"Can't you read my thoughts?" he teased.

She glanced up at him, her eyes shining so green under the old streetlights. Batting her lashes, she replied, "Well, that's fine with me, if you're sure you don't mind missing dinner."

Laughing, something he did a lot lately, he said, "Other than that."

"*Do* you think about anything other than that?"

Didn't seem that way. Especially lately, since Lexie had finally landed the job she'd been after and moved here to Savannah. And right into his place with him.

She still sometimes talked about getting her own apartment. He had every intention of talking her out of it and, in fact, changed the subject whenever she mentioned it.

She mentioned it less and less now.

Good.

He liked sleeping with her in his arms. In fact, when she was in his arms, he was actually able to sleep, as if as long as his subconscious knew she'd be there when he woke up, he could let himself go.

He also very much liked being awake with her in his arms. Their sizzling sexual attraction hadn't decreased with time, it had only grown stronger as they became more and more connected in every way.

Aidan didn't want to lose that and would do whatever it took to keep Lexie in his bed, in his home, in his life. They'd exchanged no rings, made no promises, but their feelings ran so deep, he knew he never wanted to live without her. He also knew she felt the same way.

They didn't say *I love you* out loud every day. But they whispered it every night, when they came together in the dark. Sometimes they said it without ever really saying a word.

"To tell you the truth, I was thinking life is pretty good," he admitted.

"Yes, it is. I wouldn't have imagined it six months ago, but it is."

He squeezed her again, knowing how those memories still tore at her. Moving away from Walter and his family, and from Vonnie, with whom she had become very close, had been hard for her. But they all knew she'd go back and visit often.

The Kirbys were doing okay. Getting ready for Taylor's and Vonnie's graduations, preparing Ann for her junior year, and Christy, the youngest, to start high school. Living life. Not necessarily living the life they wanted, the one they'd dreamed of. But they were surviving.

Vonnie was surviving, too. She'd gone home from the hospital with Taylor, who had refused to leave her side, and the Kirbys had asked her to stay on to finish the school year.

She hadn't replaced Jenny; God, no. But helping the

girl, giving her a place to go, rather than back to her abusive mother, and giving her a chance at the life she deserved, seemed to help Walter and Ann-Marie deal with their own grief.

Vonnie had saved their daughter's life. Just as Taylor had saved hers. Nobody would ever forget that. No matter where any of them went, that bond would always remain.

"Are you glad you moved here?" he asked Lexie. "No regrets?"

"Are you kidding? Think I miss the wives of all those men glaring at me in the grocery store, like it's my fault their pervy husbands ended up charged with everything from statutory rape to murder?"

He hated that she'd gone through that. But he also knew things hadn't been all bad. "Most people thanked you. And they'll miss you. Dunston looked ready to cry at your going-away party."

She chuckled. "He's a big teddy bear."

Another thing he couldn't have imagined hearing her say six months ago. Especially not with such affection.

Aidan had just opened his mouth to tease her about it, when he noticed the couple walking toward them on the narrow, cobbled sidewalk. The loud man wore an expensive suit, the thin, pale woman a designer dress.

He knew them instantly.

Aidan's heart thumped and his first instinct was to step onto the road, out of the way.

Ted and Caroline Remington hadn't seen him yet, and it would probably be better if they didn't.

But traffic had picked up, and Lexie was closest to the street. No way would he let her step off the curb, and he couldn't get around her fast enough. There was no escape.

Only a few yards separated them now, and at last, Remington stopped listening to himself talk and glanced ahead. Their stares met. Aidan's, he knew, filled with regret. Remington's with . . . *Fear?*

The man's face tightened and his gaze shifted frantically. His jowly cheeks shook and he reacted as Aidan had—immediately looking to the street for an escape, blocked on that side by traffic, on the other by an iron fence surrounding a beautiful old town house.

Caroline Remington seemed oblivious, her jaded, pinched look hinting that she didn't notice much of anything, including her bore of a husband. She continued walking, drawing closer, until just a few steps separated them.

Suddenly, Remington jerked her around, ignoring her gasp and her protest. Trading places, he pushed his wife over toward the fence so he was the one Aidan had to brush past when they finally came face-to-face on the sidewalk.

They drew abreast. Their eyes met, locked, all in the length of time it took to take one step. Then they moved apart. But Aidan hadn't gone more than that one, single step when something made him freeze.

A scent. Peaches.

He whirled around, driven by some force he didn't fully understand, his senses taking over for his brain. "Mrs. Remington?"

The woman stopped and looked back at him, apparently not noticing that her husband's eyes had grown huge and desperate as he tried to tug her forward. "Yes?"

Aidan reached for her, watching his own hand rise as if it belonged to someone else.

Peaches. So strong.

It wasn't a phantom smell, but a real one. Her lotion? Her shampoo?

"I just wanted to tell you how sorry I am," he said.

Another inch and he touched her, his fingers brushing ever so lightly against her arm. Just a touch, the faintest connection.

But that was enough. That was all it took.

Mommy, please! I'm sorry. I'll be good. I didn't mean

to forget to wash my hands. Please don't spray me. No, please don't put me in the dark. I don't like the closet. Mommy!

Peaches. Spraying water. Wood. Splinters.

Teddy.

Remington, watching in horror, saw the moment it happened. His expression told the tale—he knew Aidan had touched his wife and seen the truth.

Which meant Remington, himself, already knew the truth.

"Come on, Caroline, we're late," the man snapped, his hands tightening on his pale wife's arm, his eyes venomous as he glared at Aidan, silently threatening him not to say a word about what he had discovered.

The woman let herself be dragged away, though she looked back over her shoulder once, obviously not recognizing Aidan, confused, having no idea what had just happened.

Lexie, though, knew. Standing beside him, she watched the other couple depart, then murmured, "That was them."

"Yes."

"You felt something."

He nodded. "She did it."

Lexie said nothing, she merely curled her hand into his and squeezed, tight, knowing without further explanation what this meant.

That cold bitch Caroline Remington had done it, and Ted Remington *knew*. The bastard had, at some point, found out his wife had killed their child, and he'd covered it up. Let Aidan hang out to dry, probably paid off someone in the medical examiner's office.

He'd covered up his own son's murder.

"What are we going to do?" Lexie asked, her voice quiet, introspective.

He focused on the *we*, realizing they had become a solid unit, the two of them a unified front against anyone who threatened them. God, he loved having this woman for his partner.

He loved her, period.

"They're not going to get away with it," he swore, still staring at the couple as they disappeared into Savannah's shadows.

"Will Julia and the others be able to help?"

"Absolutely. I know they'll want to," he said. Then he added, "It's going to get ugly."

"Murder always is."

"Yes. But they won't get away with it."

Whatever it took to bring those people to justice, he would do it. He was back in his town, back in his job, back in his *head*. And ready to take on the world. Or at least two murderous residents of it.

"Okay," she told him without hesitating. "I'm with you."

He turned to her, looking down at her beautiful face, so serious, so supportive, so full of emotion for him. Worry, fear, tenderness. Love.

And with every part of himself he told her exactly what was in his heart.

"As long as you're with me, Lex, I can do anything."

Don't miss the second book
in Leslie Parrish's exciting new
Extrasensory Agents series!

With her dark gift, eXtreme Investigations
agent Olivia Wainwright has experienced
the deaths of dozens of other people. But
now her past is catching up to her and she's
forced to confront dark, painful memories
of her *own*.

Turn the page to read an excerpt from

COLD TOUCH

Coming from Signet Eclipse in April 2011

Twelve Years Ago

"He's gonna kill you."

The boy's voice shook with both sadness and fear. And with those four whispered words, Olivia Wainwright's faint hope of survival disappeared.

The boy—Jack. Her captor, or another victim? She wasn't sure. She knew only that during the three terrifying days she'd been tied up in this hot, miserable barn, his was the only face she'd seen. She'd caught brief glimpses of him in the shadows when he shuffled in to bring her water, and sometimes a handful of stale nuts that she suspected he wasn't supposed to share. Once he'd even come close enough to loosen the ropes on her wrists and ankles a little so she had at least some circulation.

But he hadn't let her go. No matter how much she'd begged.

He was a couple of years younger than her—twelve or thirteen, maybe. Skinny, pale. While he was free to go in and out, she suspected he was a victim, too—of abuse, at the very least. The kid looked beaten down, his spirit crushed, all memories of happiness long gone.

Olivia began to shake, long shudders making her bound legs quiver and her stomach heave. She'd eaten almost nothing for days yet she thought she was going be sick.

This wasn't supposed to happen. She'd tried so hard to be strong, to think positively. Her parents loved her, and they had a lot of money. Of course they'd pay the ransom. She'd told herself it would all be okay. But it wouldn't be okay. Not ever again.

"When?" she finally asked, dread making the word hard to push from her mouth.

"Once he makes sure they left the ransom money."

"If they're paying the money, why is he going to kill me?" she asked, the words sounding so strange in her ears. God, she was fifteen years old; the very idea that she would be asking questions about her own murder had never once crossed her mind.

Four days ago she'd been a slightly spoiled, happy teenager looking forward to getting her driver's license, and wondering how much begging it would take to get her overindulgent parents to buy her a Jeep.

Now she was wondering how many minutes she had left on this earth. She could hear a clock ticking away in her mind, each tick marking one less second of her life.

"He doesn't want any witnesses." Jack leaned back against the old plank wall and slid down it as if he couldn't hold himself up anymore. He sat hunched, watching her. A shaft of moonlight shining through a broken slat high in the barn wall shone like a spotlight on his bony face. Tear tracks had cleared a path through the grime on his bruised cheeks and his swollen, bloodied, quivering lips. "He's afraid you can identify him."

"I can't! I never even saw his face."

That was true. She'd never gotten a glimpse of the man who'd grabbed her from her own bedroom. Liv had awakened from a sound sleep to find a pillow slapped over her face, a hateful male voice hissing at her not to scream or he'd shoot her sister, whose room was one door down from hers. Their parents' room was on the other side of the huge house, and Liv didn't doubt that the man would be able to make good on his threat before anyone could get to them.

A minute later, any chance of screaming had been taken from her. He'd hit her hard enough to knock her out. By the time she'd regained consciousness, she was already inside this old abandoned barn. Jack was the only living soul she'd seen or heard since.

"I'm sorry."

"Let me go," she urged.

He shook his head, repeating, "I'm sorry."

"Please, Jack. You can't let this happen."

"There's nothing I can do."

"Just untie me and give me a chance to run away."

"He'll find you," he said. "Then he'll kill us both." His voice was low, his tone sounding almost robotic. As if he'd heard the threat so many times that they had become ingrained in his head.

"When did he take you?" she asked, suddenly certain this boy was a captive as well.

"Take me?" Jack stared at her, his brown eyes flat and lifeless. "Whaddya mean?"

"He kidnapped you, too. Didn't he?"

"Dunno." Jack slowly shook his head. "I've been here forever."

"Is he your father?" she persisted.

Jack didn't respond, though whether it was because he didn't know or didn't want to say, she couldn't be sure.

"Do you have a mother?"

"Don't remember."

"Look, whoever he is, you have to get away from him. We have to get away." She tried to scoot closer, though her legs—numb from being bound—didn't want to cooperate. She managed no more than a few inches before falling onto her side, remnants of dry, dirty hay scratching her cheek. "Come with me. Untie me and we'll both run."

If she could run on her barely functional legs.

She thrust away that worry. If it meant saving her life, hell, she'd crawl.

"I can't," he replied, looking down at her from a few feet away. His hand rose, as though he wanted to reach out and touch her, to help her sit up. Then he dropped it back onto his lap, as if he was used to having his hand slapped if he ever dared to raise it.

"Yes, you can! My parents will help you. They'll be so grateful."

"I can't."

Again, that robotic voice. As if the kid was brainwashed. If he'd been a prisoner for so long that he didn't even remember any other life, she supposed he probably had been.

He reached into the pocket of his tattered jeans, pulling out two small pills. "Here," he said. "I swiped 'em from the floor in his room—he musta dropped 'em. I think they'll make you sleep, so maybe it won't hurt."

A sob rose from deep inside her, catching in the middle of her throat, choking and desperate. "How will he do it?"

The boy sniffled. "I dunno."

"Not a knife," she cried, panic rising fast. "Oh, please, God, don't let him cut me."

She had a deep-seated fear of knives, of being stabbed, a fear that bordered on phobia. In every horror movie she'd ever seen, it was the gleam of light shining on the sharp, silvery edge of a blade that made her throw her hands over her eyes or just turn off the TV.

"He don't use a knife. Not usually," Jack said.

His misery didn't distract her from the implication of Jack's words: She wouldn't be the first person to die at her kidnapper's hands. He'd killed before. And this boy had witnessed those killings.

"Don't let this happen, Jack. Please don't let this happen." Tears poured out of her eyes, and she twisted and struggled against the ropes. "Don't let him hurt me."

"Take the pills," he said, his tears streaming as hard as hers. "Please take them."

"You should have brought the whole bottle," she said, hearing her own bitterness and desperation.

"If I could get to a whole bottle, I woulda swallowed them myself a long time ago."

That haunted voice suddenly sounded so adult, so broken. The voice of someone who'd considered suicide every day of his young life. What horrors must he have endured to so easily embrace the thought of death?

It was his sheer hopelessness that made her realize she hadn't given up hope. She was terrified out of her mind and didn't want to die, didn't want to feel the pain of death—oh God, not by a knife—but she wasn't ready to give up, either. No matter what she'd said, if he had a bottle of pills in his hand, she didn't think she would swallow them, not even now, with death bearing down on her like a car heading for a cliff.

She wanted to live.

"Where you at, boy?" a voice bellowed from outside.

Jack leapt to his feet, his sadness disappearing as utter terror swept over him. That terror leapt from his body into hers, and Olivia struggled harder against the ropes. Like an animal caught in a trap, she could almost smell her own destruction barreling toward her.

She tried to keep her head. Tried to think.

If her captor didn't know the boy had warned her, maybe he'd let his guard down. Maybe she could get him to untie her, maybe she could run. . . .

Or maybe she really was about to die.

"Please," she whispered, knowing Jack wanted to help her. But his fear won out; he didn't even seem to hear her plea. He had already begun to climb over the side wall of the stall, falling into the next one with a muffled grunt.

No sooner had he gone than the barn door flew open with a crash. Heavy footsteps approached, ominous and violent like the powerful thudding of her heart.

Through the worn slats, she could see Jack lying in the next stall, motionless, watching her. She pleaded with her eyes, but he didn't respond in any way. It seemed as though the real boy had retreated somewhere deep inside a safe place in his mind, and only the shell of a human being remained.

Her kidnapper reached the entrance to the stall. Still lying on her side, Olivia first saw his ugly, thick-soled boots. She lifted her eyes, noted faded jeans pulled tight over powerfully muscled legs, but before she could tilt her head back to see the rest, something heavy and scratchy—a horse blanket, she suspected—landed on her face, obscuring her vision.

Confusion made her whimper and her heart, already racing, tripped in her chest. She trembled with fear, yes. But there was something more.

Hope.

He didn't want her to see him. Which meant he might have changed his mind. Maybe he knew she couldn't identify him and he was going to let her go.

"Up you go, girl," he said, grabbing her by the back of her hair and yanking her to her feet, holding the small blanket in place. He pressed in behind her, and she almost gagged. The cloth over her head wasn't thick enough to block the sweaty reek of his body or his sour breath—the same smells she'd forever associate with being startled awake in the night.

Forever? *Please, God, let there be more than just tonight.*

"Looks like your mama and daddy aren't sick 'a you yet. They paid over a lot of money to get you back."

"You're going to let me go?" she managed to whisper, hope blossoming.

"Sure, I am, sugar," he said with a hoarse, ugly laugh.

Olivia forced herself to ignore that mean laugh and allow relief and happiness to flood through her. She breathed deeply, then mumbled, "Thank God. Oh, thank you, God."

Ignoring her, he kicked at her bare feet so she'd start moving. She stumbled on numb legs, and he had to support her as they trudged out of the stall. His grip on her hair and a thick arm around her waist kept her upright as they walked outside into the hot Georgia night.

At least, she thought she was still in Georgia. It smelled like home, anyway. Not even the musky odor of the fabric and her attacker's stench could block the scent of the night air, damp and thick and ripe like the woods outside of Savannah after the rain.

Maybe she was still in Savannah. Close to her own house, close to her family. Minutes away from her father's strong arms and her mother's loving kiss.

Despite everything—her fears, the boy's claims—she was going to see them again.

Suddenly he stopped. "Where you been at?"

A furtive movement came from nearby. Jack had apparently scurried out of his hiding place. "Watchin' the road."

Suddenly Olivia was overwhelmed with anger at the boy, fury that he'd scared her, even more that he hadn't helped her escape. Over the past few days, there had been any number of times when he could have released her, but he hadn't done it.

Then, remembering the blank, dazed expression, the robotic voice, she forced the anger away. He was a little kid who'd been in this monster's grip for a whole lot longer than three days. She couldn't imagine what he had endured. Once she got home, she was going to do what she could for him. Help him to get free, to find out who his people were. She had to; otherwise that blank, haunted stare and bruised face would torment her for the rest of her life.

"Good. I'm gonna need your help in a li'l while. Once I take care of this, I want you to get some plastic and roll her up good and tight to bury her. You know what to do."

And just like that, her fantasy popped. He wasn't hauling her into the woods to let her go. Jack had been right all along. Olivia shuddered, her weak legs giving out beneath her as the world began to spin and the faces of her parents and little sister flashed in her mind.

"Get me my hunting knife."

Every one of her muscles went rigid with terror. A scream rose in her throat and burst from her mouth. He clapped a hand over it, shoving the fabric between her split lips. "Shut up, girl, or it'll go worse for ya." Then, to the boy, he snapped, "Well? Get goin'!"

"Knife's broke," Jack mumbled. "I was usin' it to tighten up the hinges on the barn door and the blade snapped."

Her kidnapper moved suddenly, the hand releasing her mouth. A sudden thwack said he'd backhanded the boy. Jack didn't cry out, didn't stagger away, as far as she could hear.

"What am I supposed to do now?" the man snapped.

Jack cleared his throat. For a second, she thought he had worked up the courage to beg for her freedom, that he would try, however futilely, to stand up for her.

Instead, in that same brainwashed voice, he made another suggestion. And her last hope died.

"Why don't you drown her?"

LESLIE PARRISH

THE BLACK CATS NOVELS

"HOLD YOUR BREATH ROMANTIC SUSPENSE."
—*New York Times* bestselling author JoAnn Ross

FADE TO BLACK
After transferring out of violent crimes and onto the FBI's Cyber Action Team, Special Agent Dean Taggert is shocked to encounter a case far more vicious than any he's ever seen. A cold and calculating predator dubbed The Reaper is auctioning off murder in the cyber world and is about to kill again—unless Dean can stop him.

PITCH BLACK
Alec Lambert desperately wants to catch The Professor, a serial killer who lures his victims with Internet scams. Now working with scam expert Samantha Dalton, he finally has his chance. But as they draw ever closer to discovering The Professor's identity and stopping his murderous rampage, they realize Sam is the killer's new obsession—and possibly his next target...

BLACK AT HEART
After the loss of a vulnerable young agent for whom he cared deeply, Wyatt Blackstone is starting to crack. For not only does he have a vigilante murderer to track down, but the clues to the crimes lead to an impossible suspect: the very woman he thought he'd lost.

**Available wherever books are sold or at
penguin.com**

S0093

Penguin Group (USA) Online

What will you be reading tomorrow?

Tom Clancy, Patricia Cornwell, W.E.B. Griffin,
Nora Roberts, William Gibson, Robin Cook,
Brian Jacques, Catherine Coulter, Stephen King,
Dean Koontz, Ken Follett, Clive Cussler,
Eric Jerome Dickey, John Sandford,
Terry McMillan, Sue Monk Kidd, Amy Tan,
J. R. Ward, Laurell K. Hamilton,
Charlaine Harris, Christine Feehan...

You'll find them all at
penguin.com

*Read excerpts and newsletters,
find tour schedules and reading group guides,
and enter contests.*

Subscribe to Penguin Group (USA) newsletters
and get an exclusive inside look
at exciting new titles and the authors you love
long before everyone else does.

PENGUIN GROUP (USA)
us.penguingroup.com